TRIAL OF SPIRIT:
Elf Queen of Kiirajanna
(volume 3)

STEPHEN H. KING

(TOSK)

ISBN: 978-0-9989355-5-3

CONTENTS

Acknowledgments

It's still amazing to me, after all these pages written, how much goes into writing a single novel, and also how much help is needed to accomplish this feat.

To my beloved bride, Heide, for all the lonely hours you put up with while I'm banging away at the keyboard, and for all the times you've listened to drafts and had the wisdom and the tact to tell me how it could sound better, I give my utmost of thanks. I couldn't do this without you.

To the magnificent students, and their teacher/leader Pam Manning, of the Graphics Technology program at the Washburn University Institute of Technology, I owe a deep debt of gratitude. You all took a graphics project from conception to reality and gave me several outstanding options for a cover.

To Noah Spencer, specifically, thank you. Thank you for taking a vague description of the book and turning it into fantastic cover art. Thank you for revision after revision as a writer's mind tried to grab hold of graphics perfection. The cover for this work is beautiful, and that is entirely due to your efforts. I have no doubt that your future as a graphic artist will be both bright and fulfilling.

Finally, and most recently, thank you to my Kickstarter supporters: Chris McMahan, Sheri Cox Bowling, Jaime Baur Layman, Leslie Ghoorahoo, and Rae Smith. Your support has enabled me to move this novel and my writing business to a new level.

SPECIAL ACKNOWLEDGMENT

A very special acknowledgment and thank you to Rae Smith, whose support stands out among all the rest. Rae's contribution to my campaign came at a time when I needed it the most.

Opening

I've always had a thing for dogs, but not when they tower nearly my own height, have long, sharp fangs, and want to kill me.

Okay, fine, I'll admit that the dog wasn't acting much like it wanted to kill me, but it hadn't been that long since several others that looked just like it had tried very hard, and that was a bit of a challenge to overcome. And to be fair, the dog wasn't acting much like it didn't want to kill me, either. I stepped back and raised my hands defensively, one out front to physically stave off the imminent fang-led charge, and the other to my chest, pressing Draignerthol against my skin through the thin fabric of the blouse I wore. I felt the relic's magical power swell and surge within me, thrilling me with the possibilities. Then, with supreme force of will, I stopped and bottled it up, knowing I'd likely cause a riot if I let it loose in the busy town square.

"Don't be scared—Cuddles would never hurt you, Princess," Gwenda said. She flicked her eyes about before bringing them back to rest on my face, her expression pleading. She licked her lips in a nervous gesture. Apparently meeting the crown princess of Kiirajanna wasn't something she'd been prepared to do.

"Cuddles? You named a dire wolf *Cuddles*?" I was incredulous, myself.

"Of course. He's..." Gwenda began to argue, but then she looked over at my cousin, her eyes begging for help.

Sephaline did help, stepping up to scratch this monster named Cuddles a couple of times behind the ears before turning a kind, peaceful smile my way and gently explaining, "Gwenda, the only experience Alyssa has with dire wolves is from our now-fabled dash across the blight to the library. It's not surprising that she's a little bit hesitant to accept Cuddles as a friend. Give her some time, okay?"

The dash to the library—that was fabled, alright. Both widespread and fabled, already, just a few months after it had happened. I'd been dead-set on reading the prophecy related to me, and so I'd talked Seph into making the journey. That was when we'd discovered the Cult of the Wyrm, who started out just trying to hold me, but then they decided to kill me.

What a nice welcoming party, right?

So my answer? Oh, I just—accidentally, I swear!—burned the entire library down, using powers I'd never even dreamed I had. That's what made the trip fabled. It wasn't the numerous waves of attacks by dire wolves and ravens we rode through to get there, nor was it the wyvern that Seph had to defeat. No, it was the whole "she used magic!" bit. Fabled, in this case, meant that I couldn't walk into a normal elf village again without people looking at me sideways, fear filling their eyes over a power they just didn't understand.

Seph succeeded in convincing Gwenda that the pet dog thing was a bad idea, and so Gwenda pushed Cuddles away with an order to "go play!" The massive beast thundered off into the nearest tree line, its tongue lolling out to the side like Old Yeller. I shook my head as I watched it run. It made sense that Gwenda, who was abnormally tall for an elf—and elves are tall folk, anyway—would claim something bigger than, say, a Chihuahua, as a pet.

"So, Alyssa," Gwenda tried the friendship thing again, "who's your favorite team in cylchoedd?"

I had no answer. I'd never even heard of cylchoedd, much less its teams. Well, once, or maybe twice, back when Prince Keion was grumbling over how our trip to the north threatened to make him late in starting cylchoedd practice. But I hadn't held any desire at the time to discuss the game, the league, or its teams with the guy who was constantly grumbling about it.

It was a strange way to start a conversation, but to call Gwenda strange would be an understatement. She'd walked up to greet Seph, who I'd been told was her only friend since childhood, wearing a dapper-looking long tunic over embroidered pantaloons. It was the kind of outfit I'd expect to see on fancy days in the castle—only, on a guy. And her shoes! Elves normally wore moccasin-like things that only become fancy in court, and then only by applying a little paint and polish in places to make them shiny. Gwenda, though, sported bright red built-up platforms on her feet, and that just made her abnormal height even more pronounced.

Because of her friend's strangeness, I watched my cousin closely for cues. Seph wasn't much help, though; she just rolled her eyes.

Cylchoedd—that's the elf word for hoops. Hoops meant basketball to me, normally. I couldn't see the elves having any sort of national basketball association, though. I decided to go ahead and bite on the verbal lure. She was, after all, just trying to make conversation.

"What's cylchoedd like?"

Gwenda looked shocked and injured at the same time. "You've never seen cylchoedd?" she challenged.

"No. No, I haven't. Keep in mind that just a few months ago I was a normal Earth-bound teenager who would've thought 'cylchoedd' was a strange cough. But I would love to hear all about it," I finished in my sweetest voice, noting how Seph's expression was begging me to make nice with her old friend.

"They probably don't have any organized sports in the primitive region Alyssa comes from," Seph said with a wink. "Missikippi, right, Crown Princess?"

I sighed playfully. "It's Mississippi, and it's not that primitive, Cousin. Well, okay, maybe it is in some ways, but we do have our sports teams. No professional ones, of course, but on Earth those only exist in big cities, and anyplace with a population more than a few thousand scares the daylights out of me." I wasn't kidding; the trip to Graceland had been fine because I was with Dad, but my friend Sarah had been talking about taking a trip to Chicago after we graduated, and I'd had to tell her there was no way I was going. Absolutely no way at all, in fact. Just the thought of all those people made my skin crawl.

Then Dad turned that on its head with a trip to New York City over Christmas. Granted, it was a little different being supported by all the crown's immense wealth, staying in the nicest of hotel rooms, and experiencing the nicest that the city had to offer. It was, I was certain, a completely different experience from what Sarah and I would have had on a tiny budget in Chicago. But the idea of being in a huge crowd of people still scared me. That was one good thing about the crown princess gig, I guess. After all, the biggest city on Kiirajanna was the crown complex at Cysegredig, and it just felt like a large village with a couple of huge buildings in the middle. Ganolog, capital of the north, had seemed bigger, but that was only because its population of a few thousand was all enclosed in a fortress. There were other cities that felt a little different than either Ganolog or Cysegredig, according to my teachers, to the south and the west, and I actually looked forward to journeying there as I sought the clans' approval. Once the holiday was over, I knew it was coming.

For the time being, though, I was enjoying the end-of-year holiday, Yule in English but *amser calan* in elf, in the tiny village where both my father and my cousin had grown up.

It is a strange holiday, but it does make sense. The name literally means "time period at the renewal of the year." It works out to be the days left over in the solar year of three hundred sixty-five days, plus a bit more, after the elves' regular six-day week is cycled through. Nobody, not even the king and queen, can work during that time other than simple tasks of lighting cook fires and such. Everybody pretty much just abandons the massive castle and cathedral complex and goes home.

A throat cleared, bringing me back to the present. "So how is this cylchoedd played?" I asked.

"Like that," Seph said with a shrug and a confused look. I followed her pointed finger with my gaze. Oh, right, of course. Every elf village I'd visited had featured kids by the twos and threes or even by the dozens rolling hoops along the ground with sticks. "Only with some adult rules, like the need to hit each other. That's usually the one with the hoop, but not always. It's really fun to watch."

Gwenda's face lit up in the too-big smile that is a standard fixture on elf faces. Seph's description had made her very happy, it seemed. She said, "I love the Bees. You'll have to go to a game with me."

"Why would you name a sports team after an insect?"

Seph and Gwenda both looked blankly at me. Oh, right. I was still thinking mostly in English, despite the fact that I was speaking in the elf tongue. Bee isn't a word in elf. It's a letter.

"I mean, a letter. Is there a Ch team?" Yes, Ch is an elf letter; it's one of my favorites, in fact, because it's so much fun to say. A good girl, even one everybody regarded as a tomboy like me, would never have hocked up anything in public in Mississippi, but that letter let me do it repeatedly in Kiirajanna.

"Of course there is," Seph said, and Gwenda added, "but they suck. They always cheat, and their fans are so obnoxious. Tell me you'll cheer for the Bs with us."

"Okay, I'll cheer for the Bs with you," I agreed. What difference did it make, really?

"No, no, no. She can't," Seph told Gwenda, shaking her head. "Remember, she's the crown princess. Royalty doesn't choose sides in cylchoedd."

Oh, right. It made that difference.

Gwenda looked disappointed for just a second and then brightened up. "Say, when you're crowned queen, don't forget that I'm the one with the dragon birthmark."

Well, that got my attention. The prophecies we'd gone to the library to read spoke of someone born with a dragon birthmark. Someone, it seemed, who would turn elf society over onto its head, someone who would bring sorcery back and not in a good way, someone who would somehow involve the now-mythical dragons of old.

Someone like me, who'd actually been born with a dragon birthmark on my right shoulder blade. I wondered about the thing growing up, but Momma just smiled and shrugged whenever I asked. When Dad waltzed back into my life, he'd proven himself my father by knowing about it. It seemed a big deal to him then, and it was an even bigger deal now that I knew what it meant.

Yes, I had it, but I really didn't want it.

"You have a dragon birthmark?" I asked, ignoring Seph's look of alarm. My cousin rolled her eyes as her old friend nodded, skipped over to me, and hauled the back of her tunic up for me to see.

It was a birthmark, for sure. It was kind of cute, too. Sitting right above her hips in the middle of her back as it did, it looked like one of those tribal tattoos people on Earth get. Only…

A heart. It was a cute elongated heart, not a dragon. I caught Seph's frantic wiggle of her head, though, and so I chose my words carefully. After all, mirrors weren't common outside the palace in Kiirajanna, and so how was Gwenda to know that she didn't have a dragon birthmark?

"It's—nice, Gwenda. Very clear. I will most assuredly keep this birthmark in mind when I gain the throne."

"Yay!" Gwenda said, letting her tunic fall back down and then bouncing for joy. "It's my lucky day to have met you, Princess!"

"Yeah," I said, not sure what else I could add.

"And now, I have to go. Chores, Your Highness. I hope to see you upon the morrow," the weird one said. She slipped me a precarious combination of curtsy and bow, one that her height combined with the platform shoes made grotesque, and then she spun back around to run home.

Only she didn't get far. She tripped over her own feet.

"Oopsie," she said, and it was even more irritating thanks to the way she raised her high-pitched voice even higher. She must have been nearly seven feet tall and yet she sounded like a pixie.

She dusted herself off as Seph helped her up.

"Oopsie, indeed," Seph said, watching her long-time friend jog away. "That was what everybody called her growing up: Oopsie. It was what we heard her say most often."

"She seems nice, bless her heart" I said.

"She is nice. She's just a little bit eccentric."

Pot, meet kettle, I thought but decided not to say. Seph was the queen of eccentric herself, a ranger whose familiar was a wolverine named Booboo and whose battle cry was *eep*. But she was the first cousin I'd ever met, and as far as I knew the only one I had, and so that made all the eccentricity okay in my eyes.

"How come she wears that getup?" I switched to English in case her friend managed to hear.

"She's going to be the Dragon Queen, at least so she believes. The Dragon Queen should dress nicely, and wear masculine clothing because the aspect of the dragon is masculine, she says."

"The aspect of the dragon is—what? Are dragons masculine?" I was having a hard time separating what sounded like astrology talk from the reality that dragons had once actually existed on Kiirajanna.

"How should I know? She's the one who constantly says dragons are still around, thanks to her strange queenly dreams. By this point you know as much as, if not more than, I do about them," Seph reminded me.

"Right. I guess. So why the shoes, then?"

"She wears tall shoes to look down upon her subjects, like a
—"

"A dragon. Right. Makes sense." It didn't, not really, but whatever. "Why red?"

"Dragon, remember?"

"We don't know what color dragons were, though."

"She does. Or at least she's convinced herself that she does. Look, now we both know that my old childhood friend is—what's your word?"

"Kookoo sums it up pretty nicely." I added the standard Earth hand gesture, my index finger circling my right ear.

"Kookoo. Fine," Seph said, sounding dejected. I realized belatedly that I was, after all, attacking a long-time friend of hers.

"So does she have, like, a boyfriend? Or is she promised to one from a faraway village like Prince Charming?" I asked, trying to lighten the mood.

"Um," Seph stalled, not answering. It was clear I'd hit a nerve.

"Is she—is she gay?" I'd never thought of the elves being like that, but it didn't make sense why I wouldn't have. Nothing wrong with it, certainly, but—well, it just hadn't occurred to me.

"Gay?" Seph shook her head in confusion.

"Sorry," I continued in English, and then tried in elf after searching for a moment. "*Hoyw?*"

If you're new to elf, the best I can say is that it's based on Welsh, from Earth. Or, if the history is to be believed, Welsh is based on elf. Whichever is true, it's a beautiful language. But w's and y's are both vowels, which takes some getting used to. The word I'd just said is, phonetically, ho-ee-yoo.

Seph shook her head, still clearly not comprehending my meaning. Then I remembered the word I'd been taught once in one of my more private lessons.

"*Gyrywgydiwr?*"

As fun as the word is to say—phonetically, goo-roo-goo-dee-oor—it literally means grabber-of-man. That works fine with gay men, though I couldn't get anything different from my teacher for gay women. But at least Seph finally got it. Her face lit up with horror.

"No! No, she's not. Well, maybe. She, um, isn't certain. Look, that's not something we talk about."

"Ah, okay." I gave up, chalking it up to repressed elf society.

"So what's with the birthmark thing?" I asked in English, trying to venture into more comfortable territory.

"When she was young, somebody joked with her that she was special, that her birthmark was a dragon. She took it to heart, and nobody's been willing to break that since. We even go so far as to hide the mirrors when she comes around. She's convinced that she's the one with the dragon birthmark."

"Well, she can have it."

"What?" Seph turned to face me, scandalized.

"No, really. She can have it. The birthmark, the castle, the crown, everything. I love Kiirajanna, and I love the elves, but—me? Queen? Seph, you saw me in Ganolog. I started a war, Seph. I'm a Mississippi girl. A rabid dog's got more diplomacy skills than me. I did well in school, and was headed to college at State to study engineering, or something. Now here I am, learning to be all regal and stuff, and—and I burned a library down, Seph. I burned a library down. And not just a library—*the* library." Seph's face clouded over at that; she apparently remembered the scene as vividly as I did, with me standing in the middle of the most ancient, well-stocked, library in the land, my newfound magical powers swirling about me as I threw tendrils of energy this way and that. Oh, yes, we won, Seph and Booboo both survived, and the Cult of the Wyrm was defeated, rounded up, and imprisoned, but all that paled in comparison to what I'd done. I'd used magic, something forbidden to elves for countless centuries, and worse, I'd used it to burn a library down.

"This conversation should not take place out here in the village commons," a strong, familiar voice interrupted my rant. Seph and I both turned to face the elf king, who was standing with his hands on his hips casting a royal shadow over the pair of us. His expression made it clear that neither of us had any choice but to follow him.

"English is rare outside of the royal family, but it is still known throughout the realm, and you must remember that for your own safety as well as that of the crown," he chided us.

"Yes, Daddy," I said meekly as Seph and I let him lead us into her father's house.

The People

My father rounded on us as the door closed.

Me, that is. He apparently completely forgot that Seph had come in too, and rounded on and then focused the brute force of his royal bearing on me.

"What, precisely, did you mean by 'she can have it,' Alyssa?"

I tried to meet his gaze directly, but it was impossible to shield from the glower. When my eyes finally settled comfortably on the tops of his boots, I said, "I meant that she can have it. Just that. Pure, simple, direct, no strings attached, give me a marker to color in a dragon on top of her tramp stamp and I'll just be heading home to Momma. Y'all will have your queen, and the elf lands will be happy, and you can come home to Mississippi and live with us, and...."

My voice trailed off, as I hadn't any idea how I was going to finish that little rant. I'd figured he would jump in and start yelling. He didn't, though, and after a few seconds of silence I pushed my eyes back up to his face.

He was crying.

Okay, I admit, crying is a stretch. But I saw a tear; I know I did. Slowly, his hands reached out and grasped mine. He led me gently over to the table in the middle of the small home, and together, as one, we sat. With one hand Dad pushed a tiny lock of my hair out of my face from where it'd fallen.

Finally my father, the ruler of the entire realm of the elves, spoke, his voice rumbling out of his chest like the muted thunder of a spring rain. "Alyssa…. It—it is not fair, what Kiirajanna has asked of you, my daughter. I know, because I said the same thing many years ago in my own training to take the male throne. The idea of being a ruler, of having servants, of everyone bowing and saying, 'Yes, Sire,' and 'Your Majesty' all the time, is but a siren's song compared to the reality of the burden of leadership. You, my daughter, are just starting to step into that burden, and yet if the prophecy is to be believed—and I have no doubt that it is—then you have to look forward to the toughest monarchy in our entire history, all four epochs combined. It would be absolutely terrifying to an experienced ruler. I can only imagine how daunting it must be to you."

"It is, Daddy." That wasn't the biggest problem, though. I figured there was no point beating around it. "But my real worry, over and above the weight anyone would feel in the crown on her head, is that this society that I'm destined to lead despises me. Remember the talk we had last time we were sitting at this table?" He nodded; right after we'd returned from the disastrous library-burning trip, his brother had verbally, and strongly, taken me to task over accessing the forbidden powers of outright, visible, magic. I'd satisfied my uncle, and my father had helped me convince High Priestess Naissa that I shouldn't be banished because of it, but the battle of Ganolog as well as the shunning I'd received in more nearby villages told me that the people hadn't followed their lead quite like Dad and I hoped they would. Outright attempts on my life had stopped, granted, but the quiet and secretive whispers and the glares cast my way were sometimes even worse than that. At least an attack on my life was overt, and I could see it and deal with it. What had happened up in the northlands, with the outright challenge not only to my own life but to the leadership of my father's most loyal chieftain, terrified me for the future of my reign on Kiirajanna. There were a group of elves—a large group, it seemed—who were willing to take up arms against what they viewed as a challenge to their traditional way of life, and I wasn't sure if there was anything I could ever do to convince them that I was not the dire challenge that they imagined.

Heck, sometimes I couldn't help wondering if they were right. Would I actually become that challenge?

Even here, my father's own home village, there was a hidden resentment problem. I'd learned enough in my studies on the history of elf government to suspect that Dad was the most popular king there'd ever been. Before my use of magic, that popularity seemed to rub right off on me, with elders and children alike flocking to shake the Earth-born princess's hand, sharing in an alien-feeling gesture from the exotic and far-off realm of Mississippi. Ever since word of magic had reached their ears, though, they avoided me entirely, only gathering around my father when I wasn't there.

I saw it, clearly, and it hurt. Just as clearly, it hurt him a little, too.

"Do not worry, my dear daughter; they are only afraid of what you represent," my father's favorite attempt at comfort sank sloppily. The logic only went so far. I was afraid of what I represented. If the prophecy were to be believed—and, according to everybody who mattered, it was—then I was bound to absolutely, personally, violently decimate the countryside. I would lay waste to their customs, divide the elves brother against brother, and all sorts of other miserable things. "Alyssa" would soon, if prophecy were to be believed, be the Kiirajanna version of the cursed name "Adolf Hitler." Back in the library I'd read all these evil outcomes of my reign and figured there had to be some way out of it all, but then I managed to fulfill the first one right then and there by burning the dang building down to the ground. A library. To me, a nearly *sacred* space. I burned it completely down, and that I hadn't done it on purpose didn't matter much. Then I'd gone and answered other prophecies, like lighting the sky up with radiance and starting wars among brethren and so on.

It was really darn depressing, all things considered.

"Alyssa, they do not—" Dad started, but I interrupted.

"Oh, yes, they do, bless their little hearts. Don't tell me you don't see the dark looks. Don't tell me you don't sense them holding back and away from me. I'm going to be the first elf queen to be ruler of a people who don't want her rule at all."

"Not the first," Dad joked. At least, I hoped he was joking.

"Right. What, the second?" Hey, I'd studied elf history nearly as thoroughly as he had.

"Third, I think, but that is not the point. Do you really believe that I was Mister Popularity when I was crowned?"

He had me there. "Well, yeah. I do, Dad. You're a pretty cool guy. And you've never, that I know of anyway, used magic."

"You are right, but you cannot keep dwelling on the use of magic. I know, I know, it has been forbidden by your High Priestess Sternyface, and by others," he said, grinning with me as he used my epithet for Naissa. "And yet, at the same time, it has been prophesied, and it was done, and there is no possible path from where we are except forward through time. It gladdens me more than it should, I must admit, that you think I am a pretty cool guy, but I have not always been labeled so, nor ever by all. It is the nature of being in charge that you garner dislike as you move along. When I was young, it was even worse."

"He was an arrogant asshole when he was young, I'll tell you what," his brother, my uncle, chimed in as he moved past the table. "Like some tea?"

"Oh, yes," I breathed. My uncle was a smith of soft items—leather and wood—by trade, but he also had a knack with herbology that made his tea incredible. His concoction would make the saddest sad happy, and the gladdest glad even happier. And, as I'd learned the hard way in my first trip to the village, it makes the worst hangover—well, it made it a little less painfully horrible, a feat that I have come to believe is pretty much legendary.

"He is right," Dad nodded as his brother got busy with the water. "I was—I suppose, an arrogant asshole when I was young. And some would say the same about me even now. That is my point, in matter of fact. You see, it is the norm for rulers to be regarded as arrogant at first, especially when they follow behind someone who is popular. That is the curse of taking over when things are going well. You cannot adopt the same behavior and policies as the one who governed before you, or else you are considered weak and unoriginal. At the same time, doing your own thing marks you as an agent of change, and change is both feared and rejected whenever it is not seen as absolutely essential, and it is often feared even then. That is likely a significant part of the angst you are picking up on, my lovely daughter. You are already taking over for a very popular queen, and it is the change you cannot help but bring that they fear."

"That, and the magic," I reminded him.

"Well, there is that," he agreed, and then the table grew silent as we stirred the tea that my uncle had just warmed up for us.

He finally broke the tea-infused silence by continuing, "Alyssa, as difficult and even painful as it may prove, you must continue to move forward and become the queen you are destined to be."

I ignored my uncle's disapproving grunt as I said, "I know, Dad." I did, really. I knew none of us had a choice, but I didn't have anywhere near as much to complain about as he did. Here was a man who'd given up years of his life to train to be king, and then years of his life to find a human woman to love and to bear his child as elf custom required, only to be followed by nearly two decades away from that woman, and the daughter they'd made, in order to return to his duty as sovereign over his people. Sure, I'd hated him for it at first, but we got past that as I came to understand the burden he was carrying. Now, the only thing that stood between him and the love of his life—my mother—was for me to put on my big girl panties and take the throne, and then for his own successor to be appointed and trained. If I were to step aside in someone else's behalf, bless her heart, custom as well as reality said it would be years, if ever, before Dad could join Momma full-time at home.

"And no more public outbursts, okay?"

"Can't promise that." I gave him my most precocious smile, but he ignored it.

"You must. For it is that degree of discipline that is required of a queen, dear."

"Okay, Dad," I said, getting serious. "I'll promise, no more public outbursts. Now, drink your tea, and I'll drink mine, before the water gets cold again."

"Yes, Your Highness," Dad said with a smile. I couldn't quite tell if he was lightly mocking me or gently deferring to me, but to be honest, I liked it either way.

"Maybe her standing among the people will be helped once she has completed her hunhymgais," Seph offered from behind the safety of her own cup of tea.

Dad nodded tentatively and said, "It should, definitely. I cannot say by how much, but our peoples' opinions should certainly rise once you become truly one of us, Alyssa."

"Yay." One corner of my lip twisted up into my best, most sarcastic, smile. "Into the woods naked go I." Literally, hunhymgais means "quest for self," and it is the rite of passage to adulthood for the elves. I hadn't had one, of course. In Mississippi they frown on prepubescent children running off "*nekkid* as a jaybird" into the woods by themselves. The elves' quest for maturity, on the other hand, required a young elf to fend for herself for six weeks—thirty-six long, cold, and probably hungry days—using just her wits and nothing else, not even clothes—and then return, hopefully with a story to tell of facing down one or more of her worst fears.

My worst fear? That would be running off into the woods *nekkid*, especially in the wintertime. That was just not my kind of thing.

"Not naked," Dad argued, shaking his head. "A child leaves naked and is expected to return an adult in whatever attire pleases them—fashioned, of course, by their own arts. You, on the other hand, come a bit late to the questing, physically well past your childhood, and I will not have my daughter, our future queen, run off into the woods with her womanhood displayed for all to see."

"But if I don't do it just like an elf, won't that diminish the effect? Won't people just gripe that I didn't start it naked like everybody else?"

"No. Well, maybe. But I invited the counsel of the High Priestess before we left, and she informed me that there is precedent for beginning the hunhymgais clothed, especially insofar as the crown princess is concerned. It has always been done, in fact. We will make sure to inform everyone that you wanted to run off naked like your brethren but were prevented by tradition. How is that?"

"Great, Dad. Anybody who knows me will believe it when you say how much I wanted to run off naked like everybody else, or, for that matter, how I was prevented from doing it by that thing I cherish most—tradition."

"Sarcasm, dear?"

"Ya think?"

My uncle's snort sounded from the tiny pantry-kitchen combination that was the third room of the house. When he stopped chortling, he added, "One additional thing to consider, my brother, is that she cannot leave Draignerthol behind when she undertakes the quest. It is too precious a relic, and even under the castle's own vaunted security it's too inviting a target for thieves. She should wear it with her quest, and of course that means she must wear something to cover it up."

"Right, Dafydd," Dad said, his eyes going to the lump on my chest that indicated the hidden presence of the legendary elf pendant. It had been fashioned in the early days of elf civilization, back when magic was cool, by some of the most powerful sorcerers in Kiirajanna. Then, when the great priestess-queen Rhiannon had crossed over to Earth, intending to forever seal herself away from the land of magic and the elves, she'd taken it with her, and the entire elf race had assumed the pendant lost to the hands of time and humans. Somehow, thousands of years later, the striking dragon-shaped pendant had been handed to me by Momma the night before I crossed back into its original homeland. Its blue gemstone eyes flared to life when touched by anyone who could wield magic, and it seriously magnified my own puny grasp on the power. It had protected me from poison when I didn't even realize it was doing so, and later I'd pulled enough power through it to save us in a fall from a cliff, to defeat Padrig's foes' sorcery, and yes, to burn the library down. I treasured it and cursed it, both at the same time.

"Can we at least wait till after Yule?" Since we were talking in English, still, for security, I used the English term. "Like, a few months after Yule? I doubt the people would believe the claim that tradition made me wear an overcoat, too." In truth, the area of Kiirajanna the castle was located on was pretty close to the equator, and so it wasn't all that cold, but the possibility of being out in real winter weather without overgarments still terrified the Mississippian in me.

Heck, the whole bit terrified me—all of it, especially the part that involved traveling to the other three clans to gain their approval, after the little war I'd started with Padrig's clan. That scared me every bit as much as the hunhymgais thing. It was just that I didn't want to die of hypothermia along the way.

My dad chuckled. "No, Alyssa, we do not specify the timing of hunhymgais to suit ourselves. That is part of the challenge. You must go when the time is right, once you have marched yourself into the hearts of the eastern, western, and southern clans, whether that requires a month, or twelve, to complete. Besides, you can never know where you will end up, so judging the time to leave based on the weather pattern near the castle is an exercise that is entirely useless."

"What do you mean I never know? Don't I just run there?" I hadn't gotten too much into the details; all I'd heard so far was "naked," "alone," "woods," and "six weeks." That had been quite enough.

"Absolutely not. We hold a ceremony, you take a special staff with you, and you step into one of the ley-gates. It transports you to wherever you need to be to successfully complete your quest."

"Earth?" I asked, confused. "Or do they go to random places on Kiirajanna?" The ley-gates were the system of energy spots used to transport people from Earth to Kiirajanna and back, as far as I knew. We'd taken one from Memphis when I'd first made the transition. There was another used by trappers far to the north that had both entrance and exit in the same realm, but I'd been led to believe it was a rare one. That, and it always ended at the same two points, just as the other I'd taken did.

Dad nodded and said, "Maybe Earth, but most of us, I think, end up going to another location on Kiirajanna. At least, I did." Seph nodded from behind her cup; she'd stayed on Kiirajanna, too, apparently.

"How do you know it's Kiirajanna?"

"Most elves do not know the difference, I suppose, but those of us who have made the journey to Earth do, as do you. You recall the emptiness you felt when you made the trip back to the world in which you were born, yes? It is less a sensation, and more a lack of sensation, the lack of awareness of your surroundings that you have already become accustomed to here."

"Oh, right. Magic," I said, and then I wished I hadn't. Dad had sprinkled the term freely through our first conversation to get me excited about coming back to Kiirajanna, describing the magical realm of magical creatures and magical elves and magical this and that, but as soon as I'd crossed over I'd found that using the word magic was nearly as taboo as the act of using the power itself. They still held that singing the trees to shape and healing each other, in addition to all their ranger powers, were somehow different from using magic, but I knew the distinction was fake. Part of the reason I hated using the word myself was my frustration that nobody would listen to me about what I already knew to be true regarding the true nature of magic.

"Yes," Dad said, pursing his lips to make it clear he was not using the word on purpose. He rose. "Well, Brother, thank you for the tea. It was wonderful as usual. Do you believe that we could get the men of the village together for some wrestling fun?"

I looked across the table and caught my cousin's eye; she was as bored with the idea of watching wrestling as I was. She rose, shrugged, and said, "I'm going to head into the woods with Booboo for a while, Alyssa. Would you like to come with?"

I nodded a lie. No, I had no desire to walk through the woods for a while, with or without my cousin and her familiar. The wolverine still scared me, with his looks and actions both. He reminded me of a small bear. He'd proven himself an incredibly powerful, fast, agile, and strong ally, though.

Sometimes he made me wish that I had my own familiar, one just as powerful, fast, agile, and strong, but only a little bit cuter and fluffier. My tree didn't count. As much as I cherished, and was cherished by, Little Treebeard, my potted elm that I'd somehow found a weird, magical connection with, it was still just a tree, growing in a pot. Oh, it could make its intentions clear enough, and loudly, by smacking the walls with its ever-lengthening branches, but it couldn't go on vacations with us like Booboo could. I'd had to leave it in the few remaining palace guards' care, and, weird as it sounds, I missed the little guy.

We stepped out of the village into the open forest. The elves loved their forests to look more like well-manicured lawns, and rangers like my cousin were tasked with keeping everything growing in a neat and orderly manner. Even the grass grew to a uniform height and no farther. It really was pretty, if you weren't looking for the mangled wildness that a good Southern old growth forest contained. I wasn't, so it was good.

As we stepped lightly through the trees, I couldn't help noticing with pride that my own stride was matching that of the elves more and more every day. They were very good at passing through the woods silently, and my cousin, trained as a ranger, was exceptionally good at it. When I'd arrived I had felt like an elephant compared to her cheetah walk, but even she occasionally commented on how much more like an elf I was moving.

As we walked it started snowing lightly. Strangely, I didn't feel all that cold. Then again, I'd spent much of the winter so far outdoors, with a lot of that in the far northlands. I figured my body was becoming used to the lower temperature, at least more than it ever had in Mississippi.

"Cousin?"

"Hmm?" I could tell from her quietened, serene reply that she was in her attuned mode. Somehow, out in the woods, I could lightly whisper something and she'd still hear me, thanks to the same powers she used to know exactly where I was without looking. I could do it, myself, out to a limited distance, but her sensitivity was—well, not to overuse the term, but it was magical.

"Gwenda's not a ranger, is she?"

"No, she's learning to craft with leather. From my pa, in fact."

"How does she have a dire wolf as a familiar, then?"

"Oh, Cuddles isn't her familiar. He's more of a pet."

"That's—not what I expected," I admitted. "In fact, that's a little more unnerving than if he'd been a familiar. How does she keep a dire wolf as a pet?"

Seph shrugged as though the answer should've been plain to see all along. "She feeds him. Same way you keep a tree as a pet, though I'm certainly not one to judge."

"L.T.'s not a.... So, what does she feed him? Never mind," I added quickly, correcting myself based on the glare she shot my direction. Obviously, whatever you feed a dire wolf to keep it as a pet wasn't something I would want to have described to me.

We walked along in silence, leaving me to contemplate my upcoming vision quest, whenever that would be. We still had a couple more days of relaxation and frivolity left in the holiday for me to worry about it. I planned to spend a few days at some point out camping with Seph learning all I could about which parts of which plants were edible, but not knowing which part of the world I'd end up in made that seem mostly useless. The thought briefly flashed across my mind to ask Seph to start teaching me a little of what she knew now, but it was Yule, and we weren't supposed to do such things at the end-of-the-year celebration.

Yule time was party time.

In fact, when we'd arrived, Dad had physically, publicly, symbolically, doffed the crown of the Elf King in order to just be himself for the one and only true holiday of the year. I figured it would probably end up being my absolute favorite holiday once I became queen.

If I became queen.

COEDWIG

a forest—one of the most beautiful

creations on Kiirajanna

The Challenge

"Ych a fi!"

I spun my head toward my father, stunned. From what I could see of Seph's expression in my peripheral view, I could tell she was as shocked as I was. My dad, the high king of all Kiira-janna, the elf whose speech *patterns* were always exorbitantly formal whether in English or his native tongue, had just cursed. And it wasn't a nice curse, either; it was the most disgusting of the disgust phrases that the beautiful elf language has available to it. It involved, literally, something about an ox and a person, I think, but I'd been taught never to say the phrase unless I wanted my mouth washed out with soap.

Granted, that lesson was with the five year olds, but it stuck pretty solidly with me. I could tell from Seph's mirrored reaction that my memory was accurate.

I didn't understand, though. Coming back to the castle for the last couple of ceremonies related to Yule, we'd just rounded the final corner to make the approach straight in to the front doors. It was a gorgeous final approach, as always. Huge expanses of grass mingled amongst the trees, not a single discoloration in sight despite it being the dead of winter. The only thing out of the ordinary was a ring of gaily decorated tents arrayed about the main courtyard in front of the castle, but that, in turn, looked spectacular to me. The vibrant colors of all the pendants were spectacular, and the variety and decoration of clothing worn by all the elves gathered about them was also spectacular.

It was, in a word, spectacular.

What, then, did my father find so disgusting?

"Alyssa, Sephaline, get inside and up to your rooms as quickly as possible," he growled in English just as the horseless carriage rumbled to a stop. He punctuated the order with an adamant little gesture down low, below the edge of the carriage so that it couldn't be seen by onlookers. Seph obediently grabbed my arm and rushed us inside and straight up the stairs.

"Wait," I ordered, pulling her to a halt at the first landing. "It took me a second, but I know those colors. Some of them, anyway. They were here last summer at my coronation. But why would my father be so put out by seeing Swadda's arrival?" Seph shook her head mutely and raised her shoulders in a shrug of ignorance. But I vividly remembered meeting the *penna* of the western tribe back then, along with the leaders of the other tribes as well. It had seemed like a great big elf party, with the huge drums of the eastern clan mixing in with the undulating song of the southern clan and the weird multi-voice guttural harmony from the western elves, and a whole lot of dancing and drinking to go with it. They'd all seemed pleased to meet me at the time, too.

What could be going on now?

"I am not entirely certain, but it could have something to do with their stated desire to put your head up on a pike to parade back to their people," a slitheringly amused voice cut in from the side. Seph, whose ranger gift of sensing approaching elves didn't work in stone structures, jumped in surprise, but it gave me a little pride to have sensed the royal trio approaching.

"Greetings, Meriel. Glad to see you three made it back safely from your amser calan festivities. We had a marvelous time; thank you so for the kindness of asking. Tell me, did you have a chance to stock up on the wine of nastiness while you were away?" I tossed the queen's youngest daughter a smirk.

Of the three, Meriel showed the most reaction as her eyes squinted ever so slightly and her lips pressed together. I was proud of myself for advancing in the ability to read elf expressions as much as I had in less than a year; when I'd arrived her expression would have seemed stolid. Now I could read the anger right off her eyelid lines, see the speechlessness on her lips, and watch the anger intensify as a result of her inability to make a comeback.

After all, I reckoned, very few had ever sniped back at the Light of Queen Talaith's Eyes, or whatever the youngest brat was calling herself.

Seren, the eldest, allowed herself another moment of calm serenity before rolling her eyes at the antics. "It is so nice to see the peace of Christmastime lasted so long before being smashed asunder." She split her regal glare between me and her sister. Her point was valid, I had to admit. Ostensibly to give the queen's kids a cultural rounding-off with a taste of a Southern Christmas, Dad had led us back through the portal to Memphis a couple of days before Christmas Eve, and we'd spent a wonderful Christmas with Momma. Of course, I and the brats had all decided that the trip was mostly of benefit to the king himself, and of course we'd had significantly different reactions to that. Still, the castle in Wales had been alerted of our impending plan, and so the queen's kids had been shown pretty much every possible imaginable joy, right up to a first class flight up to see Times Square in New York City. And, hey, Momma and I got to go along. And they'd still complained about being asked to do it. Meriel had, anyway, in a supercilious manner that obviously included her siblings as complainants.

The upshot was that it had actually been harmonizing in a strange, superficially joyful sort of way. Meriel, the same elf who'd just gleefully described my head on a pike, had actually grinned widely at and along with me as we watched a huge tree flash its lights at us in Rockefeller Center. Later, as we sat around the kitchen table and enjoyed Momma's Christmas morning breakfast, I finally saw Seren let slip her royal guard on her expression. She smiled, she laughed, and she even joked. The gift giving had been delightful, too.

It had all been beautiful, if obviously short-lived. But that's another story.

"Sarcasm, sister? You are so far above the low-brow humor of the half-human," Meriel purred. That made it my turn to glare.

Keion remained silent. The middle child and only son of Talaith, Keion was a smoldering mass of testosterone-based sexiness who had even gotten my really selective engines revved up once. Or, maybe twice. Okay, truth be told, he's the only member of the male half of the species who ever brought out such a visceral hunger in me. Problem was, he knew it, and he gloried in the knowledge, and I knew it, and I hated him for the glory. It was all so high-school-ish, and yet I found it impossible to keep my heart from leaping into my throat when I saw him.

For his part, he managed to maintain the same perfectly neutral expression that his elder sister held. I didn't doubt for a second that he was on my side; he'd saved my head, and my neck, and literally the rest of the body it was attached to, too many times already for me to question his motives. He'd even sworn personal allegiance to me in a strange spur-of-the-moment ceremony up in the north under the incredible northern lights. But those times were all when his sisters weren't present, and who could know what he'd decide if he had to choose between us?

"So what about you, Prince Keion?" I teased. "Do your toes curl in excitement at the idea of seeing my head on a pike, too?"

That earned a flush and a glare, both at the same time, before he answered with a fair amount of heat in his voice, "I believe, Princess, that my sister was engaging in hyperbole regarding threat to your physical form. However, the clans gathered have brought quite a solid argument, in light of all the cursed magic we have been witness to, that Seren, the well-trained, well-bred daughter of Talaith herself, would make a demonstrably better choice to succeed her mother than a gangly Mississippi girl with no royal upbringing whatsoever."

"I—I see," I murmured, feeling my control slip away in the crushing agony that his words brought with them. He was absolutely correct, and I'd wished for someone else to take the crown in my place many more times than anybody else knew. None of that mattered, though, when it was him standing there offering the damning opinion. I bravely wrestled what control I could back to my face and my spine and my knees, somehow preventing the latter from buckling. "Well. Thank you for your—opinion, Prince. I shall take that under advisement, and—now I must seek rest after a long journey back. Sephaline, would you please retire with me?"

The two of us left the trio preening in the stair landing by themselves. I marched slowly, deliberately, to my room, opened the door, and firmly but quietly shut it after Seph and Booboo, who had crept up behind us in an impossibly silent way. Then I slumped onto the bed, suddenly feeling as exhausted as I'd claimed to be.

I ignored the excited rattling and the rustling in the corner as long as I could, which wasn't very long. "Hi, L.T.," I called out in the sing-song I used to communicate with my new, strange friend. "We weren't gone all that long. I trust you were well tended?"

Another rattle, one I somehow recognized as an affirmative.

Little Treebeard, or L.T., is a very small tree. He's—or she's—my best friend, I guess, though I still hadn't figured out how to tell the tree's gender. Regardless, using *it* seemed wrong. The priests gave me the small potted elm as part of my lessons to connect to nature, and I'd connected after a long, tough run of effort. While that was a tremendous academic achievement, it was also the moment the tree latched on to me, and hard. When I went to the north, I'd only been gone for a couple of days before Dad was forced to send a squad carrying L.T. after me.

The only communication the tree and I had was the rattling of L.T.'s branches and the sing-song of my voice. In spite of that, the tree had managed to warn me of an impending attack a couple of times. And I—weird as it sounds, I kind of enjoyed singing to the little creature, who would occasionally swoosh his branches in appreciation. Seph, who was more of an animal person, just watched wide-eyed in wonder at the connection we had.

"Some day, Alyssa, you're going to have to deal with the hold that boy has over your spirit," my cousin interrupted gently from the corner.

"Was it that obvious?" I asked, dreading the answer. I looked up from where I'd buried my face in my hands and gently wiped the tears that I hadn't realized were falling.

"It's always been that obvious, but just now you seriously overplayed it. 'I shall take that under advisement, Prince,'" she mimicked, though her smile was genuine enough to remove the sting. "Look, it's obvious that you care for him, and that he cares for you, too, but seriously, Alyssa. He's most likely to become king after your father returns to Mississippi, and you're still quite in the running to become queen, no matter how much you wish differently—yes, that's obvious, too—and you know that the king and queen cannot be involved in that way. You also know that he's already promised. You need to admit it, and quit torturing yourself over it, and—what's so funny?"

She asked the question in such a piqued way that it made everything seem even funnier. Suddenly I was guffawing on the bed, rolling around clutching my side. She started giggling, too.

Finally the fit died down. "So, what was so funny?" she probed again.

"Mississippi. You said it right. That's the first time since I've been here."

"I've been practicing."

"Why?"

"Why do you ask, why?" she asked, confusion spread across her face.

"Nobody on Kiirajanna cares how you pronounce it. It's just a state back home."

"You do. It's where you were born."

"Well...." She had a point. I'd corrected her every time she'd mispronounced it because I guess it really was important to me. "I appreciate it, Cousin," I said, earning me another radiant smile. Then I took the mood down a notch with a question, "Do you think that crowd out there is really after my head?"

"No, of course not. Well, maybe. I'm not sure, Alyssa. Your father seemed awfully perturbed, and he's still out there now."

"True. I've never seen him like that." Granted, I'd only seen him for a few months of the time I'd been on Kiirajanna, but I couldn't imagine it otherwise. Seph nodded confirmation. "So what are we going to do if they are?"

She shrugged. "We'll do what we've been doing, Alyssa. We'll figure out a way around it."

"It may not be that simple, though."

She shrugged again and held me in a stern gaze. "It may not be that complicated, actually. You don't know. You've got to stop worrying about what you don't have any control over. You're smart, and you're already one of the most powerful elves in the realm. You have powerful people on your side: your pa, the queen, the high priestess, and me!"

"Why would the queen be on my side? It's in her daughter's best interest to be on their side."

"Maybe. I doubt it, since she would not have graced you with the invitations to tea or anything else if she weren't on your side. But you're still worrying about something you can't control. Stop it!" She punctuated her last sentence with a clap on each word.

"Okay. I'm tired, anyway. Maybe a night of sleep will help clear this all up."

"Maybe. Probably! It must." She nodded decisively and walked out, the shaggy wolverine padding quietly behind.

The Audience

"Highness, your presence is requested in the throne room," the little servant girl said. It was pretty easy to tell from the way she kept her eyes glued to the ground, and then how quickly she darted out again, that I didn't have a pleasant visit ahead of me.

I sighed.

"You'll be fine, Princess," a droll voice carried from the corner. I glanced over, pushing my eyes as far to the side as they would go without moving my head in an attempt to cast a dark, meaningful glare at my guard. It didn't work; I'm not sure if the failure was due to my inability to move any of my facial muscles or the old battle-axe's inability to be glared at.

"Thanks, Aerona," I said through pursed lips, earning me an affronted gasp from the makeup lady who was trying to cover up my lack of sleep by intensively pinching and pushing and prodding and smothering the skin on my face. I wasn't even certain there was all that much left of it, but I hoped what was there would be presentable.

So, apparently, did the queen, who had insisted on providing me the services of her personal retinue of makeup and wardrobe artists. It was that insistence, in fact, that had told me all I needed to know about how the day was going to go.

"I have done all I can," the makeup artist spat and walked from the room. Seph raised my spirits a little by visibly giving me a once-over and raising two fingers in the gesture my human friends would raise two thumbs to make.

"Thanks. You coming with, Cousin?"

"No! No, I was not summoned, Alyssa. I wish I could, but—"

"I know. Well, let's face the jungle, Aerona." The two of us stepped out of the dressing room, me in a resplendent yellow beaded blouse that came down nearly to my ankles, and her following in her much darker bodyguard attire.

"The word is *goeddgwyllt*, Princess," she murmured from behind me as we made our stately way down the third-floor hall.

"Thanks, Aerona," I said, trying to keep sarcasm out of my voice, but failing. I didn't need the grammar lesson when something so significant was happening just two floors down. Granted, she was right; I'd used the proper word for jungle and so it didn't make sense in the elf idiom. The correct way to get the point across was to suggest facing the crazy trees—which would, granted, have made a native elf a lot more nervous than merely facing a jungle like they had in the southern part of the continent.

At least she had gotten my point.

"You're welcome, Princess."

"So how was your vacation?" She and I hadn't had any time to chat; she'd been away for the entirety of Yule since I was safely tucked away at my father's native village—and since, I suspected, he'd ordered her to take time off. Otherwise, she'd have continued standing just past my shoulder glaring at the shadows on my behalf for the entire time. But she'd spun into my room as the door was closing behind Seph the night before, and as far as I knew she stood in watch over me all night, just as she had every night since the ill-fated attack on me during my first few days in Kiira-janna.

"I enjoyed it," was the simple reply.

"Did you go home?"

"Yes."

"Are you willing to supply me with any details?" In addition to the fact that I was anxious for anything to take my mind off of the upcoming meeting, I was really genuinely curious.

"At the moment, such details would be frivolous."

"Thanks," I grumbled.

Finally the long walk ended, as it eventually had to. I found myself standing in front of the doors that were so seldom closed, hoping that they could somehow just remain that way and it would all just disappear. Only, I knew it wouldn't, and so I took a deep breath and nodded to Aerona, who pulled one of the doors wide to let me in.

I stepped into the throne room and just barely kept myself from shivering as the temperature seemed to plummet. My father's eyes met mine briefly, and in that fleeting microsecond I watched a host of emotions flash by. The first was genuine surprise; I suppose Aerona's door-swoosh had been a little bit too abrupt. It was followed by deep and sustaining love, a dash of pity, a whole mess of sorrow, and even a little pinch of personal humiliation.

Great. I suppressed a sigh, but only barely.

The queen, for her part, wore her own mask of consternation. Her eyes betrayed absolutely nothing as they flashed over my presence and returned quickly to the assembled guests around me. She sat easily, entirely regally, on her throne, chin high and hands relaxed on the arms of the chair. Her face looked like it was ready to freeze a fireball, but every other detail about what she could have been thinking was hidden behind a firmly-fixed mask.

I made a mental note to ask her how she developed that skill.

The royal pair were as resplendent as I'd ever seen them. Dad was regal in his darkest black velvet robe complete with purple slashed openings down each arm and a purple sash under the magnificent golden stag and raven pendant. His hair was carefully molded into the perfect black mane, swooping around and to the side like Prince Charming's—Keion's—did when the prince flipped it that way. But Dad was sporting the look on purpose. Similarly, Her Majesty's hair was up in a magnificent maze of actual hair and ribbons with pearls and rubies interspersed every so often. Her luxurious dress was a formal full-length gown of purple with deep green panels inset across the bodice and down the skirt, which spilled onto the floor all about her feet. She must, I realized, have been sitting that way since before the meeting, since there was no way gravity could've placed the hem where it lay.

From her perch standing between the pair, Sternyface glared at everybody, though she seemed to take great joy in adding a little extra heat to her glare at me. The High Priestess Naissa and I had shared a special relationship since I'd arrived in Kiirajanna, new as I was to the elf lifestyle. She was special to me as one of only two people I'd ever punched in the face, and even more so as the only one who hadn't even shown the slightest bit of injury from the incident. At the same time, I was obviously special to her, thanks to the weaknesses apparent in my temperament, in my maternal genetic material, in my native state of Mississippi, and in everything else I happened to be involved with. Still, my spirits were buoyed as her glare suddenly softened to a look that actually seemed calming and understanding, if that was even possible from Sternyface herself, bless her heart.

Meanwhile, I sensed nothing but anger tinged with hatred from both sides of me. I didn't spare it a glance. I couldn't; the Queen's Lady had been extra-firm on that point both at my coronation ceremony and this morning. At the earlier ceremony it would have merely been a minor slight to the ruling pair, as everyone in audience to the king and queen are supposed to pay attention to them and to them alone. Today, though, it would represent a significant psychological victory for my new detractors.

It was okay. I didn't need to turn my eyes. My spidey-senses were on maximum overdrive anyway, thanks to the stress of the moment, and while I'd never been able to sense anything but location and identity, I found myself at that moment able to discern raw emotions, too, probably thanks to the intensity of those emotions. Hefin, the barrel-chested leader of the eastern elves, stood furthest to my left. He stood calmly and felt the least angry of the bunch.

The faint whiff of woodsmoke he carried in his tunic was nearly drowned out by the pungent incense that Swadda of the Serpent Veils exuded. I can never remember the name for the incense that her tribe, the elves of the western desert, use not only for ritual blessing and cleansing but also to cover the fact that they don't take many showers. It was described by the Queen's Lady, before I'd experienced it personally, as a strong earthy presence bearing gentle floral and citrus overtones, but to me it smelled like I was sniffing pine needles and eating an orange while somebody nuked a microwave full of popcorn into charcoal nearby.

Swadda was the most agitated of the bunch. I didn't need any extra senses to feel the air jiggle thanks to the quivering angst of the massive veils she wore. She was furious, and probably more than a little bit scared, and only barely holding those emotions in check.

To my right stood a darkly-brooding elf I'd enjoyed meeting last summer. Glynis led the southern tribes, a loose collective of jungle dwellers who perfectly personified the Amazonian archetype. The tribes were strongly matriarchal, I recalled, and—I'm not kidding—ran around in loincloths and leather bikini tops looking like contestants on a survivalist reality game show back home. They even applied war paint to their visages when they were looking for a battle, which was bad news considering I'd caught a glimpse of Glynis's striped face on my way in.

That she stood rigidly wearing an enforced calm scared me the most, if you want the truth. I'd enjoyed meeting her and her tribe mostly because of the pure, simple joy they brought to most of life's events. She'd greeted me back then with a genuine smile and a genuinely pleasant air, and then she eagerly, almost childishly, dragged me to meet nearly everybody in her camp, grinning widely the whole way. Every one of her companions invited me down to run through the tree tops with them, as others had told me that their idiom went. In a private moment afterward, while she and I were sharing some wonderful southern mead, Glynis explained to me that it wasn't just an idiom—the southern elves could literally run through the treetops, thanks to the thousands of pathways they'd developed.

That was all before news of the library thing took hold, unfortunately. Now, they were all here to see me go down, if the queen's kids' rumor held true. My senses, unfortunately, were shouting at me that the rumor was pretty much spot on. I forced that thought from my mind, wrapped my face in a true, practiced elf-grin using nearly every facial muscle I owned, curtsied with the most appropriate hand gesture of respect, and greeted the royal pair.

Then my worst fears gained form and laughed in my face.

Call for Exile

The high priestess cleared her throat to do her standard duty as herald/bailiff. Then she intoned in a loud, clear voice sharp enough that it should have slashed through Swadda's veils, "We are present to hear the discussion and receive blessing of the king's and queen's combined wisdom in the situation before us involving the Crown Princess Alyssa," Naissa paused momentarily to allow the briefest of glares toward the serpent veil from which an audible hiss of disgust had shot, "and the accusation before us that she has, on numerous occasions with wanton disregard for our traditions and most fundamental beliefs, abused the arcane powers that flow through the land."

"Accusations," the word slid through Hefin's teeth. "It is well known—"

"It is well known that none but the king and queen speak without being granted leave to do so in their formal court," Naissa cut him off curtly.

"Hefin," my father said, his voice deep and serious. I saw his knuckles whiten under the tension he was applying to the arms of his throne, and after a few months being with him an awful lot I noticed that both his eyes and his nostrils flared. "Glynis. Swadda. Have any of you ever known me to act unjustly?" The last word shot out, accusatory in its own right.

"Toward your own daughter?" Swadda hissed.

"Toward anyone?" his low-pitched reply thundered through the room.

After a long silence, during which I didn't dare cast a glance around, he continued, "So which of you were present, or had personal agents present, at the battle during which the Cult attempted to kill my daughter and her traveling companions at the library?"

"Cut the legal maneuvering, Cadfael," Hefin barked. The use of the king's traditional first name earned him a glare from Naissa, but my father merely crooked an eyebrow and gestured in a slightly condescending movement. "It is widely known that your daughter drew upon the forces of magic to set fire to the library and burn it down around the librarians, whose guilt we have still not seen evidenced."

"I must have misunderstood you, Hefin," my father replied. "Surely you did not just call me a liar?" His knuckles actually got whiter. I wondered whether the great golden chair arms or Dad's hands would win the strength contest.

"A liar?" Hefin challenged.

"It is—well known—that my men, and at times I, personally, questioned the few survivors who we captured and in doing so ascertained that my daughter's allegations were true regarding their intent. Had you not heard of that questioning?"

Hefin's presence, the aura I could sense, shrank a little. I still didn't dare glance around for fear of insulting the three who were on my side, but I desperately wanted to see Hefin's expression. After a few moments, his voice, shaking ever so slightly, came back with, "I humbly retract that statement, Cadfael. But the rest still remains. It is known that she used magic to call about fire."

"Is it? It has been my understanding that the librarians maintained ill-advised torches that were blazing at the time the library caught fire."

Dad wasn't actually twisting the truth very far. I didn't call down fire in the library. I wouldn't have called down fire even if I'd known that I could. It was wind, to be perfectly honest. This Mississippi girl recalled seeing the aftermath of a tornado or two and knew the value of a good whirlwind, and so that was what I'd reached for. Unfortunately for us all, the attackers had brought torches, which got smashed up against books, and then the wind fanned the flames.

So, no, I am not a firestarter. Firespreader, maybe. Yes, I do have my faults. And yes, I have been wanton with occasional magic usage, but not with fire.

Not that that matters a whole lot, when libraries have been burnt to the ground.

"I—" Hefin started to argue, but my father forestalled him with a hand.

"Were you there?"

"No."

"Were any of your agents there?"

"No."

"There is the matter of the battle in Ganolog," Glynis purred dangerously from behind me.

"Were you or your agents present to witness the act you accuse my daughter of?"

"No, but you already knew that, Cadfael. Padrig might be here to support us, but your daughter's antics actually led to war between you and his tribe, if I recall."

My father flushed at that. It was true; I'd stepped right into a hornet's nest of Cult members and the resulting battle had brought out my temper. Worse, it had put Dad in a position where he had to invade the land of the northern tribes to capture a Cult ringleader, thus leading to a war with the entire clan. That it had been a bloodless war, and was now over, wasn't my place to bring up since I still had a gag order on me.

"We could just ask the little girl herself," Swadda suggested innocently.

"She would probably just lie to us," Hefin pointed out.

The anger that now freely flowed across Dad's face told me that the insult had raised his blood pressure as much as it had mine, but seeing that helped me hold my own temper in check.

"Those who stand before their king and queen insisting on honoring custom should, of course, recognize the custom of not requiring self-incrimination," the high priestess pointed out, touching the king's shoulder subtly but meaningfully. It worked; his grip loosened enough that color returned to his joints, and he lost the mask of someone who was envisioning someone else's insides being ripped out.

"Well, there is Prince Keion. He's not grown too fond of the girl yet, has he?"

"My son is indisposed at the moment," the queen replied and shot Hefin an icy look.

"Of course he is. As is your niece, Cadfael?"

When moments ticked by without my father gracing the eastern elf lord with a reply, he growled and continued, "Look, it doesn't matter. My clan will not support her as queen."

"Nor mine," hissed Glynis.

"Nor will mine," added Swadda. "And if you insist on continuing with this charade, you will find yourself at war with more than just the northern elves."

"War is what it may come to, then?" my father asked, his already-long face lengthening even further.

"Cadfael, you know that we mean you neither harm nor ill will. It is just that we must be the mouthpieces for our clans, as you yourself have expected us to be for all these years. You have but to replace your daughter with Seren, and my clan will be satisfied. Otherwise...." she left the repercussions hanging.

I wasn't surprised to hear the queen's eldest daughter's name floated as a better candidate for queen than I was. I'd suggested it, myself, a few times after I'd arrived. What surprised me was the queen's reaction.

"No!" her majesty snarled, leaping to her feet. Keeping her anger in check with visible effort, she continued, "Swadda, how dare you come to us demanding what you know to be impossible, hanging your expectation on tradition while breaking another tradition in so demanding. You *know* that my daughter is off-limits in this discussion, yet you bring her name anyway. I am shocked and ashamed in what this discussion has come to."

Into the silence that followed, Sternyface tried to insert some calming words. "The prophecy has long foretold—"

It was a mistake. Apparently Swadda's inability to directly confront the queen's anger made her even more willing to verbally snap the high priestess's head off. "Prophecy! Ha! You and your useless priests and priestesses have spent centuries preparing us to face the perils of this prophecy, with no thought given to merely avoiding the outcome from the start. Well, I say it is time for the people to stop listening to the whine and murmur of our *spiritual* leaders and take action to prevent this upheaval. Let's nip it in the bud, and if Naissa and her pets get cut in the process, so be it."

"Prophecy or no prophecy, doesn't matter to me and mine. What's important is that we remove the little whelp from her *glorious* future of having power over us all," Hefin added angrily, and suddenly my father was out of his throne, his expression matching the queen's.

His hands shook as he pointed two fingers at the chieftain who's just insulted me. "You will not speak of my daughter in such a manner," he growled. To be fair, the word Hefin, bless his foul heart, had chosen was *lesgenau*, which carries a whole lot more derogatory connotation than whelp does. It refers to a depth of weakness and listlessness that cannot operate without a parental figure over it, and to the elves that's a very bad thing.

"Stop!" I heard my own voice ring out. Suddenly the entire room—and all of its anger and contempt—was focused directly on me. That's okay, I thought; at least now they'll be vicious *to* me rather than *about* me. I allowed myself to turn about, finally taking in the adversaries on all sides. They were all glaring directly at me, now—Dad looked like he wanted to rip my tongue out.

I caught the briefest of twitches on Sternyface's lips, though, and in that one fleeting moment I got the support I was hoping for.

"Penna Hefin," I said, using the formal address and doing my best to make my voice come out as a purr. "Last summer you eagerly accepted me, cheering my coronation and even suggesting that I might consider one of your sons as a consort. I don't think I am misremembering that, am I? No, no, let me finish. I have held my tongue long enough, now I ask you to hear me out," I continued, turning the purr into sharpness. "I was your favorite then, and yet now you call me—I cannot bring my own lips to utter that word around our king and queen—and why? I have done nothing but act to protect the lives of those I hold dear. In anyone else, would you not consider that strength? Why is the situation so different now?"

"It is clear—" Swadda started to interject, but stopped when I held my palm up to her and shot her a glare. Her eyes grew wide; apparently she feared I might use Draignerthol to lash out at her. Fine; I didn't mind her fear at that moment.

"Penna Hefin, I asked a question of you."

"Alyssa," he started, ignoring my title but at least using my name instead of the pejoratives he'd been casting about. "It is the will of my clan."

"The fear of your clan, it sounds like to me. When have the eastern clan been so fearful of one little girl?"

"One little girl who threatens to throw us back into civil war," Swadda spat.

"I am not the one who stood here in the royal throne room, threatening war," I reminded her, and then turned back to my father and the queen, who had both relaxed slightly. "What Swadda says holds some truth, however. I am yet a little girl according to elf custom. In fact, technically, I believe—and I would be glad for your input if I am incorrect, High Priestess Naissa, you cannot exile one who is but a child, and I am still considered such. May I suggest, for the benefit of the temper of all here today, that we put off this discussion until after I have completed the rituals of the hunhymgais, at which point you can determine what to do with me as an adult, as is proper? Would your clan consider that acceptable, Penna Hefin? Penna Glynis? If I begin preparations immediately at sunrise tomorrow?"

I left Swadda out of the deal-making on purpose, and I could tell it angered her. She seemed to be the ringleader, though, so that felt like the right thing to do. I just hoped it wouldn't backfire later. Still, it got the result I was looking for as first Hefin and then Glynis nodded.

I turned back to the royal pair. "Father. Talaith. I seek your agreement with my recommendation, and subsequently your leave to begin preparation for the arduous ceremony I am to undertake."

Naissa actually smiled at that. I'd used the informal address for the king and queen to point out my own relative status as a child among them. First my father, and then the queen, nodded their acquiescence. Swadda spun on her heels and stormed out, followed closely by Hefin. Glynis remained just long enough for the other two to exit, and then she whispered quietly to me, "Impressive turn, that was, but I believe that you are merely putting off the inevitable."

I gave her my best guarded smile, the one that doesn't include every facial muscle, and she nodded in agreement with my unspoken sentiment. She rapidly removed herself from the throne room.

"Well," the queen said, collapsing into her throne in an unroyal manner.

"That was—effective. I fear that what Glynis said will come to pass, but at least when you return from your hunhymgais, we can be prepared for the battles to come," Dad said. Still standing, he met the queen's and then the high priestess's eyes. "I would like some time alone with my daughter, please."

The queen nodded and left. Sternyface followed, but only after a very uncharacteristic smile and nod my direction. Once the door closed behind them, Dad led me through the curtain into a hidden lounge that was solely for the use of the king. In fact, he'd told me that he was the only elf allowed in there, which made me wonder who filled the ice cube bucket, the first time he brought me in for quiet, private conversation. It was the only place, it seemed, where he could let his guard down completely.

"That was impressive indeed, Alyssa," he said as he tossed a couple of ice cubes into glasses and covered them with a brownish liquor.

"I just got tired of being talked about instead of talked to," I argued. I took a sip and then grimaced. "Ooh," I exhaled. "I don't think I'll ever be used to your whiskey, Dad."

"That is fine. Children should not drink, anyway," he said with a grin.

"I wanted to calm down an escalating argument," I argued again. "I didn't mean to go back to being treated as a child. Are you going to put me in class with the first graders again?"

Dad chortled, and I joined in the laughter. When I arrived the priestesses put me into an intensive class to learn the elf language, and the only one of those available was full of five-year-olds. It was weird, but since I'd learned elf as a young child I caught up quickly enough and escaped.

"The hunhymgais is difficult, Alyssa. Let us not make light of that important ritual."

"Not making light, Dad, but so far I've faced down a wyvern, a few different groups of Cult members looking to kill me, and even an angry Sternyface. I'm not certain how going off by myself to survive for a while could be much of a comparative challenge."

"You are probably right, my daughter. At least, I hope it is thus with all my heart. You will, of course, begin preparations tomorrow, and that will require most of your time and energy. For tonight, though, you should relax."

"Well, this is a good start," I murmured, amazed once again at how much smoother the second sip of whiskey was than the first. "But why did the queen object so angrily to the suggestion that Seren would make a better choice? It's true, I'd say."

"Hmm." Dad gave me an appraising stare. "It was probably true this past summer, but I believe that, as you have already pointed out, you have earned your tiara since. But to answer your question, I believe that there are two matters that stirred the queen to anger. First, of course, is the prophecy; both she and I have a responsibility to uphold the integrity of the priesthood, which, though we claim tradition to be our savior, is truly the primary agency that has protected us from civil war all these centuries. To brush off the validity and import of the prophecy would in turn brush off the authority of the priesthood. We both believed that to be the worst possible outcome of today's discussion. More importantly, though, I suspect she loves her daughter too much to subject her to ruling through the times to come."

"Oh. I see. And you don't love me enough to protect me from the same?" I let my voice lilt up at the end to take the sting out of my words.

Dad chortled again around another sip. "Daughter.... Alyssa, I love you more than I love any other being in this entire realm. I hope that you know that. If I could spare you the turmoil that is to come, I would. Yet I also love this realm, and I am in firm agreement with both *Sternyface* and Talaith that you are the only one capable of leading it through the dark times to come."

"Help me, 'lyssa One Kenobi, you're my only hope," I quipped.

"A movie quotation?" Dad asked, and I nodded. "Well, in this case, it seems apropos, whatever it meant in the movie. As much as I hate to place this upon your shoulders, you are the realm's only hope. Seren, for many reasons, some of which are likely not apparent to you yet, cannot do what you must do." He drained his glass. "And now, might I suggest that you enjoy the remainder of your evening? The next few days will be challenging."

"I'm going out for a run," I announced to Seph and Aerona once I'd changed out of the court finery and taken my hair down. It sounded like a good thing to do; I hadn't been on a run since my arrival in the elf realm. Oh, I'd run several times, but running because you have to get somewhere fast, or because a legendary grizzly bear is chasing you, is vastly different from jogging along just because you can.

"Okay, let me change to my running clothes. It will only be a—" Seph started, but I interrupted her with both my voice and my gesture.

"No. Please, I need—I'm not certain what I need, exactly, but I'm pretty sure it doesn't involve my cousin and her wolverine and my guard loping along with me. I'm sorry, Aerona, but I need to go out by myself."

I was shocked to see her nod, and then she grinned. "I do believe your father would approve, at this point," she said, and then she pulled a dagger from one of her many hiding places and held it out to me. "Please, though, take this along with that pendant of yours. You never know which might be more useful if either is needed."

I hefted the knife. It felt—professional. The handle was smooth, its leather turned dark in stripes from a great deal of handling. The blade, somewhere around eight inches long, was simple, thin, and looked incredibly sharp on both edges. Even the point at its tip looked clean and precise. I raised a hand to the blade to test its sharpness.

"Don't!" she interrupted, and then grabbed the hand that was apparently headed for a slashing. "Sorry, Princess, but you still have some to learn about weaponry. You test a blade by flicking your finger sideways across it, not long ways. A sharp blade will feel—like this," and she demonstrated and then gestured for me to copy. I did, flipping the pad of my thumb gently across the sharpness of the blade and feeling the little *ting* it made on what seemed like a single ridge of molecules.

"Thank you," I said, and then looked to slip it under my belt. Once again Aerona sprang to my rescue, showing me how to fold a scrap of leather into a pouch to protect the belt, the clothes, and my underlying skin from the incredibly sharp edges.

I pulled the knife Keion gave me for Christmas out of a drawer and showed it to her.

"That is a nice piece of work," she complimented it. "But it is intended to go under boots, not those *tennie* things you are so fond of wearing. Keep mine instead for the time being."

"If you need me, tell the trees," Seph said as I left. Confused, I nodded anyway, assuming I'd figure out what that ranger mumbo-jumbo meant if I needed to.

COEDOLIAETH

literally, "tree community"—an acknowledgement of the forest as a living entity.

The Run

I ran.

It wasn't the all-out run of being chased by a bear, not even close. It didn't even truly start out as a run. At first it was a quick, stealthy attempt to slip past the camps of the elves from the east, west, and south. I knew they'd have rangers with them, so there was no way I could go completely undetected, but I tried to make my passing as uninteresting as possible while still passing rapidly through their area.

They all wanted to see me gone. I wanted the same, only not in quite the same permanent manner.

It worked. Soon I was past the circle of tents, and then I was jogging.

I pushed it faster.

I didn't set out for any place in particular. I hadn't been to all that many places, for one thing. Back home I'd explored nearly every nook and side street of my neighborhood before I really knew what I was doing, but the training to become an elf queen is just a little more arduous than that. I'd managed to explore the grounds to the south of Cysegredig three times since my arrival, each time with my father, my cousin, or both. Heck, every time I'd been anywhere on Kiirajanna it was in the company of someone else, most often several someone-elses.

This time, it was just me.

I was alone. Happily, gloriously, alone.

I ran, exulting simply in the silence of being alone.

Thoughts, some dark and others not, tried to cloud over my mind as they had all day. Each time they tried to take over, though, I'd focus on one of the perfect-coiffed bushes nearby, or one of the trees, and the thoughts went away.

What did Seph mean when she said to tell the trees if I needed her? I wondered if I could test it by telling the nearby elm. I didn't try, though, out of respect for my newfound—or re-found—self-presence.

It was good to be with myself, and just with myself.

I ran.

Before long the sun disappeared. The shadows were already at their longest when I left the castle, so the sunset was no surprise. No surprise, but a grand revelation. The darkness on Kiirajanna is alive. I don't mean like at home, aurally alive, with owl hoots and animal calls, though those are present in the elf realm as well. I mean physically alive, ringing and zinging about with a charged energy as ancient as the realm itself and more powerful than anything imaginable.

I stopped, allowing the energy in, letting myself become filled with a sense of anticipation and awe.

The energy was tremendous. I checked to see whether Draignerthol was somehow causing it, funneling it from wherever the pendant found its well of magical force. The ancient relic was silent, cool, dark. It was waiting on something.

A gaze upward confirmed that there was a full moon. That didn't mean anything in the elf lore I'd studied. Still, I felt connected, somehow. It seemed like the flowing power that surrounded me was pulsing along to the shimmers of the great white orb in the sky, though I couldn't figure out why. Strangely, for me, I didn't want to figure it out just then. It felt right, and that was enough.

I gazed.

It was dark, but I could see well enough when I relaxed and let my eyes and subconscious work together.

There was a tree nearby. Yes, there are always trees nearby in an elf forest, but this one was special. It called to me, though of course I know how silly that sounds. Suddenly, Seph's comment resounded in my head: "tell the trees." I didn't actually need her, but for a few bizarre moments it seemed completely natural that I would tell the trees—that tree, in particular—anything that needed saying. It stood strong, and tall, its bark perfectly uniform as it raised its arms to the darkened sky.

I reached out with both hands and touched it, fingers splayed out along the bark ridges.

I gasped.

Maybe, anyway; I don't remember whether I actually made a sound or not as the wonderment spread through me. It felt like I was suddenly split open, turned inside out, becoming one with the trees just as they were part of me.

Walking no longer made any sense whatsoever. Why would anyone want to change locations when sturdy roots were available to keep you safe and fed?

Wind rippled gently through my hair, tugging at the branches growing upward and away from my core. It rippled among my brethren and me as we all stood in its path, rattling leaves and rapping limbs against one another: an intricate symphony that played the breeze's energy out.

I understood.

Trees are one—all of them. Suddenly that was obvious, like saying the night is dark or the bedrock is hard. While some trees—the ones nearby, I thought?—whispered in the chill wind of the central region, I could sense the freezing cold as others—brothers, almost twins, but definitely siblings—gently shook off freshly fallen snow. I reached down, behind the murmur, and found the bushes there as well. They weren't nearly as powerful, or capable of drawing their sustenance from as far down in the soil, or as happy in the wind. They were the little baby brothers.

Off in the distance, I heard a surprised, overjoyed shriek. Only, it wasn't a sound, rather a sensation, and it felt strangely familiar. I opened myself to the voice, and then I realized what—who?—I was hearing. It was Little Treebeard, all the way back in my room in the castle. L.T. had sensed me joining into the meld, entering his world, and was overjoyed. The L.T. in the pot could only shake his little leaves and smack his branches against whatever was nearby. The L.T. in the meld danced and cavorted in joy.

In spite of the miles I'd run, I could almost see him. Her. Suddenly I realized that the gender thing was a really dumb question. L.T. was both him and her, and neither as well. As I came to that realization, all the trees around me—smiled.

I smiled.

That's how it felt, anyway. The elf smile is one of complete radiant joy, using nearly every single muscle in the face, but the trees have neither faces nor muscles, nor did I feel my own facial muscles moving. Still, it was the same internal sensations: joy, happiness, and for that moment, perfect and total serenity.

It was a wonderful moment. Beautiful, in fact. I'd suddenly realized that I could commune with the trees pretty much across the entire continent, and that was amazing. But when I left the castle, I reminded myself, it was for a run, not for standing with the trees.

I disconnected.

I expected it to be painful to separate from the newfound bond I'd created with the trees. That somehow a part of me I hadn't known before would be suddenly, tragically ripped away, never to be whole until I found that unity once again. At least, that's how it seems like the sensations should feel. It's not how they felt, though. I disconnected, and that was that. The trees were all still there. I knew—somehow—that they would always be there, if and when I needed them. And while the long-distance group thing was nice, I didn't miss it as I gathered my human senses about me once again.

A couple of loping steps later, I stopped again. Curiosity enveloped me, and I knelt slowly and put both hands on the ground, wondering if I'd sense anything different.

Suddenly, I was touching the entire world.

With a gasp, I raised my hands to collect my thoughts, and then my breath. I checked Draignerthol for participation or for blame; no, the pendant was still chill to the touch.

I reached down and touched the ground again.

If all the trees seemed like a tremendous breadth of sensation, it was nothing compared to pretty much the entire world. The sky was dark, so my eyes saw nothing, yet my internal vision connected into a seemingly infinite pool of sensations. It was overwhelming, at least at first.

By exerting a little concentration I found it easy to localize. A bug creeped along the ground a few meters from me. What moved and acted like a snake slithered by on the other side, which startled me a little. I guess it's hard to have the people of the west actively worshiping serpents, with a leader known as Swadda of the Serpent Veils, without acknowledging that there actually are snakes in the realm. I'd just never really thought about it.

Luckily, for me and for it, I could tell that the creature really was more afraid of me than I was of a little snake.

Off in the distance, roughly in the same direction as the now-destroyed library, I saw and acknowledged a dark patch. It wasn't barren, but rather dark in a malevolent sort of way. It was huge, and it seemed to be growing, alive even. Dark animals roamed across it in spite of the hour, and that brought a shudder as I remembered being chased by dire wolves and dire ravens across the blight. I made a note to check that portion of the continent out more thoroughly some day, to see if there was anything the rangers of the realm could do. Granted, they had probably already done all they could do, but perhaps there was something I could accomplish as queen of the realm.

Once I got there.

If I got there.

My musings were interrupted by a shadowy flash across my consciousness. It was faint, as though something—or someone—was hiding from me, and using the earth itself to do it. It was close, though, no more than twenty or thirty feet away. It didn't hold anything like the malevolence of the blight, but it was anxious—scared?—agitated and perturbed, at least a little? It wasn't like the snake, though, nor any other creature. The conscience, the mind—the footprint, if I can call it that—was too big, too grand, to intelligent. It wasn't a creature at all, I realized.

It had to be an elf.

Curious to learn who was watching me, I leaped up and darted toward the spot. I was rewarded with a gasp and a light thud as whoever it was tripped. We came face to face, and it was my turn to gasp, loudly, in shock.

It was a child. A girl, somewhere between five and eight years old, near as I could tell. But that wasn't the shocking thing.

She was clad in hand-fashioned, primitive clothes. Her tunic looked, in the glow of the moon, like supple leather, and it was bound together across the tops of the shoulders and down the sides with crude lashings. On her feet were bound simple leather flaps folded up and around. Her hair was a mess, all frizzy and jutting out. But that wasn't the shocking thing either.

What brought a shocked gasp to my lips was that she was black.

I'd seen black people before, growing up in the South. All the comments about Southern racism aside, though, we kids never really thought much about it. I had black friends, and my white friends had black friends, and my black friends had white friends, and we all just sort of ignored both the color of each others' skin. At the same time we also ignored—or perhaps we just didn't know—how the rest of the world seemed to think we ought to think about it.

But I'd left all that behind. I'd been in Kiirajanna for well over half a year, and I'd never seen a black elf. I hadn't noticed that I'd never seen one, unfortunately, because to be honest I wasn't looking for any sort of racial makeup. But now that a definitely dark-skinned elf sat sprawled in front of me, I couldn't help but notice. Even Swadda, coming from the desert as she and her people did, carried her skin as pale as notebook paper. I'd been around Cysegredig many times with my father, to the point that I figured we'd visited every village there was to visit, yet not once had we seen a black elf.

I was going to marvel at my discovery a little while longer, but the little girl decided she'd had enough. She sprang to her feet and turned to run.

"Hi! Don't—go…" I called after her as she took one step and then disappeared with a *pop*.

Teleportation! My mind screamed at me that this was important, but at the moment I was more interested in catching up to the girl and worrying about the implications later. I snapped my hand about Draignerthol and pulled upon the pendant's power. With a matching *pop*, I teleported to right behind her, and then pressed my long legs into sprinting after.

Pop!

She teleported away again.

Pop!

I teleported right after.

She darted around a tree and angled slightly away. She was quick, but I had much longer legs and was pretty sure I could outdistance her in a straightaway. Not that she did much straight-line running; every time she came close to a tree she darted at some angle behind it. It was hard to keep up, but not impossible, and I started to gain on her. She could teleport, but so could I, and with Draignerthol around my neck I was pretty certain I could keep it up much longer than she could.

Before, back on Earth, she would've been nearly impossible to follow in the darkness of the night, camouflaged as she was by the darkness of her skin and clothes and the softness of her footpads. Here, though, I didn't have any trouble locating her even after a teleport, thanks to Draignerthol's power.

Pop!

She teleported just as my fingers neared her shoulder.

Pop!

I teleported right after without losing stride. Three more long paces, and...

Slam!

I hit something solid, something unseen that stretched impossibly rigid between the trees. It hurt like heck, my momentum rebounding backward and downward onto the forest floor.

As I lay there gasping for breath, not sure if I would ever again be either capable of or interested in rising to my feet, a heavy weight was dropped over my limbs. I tried wiggling a finger, but couldn't. I twitched my head, trying to move it from side to side, but it was stuck in a vise as well. I panicked, trying to get my hand up to touch Draignerthol, to awaken the pendant and gather in the ancient power that might help me press out of the bonds that held me down, but the more I twitched the tighter I was held.

Finally, not having any other option, I relaxed. As soon as I did, a face—a black elf's face, mature this time—popped into view. The eyes in the face examined me closely, obviously taking in every detail in the dim moonlight. Eventually the eyes closed and the head nodded. She—I could tell it was a she from her rich, melodic voice—spoke to someone else I couldn't see in a heavily accented version of the elf language.

"Yes, congratulations be upon us all. We have undoubtedly captured the crown princess."

POBL'GDWIG

People of the Forest. An ancient group of elves who lived the entirety of their lives among the massive trees of the land, tending and caring for, and dancing with, their brethren. They have not been seen for centuries.

Captured

Others joined us. They came up quietly, but my senses were on high alert. First there were eight, and then ten, and then an indeterminate more; that turned out to be about the limit of my ability. They were all quietly muttering, though, and they didn't sound happy.

Finally I found enough air in my lungs to speak. "My father—will rescue me," I promised. No, that never seems to be the right thing to say in action movies, but it was the only thing that came to mind.

A muted bark of laughter came from the same older woman who'd pronounced my identity. "Rescue you? From what?"

"You said I was captured. Everybody else seems to want to capture me, and now you have succeeded. Congratulations. But—"

"So why were you chasing young Ilya?"

"I...." It was a good question, one I wasn't sure whether to answer honestly. After a moment I decided it really couldn't get much worse. "I was curious. I wasn't expecting anyone to be out in the woods tonight, and she's—you're—"

"*Groendu*." The older woman completed my thought. Black-skinned. So it was as obvious to them as it was to me.

I tried to nod and was happy that my bonds allowed it. With what I hoped was a winning smile, I said, "Yes, that is correct. I have not seen anyone else here who is black-skinned."

"You have not been raised to fear us." It was more of a statement than a question, but I still nodded.

"I was raised in a land called Mississippi, where light-skinned and dark-skinned people all live in peace and harmony." Okay, so that was a huge lie, but I doubted these elves had access to CNN.

She snorted. "The light-skinned people have not yet subjugated the dark-skinned people in your world? I cannot believe that." Apparently nobody else could believe it either, as they all laughed.

"No! They..." I let my voice trail off. Why was I bothering to lie to these elves? "Okay, so they have, in places, and during times in the past. And there is tension now, according to the realm-wide news-runners." So, *you* try communicating the concept of national TV broadcasts in a several-thousand-year-old elf language. "But I, personally, have stood for equality," I continued, realizing that I was stretching the truth once again but feeling like it needed to be said. "Why—why are you all laughing?"

"Because, Princess, the idea of one of your type bragging to us about standing for equality is like the hunter facing the mighty grizzly saying he has stood for vegetarianism."

"Look, I didn't even know your people existed until tonight. I don't even know your people's story. I'd love to learn it, though, if you would just let me get up on my own. And on that I must insist. Either let me up, or just kill me now, for this is undignified."

I was pretty certain, based on the conversation we'd had so far, that they wouldn't choose the latter option. I was, after all, the crown princess, and they knew it, and they seemed to place at least a little importance on that. I wasn't sure if they'd let me have the former option, but the call to dignity was my best guess.

It worked. Suddenly the weight holding my limbs to the ground disappeared, and a dark-skinned hand was thrust from the other side, away from the older woman, to assist me to my feet.

I took the assistance and thanked my helper with a flourish that, in elf custom, indicated equality. He snorted.

"We do not play by silly court rules here, Princess," the older woman sniped.

"Well, those are all that I know," I shot back at her. "I would be happy to learn your rules for showing appreciation for assistance."

"Like this, Princess," the man who'd helped me up said, and then he launched into an elaborate process of what would be called patty-cake on Earth. I paid as much attention as I could, but was glad to finally be able to read the mood of those around me once again, and thus I picked up on the joke.

"You've *got* to be kidding," I said.

"Perhaps a simple shake of the hands?" he offered and held his right hand out to me. I took it, and he pulled me in for a bear hug. Beside my ear I could hear his deep voice chortling, while similar laughter sounded around us. It seemed I was the butt of a very funny joke. Funny, to them, anyway. But then again, I was alive and probably going to remain that way, and so I didn't mind the joke much at all.

"So," I said after detaching myself from the fairly strong grip, "tell me about what has happened to your people."

Apparently, accepting the bear hug was what I needed to do to win over their trust, because they led me a few miles at a light jog to their little campsite. It barely qualified as that, with a few primitive lean-tos built into the side of a hill so that they would be virtually invisible from any distance whatsoever. Even their campfire was shielded by a pile of stacked logs and branches. I had no idea we had arrived till we stopped.

"Artfully hidden, but wouldn't the king's rangers know right where it is?" I asked the older woman, who shook her head.

"Look."

"I don't see anything. That's what was so impressive."

She shook her head more aggressively, the motion accentuated in the flickering light of the fire. "No. Look, but not with your eyes. Or are the rumors that have reached us untrue?"

The comment about rumors clued me in. I reached up and touched Draignerthol, a move that drew gasps from everyone nearby. I peered around, looking through the eye of the magical pendant, and suddenly I was nearly giddy from what I'd seen.

"You—you shielded your camp from the rangers. And then— you shielded the shielding?" I asked, not entirely willing to believe what I'd seen. "You—you use magic."

"It is Gaia's gift to her children," she explained in the same tone I'd use to explain to a child that the sky is blue or that a rock is hard. "We must not squander."

Flabbergasted, I turned to face her directly. "Gaia?" I'd heard of Gaia before, of course. She was some sort of—weird sort of deity that New Agers worshiped on Earth, I thought. The Earth Mother, Sarah had read when we'd discovered a book about it in the library. But that was in Mississippi, and in English, and we were speaking elf here in Kiirajanna, and she'd plainly said Gaia.

She just smiled, and I shook my head to clear it. Sternyface had taught me absolutely nothing of true religion, mainly because the elves didn't have one. The titles priest and priestess had even come to have no religious context at all; instead, her minions were teachers, healers, scribes, and acolytes. Worship just wasn't done.

I'd never been particularly religious, myself, so I hadn't bothered probing about it. There were plenty of opportunities the past summer to read histories in the smaller library at Cysegredig, and I'd loved them, but nothing I read had held mention of any sort of religion, one way or another.

"Who—who is this Gaia?" I finally found myself asking.

The older lady had been anticipating my question, and now she nodded eagerly. "Yes, yes. I am not surprised that you have not heard of the Mother. It is good, though, and right, for our Dragon Queen to hear of it. Come, let us sit by the fire, where we may talk comfortably."

"I am not the Dragon Queen yet," I argued as she led me to the center of the camp. We sat on plain logs laid out about the warmth of the bonfire, and I was once again amazed at how hidden the sizable and well-tended fire was hidden from outside of the little ring.

"Perhaps not yet, but you will be. Sooner than you think, I believe, if I am hearing the Mother's voice correctly."

"You can hear her?"

"Yes! Yes, of course, and you can, too, if you know what you are listening for. Sit for a moment, silently. Be at peace, and let your breathing slow. Listen. Listen closely, for the whisper of the moon and the gentle breeze. Do you hear it?"

I did as she instructed, sitting for long enough that my butt started to hurt from the roughness of the log. Soon, though, I could sense what she referred to. "Yes, I think I do."

"What is she saying to you, my young princess?"

"I—I don't know. All I hear—sense—feel—is a presence. It's like it's moving, but it's not."

She nodded again, her face brightening into a huge smile. "Yes! Yes, that is Gaia. I am glad you did not make anything up, because hearing anything specific the first time is quite impossible. You will come to know what she is telling you, the longer that you listen to her. And I am hearing her say that you are worthy to receive our greatest gift."

"Your greatest gift?" I looked suspiciously; it sounded too much like an infomercial on Earth's TV stations.

"Yes, absolutely. Our greatest gift. Our lore. Are you prepared to receive it?"

It hit me what she was about to do, and I gasped. "I would be honored to receive it."

She nodded, once, and closed her eyes. Slowly, softly, she began to croon a song that spun itself into a tale of beginnings.

The Pobl'pridd *were not of this land*

But we were of a land

And we were of all the land

And the land was within us

I looked into her now-open eyes to see a vast pool of emotions. She was proud of her people, the *Pobl'pridd*, which is elf for People of the Soil. It also means people of the dirt, depending on how you want to interpret it, but I'm sure that all the pride she pumped into her voice when she said it implies the nicer meaning. She also seemed glad to be telling me the tale, one that clearly sank to the center of her being and then wrapped that being around the entire audience of its telling.

The song continued in a slow, minor key for a long time. First it told of a faraway island where elves, beasts, and plants lived in harmony. Then they heard of neighbors to the west who needed them desperately—heard through Gaia, apparently, but the how part was glossed over. I thought briefly about all the other "…and God talked to us" stories I'd heard, wondering if Gaia had spoken with the Pobl'pridd through a burning bush, or maybe a serpent. But then I realized the story was moving too fast for me to start thinking such silly stuff, so I pulled my focus back to follow her lovely alto voice.

The journey across the sea was difficult, thanks to the other, opposing, deity, whose name I had missed while thinking about burning bushes. He was a pretty wicked guy, though, tossing up storm after storm to prevent the People of the Soil from doing Gaia's wishes by journeying to Kiirajanna. The people were strong, and they were strong in Gaia's gift, which I took to mean magical power, though, so they made it. Their boats didn't do so well, though, crashing into the cliffs on the eastern side of the continent.

The tenor of the song changed a little at that point. What had been a slow, moving minor key quickened and brightened slightly as she sang of meeting the elf princes, of being shown into the high courts of the land. This was back before Cysegredig existed, and what it had replaced was, according to the song, a flowing, tall building sculpted of stunningly white rock that had been sung from the depths of Gaia herself.

The land was at war, though, which was why the pace of the song picked up. Battles were raging across the land even while the people were meeting the greatest of elf queens, Rhiannon. Attuned to Gaia's body as they were, the people could sense the tumult, and many wept openly even in front of the queen herself. It made an impact, apparently; she accepted them immediately into her highest rank of guardians, soldiers, and even advisors.

It did not go well, the song recounted as it slipped back into a slow, mournful key. Rhiannon's forces were besieged, attacked from all sides, by armies that had joined together against them in response to the arrival of the dark elves. Every attempt to broker peace was met with silence, derision, or worse, deceit. Queen Aleah'la, the last ruler ever anointed by the Pobl'pridd, gave her own life defending Rhiannon from an assassin's spell at what became an abrupt ending to a white binding forgiveness ritual. The people of the soil mourned, and they fought, for at that point it was as much about vengeance as any thought of peace on the land.

Aleah'la was strong, and she was kind, and she was filled to effervescence with Gaia's gifts, and so on went the dirge, but I tried to pay close attention regardless. It seemed like she was building up to something.

Finally the pace of the song picked back up, taking on a staccato quality. I could hear the drums of war in her voice as she spoke of a decade more of battles, of this elf clan and another bonding together against Rhiannon's forces and then, upon the eve of victory, turning and battling each other. Gaia's hand was felt more than once, as both dark elf and light and even the queen herself celebrated the noble goddess's intervention. In one battle a company of unicorns joined in, using their magic and their horns to get effect. They were, the song explained, not creatures who could use Gaia's gift, but rather creatures wholly created of Gaia's gift, and there was no killing one without intervention of the Dark One himself.

She told of one battle that floored me. Rhiannon's forces were on the verge of being defeated by dark sorcery and powerful weapons when suddenly a flight of wyverns appeared. I barely held back from interrupting her lyric tale as she spoke of the majestic and intelligent creatures who swooped in and vigorously protected the elf queen. My own experience with a wyvern had left me with the sense that they were fairly evil creatures, though, so I had a hard time matching up her beautiful words with the terrifying images in my head.

They won—slowly. The song hit a martial stretch in which she recanted each of the enemy elves' names as they surrendered their forces to the queen. Each time, the song made a point of telling us how graciously the queen handled their defeat, how they all received their lives and lands back with only one promise, made over a binding relic. The oath they took was that never again would their tribes practice the art of magic against fellow elves.

As the surrenders continued and the land returned to peace, the Pobl'prinn became worried. Their foes were willing to give up magic, to walk away from Gaia's gift, and the people of the soil started to sense what might come next. It was not surprising, then, that after the last tribe had laid down its arms and vowed to leave their powers unused, the queen turned to the council of elders who had taken up leadership after Aleah'la's death.

"Come with me," she requested, urging them to join her in a self-imposed banishment on Earth, away from the lure and temptation of magical energy. They could not, though; the song repeated its initial verse about them being of the land, and the land being in them, and then it repeated again. That drove the point home. But the price of their unwillingness to turn their own backs on Gaia was banishment, and they accepted the judgment without resistance. Their elders' last act among their light-skinned brethren was to assist Rhiannon in breaking all the relics save one—the one I wore around my neck—and then helping her seal off the portals behind her.

The song went back to dirge then, its people cast out and wandering alone and their favorite queens dead and gone. There were several more verses about the split-up, and the work they'd done in the thousands of years since, but the singer seemed as uninterested in performing those as I was in listening to them.

My heart was broken, and not just for the Pobl'prinn. The loss to my own people, those I would be ruling soon enough, was tremendous. I couldn't begin to imagine all that they had missed out on, in spite of what I could see now as efforts to circumvent the ancient oath by using "earth energy" to heal and to work with the land, and refusing to call it magic.

I understood.

That understanding didn't make it any easier to face, though, I realized as the post-song silence stretched out. In being the one to bring back magic, I was going to force many of them to break a whole lot of oaths.

I didn't see where I had much choice, though.

Part of that would be positive, I figured. High Priestess Sternyface's minions had included just a little bit of religious theory from their own standpoint over the past summer, more as a historical lesson than anything else. There were no single causes to any of the great elven wars of previous epochs, of course, but religion seemed to play a central role in all of them, and the priests had made it their mission to show me how. Thus, they were proud to be priests over a somewhat atheistic order, if that makes any sense—it didn't, at the time, and it still doesn't. Atheist—*anffyddiwr*—was the word they'd used, anyway, but agnostic is closer to the truth. They're fully willing to acknowledge that their power over the forces of nature—*not* magic!—comes from somewhere or someone, but they don't really want to talk about where, or who, that somewhere or someone might be.

In other words, my people are so scared of warfare that they're willing to walk away from their god—or gods, actually—to prevent it. That made me ashamed. And I would end that shame, bring back Gaia to a people who needed her the most.

"Wow," I breathed as the enormity of the task ahead of me finally hit.

That broke the spell of silence, anyway. At that point everyone crowded around, insisting on seeing and, in a couple of brave cases, even touching the relic that I now wore on a chain around my neck. Their reactions, the faces lit with happiness, made me feel a bit like a hero in spite of the initial intercultural standoffishness.

"How many of you are there?"

"Thousands. Scores of thousands. We are spread out across the continent, keeping to little camps of no more than what you see here."

"You communicate?"

"Of course. You do not?"

"Probably not the same way you do."

"We let the dragons carry our messages to other camps," the bear-hugger volunteered from beside me.

"Dragons?" I asked. "That's funny. I haven't seen a dragon since I've been here, and I can't imagine you could hide something that big."

"Elaithim is joking, young one," the old woman answered me, using the maternal version of the term for a child, while sending him a glare. "There have been no dragons since what the history you have studied calls the Third Epoch."

"The history I studied didn't mention dragons in any epoch, actually." My interest shot up. "I've been told that the Cult of the Wyrm, the group which is attacking me, is named after dragons, but that dragons haven't existed in a long while, that they were all killed off. And there's nothing about dragons written in the histories I've read so far."

"That is probably for the best, Alyssa. You have met wyverns, if what I have heard is correct?"

"Wyvern. Just one. It was quite scary, though."

"Indeed. A young dragon is ten times larger than a typical wyvern, and will double in size every century or so of its incredibly long life, but that is not the scariest part. Gaia gave them the same gift she gave us, in her eternal wisdom, and so a dragon can perform any feat you can attempt, and likely any feat you can imagine, using its arcane ability. It is said that during the third epoch they controlled the minds of some of the rulers. Your people slipped back into the use of magic, in fact, to protect themselves from such powerful beings."

"Interesting. I was told it was in pursuit of power and wealth that they started using magic again."

"Well, there is some truth to that, to be certain. But when your only chance for survival is to embrace the powers within you, then you—make compromises."

"Do dragons still exist, then?"

She shrugged, a gesture I realized I could see too well in the glimmering morning light. "What evidence do you have that they do not?"

"There haven't been any attacks in centuries."

"So because there have been no attacks, there must be no dragons, because a dragon would have attacked by now. Yes? That is supposition, not evidence. My ancestors fought and killed the last known dragon several centuries ago, but if that dragon managed to lay an egg, and that egg hatched, the offspring would just now be reaching mature state."

"And where would it be, to have hidden from your people all this time?"

She shrugged. "That is a good point. Still, we remain vigilant."

I looked up and noticed the fact that I could see the trees and the structures a lot more clearly. Panic hit first, but then I relaxed back into the sense of ease that the camp created. "Speaking of vigilant, it is now daylight. I must get back to the castle."

"Yes. You must. Thank you for listening to the tale of my people. It gives me both great honor and a glimmer of hope for the future that you have now heard it."

"It was—it was my pleasure. I will try to come back again, if I am welcome."

"You will not find us, Princess. We must continue as we have for centuries, and you should rejoin your own tribe. We are pleased at the connection, and hopeful at the future your openness promises, but we remain wary nonetheless. No matter how popular you may be among your own, not even a queen can erase centuries of prejudice."

"I will try, nonetheless." I promised, and then took off toward Cysegredig at a lope. A couple of hundred yards away I stopped, briefly, and turned around to see nothing. There was a slight hill, but of the lean-tos, and the fire, and any life form, nothing was visible.

Shaking my head in baffled wonderment, I returned to my home.

POBL'CUDD

"Hidden people"—the dark elves once they had vanished into the trees, from the trees' points of view.

A Father's Words

"They do not exist," Dad argued.

"How can you say that? I was just talking to them!"

"I just said it. They do not exist. I am not certain whether you had a bad dream, or fell down and knocked yourself out, but the People of the Earth are fiction. A popular fiction, granted, but they are entirely not real."

I felt like stamping my foot in irritation, but was too tired. After a full afternoon of being told that three of the four major clans wanted me banished, and then all night spent talking to and learning about the strange race of black-skinned elves, I'd run home to find him, Aerona, and Seph all waiting for me in my room. Seph was worried, of course, while Aerona was mostly just irritated over having been left without a charge to look over all night. Dad was—well, he was the king, and he was doing his best to make sure that I knew it.

"Okay, so maybe I knocked myself out and didn't realize it. I'll know more after I sleep a little. Please, may I have some privacy for just a few short hours to catch up?"

"Under normal circumstances, my daughter, such a request would be warmly met by my approval. Unfortunately, it appears that you have forgotten your promise to begin preparations for your passage to adulthood at sunrise on this day. Certainly there was no plan on your part to renege on this important point from the negotiation yesterday, was there?"

"No! No, I just—I'm tired, Dad, and want to get some sleep."

"Perhaps you should have considered that prior to—"

"I know, I know. Okay, look, I'll put it off. I don't need a lecture. Where do I need to go to get the preparations started?"

"I believe the high priestess herself is awaiting your arrival in her office. As she has been, since sunrise. I am certain that you will find her in the most pleasant of moods when you arrive."

I shot Seph a glare as penalty for her snicker, and then I spun on my heel and marched out of the room toward the castle's passage to the cathedral. I resisted my own intense desire to hurry; Sternyface would already be as angry as she was likely to get, and sprinting through the cathedral to get to her office quickly would counter everything I'd done to prove myself worthy of the title of crown princess and its requisite respect.

Well, that, and I really was bone-tired. My legs felt like rubber. I was barely able to keep plodding along, one foot in front of the other, while my fear-addled, sleep-deprived brain kept sending irritated signals to my feet to turn around and run the other way.

Eventually, I made it anyway. I knocked, and after a long, long wait that was probably only a few dozen seconds in reality, the response filtered through the door.

"Come!"

I opened the door and marched in, wondering what I was in for.

"Please close the door behind you," made my heart skip a beat. She'd never had me close the door behind a meeting with just her and me before. We'd had a few closed-door events with my father present, but not with just me.

"You're late. Very late," she chided me once I'd returned to my spot in front of her desk.

"I went out for a jog last night to clear my head and lost track of time," I explained, as unapologetically as I could manage.

"Lost track of time?" she asked, giving me a doubtful look. Obviously, she hadn't heard the real story. "How do you lose track of sunrise when you are outside?"

"I got into a conversation," I answered, trying to make it sound like the most natural thing in the world.

"What sort of conversation?" she probed.

"I met some dark-skinned elves, who told me the history of their portion of the race. Dad told me this morning that they don't exist, though, so I probably imagined the whole thing while I was busy not noticing that the sun was rising." I gave her my sweetest smile to emphasize the level of sarcasm I was attaching to the statement.

"Dark-skinned elves," she repeated, her mouth dragging the words out acerbically. "Yes, there is certainly a—constraint— upon your father and what the king can and cannot say within the castle's walls."

"So he knows about them?"

"I am not at liberty to say what the king knows about and what he does not. I would, however, recommend that you try to use some of the sense that your birth lineage gave you and avoid introducing topics like that where they should not be discussed."

"So you know about the dark elves." I didn't let it slip into a question at the end.

She shrugged, making the gesture into a luxurious show of ostentation, with a sideways sneer on her face. "What I do or do not know is not a matter to be questioned by a child, even one as privileged as the crown princess believes herself to be. You came here to prepare for the hunhymgais. Now, let us begin."

By lunchtime I was convinced that the preparation for hunhymgais was likely to kill me from stopping my breath due to boredom. Sternyface, who apparently hadn't gotten over my tardiness or my putting her on the spot, seemed to delight in droning on about what makes an adult, an adult. She refused to let me sit through the process, too, so I had to stand, shifting my weight occasionally as one leg or the other fell as deeply asleep as I wished that my entire body could. Lunch was brought to me, to be eaten in a special side room, where the furniture consisted precisely of one small wooden table and one wooden stool. Apparently Sternyface had "business to attend to," in her sparse terminology. The fruit and slices of meat were welcome, though, since I'd skipped breakfast completely. At least I got to sit down to eat.

After lunch the high priestess announced that lecturing me was too boring for Her Holiness, and suddenly I was rushed off to a smaller office where an even more boring set of lectures were delivered by a male priest with a high-pitched voice and a slight lisp. I was actually glad that he wouldn't let me sit, because I'm pretty sure I would've fallen right to sleep given the chance.

"That sounds awful," Seph comforted me as I told her the story that evening at the table in the common dining room. I didn't have to be seek any privacy, since nobody other than my cousin was willing to sit anywhere near me.

I nodded and chewed another bite. Finally I asked, "How did your preparation for hunhymgais go?"

"What do you mean?"

"You know, when you were getting ready to go for your ceremony. How many lectures did you have to sit through?"

Seph looked incredulous. "None."

"None at all? What did you do to prepare?"

"I stripped my clothes off."

"And then what?"

"I stepped in to the portal."

"That's all?" I couldn't believe the difference between her and my experiences so far.

"Alyssa, I'm just a regular person. Growing up, I observed everything that the high priestess and priest have been lecturing you on. So when the time came, I just did it."

"Oh. Wonder how my father's hunhymgais went."

"About the same as your cousin's," my father's voice answered from behind, surprising me enough to earn him a jump and a gasp. I've bragged about my spidey-senses, but my father is the one exception I've found. Luckily I had no fear he'd ever sneak up behind me with a dagger, because he's the one guy who could actually do it.

"Your Majesty," Seph said with a flourish, and then she kept eating at his gestured command to do so. She looked a lot like she wanted to escape, though.

"Dad, I get the desire to see me safely through the hunhymgais, but why all the lectures?"

"That is not mine to explain, my daughter."

"I'm just—tired," I said, and unbidden came a yawn to accompany my pronouncement.

"I can imagine. You had a long and exciting night. Perhaps we could discuss it further in privacy?"

"I'd like that. Only, not for too long," I said, yawning again. It was catching; Seph mirrored the action.

"Not for too long," Dad agreed, and then headed into the throne room. I said good night to Seph and then followed him in, taking my food tray and its few remaining bites with me.

"So. Dark elves," Dad said in English after silently pouring each of us a whiskey.

"I'm a little nervous about drinking that, as exhausted as I am."

"Drink it. Slowly. It'll help you sleep."

"Okay. So there really are dark elves," I said, unable to make my voice do anything, accusatory or otherwise. I was impressed with myself over merely being able to form a coherent sentence. At least, I thought it was coherent. It was getting harder to speak in English, believe it or not, after so many months of speaking mostly in the beautiful, complex elf language.

"Yes. As your father, I am not very proud of it, but as your king, I cannot admit to their presence where such admission could be overheard."

"Why not?"

"They are—*aflan*," he said. I searched for the meaning of the elf word he used, but couldn't find anything. To my confused look, he added, "not—not clean, I believe is the best translation."

"I'm sure they could be clean if you let them into the castle to take a bath."

Dad grimaced. "It is not a bath-scrubbing sort of clean that we are talking about, Alyssa. They are wild—untamed—untamable."

What he meant slowly came to me. "Wait—you mean unclean, as in a caste sort of thing, don't you? Like what Ghandi saved the Indian people from, or something." I was so tired it was just spilling out, and besides, Dad wouldn't know the history either. "You're saying that because they're dark-skinned, they don't have any worth and so they can't be in your presence. That's disgusting. That's racist."

"No, no, it is not because of their skin color."

"That's what all racists say."

"Alyssa—"

"Racist."

"No! That is not it at all. Please listen to me."

"Okay, racist." I was completely, totally disgusted with my father at that moment.

My father inhaled, his nostrils flaring in agitation, giving me the cue I needed to stop prodding him. With a measured voice, he said, "The dark elves refuse to follow our tradition. They use magic freely, wantonly, repetitively."

"So do I. Are you going to call me unclean, too?"

He leaned forward, anger flashing in his eyes brightly enough that I shrank back a little. "Did you miss the brunt of the conversation a few days ago? The one where three major clan chieftains were suggesting just that? You are far from stupid, my daughter, so I can only assume it is your exhaustion making you speak so illogically."

"Oh." He was right, I guess. Still, it went against every fiber of my being to ostracize an entire segment of society—one that just happened to be identified by the color of their skin—over a social more that I already considered dumb.

I said exactly that, only in a little bit lighter tone than I'd been using.

He relaxed slightly.

"It has nothing to do with their skin color, Alyssa. Their presence, their beliefs, run foul to a true elf's sensitivities and sensibilities. Remember the boy you met in the village?"

"Gwyn?" Of course I remembered the boy. It's not every day you meet the body double for Legolas, and he had just the sort of impish grin that I liked staring at.

"Yes, that boy. He is trouble, precisely because he has ingratiated himself and apparently has visited numerous times and at length with the dark-skinned ones. It has gotten him shunned by his whole village, and for good reason. Yes, I know you were attracted to him, but to be honest I would rather you pursue even Keion than that rascal. You have a very real, very pressing challenge to your future throne mounting, my daughter, and the last thing you need to do is make your claim worse by raising the specter of *aflan* against you. Please tell me that you will not again make contact with—those."

"Dad, you're still a racist. You know that?"

He looked at me for a long while, just shaking his head in a tiny side-to-side arc. Finally he replied quietly, "I am obviously not solid on what the term racist means, my daughter, but I can tell that it is an important concept to you. For my part I will admit to whatever you accuse me of, in the name of effectively governing my land. You may see things differently, and that is fine. You may feel free to violate that tradition once you become queen, just as you are apparently slated to violate every other tradition that my—our—people hold dear. But for my sake, and for that of your mother, as well as the queen and the high priestess, please pretend as though last night did not happen until you are safely and securely crowned. Even then, I must warn you, accepting the *aflan* into your presence and society will likely cost you a large part of your following, if not the throne itself. Tread with wisdom there, please, my daughter."

"I will, Dad," I said, nodding. "But for now, I just need to get to bed."

"Sleep peacefully, then, and please, no more night runs."

A Queen's Words

"Good evening, Crown Princess. How may I be of assistance?" The Lady of the Bedchamber stood with a glare, blocking the narrow opening that the partly-opened door made into the queen's chambers. Her tone, meanwhile, said she would be happy to be anything other than assistance.

"Good evening. I need to speak with Queen Talaith." I figured the direct approach was the best.

"It is late." She sniffed. "And you have been drinking. Perhaps now is not the best time for an audience."

I was about to reply when a clear voice tinkled from behind her. "It is okay. Now is a fine time. I have been expecting a visit, after all. Please, come in and have a seat, Alyssa. Meredydd, would you mind fetching us a couple of cups of tea? My favorite herbal, I would say, but add some *balan* root to help our poor crown princess counter the effects of her father's whiskey."

The Lady did as asked, her glare instantly disappearing. I stepped in to see the queen sitting regally on one of her carved couches, motioning to a spot on the opposite one.

"You are here to ask about hunhymgais." It wasn't much of a question, but it was correct.

I shrugged. "You're the only person I know who went through it at about the same age as me."

"Age makes little difference in the trial, Alyssa."

"I know," I lied. I didn't want her to see the truth, though, which was that I was completely ignorant, and that terrified me. "But you came from a human life back on Earth, just as I did, and so I am curious what, if anything, you found that did make a difference in the trial."

"There are two words—I do not know the proper elf translation, so I shall speak them in English. You will need to hold these words close to your heart as you go through the challenge, as they are teh only thing I found that made a difference."

I nodded, looking forward to the revelation to come. "I am ready."

She leaned closer slightly, inhaled the aroma from the still-hot cup of tea that the Lady had just brought, and smiled pleasantly.

"Intestinal fortitude," she said slowly, in English.

I tried not to let my disappointment show as I nodded my acceptance.

"You mean, the ability to tough it out through whatever comes my way?"

"I mean precisely that, yes, only—maybe a little bit more elegant language could be selected by one who will soon be queen."

"Well, I—yes, ma'am—I mean, Your Majesty."

"Are you always this far off your game, or did you consume a little too much of your father's whiskey?"

That brought me up cold; I'd never been told I was doing a bad job before. Well, except by Sternyface, but I figured that it was her job to be mean. I took a slow sip of the tea to hide in my own head for a moment and collect my thoughts before speaking.

"No, Your Majesty. To both, I would like to think. This is very good tea, by the way. The aroma is both heady and pleasant. Thank you." She nodded briefly and I plunged on. "I apologize for my out-of-sorts reply, but I admit that I was looking for something a little more—"

"Useful?" she interjected, and I nodded. It was close enough, anyway. "Yes. Relax, Alyssa. At your age I was looking for things that were more *useful* as well. But the good thing about the hunhmgais—mine, at least, and I hope for yours, as well—is that it throws some perspective at you, tosses it crashing rapidly into your field of view. You will likely not enjoy it, but through perseverance you can make it through the trial, just as I did. Remember, intestinal fortitude."

I sipped the tea again, using the obvious breathing rhythm as a conversational shield while I thought of what to say next. Besides, the tea really was unfurling a few strands in my brain that Dad's whiskey had twisted up a little.

"So what was it like?"

She shrugged. "Alyssa, I do not say this to sound like—I believe you call her Sternyface?—but rather as a simple statement of fact. It is personal. What you go through will undoubtedly be vastly distinct from what I faced, which was in turn vastly distinct from whatever Talaith before me experienced. And before you ask, yes, I did ask her, and yes, I received the same response." She flashed me a sweet smile, disarming the shock I'd felt over the realization that she knew my nickname for the high priestess.

"I would just like to know what to expect, is all." I tried not to sound petulant, and for the most part I succeeded.

"As trite as this sounds, you must expect the unexpected. That is all I can tell you. All I can tell you about the hunhymgais, at any rate, but you, Alyssa. You," she paused to nod in emphasis, "are a strong one. Far, far stronger than I was at your age. If I'd had to stand up to the collected clan chieftains as a crown princess, I do not know whether I would have pulled out nearly as solid a performance as you. You do not need to worry about the unexpected. In fact, I would suggest that the unexpected should worry more about you."

I giggled at the way she'd phrased it, and was surprised when her laughter joined mine. Talaith wasn't prone to fits of it, from what I'd seen and heard, so the rare joy was nice.

"That was a little—trite—of me, was it not?"

"I don't think so. It was inspiring."

"Inspiringly trite, then."

"If you say so, Your Majesty."

She nodded and finished her tea, and then put the cup down meaningfully. Lady Meredydd stepped forward to collect both cups, obviously, and so I took the cue and rose. "Thank you for your wisdom. I cannot say I look forward to the experience with great joy, but I am somewhat more confident now."

She nodded. "Intestinal fortitude," she said one last time, her voice sharp, and then she strode regally into her own chamber farther back. Meredydd helped me to the door, her face a mask of neutrality the whole time.

By the time I reached the opposite end of the hall I knew I was in trouble. It wasn't my father's stance in the hall or his glare that told me so, but rather the *whump whump* sound from inside my room. I marched up to my door, put my hand on it, and met my father's eyes.

"Your tree," he said simply, anger resonating in the two short words.

"Missed me," I finished the thought, nodding with a smile and then ducking into my room to avoid any further glare.

The noise stopped immediately as soon as I shut the door behind me. I turned to find myself alone in a room with a quivering potted elm on the opposite side. The air in the room zinged and crackled with an agitated energy, and I rushed over to tend to my—my what, I wondered. L.T. had become more than a potted plant, to be certain. To call an elm tree a pet was absurd, though. To call it a friend seemed even more so, but at the same time it felt closer to the truth.

Calling up the gentle sing-song voice I'd learned to use around L.T., I asked about him—it! When talking *about* the tree, it's easy to use a genderless, personless pronoun, but when talking to him, the tree is full of identity and even gender, though on a shifting basis. My mind flashed back to the night we'd connected through the strange tree-link, when I'd found that it, she, and he hardly mattered—or sufficed, for that matter—as a label, and I smiled. My little tree-friend had a big heart, no matter that it didn't actually have any organs.

That heart was as close to broken as I can imagine a tree's being.

I sat and listened as the gentle tree communicated with me. He couldn't speak, of course, nor could he sing in the same pattern I'd been doing. Nor did we open a channel between us like we'd had the night before. It was more of a rhythmic pattern of branches swishing against the air, soft breezes in patterns that were recognizable as long as I tried.

Little Treebeard was sad. He knew, from a communal memory sump he held with his brethren as well as from mental images from me, what a hunhymgais was, and he wanted to come with me, while he knew he couldn't. He, like Seph before him, sensed danger coming my way, but neither of them could identify its source.

I spent the next long while—several hours, it felt like—crooning softly, reassuring my tree friend that all would be okay. I had the guts to make it, the queen had said, and all I had to do was apply intestinal fortitude and I would be fine and back to be with him in no time.

It calmed him down, and it calmed me down as well.

I don't know how I got to the bed that night. I vaguely remember strong arms that carried Dad's scent lifting me up, but I'll never be certain.

Argument

"It is customary," Dad stated flatly and went back to making a show of examining the trees and shrubbery as we passed by.

"I don't really care. I want to get on with the hunhymgais. I don't need a grand celebration in the village of my birth—or of your birth, anyway. I don't even know where I was born."

"The document of your birth says Wales. You could be a Welsh citizen if you wanted to."

"It's called a birth certificate, Dad. At least, it's called that in the United States. And I knew where I was born; kids at school somehow knew it too and made fun of me for it. And you can't be a Welsh citizen any more; they're part of the UK. And why would I want to be a British citizen anyway, when I have such a loving, kind, and nonjudgmental kingdom of elves here on Kiirajanna, bless their kind, nonjudgmental little hearts, that I will some day rule?"

"Falling back on your old sarcastic ways, dear?"

"Ya think?"

The rest of the ride passed quietly, Dad giving up the argument in favor of glaring at the trees as we passed. I glanced back to see Seph pointedly ignoring us from her perch in the back seat. Meanwhile, Aerona's eyes twinkled with a mirth that she didn't dare allow to spread across the rest of her countenance.

"Racist," I reminded him with a whisper that was rewarded by continued stony silence as the carriage rumbled into the village, which was, itself, quiet due to the early hour. Dafydd ambled out with a huge smile on his face that quickly flattened as he read his brother's dark expression, and then he quietly helped us into his cottage.

Seph turned to the right and headed out into the woods. Hoping for a reason to pick my own cloudy mood up out of the sewers, I followed her, tentatively at first. She seemed a little off from her normal self, both in the determined setting of each step and in the flatness of her usually cheerful expression.

With a little effort I caught up to her so I could stride side by side. "What's wrong, Cousin?"

"Who says something is wrong, Princess?"

"Your face, for one thing. And you haven't called me Princess in years."

"I haven't known you for years."

I shrugged. Her stony face had cracked, at least a little, so the comment had accomplished what I'd wanted. "Right. So, what's wrong?"

"You."

"Me?" My surprise pushed into my voice, and I let it through.

"Yes, you." She glared at me as though the answer should have been obvious.

"Aren't you going to explain?"

"Only if you ask me to, and promise me you won't bite my head off if I do it."

"Okay, sure. I won't bite your head off. So why am I what is wrong with you?"

"You're in such a bad mood, all day, every day. And when you're in a bad mood, everybody around you knows it. You broadcast it, radiating it like heat from a bonfire. You don't even have to say anything, though when you do, it's almost always in a nasty tone. I recognize that we are family, and I love you for it, but you make being around you a very hard thing to do, Cousin."

I stopped, and she did too, and we both turned to face each other. I could tell from the set of her jaw that she had spoken the absolute truth as she saw it, but I couldn't see that truth at all.

"I am not. At least, I am not in a bad mood today."

"No, of course not. You call your father a racist out of love, respect, and an overall sense of contentedness."

"Sarcasm, Seph?"

"I learned from the best, Cousin."

Her peevish tone mixed with her screwed-up, angry expression struck me suddenly as one of the funniest situations I'd ever faced, and I couldn't help breaking out into a series of guffaws. She seemed hurt, immediately, but that faded as she, too, morphed an angry expression into a slight smile and then joined me in laughter.

"Why is this so funny, Alyssa?" she finally asked once she'd managed to catch back up to her own breathing.

"I don't know. It's just—it is."

"Well, I needed the laugh. And so did you. Your entire being changed."

"What does that mean?"

"What do you mean, what does that mean? You changed. You became happy again, and the negative you transitioned out. It will probably be back, of course, but for the time being its absence is beautiful."

"The negative me? What negative me? And how do you see anything like that? Are you talking about some strange— presence?" The elf language didn't, as far as I knew, have any word for aura, so saying presence while waving my arms all around me was the best I could do.

It wasn't good enough. Seph glared, confused. She shook her head. "I don't know what this presence," she said, mimicking my gesture by waving all around, "is, but have you never been around someone whose moods you could sense?"

"Well, sure. Momma, for example. I could tell just by walking into the room what sort of mood she was in. You're not saying—"

"That you and your Momma share a power of broadcasting your feelings? That would not be entirely unheard of, Alyssa."

"No, I guess not. Have you sensed it before?" *Have I always been a jerk?* I wanted to ask, but I decided to keep it as logic-based as possible, at least till I figured it out.

"Sure. Sometimes. Often, I suppose. I've been around you an awful lot, after all. It took me a while to figure out what the feeling was, that it was coming from you rather than from my own being, and much of the time you've just been broadcasting confusion."

"Confusion?"

"Don't get upset. At least, don't get upset over that. Look, you didn't grow up here, so nobody expected you to understand us immediately. If you hadn't felt a little confusion at first, everybody would have wondered why."

A perverse thought occurred to me. "What about when I'm around Prince Keion? Do I radiate anything then?"

"Well, yes, but—"

"What? What do I radiate?" I felt myself getting agitated once again.

"You don't—"

"Tell me. The truth!" Without realizing it, I leaned in closer to her, my anger-laden face nearly touching hers.

"Alyssa, stop it. Back off, okay? You're—too intense, okay?" Her voice took on a pleading tone as I moved away, confused.

"I'm sorry. I just—I fear—I don't—I'm not sure how to say what I'm feeling." I was terrified, for one thing, but the potential that I'd radiated anything about Prince Charming mortified me.

"Relax, Princess. You haven't—nothing unexpected has come from your radiating, anyway. He's a handsome prince, after all—the handsomest of handsome princes, in fact—and you're sure not the first girl to have the hots for him. You just make it a little easier to read, that's all."

"A little easier to read? And you didn't think to tell me?"

"Tell you what? That the whole castle could see you were attracted to the guy? It surprised nobody."

"Well, you still should have told me I was—radiating, or whatever you call it."

Seph set her face and crossed her arms obstinately. "What would that have accomplished?"

"Well—I—maybe—I—look, I don't know, but it would have been awfully dang nice to know so you weren't laughing at me behind my back, bless all your little hearts."

"Nobody was laughing at you. Well, okay, maybe the prince's sisters were. But you already knew that! You did, didn't you?" She paused long enough for me to switch from an angry glare to a glum nod, and then continued, "So stop blaming me. Now you do know, and maybe you can do something about it. Probably, you can't, though. I can't see where anybody could do anything about that prince's spell. In fact, now it will just make you more self-conscious than you already are, I bet. But the more important question, at least to me, is why you're treating your father like such a jerk."

She didn't actually say *jerk*; there's no direct equivalent in the elf language. The word she had used, though, is much more profane than I can repeat here.

"I am not treating him like a—like that. Am I?" I asked, getting unsure when she turned a knowing expression on me.

"Well, you called him a racist, for one thing, and not in a very nice tone of voice. And like I said, you were radiating—more than anger."

"Well, he is a racist!"

"No, he's not. Where did you get that?"

"He refuses to even acknowledge the presence of dark-skinned elves, just because of their skin color, that's where!"

"What dark-skinned elves?"

"Not you, too!"

"Slow, Alyssa. You're stepping into a part of society that has been the way it is for eons, and expecting it to change overnight."

"But it will change overnight, the moment I'm queen! That is, after all, what the prophecy said, and you can bet Sternyface isn't letting me forget it."

She considered me for a minute and then shrugged. "Okay, so maybe it will. But why do you think you can expect your father to change it? And why do you expect him to like the idea? Kiirajanna is all he has ever known, and the same goes for me. I—I will admit, as a ranger, to—well, to occasionally sensing something out there, something hidden, something moving and even—even elf-like. But that doesn't make me want to run out and welcome them into our camp. We're here, and we're doing okay without them, and they're there, and they're doing fine without us."

"How do you know that they're doing fine without us?"

"Well, it isn't really mine to know, Cousin. Now you're radiating again."

"Well, I'm angry. I'm angry that everyone refuses to even look at them as the allies they are—"

"So you just wish to use them against the Cult?"

"I—well, no—not use them—um—I—I want to see the two groups reunited, is all."

"Uh huh."

"You've gotten way too good at sarcasm. You know that?"

"Yep. Continue." She motioned me on with a wicked look in her eyes. I could tell she was very pleased with herself.

"So that's why I'm angry at my father."

"That's not all of it. You were angry before you found out about the dark ones."

"How do you—radiating again, wasn't I?" She nodded, and I continued, "I was trying not to make a big deal out of it."

"You didn't make a big deal out of it. I only barely noticed. It's not like you're furious at him."

I nodded, relieved that at least it wasn't likely to become a matter of state concern.

"So what is it you're angry about?"

I wanted to reply with a curt "none of your business" but held it back. It was sort of her business, after all, not just because she was my cousin, but also because she was an elf of the realm, and it had been drilled into both of us—her as a child, and me in those classes I'd taken with children—that elves of Kiirajanna should be concerned about all matters of the continent, including its rulership.

"It's just silly, to be perfectly honest. No, it is," I argued as she started to roll her eyes. "I—do you love your father, Seph?"

"Of course I do." She shrugged; it was the most obvious answer she'd given. "Don't you?"

"I—I think so. I respect him, of course. He is the king. And Momma loves him. But I've—I never knew him. Not growing up, at least not in any of the memories I can dredge up. I didn't even know who he was until about six months ago. He was gone. He left Momma to raise me by herself. I know, I know," I waved her down as she started to object, "he was doing his duty, to the realm and to Momma and to me and to everybody else. I know how hard it was for him, and I know how much he loves me and my mother. At least, I know these things up here." I pointed to my head, and then to my heart as I continued, "if not down here. And I don't know how I'll ever know those things down here. I—I understand why Dad had to do what he did, but it doesn't stop me from being angry about it, and then I get angry because I'm angry, if that makes sense. So—so maybe it doesn't, at least not as I'm poorly explaining it, but that's the way it is. Dad had great responsibility, but part of that was being there for my childhood, and he wasn't. And he'll—and I'll—never get that chance again."

She stared at my face for a minute, and then looked into space over my shoulder, her expression thoughtful. She nodded, slowly at first. "I understand, Alyssa. Have you told His Majesty these things?"

I snorted. "No. Why would I tell him, go out of my way to inflict these thoughts upon him? Why would anybody believe that he is in a position to understand my point of view, anyway?"

She shrugged and smiled, her gaze still held to the space beyond my left ear. "Oh, I think he would be in a good position to understand your point of view."

I finally realized what she was looking at over my shoulder, but I refused to turn around. "How long has he been standing behind me?"

"A while. I'm surprised you didn't sense him coming up behind you. Heck, I'm surprised you didn't hear him. You're a warrior, not a ranger, right, Your Majesty?"

"Hi, Daddy," I said as I turned around, giving him my best don't-hate-me-for-what-you-heard look. I tossed an explanation back to Seph, "I have a blind spot where he is concerned."

"No kidding," she said with a snort. "In more ways than one, I'd say."

"You two were engaged in a deep conversation. I came out to invite you to dinner, but did not wish to interrupt."

"It's okay. I—"

"No, Alyssa. No, it is not okay." As he continued, I saw a single tear form in the corner of each of his eyes. "You have every right to be angry for missing your childhood, my daughter. You should be, in fact. I have been so utterly focused on being the well-respected king that Kiirajanna demanded, to the point where it blinded me to my other responsibility to be the beloved father that you needed, or the husband that your mother deserves with every ounce of her being." He broke, and crumpled me against his chest with both arms, continuing with a whisper into my hair,"You are correct that I can never have the chance to enjoy you growing up into the beautiful young lady you have become, and that is a loss that I hope you believe is dear to my heart. More important to me, though, is your heart. Can you forgive me?"

By the time he unfolded and let me slip away, Seph had vanished into the forest. Dad and I walked silently, but entirely together, back to Dafydd's home.

WYNT YN EI DDWRN

literally, "wind in his fist"—in a hurry, which is how these cylchoedd players seem to be all the time, and far different from the peaceful wind in the branches that trees enjoy.

Cylchoedd

"Not so fast, Princess Alyssa!"

Oh, boy. I recognized the high-pitched voice before I turned around, and it made me not want to. But turn around I did, and saw that I was right. Toward me strode Seph's childhood friend Gwenda, Cuddles loping along by her side.

"Hiya," I said, my best fake smile glittering on my face. "Glad to see you." That was an unfortunate lie. What I was hoping to see was the stones of Cysegredig so that I could start my adulthood trial, which should have started the day prior except for the celebration that my father had insisted on. We'd been there overnight, and had quite a party in the village green, but I was done with celebrations and just wanted to get it over and done with.

"Hey, Cousin," Seph said, bounding out of her father's house with the last of her luggage to load in the carriage to go back home. "Gwenda has a surprise for you."

"Oh. Well, bless your heart, I can't wait to find out what it is."

My cousin, who had long since figured out that me blessing somebody's heart wasn't really much of a blessing, gave me an exasperated look. Gwenda, who hadn't, beamed.

"I'm so glad you're looking forward to it, Princess. You probably didn't know that today is the first game of the cylchoedd season, and today my Bs are playing close by! I've arranged for all three of us to go together so that you'll learn to love the sport as much as I do. Isn't that exciting?"

"Yeah," I said. It wasn't. Not really. Watching men running around rolling a hoop that I usually saw kids play with sounded about as exciting as watching a tree grow.

Not that I have anything against trees, mind you. Men rolling hoops, maybe. Not trees.

Another carriage wheeled its silent way down the street as Dad came out of the house and hugged his brother Dafydd goodbye. He'd put his cowl and his crown back on, and now appeared every inch of the king he was. The two men spoke in quiet tones, thumped each others' chests in the strange way elf men who are close to one another have of wishing each other well, and parted, my uncle back into his home and Dad to the royal carriage.

"Everything packed up, Alyssa and Sephaline? I understand you will be enjoying a bit of a detour with this fine young lady," he said.

Seph nodded eagerly, and I tried to smile the same way. Dad caught my failure and managed to hide his grin so that only his eyes lit up.

"Alyssa, you are in for a rare treat," he said. "Every time the Bs and the Chs play it is always a close game. I wish I could go with you."

"Why can't you, Dad?" I asked, trying not to lose my cool and bust out in laughter at the team names. The Bs he'd said as though the insects were playing: 'bees." The Chs, though, sounded like somebody back home who didn't like okra and wanted to let everybody know it: 'echs' only with plenty of 'ch' from the back of the tongue. It sounded like phlegm, to be honest.

I couldn't wait to hear their fans cheer for them. "Gimme a *phlegm sound*!"

"Official business, my dear. The end of Yule and the start of a new year is always a big deal at the palace, and we hold a special court tonight to rule on some of the most important annual issues. At the end is a great big party, but you will probably be there by then to see for yourself. Enjoy the game!"

It was, truly, the end of the Yule season, it turned out. I'd thought Yule was over the first time we returned to Cysegredig, but that was just the end of the main holiday. The celebration went on for another week, during which time I'd gotten into the trouble you already know about, followed by a few days of gripping lectures on what it means to be an adult in Kiirajanna. Then back to Dad's village, and now here we were.

"I still don't understand," I said as the carriage launched itself down the trail, "why the teams are named after the letters of the alphabet."

"What do you name teams after on Earth?" Seph asked.

"All sorts of things. Cowboys, buccaneers, pirates, animals like broncos and colts and panthers." I searched my memory for more references to sports teams. "We even have teams named for the color of their socks."

"That sounds random," Gwenda said, crinkling her nose in disapproval.

"It is, I suppose, but what's wrong with that?"

"It's random."

Oh, right. Random is bad. I did mention before that the elves won't let a single blade of grass grow too tall in the forest, didn't I?

As that conversation died a quick death, I gazed around at the woods on both sides of the path. It was very pretty, with little tufts of white snow still hanging around in shady spots. It felt like one of those old-timey sleigh rides I'd always imagined would be, except that it was completely silent without the punctuation of the clop-clop of hooves. The elf carriages had freaked me out at first, moving under their own magical power as they did, but Dad had assured me that it wasn't really magic but rather earth energy that powered them.

Uh huh. Earth energy *was* magic.

I was starting to figure out that the prophecy we were seemingly all enslaved to was just a fancy way of saying that, once I was queen, I'd have to knock some sense into everybody's heads.

"So how long is a game of cylchoedd?" I asked Gwenda, trying to be nice.

"Oh, it's as long as it takes, Princess. Sometimes they're just a few minutes, and sometimes they take all day and all night. One game a few years ago took nearly a week."

"A week? How many overtimes was that?" I was still imagining soccer with hoops.

"Overtime? I'm not sure what that is. The teams play to fifteen, and whoever gets there first wins."

"Oh. How many points do they score for crossing the goal line?"

"Crossing the what?"

"Cousin," Seph said, "perhaps it would be easiest for everyone to understand if you asked Gwenda to just tell you about the game and how it is played rather than assuming the ways it is likely to be similar to your Earth sports."

"Oh. Right. Thank you, Seph. So Gwenda, what's the ultimate goal of the game?"

"To defeat your opponents."

I waited for a few seconds and then realized that she probably wasn't going to delve any deeper. It was going to take some patience.

"And so how do you defeat them?"

"I told you. Your team has to score fifteen points before the other team does."

"Oh, right. And so how do you score points?"

"The team scores three points for a ringer, two for a leaner, and one for a *moosoogle* hit."

I stole a glance at Seph to check whether Gwenda was just messing with me. Nothing. Either Seph was getting better at schooling her features, or this game really involved ringers, leaners, and whatever a moosoogle was.

"Alright, at the risk of asking a dumb question, I have to ask what this moosoogle is and how you hit it."

Gwenda looked at Seph helplessly. Seph shrugged and said, "I can't remember what the English word is. It's a little bitty plant that grows in clumps on the damp side of trees and rocks, and —"

"Moss?"

Seph's face brightened up. "Moss! Yes, that's it! While the game goes on, the archers try to hit either the hoop or the roller with the moosoogle, and they score a point if they do."

Moss. Moosoogle. I was misspelling the word in my head, I realized; it was *mwswgl*, thanks to the elf way of saying w as oo. Only the elves could have a three-syllable word with exactly zero real vowels.

"Archers?" The game was suddenly sounding a little more interesting.

"Archers," Gwenda agreed. "Oh, you were thinking of the way the children roll hoops, weren't you? No, no, that's not it at all." Suddenly my cousin's friend's voice was hot with the intensity of her explanation; she obviously loved the game. "Each team fields nine players: three riders, three archers, and three rangers. The playing area is a circle that is about the same size as the normal village, and in the middle is a well-cultivated circle with a stake in the center. The riders carry a stick with a fork at the end, used to roll the hoop along, and they're the only ones allowed in the circle. The archers begin the competition with three mwswgl-tipped arrows each, and that's all they get unless the other team is assessed a penalty."

"What kind of penalty?"

"Hitting the horse is a penalty. The archers get a point for their team if they hit either the other team's rider or the hoop, but they give the opposing archer an arrow if they hit the horse."

"Elf archers never miss, though."

"Have you ever shot an arrow tipped with—um, moss, Cousin?" Seph interjected, her eyebrows moving upward to make a point.

"No, I can't say I have. It must make it hard to hit the target with, though."

"It takes practice, from what I hear, though the professionals are very nearly as good with it as I am with regular arrows." That was saying something; I've been shooting alongside Sephaline several times, including on our race through the blight to the library, and I've never seen her miss. I said that, and she shook her head. "It's not just about hitting or missing. The arrows with mwswgl heads are slower than regular arrows, clumsier, and the riders are very quick with their rods. If the archer doesn't pick just the right time to fire, it's easy for a rider to knock the arrow out of the sky, thus wasting a possible point. And even if every archer hits every time, that's still not enough points to win."

"Oh, okay. I get it. This is going to be an interesting game."

After a few moments of silence, Seph asked, "So, aren't you curious what the rangers do?"

"Who? Rangers? Oh, I am! I am. Sorry, I just got wound up in the idea of archers shooting arrows at players. It's a whole new meaning to the term contact sport, and I was wondering what football, or baseball, or golf might be like with that component. So tell me, what do the rangers do?"

"The most important job, of course," Seph said, her nose up in the air.

"Of course."

Gwenda chortled. I looked over at her, and she filled me in. "The rangers sing the whole time, if they can."

"What do you mean if they can?"

"The archers can try to hit one of them instead of the riders. It's easier, and there's no horse to accidentally hit."

"If they get—moosoogled—then they're out of the game, I take it?"

"No, they just can't sing any more."

"So what can they do?"

"If they're hit? They can watch the archers and try to call out when shots are taken."

"Sounds like a useful tactic regardless. So what do the rangers sing for?"

"They're battling each other with earth energy, each side trying to either smooth a path to the center or throw small hills and divots or brambles in the way of the hoop. A powerful ranger really can make the difference between winning and losing, and having one out can really hurt as well."

"Huh," I said, and I sat back in my seat to imagine how the game of cylchoedd, the Bs against the phlegms, would go. My attitude had turned; I actually couldn't wait to see.

LLWYFEN

A difficult word to pronounce if you are in a hurry, but a good one anyway; it means elm tree, which is the best sort of tree.

At the Game

The carriage somehow knew that the crown princess was aboard, and that I had a special entrance to the stadium reserved just for royalty. I don't know how it knew any of that, but I was glad it did as we wheeled right past a long line of folks waiting to be dropped off at the large front gate. On the side, we pulled up to a much smaller doorway. Two guards wearing the king's livery stepped up and helped us—well, me; Seph and Gwenda were left to get out by themselves—down and through the door.

We followed a long hallway upward and through one sharp turn, and then we emerged at the top of the grandstands. The special royal box was covered and had nice cushioned seats, but it was open to all sides and a little chilly as a result. A servant met us there and asked our food and drink requests and nodded when I asked for a blanket.

I kind of liked being the crown princess sometimes, to be honest. Gwenda, meanwhile, had apparently never been treated so well in her life. She was beaming.

And then she missed the chair.

"Oopsie," she said as she climbed back onto her feet. Luckily her butt managed to find the chair cushion on the second attempt. Seph's eyes met mine and we raised our eyebrows in unison, neither of us willing to voice the thought we shared.

A few minutes later our drinks arrived. Seph had taken the liberty to order for all of us. She'd asked for a drink called *meddeglyn* for all of us, and they brought a few whole bottles in. Meddeglyn is, according to Seph, a drink of fermented honey with spices overlaid on the sweetness. When they opened and poured it, I saw that it had a little bit of fizz, and after the first sip I was hooked by the sweet, spicy, and sassy flavor.

Suddenly I sensed a presence in the room behind us. I didn't need to turn around to tell who it was, but I did anyway and smiled. "Hi, Aerona," I said. "Dad sent you, didn't he?"

The female version of an elf linebacker shrugged. "This cylchoedd stadium is a public facility, Princess. Your safety is my charge."

Gwenda didn't notice Aerona till after I greeted her, but then she turned and gasped, her normally high-pitched voice squeaking, "Hi! You're—Aerona?"

Aerona grinned at Gwenda, sort of. The grin wasn't either particularly friendly or cheerful. The sight of Aerona's lips and teeth giving one message while her eyes sized Seph's friend up like a predator sent chills up my spine.

Gwenda noticed it too and gulped, but she still rose to give Aerona the female elf gesture of respect, her right hand flickering up and then sideways and down. It gave me a chance to compare the two. I'd never realized, in the time since Dad had set the massive elf woman to guarding me, just how big she was, but she actually had a couple of inches on Gwenda, and Gwenda was extremely tall. The difference was that Gwenda was also lanky, angular as the typical elf and thin as a normal elf woman. Aerona, meanwhile, looked like she'd been carved from a redwood trunk.

Then Gwenda ruined the moment by missing her chair again when she sat down. This time I felt bad, almost sharing her intimidation at my guard's aura, and I reached to help her up. Aerona's scowl deepened as we were treated to yet another verse of *oopsie*.

"The king asked me to remind his daughter and her friends that the royal company is not to choose sides in cylchoedd games," Aerona stated, her voice flat and commanding. It felt like a traffic cop reminding us that a speed trap was set low. I shrugged; it wasn't a big deal to either Seph or to me, but I looked at Gwenda, the superfan, to make sure she was okay with it. The poor girl just nodded meekly with a terrified expression. I guess I couldn't blame her.

Marching to a trumpet fanfare, the teams entered the stadium. The Bs were in blue, and the Chs were in white, Seph explained. Why? Well, just because, she said. When I asked why the Bs didn't have huge bees embroidered into their shirts or on their sleeves, they just looked at me funny, like I'd just asked the dumbest question ever. Hey, I thought it was a good joke, at least in English.

In spite of the lack of bees and phlegm on the uniform, they looked gallant. The silk uniform tops, each split vertically in color with white or black on one side and the team's color on the other, molded smoothly to the rippling chest and arm muscles. Long hair pulled back, they treated the cheering crowd to the ferocious scowls of warriors entering a battlefield. The riders carried the long forked stick Gwenda had told me about, but each one had another stick, too, a smoothed rod a little bigger than half an inch thick. It was, Gwenda explained, the stick they used to hit each other with.

Oh, of course. One stick to roll the hoop, and another to hit each other with. Because having archers isn't violent enough.

Men just can't design a game that doesn't involve hitting each other, can they?

They launched with a blast of a trumpet, the sound followed by the roar of the fans all around. I asked which side was the Bs fans and which were the Chs, but that got the same "that's a dumb question" look that my team name question received. I gave up that attempt at conversing and looked more closely out to the stands. Sure enough, there were splotches of green mixed in with splotches of white all over the place. Apparently the elves could intermingle support while watching a game, unlike some of the sports I'd seen back home.

To start cylchoedd, the lone referee rolls the hoop out into the center between the two teams, and then he high-tails it to a little glassed-in protected area from which he just works the scoreboard for the rest of the match.

You have to admit, this is an awesome game.

The archers began the game by spreading out around the circle, alternating Bs and Chs so that the riders would have to work harder at paying attention to the arrows flying around. The rangers from each team, on the other hand, huddled together to combine their singing powers. I could sense that they were fairly powerful as they started their chants; vibrant blue energy coalesced around each group.

The horses, meanwhile, were gorgeous. Riders sat bareback, tan trousers all the padding they needed, atop sleek stallions, each horse with its mane and tail braided with bright ribbons the same colors as its rider's jersey. There weren't any bits or reins either; riders commanded through minuscule knee pressures as the tremendous horses charged about the field. It was a really beautiful display of horsemanship. And, um, manship, I have to admit.

The girls had been wrong—or sloppy, anyway—about the sticks. Only one rider at a time used the forked stick to keep the hoop hurtling across the turf, while the others actually used both sticks pretty effectively to beat on each other. As I watched, a rider from the Bs got thwacked across the arm by the long stick from a rider from the Chs, who got one in return almost instantly, leaving a red welt on both arms and a set look of determination on both faces.

Taken as a whole, it amounted to one stick to roll the hoop, eleven others to hit with. Thus, lots of hitting. Oh, and archers.

Elves definitely play interesting games.

The Chs put the first score on the board, which happened to literally be a massive wooden board perched above the stands and directly across the round stadium from the royals box. One of their riders managed a good thwack across the upper arm of the Bs rider who had the hoop, and that distracted him just long enough that an archer plunked him in the chest with moss. He grunted, the moss-tipped arrow bounced off and onto the ground, and the referee raised a white flag for a point scored by the Chs.

Gwenda moaned quietly, but she quickly remembered Aerona's order to not take sides. Her shoulders tightened as she went silent.

The Bs rider didn't seem fazed by the blow beyond his single grunt, though, as he used the moment of celebration among the Chs to charge in and flick the hoop up and over the post in the center. The ref pumped the blue flag three times: three points, Bs!

Gwenda looked like she was about to explode over that one, bouncing in excitement and just barely holding her tongue.

A rider in white galloped over to the pole. He used his stick to deftly lift the hoop back up and roll it over to his own team of rangers. It was up to them to put the hoop back in play after a score, apparently.

Put it back in play they did, rolling it out to the same rider.

Seph kept me busy with learning more rules as we watched. For example, the archers gained no points for shooting a rider in the back. That kind of made sense. I learned it, of course, by seeing it in play; one of the Bs archers sent a well-aimed shot at the Chs rider with the hoop, but the rider managed to spin his body around at the last second. The moss hit him square in the back, and no flag was raised, and Gwenda led half of the crowd in groaning their displeasure. Seph explained quietly.

Also, the horses were as protected from the rangers as they were from the archers. I watched as a ranger, clad in the same tunic as the horsemen on his team, split his energy off from his fellows and ran a line of blue energy in front of the hoop that the other team's rider had just rolled. A lump of earth followed the energy, pushing the hoop up into the air, but the ranger rapidly removed it as the horse arrived.

In general, the rangers were very careful in where they laid out their soil and grass obstacles for the hoop, and I finally asked Seph about it. Can't trip the horse, she said tersely, her attention riveted on the field where the Chs rangers managed to deflect the hoop enough that their rider stole possession of it from the Bs. Again, Gwenda and half of the crowd groaned. This time Aerona followed the crowd's groan with a growl and a glare, both directed at Seph's friend.

"Right. No sides. This is difficult," the high-pitched voice carried across the royal box as the tall girl cringed.

"You can always step out front and cheer as much as you wish," Seph offered.

"Trying to get rid of me?"

"Not at all. It's just that you love your Bs, and you love to cheer for them. Stepping just outside the box will give you that opportunity."

Gwenda growled and kept her seat. Obviously she was more interested in spending the time with us than in cheering on her Bs, which was a wonderful sentiment. I only wondered how long she'd be able to keep from doing both.

I also wondered what Aerona would do to Gwenda when she ended up violating the no-taking-sides rule too obviously.

After a moment Gwenda started making a strange hissing sound and rocking back and forth. It didn't seem like she was trying to get anybody's attention. It didn't even seem like she knew she was doing it. I looked a question to Seph, who obviously heard it. She shrugged back at me.

Meanwhile, the Chs rider managed to make it to the inner area. He flicked the end of his guide stick up and around, a movement that caused the hoop to rise in the air and sail right over the top of the score post. At the same time a Bs archer caught the rider square in the chest with more of the mwswgl, but since the rider no longer had possession of the hoop it was ruled a wasted arrow. A Chs rider galloped by on the other side, though, and in one spectacular move he twisted off of the back of his horse, caught the still-twirling hoop with the end of his longer stick, and flicked it back over and down onto the scoring post before rolling over a couple of times on the turf and then springing back onto his feet.

The crowd went wild! Half of them were screaming and dancing for joy, while the other half were screaming and shaking their fists. I saw the reason for the glassed-in referee area as rocks pelted it from all sides while he pumped the white flag up and down three times.

"Can he do that?" I asked.

"Do what?" Seph turned.

"Jump off of his horse like that to make the shot."

"Well, sure. The rules don't say the riders have to be riding a horse to play, but a player on foot isn't nearly as effective as one on horseback, and now he's got to wait for the horse to come back around to get on him. See how the Bs are hustling their advantage?"

They were hustling, actually. A rider in blue dashed by, snagging the hoop and hurtling over to his rangers. They caught it and immediately twirled it back to him.

They were hustling a little too much, though. As the blue rider stormed past the two remaining mounted riders in white, focused on getting to the pole quickly, a small flurry of arrows buzzed in and scored point after point. He managed to flick the hoop up and over the post, but only after the Chs had managed to score another five points in arrows alone.

That made the score nine Chs to six Bs. And, at the same time, it sent Gwenda into an apoplectic rage. "Bummer," I said. "Maybe we should have chosen a game that didn't feature Gwenda's favorite team to sit in the no-cheering box."

"Here," Aerona said, lifting Gwenda and her chair with apparent ease. Gwenda yelped but didn't object; instead, she gripped the arms in apparent fear of being launched out of the box. Aerona moved to the front edge of the royal's area and set her burden down just across the threshold. "Cheer to your heart's content, young lady."

Gwenda shyly peered over her shoulder, and when it became apparent that Aerona truly wasn't going to launch her into an airborne tumble over the crowd, Seph's lanky friend rose and cheered lustily. Aerona turned a toothy grin my way and nodded.

The Chs put the hoop into play quickly, but it was just as quickly stolen by a Bs player who was helped by all three of their rangers setting up a series of ridges in the grass. He took a little more time getting to the goal than the others had, and managed to bat two arrows away as he looped in to score three points.

Tie game! Gwenda was on her feet, screaming like a crazy woman, dancing and flailing in her dapper clothes. It looked kind of ridiculous, but no more so than what I'd seen of the fans at American football games.

The Bs had only shot one of their arrows, and the difference in strategy was showing. The riders were slowing just a little, nearly imperceptibly for a non-elf, but they were just tired enough that their reactions were not as good as they had been. An arrow zipped in from the side, catching the Chs rider with the hoop on the arm. Score: ten to nine. The three Chs riders danced and leaped around the circle, passing the hoop from rider to rider, and as they focused on the dance they were weaving in the name of getting a ringer, *zziiip*! Another arrow, adding another point to the Bs lead. They passed the hoop, and once again the mwswgl found its mark, raising the score to twelve to nine.

Finally the Chs rider with the hoop had had enough; he charged, brushing past the Bs rider who was guarding him and taking the hard thwack on the arm in stride. He flipped the hoop up and over the post just as an arrow caught him in the chest. Now everybody in the crowd went wild as the referee held the blue flag up once and pumped the white flag three times.

Thirteen to twelve. Anybody's game. And the Bs had the ball—or hoop, technically—as anybody could tell by watching Gwenda dance with joy.

The Bs team exploded. Their rangers tossed the hoop to their largest, strongest rider and immediately went into a loud convulsive singing. The comment earlier about a powerful ranger making the difference in winning rang true as the Bs shut out every wrinkle, every growth that the Chs rangers tried to put in their way. Meanwhile the Chs archers fired both their remaining arrows. One found its mark while the other was flipped aside by the rider who charged in ahead of the one with the hoop. Tie game, thirteen to thirteen, with the Bs having control of the hoop as well as the only arrows remaining in the game.

It ended amazingly well. The Bs rider with the hoop charged directly in toward the three Chs guarding the post, but at the last minute feinted toward the rider to his left and then passed the hoop to the rider galloping around to the right. The Chs wheeled their horses around, but there wasn't a horse alive that could cover the distance required in the short time the Bs rider took to get there and flip the hoop over the post for the win.

The whole crowd roared to its feet, the half who supported the Bs stomping and dancing and causing the entire structure to shake.

Finally the normally staid elves calmed down. The teams met each other on the field and saluted, player to player, in a show of mutual respect.

I walked up to Gwenda, who was still squealing in glee. "I see why you love the Bs," I said.

"No, you don't see yet," she argued. "They always play a good game, sure, but just wait till their captain comes onto the field to accept the win. He's so dreamy, I must some day meet him. You can arrange a meeting, can't you, Princess?"

"Possibly," I said, and waited as the crowd quieted down. Finally the stadium was settled down enough for the captains to come out, show their respects, and the Bs captain to acclaim the victory.

Both captains strode confidently out onto the field. One of them swooshed his hair across his head in a gesture I'd seen far too many times before.

I gasped.

The Bs captain was none other than Prince Charming.

Return to the Castle

"You've met Prince Keion?" Gwenda asked, her voice climbing back into squeaking range in her excitement. Meanwhile, Sephaline, my cousin, stood behind me snickering her fool head off.

Come to think of it, I believe I overheard Aerona giggling, too.

"Yes. Yes, I know Prince Keion," I said, trying desperately to hold on to my cool despite the flush that was taking over my face, and then my entire head.

"Could you—I hesitate to ask such a boon, Your Highness, but could you secure for me an audience with the prince? Just a moment, that's all, for me to tell him how well his team plays. Please, Princess?"

"The prince keeps his own calendar," I said, a little more sharply than I'd intended.

Suddenly I heard my own name over the loudspeaker. I looked down over the stadium and into the suddenly-cavernous silence and realized that they'd announced that Crown Princess Alyssa was in attendance.

Everyone turned to face the royal box.

Nobody applauded.

I waved and smiled my happiest gestures, hoping that somebody would wave back, or at least smile

They didn't.

The eerie silence gripped the stadium for several long, awkward moments before the announcer started speaking again and everybody turned away from me to go about their business.

I shivered. That reception had been so cold that it cooled off the heating that my face had gotten over the mention of the prince.

See, the prince and I had a thing. It wasn't a good thing, really. It wasn't a bad thing, either. It was just—a thing.

He'd kissed me. Once. No, twice, I guess. Both times, I'd enjoyed it.

To be completely honest, I really wanted him. The thought of Prince Keion—Prince Charming—made my knees weak.

I couldn't have him, though. He was already promised in marriage to someone else. Besides, he was likely going to be the future king, and this was the craziest of realms in which the king and the queen weren't a couple, not ever. He couldn't, and I couldn't, and that was that.

And yet Gwenda wanted him? I was startled, because Seph had told me that Gwenda was confused. Seph's childhood friend, Seph explained delicately, didn't know if she wanted boys or girls. Which, I suppose, made Prince Charming nearly perfect as the object of her desires. His long flowing black hair made him insanely beautiful, and his strong features were paired with perfectly smooth skin.

Heck, I couldn't imagine anybody in the realm not wanting to bear Prince Charming's children, even if it meant being sister-in-law to his two evil siblings, the "Lights of Talaith's Eyes," Seren the Wise and Drizella the Evil. Granted, their names were actually Seren and Meriel, but the younger one was so much like the evil stepsister of Cinderella that the nickname was completely appropriate.

Suddenly I realized I was brooding on the front step of the royal box all by myself. I turned and saw Seph, Gwenda, and Aerona helping the king's liveried servants straighten up the royal box, and so I hurried in to assist.

"No thank you, Princess," the first servant said, shaking his head as I tried to lend a hand, and Aerona reacted by pulling me out of the box and into the hall. Seph and Gwenda followed.

"The crown princess should remember that she is the king's representative when he is not here, and that if she steps in to do menial tasks for servants, that degrades the servants whose purpose such tasks are," Aerona said stiffly as we walked back down the hallway.

"I remember that," I said while trying to keep my anger down. "But I also remember a little before that, when the entire audience turned toward me with malice in their faces. I figure that if I can just prove I'm a good person, that I'm like one of them, maybe—"

"Maybe then the people will hate you even more for not being good enough to act like royalty," Aerona cut me off. She turned, and her features softened. "Princess, the current dislike you feel, founded in a distrust not only for change in general but specifically for the change you particularly represent, is just part of the path you must walk. You should stop allowing it to bother you. If you show the strength you have, the people will eventually come to love you as their queen."

Great, ruling advice from the high priestess of toughness, with long words and sentences too. Not that Aerona was dumb in any way; I'd never thought that. I just never expected her to sound like my father when spouting off advice on being a princess. Worse, it made a lot more sense than my reaction had. I drew myself up to the full height of my crown princess being and royally proceeded down the steps to the waiting carriage.

Aerona followed me the whole way down, then nodded and smiled.

The ride back was quiet; apparently Gwenda had expended all her energy in rooting for her team, and my socially awkward cousin was content as usual to ride along in silence. As we rode I practiced extending my senses out into the forest, using a hunt for Booboo as a focus. Seph's wolverine familiar had followed us all the way to the stadium and then contented itself by stalking game outside, and now it loped along in the forest on a route parallel to ours and just off of the road.

I didn't tell Seph how easy it was for me to track Booboo for fear it might upset her. That was a special trick of her discipline; only rangers were supposed to be able to track other rangers or their familiars. That was another reason I was convinced that the powers a ranger used were nothing more than an aspect of magical practice.

Thanks to Draignerthol, my magical talisman, I could apparently out-ranger the rangers.

The carriage rolled silently to a stop in Seph's home village, and Gwenda climbed sleepily out and headed off to her little home to go to bed. I expected to watch her somehow miss the ground and fall in a heap, but she climbed out as gracefully as anyone.

I looked at Seph, who shrugged back. The carriage jolted toward the castle, and at a safe distance she said, "When she's tired, or busy, or just not focusing on it, she's perfectly agile. It's when the only thing she's doing is sitting down that she'll miss the chair. I don't understand it either."

"Oh. What was that hissing sound she was making earlier?" I asked.

"A dream she's had since childhood."

"Oh? Really? What's in the dream?"

"That's—well, okay. Don't tell her I told you, okay, Cousin? She's had this recurring dream where she's turned into a cat and is being stalked by all sorts of creatures—I guess that part changes regularly. Sometimes it's a dragon, sometimes it's a griffin, and so on. Every time she has to hide, and every time she's found, and every time she almost gets away. She'll be just about to receive the killing blow and suddenly wake up."

"She likes cats, then?"

"Hates them, actually, Cousin. She's terrified of them. That's why she has a very large pet dog."

"A dire wolf is not a very large pet dog, Seph."

"You know what I meant. She adopted it as a pup with the sole purpose of raising something that would guard her from any member of the feline species, no matter how large."

"Sounds like she needs to see a psych."

"What's a psych?" Seph asked, confused.

"It's—well, on Earth, it's a person who listens to your stories about fear of cats and dreams about being a cat and tells you what they might mean, and then helps you get over them."

"You mean a priestess, then."

"Yeah, sorta. Except on Earth they have—oh, never mind." I stopped myself before I confused the matter worse by telling the little I knew of psych meds. On Earth, docs put a cast on broken bones in the hopes they would knit, while here they sing the bone back together. Momma treated a cold with orange juice and rest, while the priestesses of Kiirajanna could actually heal you.

"Never mind what?"

"Never—well, it's just that I'm still dealing with the significant differences between here and Earth. Psychiatrists on Earth can do some things, like treat you with drugs and—I don't know what else, honestly. But I can't help but wonder if the priestesses wouldn't be better at dealing with psychological issues."

Who knows, right?

She let it drop. We were able to see the lights of the castle, anyway. It was fully dark. The game had lasted just over an hour, thanks to a complete lack of halftime, two minute warnings, time outs, and those evil commercial breaks. The trip back to the village hadn't been more than an hour, I figured, so I hoped that there was a good chance I could watch the special court happen.

I jumped out of the carriage and hurried up the steps and into the castle, my eyes searching out the throne room. Unfortunately they were already breaking up, the nobles in their fancy getup exiting the chamber. A reedy sound behind me made me spin and jump. In the ballroom, an orchestra was setting up.

I stood for a minute and watched them work. It had only been a couple of months past when I'd had a gala ball thrown in there in my honor, a celebration of the fact that I'd become worthy of the title Crown Princess. I could still remember Dad's regalia as he took my hand for the first dance—the shiny buttons, the deep black satin of his sash, the gleaming golden crown with jewels splashing light all around. We danced, and he and I both laughed joyfully, childishly. I think it was that night that I finally forgave him for being absent for most of my life.

Another memory from that night popped into my head, unbidden and unwanted as it was. Prince Charming had found me on the porch, catching my breath and cooling off from the reels and spins on the dance floor. He'd stalked me like a tiger, for the moment apparently wanting me as much as—as much as I wanted him, I admit. He took me in his arms there at the end of the porch, and our lips met, and the world stopped for a blissful several long minutes.

Or seconds, maybe. Or hours. I have no idea.

We were found, and interrupted, of course, and we'd been good since then. I mean, his hand was promised in marriage to a—to a child. It didn't matter what either of us thought of that; it was what it was.

Okay, it sucked. But life just goes on sometimes, right?

"Princess," a voice cut into my head. I gasped and spun, but it was just Aerona, wearing a wicked grin. "A crown princess should keep her expressions schooled, Princess. Besides, you have a ball to prepare for."

"I wasn't that bad, was I?" I whispered to Seph.

"I think I read an entire romance epic written across your face," she said, and then she grinned. "Have fun at the ball!" She skipped off toward her room, apparently deciding a full night's sleep was better than an evening watching others dance.

She wasn't royalty, technically. Yes, she was the king's cousin, and she was my companion, but Seph wouldn't be looked upon as anything fancy until I ascended to my throne. They'd explained it earlier as the need to only have one special family at a time, and it was always the queen's that got to be special. It didn't really matter much, I figured. Because the king's daughter always became the queen according to elf rules of succession, his family would eventually become her family and thus the special ones.

It just seemed dang silly. It wasn't the only elf custom that seemed that way, mind you, but it was definitely among the silliest.

I hurried to my room to change into an outfit that would work at the ball. Honestly, after the reception I'd received from the *pennae* the other day and the crowd at the game earlier today, I wasn't sure I wanted to be there tonight, either.

DATHLIAD

A celebration, which aptly describes Yule in most cases.

New Year's Party

I ended up out on the balcony a lot earlier for this ball than the last one. For one thing, other than my father, nobody seemed to want to dance with me. It shouldn't surprise me, this whole magic thing and all. I mean, who wants to dance with a girl who might zap you to death for stepping on her foot, right?

Oh no! Evil magic user crown princess future dragon queen alert!

Fools. Judgmental fools, all of them.

I also didn't want to be around Keion. Oh, he was there, along with his two evil sisters. I'd felt so close only a few days ago over Christmas at Momma's, and then they'd all come back and found their old, mean selves.

Granted, the prince looked dashing. Meanwhile, I couldn't help but overhear, constantly, how everyone congratulated the mighty sportsman for his team's come-from-behind, skillful win on the cylchoedd circle that day. "Great work, son!" they all said.

He wouldn't even look at me.

Actually, he did, once. As the dance was getting started, we both happened to be near the same spot on the floor. He turned, and I turned, and our eyes met. I saw it, too—the smoldering intensity I'd seen before. The same one I felt.

You know, the forbidden one.

I fled.

Have you ever stood outside a party, close enough that you could hear the music and the laughter but far enough that you weren't a part of any of it? That's probably the loneliest spot in the universe. I stood up to the loneliness as long as I could, listening to the sounds of merriment just inside the dance hall. That was the room where, invited though I was, I wasn't really welcome. The room where, in gay elf tradition, everyone danced with everyone else—except me.

I fled, again.

Before long I was far enough away that I could neither hear the sounds nor see the lights of the party through the forest. I slowed down to a walk then, finally, catching my breath as I passed from tree to tree. I reached out to each in turn just as the high priestess had taught me, combining spirits and sensing the other being's identity.

Only now it was more, a greater level of understanding, a farther reach.

Oh, to be a tree, I thought. Trees know what they are, where they are. There's never any question about their role in the world. They don't have relationships, so there's nothing to be lonely from. Jealousy, fear, loneliness—all absent from a tree's sensations. It's all just joy, joy of being, joy of living, joy of taking up their appointed space in the world. The thought left me with a strange longing, a wish that Little Treebeard were a person I could dance with.

I found a tree that felt sick, its joyfulness diminished a little. I probed deeper with the song of my mind, finding some fibers in its trunk that had curled the wrong way. They'd stopped growing, which had in turn invited parasites, and a bug had moved in. I deepened my song, broadened it, helping the tree straighten its fibers of cellulose and push out the bug. Soon the tree's "voice" joined with mine, rejoicing in its new feeling of health and well-being.

"You shouldn't be out here by yourself, Princess," a voice interrupted as the song settled itself out to a whisper.

Startled, I panicked. I should have sensed anybody coming up behind me here in these woods, and tied into the tree as I was, my senses should have screamed even louder. That they hadn't gone off bothered me greatly as I spun and reached for Draignerthol, ready to protect myself.

"Cool your flames, now," the old ranger admonished, waving his hands up and down as if to physically cool me off. "I'm no danger to you."

"Owain?" I let my grip on the forces of magic drop and relaxed into the hug he presented. "What a surprise to see you."

Owain was the ranger of all rangers. Seph looked up to him as a living legend. He taught her most of what she knew, including the lesson I was most indebted to him for: how to cook ranger stew in a way that didn't taste like old shoe leather.

If anybody besides my father could sneak up behind me, it was him.

"I come by the castle every new year to report to the king and queen," he said. "If you'd been there instead of off watching that game, you'd have heard my report."

"I figured all those reports would be boring. If I'd known one would be yours, I would'a figured differently."

"You would have been wrong, Princess. My report is every bit as boring as everybody else's. They're all important to the crown, of course, in terms of the business of managing a realm and its people, but not one of them is ever really exciting. Frankly, that lack of excitement is a good thing. I'll take it any day over reports of war or strife. But tell me, Princess, why is a young beauty like you out here singing to the trees in the darkness when you should be in the ballroom dancing what's left of this glorious holiday away?"

"Nobody likes me in there," I said, realizing as the words tumbled out of my mouth how juvenile they sounded. Whatever; they were true. "Everybody looks at me like I'm going to use magic to set them on fire."

"Use magic to set them on fire, like you almost did to me just now?"

"I'm so sorry, Master Owain. I don't get startled very often, and I was startled and scared and so I panicked."

"I know, I know. I should know better at my age than to sneak up behind pretty girls who are singing to trees, no matter how beautiful their song is."

I felt a rare blush climbing my cheeks.

"Truth is, though," he continued, "you shouldn't be out here by yourself. It's too dangerous, no matter how sensitive you are or how powerful you're becoming."

I shrugged, which was probably a useless gesture in the darkness. "The Cult members are all safely imprisoned or dead, or fleeing by now if not."

"If the Cult were all gone, why is the blight still growing?"

"It's still growing?" I feigned surprise. I'd felt it growing, but I figured that I wasn't supposed to be able to do that. I also knew that the Cult members weren't all safely imprisoned or dead, but sometimes things just feel good to say whether they're true or not. Besides, I was curious what Master Owain knew, and it struck me as an excellent opportunity to practice my queenly intelligence gathering skills.

"Yes. You haven't checked, have you? That's okay. You're going to be a queen, not a ranger, so that's to be expected." I wasn't sure whether to be insulted or not over that statement.

"It's still growing, though. It's growing slower than before, I believe, but it is definitely still getting larger."

"So the Cult may still be powerful?"

"Probably. Almost certainly. There's signs to the south—rumors and whispers more than anything, but—oh, look, I don't want to ruin what should be a night of celebration. These rumors and whispers, even if true, are likely overblown. Regardless, I don't see why we'd think we could beat them all in a couple of battles, right, Princess?"

"Oh." I'd known what his answer was likely to be, yet it still felt like a wet blanket had been laid over the happiness I'd worked up singing with the trees.

"Don't get down on it," Owain said. "It means there's still more to do. There's always more to do, Princess, as long as there's still breath in our lungs. It also means, though, that you shouldn't walk through the woods alone at night. Mind if I escort you back to the castle, m'lady?"

"Not at all, Master Owain," I said formally, giving him the elf hand gesture that signified respect between peers.

He chuckled. "Thank you, Princess, but I am not royalty."

"To the rangers, you are," I said, and we turned and walked back toward the castle together.

Seph ran up to us before we saw anybody else, Booboo the ferocious wolverine at her heels, tongue lolling placidly out to one side.

"Alyssa! There you are. I've been looking for you since your father said you weren't at the ball."

Owain shrugged off the shadows he'd been using as a cloak. I made a mental note to figure out sometime how he'd managed to cloak his presence while still holding firm to my arm. "A ranger? Looking for someone?" He glared at my cousin. I could tell from his tone that it was playful, but I wasn't sure how Seph would take it.

She didn't take it well. In the glimmering light from the castle I watched her grow even paler than usual, and she stammered, "M—Master Owain. I—I—I'm honored. I c—couldn't s—s—sense—"

He interrupted her gently. "Of course you couldn't, my young ranger. Your cousin grows in power every day, though. It was only due to my own experience that I was drawn to her song. I was just tweaking your nose."

"Wait," I said. "If Seph couldn't sense my presence, and you could only barely do so, then why should I worry about the Cult?"

Owain's eyes darkened as he answered, "Your cousin has already reported the details of the flight and the battle in Ganolog, Princess, so I know that you know they have their own rangers. Plus, the Cult members use other senses than those we rangers are willing to open ourselves to. More generally, though, you must never assume that your abilities lie outside of your opponent's power to counter."

"Oh." Once again the ancient ranger proved himself wise.

"Hey, it's the celebration of the start of a new year. Both of you, smile. May I have the pleasure of you two young ladies' company to the fireworks display?"

Fireworks? I perked up; I love fireworks. "Please, Master Owain. It would be my pleasure," I said.

The ranger emeritus led us to a large open area near the castle where everyone else was gathering. We sat directly on the ground, and I enjoyed a brief flashback to going to watch fireworks with Momma. Momma and I always sat on the ground, too, but never without a blanket. Now, I couldn't imagine any of my new companions thinking to put a blanket between themselves and the soil. Being an elf was—different, in all sorts of little ways.

My father plopped down right behind us. I pointed a smile back his way as his hand gripped my shoulder in a comforting gesture.

Shaking myself out of the self-pity I had created, I started wondering about—well, about gunpowder, believe it or not. I wasn't sure how fireworks were made, but I was pretty certain it required gunpowder. I'd seen nothing to indicate that the elves knew how to make gunpowder, a knowledge that should immediately lead to that of guns and cannons and the like, and yet there were neither guns nor cannons in the realm. Thus, I wondered how their fireworks worked.

I didn't wonder for long. Soon the first brilliant streaker to shriek through the air brought a collective gasp from the elves.

It was tinged in blue energy.

Yep.

Magic.

Part of it was magic, anyway. I saw whisps of black smoke and caught the scent I'd always associated with normal fireworks. As the show progressed my ears picked up soft chanting near the fireworks base, a sing-song that called for various shapes of sparkles from each rocket. Gunpowder, or something similar, apparently existed, but of course the elves wouldn't leave the beauty of their fireworks to mere black powder.

They were beautiful, no matter how the use of magic lent itself to displays that mere physics could not. There were perfect circles of blooms of light, followed by shamrock patterns as well as this one amazing yellow display where the center bloomed upward, giving it a vague daffodil appearance. Then there was what clearly attempted to emulate a chromatic dragon, its multicolored sparkles undulating in the sky. It was chased away by a white unicorn, each sparkle of the latter holding out and vibrating to give the whole shape a quivering beauty.

The boom and zip and blam of the fireworks display built up to a crescendo, and then it died off. Finally the last one exploded into brilliant red, green, and yellow sparkles that danced in the night air, leaving little bright spots in our vision and hazy smoke hanging above us for several long minutes of silence.

At first no one seemed willing to move, but finally the elves started shaking the spell off and rising. Dad helped me up, and Ranger Owain did the same for Seph.

The old ranger turned to me and gave me the hand signal for deep respect and friendship. It was actually the simplest one, just a tiny up and down flutter of the hand with the palm down. "Princess," he said softly, his words meant for just me, "thank you for being out tonight and brightening an old man's heart, but take care in the weeks and months ahead. A dark cloud is rising with the new year's sun, and I fear for all who are caught within its shadow."

I nodded in reply and returned the gesture. He grinned, his face lighting up into the elf expression of sincerest happiness, and he mouthed a more public farewell to Seph. Then, he turned and walked into the trees, and as he passed the first one he disappeared.

No, really—he actually vanished.

"How did he do that?" I asked Dad.

"A master ranger has tricks even the monarch does not know," my father said, his voice mysterious.

"Ah. So, one more question?"

"Anything, my daughter," he said grandly.

"Right. So I know that Keion went to Earth to study warfare and tactics. Now I know that gunpowder exists on Kiirajanna. Why do we still fight with swords and archery?"

Dad chortled quietly. "It is our way. The prince was warned by his mother about the repulsively impersonal way humans have developed their warfare, which is the reason that I believe he focused mostly on the more ancient history. But he did see plenty even then, and brought us back the English term 'barbarian.'"

"So fighting without a sword or a bow is barbaric?"

"You should always be able to look into the eyes of your foe, Alyssa. To do otherwise is mere murder, and sometimes on a grand scale. You experienced that in Ganolog, yes?"

"I did," I said, and couldn't suppress the shudder that came from the memory of that in-person battleground. I had been able to look each of the black-robed Cultists in the eyes as I, reaching through Draignerthol for the power to do so, burned them into little helpless charred piles of flesh.

Dad sensed my thoughts and shot a grin my way. He put an arm around my shoulder and started toward the castle. "It is time for sleep, Alyssa, so that we may welcome the new year with open eyes and warm hearts in the morning."

"A whole helping of new year with a dash of hunhymgais?"

He turned and held my gaze for several long moments before answering, "Yes. So it would seem."

HUNHYMGAIS

Literally, "quest for self."

Hunhymgais Eve

"You could wait a few more days, you know," Seph said, glaring at me over the pair of dice that she'd just rolled a seven on. She lost; I won, and I gleefully scooped up the pebbles we used to keep bets with. They weren't worth anything in particular other than bragging rights, but between two cousins living in the royal palace as the guests of their father and uncle, the king of Kiirajanna, who needs more than bragging rights?

I tossed out five pebbles, feeling particularly lucky, and she matched mine with five from her own smaller pile. I rolled; the dice stopped with a two and a three showing. Five wasn't a particularly good first roll, but that was okay. I rolled again and got a one and a four. Nailed it!

I shrugged as I pulled in her five pebbles and left mine out as the new bet. "What can I say? I'm feeling lucky," I said with a wicked leer. I really did feel lucky, and it showed in the dice; I hadn't won this many rolls since she'd taught me the popular elf gambling game on our ride to the library.

"Lucky with dice and pebbles, or lucky with possible death in your quest for self?" she asked, her face as cross as I'd ever seen it. Booboo growled at me, the wolverine's voice reflecting just how irritated Seph was.

"Both, Cousin." I tempered my flounce because I didn't want to irritate her more, but I really was feeling pretty excited about the hunhymgais starting tomorrow. We'd talked about it at length, and then we'd talked about it again, and I was totally ready to just get it started.

"You could at least give me a week to teach you more of the edible plants so you won't starve."

"I could," I agreed. We'd been over that already, a few times. She already knew why I wasn't going to.

"Aerona," Seph appealed to my bodyguard, "can you talk some sense into the princess here? She's convinced that, no matter what I teach her to prepare, she'll need to know something else."

"Actually, ranger, that was my experience too. No preparation I did for my own quest was worth anything after I was teleported."

"Gah! Roll, then," Seph said, tossing five more pebbles out to match my bet. I did; a three and a four, or a total of seven for another win. I scooped all but three of the pebbles out of the middle and into my own pile. I could see that Seph only had three pebbles left in her own pile, and there wasn't any point betting higher than she could.

"Your roll, Seph," I said. The roll always passed to the gambler who was down to her last bit.

She shook her head. "No, you go ahead and finish it off. You know I'm going to miss you, right?"

I stopped mid-toss. Seph was many things, but gooberly emotional wasn't one. She was now sitting across the table from me barely holding back tears, though.

"I'm going to miss you, too, Cousin. But I'll be back in just six weeks."

She shook her head violently, her brown bangs leaping from side to side. "No, that's not it, Alyssa. I sense great danger ahead. It's the same feeling I got as we approached the library, but I shrugged it off then as nothing more dangerous than the effect of the evil taint within the blight on a ranger's sensitivities. Now I'm getting the same danger reading, and the blight is nowhere near. Worse, once you step through the hunhymgais portal I won't even be able to help. You'll be completely on your own, and there is a lot about Kiirajanna that I haven't had the chance to teach you yet. I'd feel so much better if we waited till I could."

I sat for several long moments, not sure how to respond. Seph was quirky and emotionally needy at times, but she had proved herself a stable companion and a solid ally to fight by my side in the battles at the library and in Ganolog. If she felt that it was important to talk about her ranger senses going on high alert, then it was important. That said, I had to leave on my hunhymgais the next morning, or else break my word to the clan chieftains as well as my father. No matter how much danger lay ahead of me, none of us could do anything about it, so talking just made it worse.

I decided to push the logical approach again.

"Seph, you and I both know that it would take me years to learn everything about Kiirajanna that you have to teach me, and even in those years, you'd still end up leaving something out, or else I'd end up forgetting part of it. You know that. The only thing I can really do to control, to prepare, is to get started soon so that I can get it done soon."

"You do know that sometimes even the most prepared of elves don't make it, right?" Seph turned extremely large eyes on me as though looking through them could let me see the true volume of fear in her very soul.

"Yeah, of course. If one or two didn't make it every so often there wouldn't be any danger in it. No danger, no point in doing it."

"No!" she pumped a fist on the table, making me jump. She could be plenty violent when called upon, but slamming the table wasn't normal for her. "Alyssa, it's more than one or two every so often." I looked at Aerona for confirmation; she just nodded once, but that was enough. Seph, seeing my glance and the nod, continued in a bolder voice, "It's become even more regular, from what I've heard, that elves don't return from their quest. It's even what some are calling frequent."

"They don't return at all, or don't return at the right time?"

"Don't return at all. Very few ever return too early, and even fewer return too late, as most of the time the elves are sitting there waiting for the sixth week to roll over so they can teleport back. The ones I'm telling you about, though, we've never heard from again."

"Okay, I get that, but see, you said yourself that 'most of the time' they're just sitting there waiting. That's good odds to bet on. I'm going to go, have this quest for self that is so vital to coming of age, one I promised the king and his chieftains I would take, and then come back like most of the other elves."

"You're not like most of the other elves, though, Alyssa. Don't you get that? You're the crown princess, you've found Draignerthol."

"Yes, so?"

"Most of the other elves haven't ever been shot at in battle. Most of the other elves haven't been poisoned. Most of the other elves haven't seen an ally's head smashed open on the battlefield. Most of the other elves haven't charged across the blight, shooting their way through."

"You're making my point, Seph. I'm uniquely qualified to handle whatever comes my way."

"You've—gah. You're special, Alyssa! If anything is floating out there in the odds or in fate or in whatever the universe wants to call it, waiting to pounce on a really special case, you're it! You're that special case."

I nodded; there wasn't much else of a reply to be made. I rolled two threes. Not a great prif, or first roll, but not a bad one either. I rolled again, and both dice came up sixes.

Boxcars, in English.

A win, in any language.

I smiled at Seph and shrugged. "See? Luck is with me," I said. I had been extremely lucky; it was rare that I cleaned her out of pebbles at all, much less within a half an hour's time.

She nodded. "Lucky, yes. I've never minded losing to you in dice, Alyssa. Losing you to fate, though, is still a possibility that drives me crazy, and as bad as it would be to me personally, it would be devastating to the realm. Won't you push back your hunhymgais just a few days?"

I gave the suggestion as much visible consideration as I could, and then shook my head. "No, Seph. I'm as ready as I'll ever be. Besides, the queen before me went through this, right? Intestinal fortitude is the key. I have to start this so that I can finish it."

Sephaline nodded, both eyes tearing up. She kissed my cheeks in the tender way of the elves, and then turned toward the door. "I pray it will end as successfully as we expect it to, then," she said as she stumbled reluctantly out the door. Booboo followed her, the wolverine's tail drooping as I'd never seen it before.

It broke my heart, that did. But bless their hearts, I was still going to start my quest the next day, rain or shine, good vibes or foreboding.

OEDOLION

Adult.

Literally, "signs of age," which is quite funny.

Coming of Age

The hunhymgais ceremony wasn't as big of a deal as Dad had made it out to be.

It was small, for one thing. The High Priestess Naissa, Sternyface, officiated, which according to my father was a tremendously high honor to the one coming of age. Then again, I was the crown princess, right? Seph was there, of course. Dad was there. The royal trio of Keion and his two sisters were there, too, in tow behind their mother. The king and queen were decked out in their standard dress of state, my dad in his long purple blouse and black sash and the queen in a beautiful long green gown, but the queen's kids' blouses only went down to their waist, which in elf attire is the formality level of cutoff blue jean shorts.

That was pretty much it, if you didn't count the small cadre of priests and priestesses who were there to help Sternyface. I could sense that the lack of turnout bothered my father, who kept glaring around the clearing at the trees as though any moment others should be striding around them. I remembered his tales of other coming of age ceremonies that brought out the entire population of one or even several villages to cheer proudly for their youth as they stepped bravely into the unknown.

That the queen showed up made me happy. She had purposely, and according to the mores of tradition, avoided the entire rest of my training and education to be her successor. In fact, I was kept from seeing her until the ceremony last summer in which I was crowned Princess of the Realm. She'd treated me to visitation over tea a few times, and then the surprising talk the other night, but we were still pretty much strangers. Yet there she stood, a weird tossed salad of emotions running across her for-once-unguarded face.

I thought briefly of asking her what she was thinking about, but quickly decided against it. She was, after all, one of the only two people present who outranked me—three if I conceded the point to Sternyface, which I wasn't keen to do—and the member of the pair who didn't have a blood tie to me. I respected her quite a lot, and to be honest, she scared me a little.

I felt a presence, and glanced that direction. Master Ranger Owain stood way back in the trees, smiling and waving. The sight of him slowly faded, as did the sensation of his presence. He was still there, I knew without understanding how I *could* know, but he'd cloaked himself once again in the mystery of the master woodsman. I glanced around, and it looked like nobody else even had an inkling that he had appeared.

I was glad to see everybody, especially so early in the morning right after the huge party. I insisted as soon as we woke up that we get to the hunhymgais ceremony immediately. I'd never felt as much of an outcast, and if the six weeks of self-questing had any chance of positively impacting their attitude toward me then I was all for it—and that meant I was all for it right now. Not the next day or the next, but right now.

That was why I stood at the ley-gate, special hunhymgais staff clutched in my hand, a light tunic hiding Draignerthol from view, and a light pair of pants and sandals my only other attire. I wasn't naked, but I wasn't wearing much, either. It was chilly; winter still held the land in its grip. Other than a few involuntary shivers, though, I wasn't about to show that I felt it.

Sternyface cleared her throat to get everyone's attention and then launched into a much shorter speech than I was expecting. "Your Majesties, honored guests, thank you all for your presence on this important, and soon to be historic, day. Now, normally I would speak highly of all that the youth standing before us has learned, and how much I looked forward to seeing an adult return to us following six short weeks of challenge and growth. Today, though, we all recognize that the one who stands before us is technically no youth. Alyssa has already blossomed into woman-hood in the culture in which she was raised, and yet now she seeks to join with us spiritually as well as physically by enduring our time-honored rite of passage. She has bravely faced the many challenges set in front of her so far, and I believe she is due the chance to complete a hunhymgais of her own. If any assembled here object, please say so now."

I held my breath as Sternyface waited for objections. None were expected, but with the elves you never know.

Finally the high priestess continued through the silence. "Alyssa, the path before you is yours to create. The only certainty is that your hunhymgais will afford you the opportunity to face down your greatest fears. Only you can know what those are, and it is most likely that as we stand here at this moment, even you do not know. You go clothed into the test, as is appropriate for an adult woman and the crown princess, but the challenge will be no less for that. Watch the passing of the sun, and count the number of days, as if you return even one day short of the six week period then you will have failed the challenge and thus be outcast from your clan forever. Do you have any questions?"

I shook my head, a chill breeze causing my teeth to chatter momentarily. Dad saw it, and his jaw tightened. He wanted to protect his daughter, and for that I was touched, but we both knew I had to go through this, and that I had to do it alone. Besides, with Draignerthol resting against my chest, I was willing to bet that I was the most powerful person at the stone.

I was ready.

Probably.

I hoped.

Sternyface moved aside as I stepped forward, bravely keeping the tiny doubts that suddenly grew into fearsome monsters in check. I walked up to the stones surrounding the ley-gate proudly, confidently, and stabbed the end of the special staff the priests had given me into the ground in the middle. Silently I willed the energy of the ley-lines into it, and the runes carved all along its length flared up with blindingly brilliant blue light.

I felt the teleportation, but it was different from what I remembered of my first trip. Before, back when Dad and I had crossed from Memphis into Kiirajanna, there'd been a lurch in my gut and that was it. I'd opened my eyes to the darkness of the Kiirajanna woods. It was quick, almost unnoticeable. The same was true of the ley-gate travel in the northlands. I hadn't actually moved in either case; I'd stepped in and through and everything in between was nothing.

This time, the travel was obvious. Still blinded by the light of the runes, I couldn't see anything, but I felt movement to the front and then suddenly to the right. Then it felt like I'd stepped aboard a strange, erratic cosmic bus, slowing and stopping for a brief moment before accelerating again in the opposite direction.

Whoosh! I felt the terrain, if you could call it that, fly by, both in my guts and in my inner ears. It was completely silent, near as I could tell, and yet the power of the ley energies roared in my ears, overloading my hearing as much as the rune light was overloading my sight.

I arrived, finally. I couldn't say what it was that alerted me to the destination coming up, but the flight slowed and came to a rest.

My feet suddenly found solid ground.

The glow of the runes faded, leaving the afterburn on my retinas, and then that also, slowly, went away.

As the light faced, so did the roar of the ley energies, replaced by a weird muffled babble of voices and noises. It sounded like an entire village was trying to speak around me, and all at the same time.

It was completely, soul-crushingly, dark. As terrifying as that was, my mind also pointed out to me in great big red letters how weird it was. Most of the time young elves stepped through the ley-line portals and emerged elsewhere on Kiirajanna. It was, according to stories, normal to pop out at a random time of the day due to the time zone thing. I'd figured it was as likely to be deep night time as it was to be high noon. But no forest I'd been in was ever completely dark. I had to be inside something, somehow, a realization that made the low mumble of noises that surrounded me seem even more ominous.

Once my eyes and ears had settled down, my nose kicked in, with a vengeance. Wherever I was, it was really stinky.

I took a deep breath to figure it out, and immediately regretted it. Mixed in with the smell of weeks-old dirty laundry and locker room was a biting aroma that could only be the ammonia of old urine. I'd never actually smelled it before, but I'd heard it described enough. It's truly unforgettable.

I panicked, but managed to catch myself before I did anything hasty. My eyes were slowly adjusting, and that was somehow comforting despite the fact that I still couldn't see anything but shadows leaning on other shadows. I reached out with my mind, attempting to use my spidey-sense on purpose, and found nothing that seemed threatening within the immediate area.

Good, at least so far, I thought. I hadn't expected to end up in a land of milk, honey, and lollipops, but it never occurred to me that a pair of rubber muck boots might come in handy, either. But other than my heels and toes I wasn't actually in the muck, which was nice, and the murmur that invaded my hearing wasn't coming from anything dangerously close, which was also nice.

All things considered, then, it wasn't too bad.

Yet.

I reached up to touch Draignerthol. They'd only said I couldn't come back before the six weeks was up, after all. There'd been nothing about not using magic. I pushed my will through the dragon pendant into the depths of the magical flows surrounding me, and out of that effort shone a dim blue light.

I blinked a few times to clear my startled eyes. It was good I'd chosen dim blue; anything brighter would've completely blinded me. I was in a mid-sized, square, whitewashed concrete room: a basement, maybe. The floor was covered with filmy, fetid water that looked like it got shallower near the corner in front of me. I hopped that direction and was pleasantly surprised that I'd been right. I hated my sandals having been immersed in the muck, but at least the spot where I landed was dry, ish.

There was a door. Unlike the elf-made doors I'd seen, this one as made of steel and had a round, shiny, metal door knob. All of which begged the question: where in heck was I? The elves of Kiirajanna aren't huge fans of shiny metal anythings other than swords. Or, for that matter, basements, especially basements flooded with filth. No, elves don't do filth, period.

Hoping I could safely assume, from the scum growing peacefully on the surface of the water, that the room I was in wasn't visited very often, I pushed the ley staff into the tiny alcove I'd leaped to so that it would be safe and out of the line of sight from the door. With the magical blue light still raised above me, I inched my way along the edge of the room, wincing every time the cold, murky, slimy water lapped over onto and between my toes. Worse, every movement seemed to stir up more of the nasty smell. By the time I reached the door I was barely holding myself back from gagging.

I reached carefully for the round metal knob, fearing the worst and not really certain what that meant. Would the door be locked, thus forcing me to decide between failing the test and staying for six weeks in a murky basement room? Or would the door open, only to cast me out into whatever group was murmuring loudly outside, and that group then gang up to hurt me? I gathered my courage anyway, and then said a prayer of thanks to anyone who was listening when it turned easily and quietly.

As slowly as I could manage, I pulled the door open half an inch and then waited. Nothing attacked through the crack, so I pulled it open a little farther and peered around the edge. Stairs—that was all. Just stairs. The door opened to a landing at the bottom of a set of stairs formed from rusted metal grates. From above, a hazy daylight filtered downward.

Daylight, and noise. As the door opened the muffled sounds of what had to be thousands of people became much more prominent.

Not wanting anybody to notice the magic, I snuffed out the blue light. Instantly the place went dark except for the hazy daylight that filtered casually, neglectfully, down the stairs.

Slowly I inched through the door, shut it tight behind me, and moved like a terrified little cat up the metal stairs toward the light. After a few steps I crouched on a metal grate landing with another door, this one thick, heavy metal featuring a glass window with security wire stretched across it. I stood slowly, carefully, and peered out through the window.

I saw people. Lots of people.

There were hundreds, if not thousands, of people out there, every one of them hastening in one direction or the other on the street outside.

The panic suddenly caught back up with me, and I started shaking. I felt like I needed to cry, wanted to cry, but my mouth was suddenly too dry to let even a sob out. My worst fear had, in fact, been placed right smack in front of me.

I was in a city.

Quest for Self

I finally managed to convince my body to stop its silly shaking. Yes, yes, I was in a city, I told myself firmly. I didn't know where, and so of course I didn't know that it was necessarily all that dangerous. All I knew was that on the other side of the door a mega-multi-person universe thrummed. I could hear them moving, and I could tell they were talking from the grunts and other sharp voices that carried through the door.

I could see them, too—thousands of people moving this way and that. They infested both sidewalks with incredibly industrious activity, hustling and bustling in both directions. There didn't seem to be any purpose other than getting from one end of the street to the other, but there didn't seem to need to be any purpose, either. Everybody was clearly, obviously, simply, on the move.

It was a madhouse.

I craned my head backward, trying to see some of the skyline through the nice, safe window in the door. I couldn't, though; with the sharpest angle upward I could get, I still couldn't even see the top of the building that towered across the street.

It was a tall madhouse.

I racked my brain trying to remember whether I'd ever heard of a city in Kiirajanna, but I found nothing. Everything I'd learned said that the elves preferred to live in small handmade huts ringed around a central green, where they could laugh and live and dance around a bonfire during the nights of celebration, which was pretty much every night in elf custom. In the north and the east they lived in greater walled communities for mutual protection, but even Ganolog, the northern elf fortress, was nothing compared to this. The largest gathering I'd heard of, in fact, was the one I lived in, and that was only big because of all of the civilization required to support the castle and the main cathedral. At that, it might be over ten thousand. In fact, I'd never heard of any elf settlement anywhere big enough to have its own Piggly Wiggly, much less its own Wal-Mart.

This place dwarfed all those, just based on what little I could see through the dirty window.

Was I, somehow, back on Earth?

Since one of my greatest fears was being in a city, maybe that was the truth of it? Maybe I was on Earth, and if so, then maybe I could just call Momma, maybe just once, and maybe say hi.

That thought brought me some courage.

Forcing my newfound courage together into a big strong bundle of hopey-action, and figuring I was never going to get anywhere if I didn't at least try, I pushed the door open just a crack. Everything suddenly got much louder. Great fun, right? And the smell—it was nearly as fetid outside as the basement had been. I looked down and found the small pebble I hoped to see. Stepping through the door, I knocked the pebble into the doorway to keep it slightly open in case I needed to dart back inside.

I did the bravest thing I think I've ever done, then. I stepped out into the flow of people.

It felt like I'd jumped into the ocean, only with a current going both directions. People jostled me—bumped right into me and pushed me out of the way, even—without the least bit of courtesy, not even an apology. No "sorry," no "excuse me," nor even a sad expression. No, to these folks I was just an obstacle to be brushed aside, it seemed, and I felt myself getting brushed farther and farther out into the flow.

It wouldn't do to be stampeded through and lost on my first day of hunhymgais, I thought, so I turned back and noted the door I'd come out of. The numbers on the still-cracked-open-door read 2713. Okay, I could remember that. I turned the same direction as most of the people bustling around me were going, my head craning side to side in the hopes of seeing someone who looked like they were in charge.

It didn't take long. I crossed one busy street with the crowd; they were a lot braver than I would've been if they'd given me a choice. They were pressing me along as part of the gang, though, so I just ignored the "No Walk" signal along with everybody else and strode across the pavement with them. As we crossed I turned my head to each direction, hoping for a landmark, but I couldn't see anything but more tall buildings stretching from horizon to horizon.

Fighting down another surge of panic, I was delighted to step into the eye of the raging storm of pedestrian crowd. Just on the other side of the road was a lone island in the busy current of people, an incredibly welcome sight for my sore eyes.

It was a policeman in a starched black uniform: black slacks, black waist-length jacket, black multi-point hat with a shiny black bill. From his wide black leather belt was hanging a pistol in its holster, an ammunition pouch, and a black wooden baton. A shiny badge sparkled on his chest.

Yep, a policeman. My newest hero.

I walked up to him, and he smiled at me. Sort of, anyway. By smiled I mean scowled. In fact, he outright glared at me for entering his personal space.

Ensconced within his personal space as I was, I could finally read his badge. It was in the shape of a shield, with a winged creature on top. In bold, black letters across the flat area, I could read what I'd most hoped it wouldn't say: "N.Y.P.D."

Great. I was in New York City.

The city that made all other cities look small and overly hospitable.

It was, in fact, my greatest fear, I realized: to be lost in The Big Apple. Though I'd been there once, it was with Dad, following a short path to somewhere he knew. But now, I didn't even know where I was, and I felt the panic rising. Was I in the Bronx? Harlem? I couldn't tell; I had no idea where those places were, or even if they were real places. All I knew was that Bronx people talked really funny, and Harlem was where the Globetrotters were from.

Tweeeeeeeeeeeeeeeeeeeeeeeeeeeeeeeeeeeeeeeeeeeeeeeeeeeeeeeeeet!

I realized he was blowing his whistle at me. He pointed down the street in the direction I'd been going, gesturing as though it was vital that I keep going that way.

He didn't understand.

I started doing the elf hand gesture of respect, but he stopped me by brandishing his blackened club. Whoa! I raised both hands to calm him down and said, "Sorry! Sorry. I'm Alyssa, and I'm just trying...."

Tweeeeeeeeeeeeeeeeeeeeeeeeeeeeeeeeeeeeeeeeeeeeeeeeeeeeeeeeeet!

He kept gesturing down the road. With a sudden flush of embarrassment I realized I'd been speaking elf, the language I'd worked so hard to master. Back on Earth, and in New York City, then, it shouldn't have been surprising that a noble officer of the law couldn't understand me.

I switched to English. Brandishing my sweetest smile, I said, "Please, Sir, I am lost. Can you please help me find...."

Tweeeeeeeeeeeeeeeeeeeeeeeeeeeeeeeeeeeeeeeeeeeeeeeeet!

The completely confused look on my face must've done it; the policeman dropped his aversion to speaking and launched into a tirade at me. Only, it wasn't English. It wasn't elf, either. It wasn't any language I'd ever heard. It was harsh, though. Brutal. Every syllable echoed like a jackhammer. Where elves relished the softer, gentler sounds of their language, the phlegm-based *ch*s and the lilting *ll*s and so on, the policeman seemed to enjoy pounding me into submission with repetitive verbal blasts of harsh consonants.

My chest started warming up, and I remembered Draignerthol. I'd been forced to bring the pendant to keep anyone from stealing it back in Kiirajanna, but I was comforted by its warmth on my chest. But then it hit me: Draignerthol could cleanse the body of poison, and could help spin fire-wads around a room. It could even shield a large group from injury in a deadly fall. Could it also translate a language?

As soon as I thought about translation I could feel Draignerthol working at doing just that. The spot on my chest where it lay grew even warmer, and the officer's words started falling into recognizable patterns. It happened slowly at first, but as I listened directly to his rant I actually caught a word, and then another. Soon I was understanding entire phrases, and then finally what he was yelling became clear.

"Move along, get out of the way, don't lollygag, loiterers must be prosecuted, don't you have somewhere to go, I'll have to take you in. Move along, get out of the way, don't lollygag, loiterers must be prosecuted, don't you have somewhere to go, I'll have to take you in. Move along, get out..." and, um, so on.

It was like he'd been programmed to say all that.

Cops probably are pretty well programmed, I realized. They always seem to have such rapid responses to everything, at least on television.

I wondered if Draignerthol could help me speak whatever language this guy was able to hear. Raising my hands to vertical, I slowly worked my tongue around the strange staccato language and said, "Excuse me for stopping. I seem to be lost, though."

His monologue stopped abruptly. "Well, why didn't you say so?" he asked.

I shrugged, not sure if I could choose the answer that would get me some help over the answer that would get me hauled off to jail. Apparently the shrug was best, though, because he barked, "Where are you going?"

I looked around at all my fellow pedestrians. I had no idea where I was going, and that thought made me wonder where all of those other people could be going.

I was hit, then, by a crazy thought of craziness. Maybe that was what living in a city was all about? Did everybody who lived in a city just walk back and forth on the streets all day, accomplishing nothing but a slight wearing down of their shoe soles?

The policeman glared at me, gripping his baton as though he was really looking forward to using it. He obviously wasn't in the mood for my crazy musings, in any event.

"Twenty seven thirteen," I said, hoping that would get me farther than—well, anything. It was really all I had.

"Twenty seven thirteen what?"

Now he had me. I looked up and around, looking for the first word I saw to give the impatient officer of the law. There! On a green sign just above the man's head was a word.

"Lexington."

It was the wrong word. His face clouded over in anger. He reached out and grabbed my shoulder, his grip digging deep and hurting. He spun me back the way I'd come, pointed, and shoved me.

I glanced back up; yes, I could see now that I'd read the street sign. Great. I'd just told him I was looking for a place half a block away, and he'd made the natural assumption that I was an idiot as a result. Obviously the N.Y.P.D. had no time for idiots.

Normally, I wouldn't have time for idiots, either. But then again, there I was, stuck in New York City with strict orders not to come back for six weeks. No, on second thought, I couldn't come back for five weeks, five and one-half days—but who's counting, right?

Whatever. I had to find something to do for what could end up being quite a long time.

With that in mind, I headed back into the building at 2713. Maybe—hopefully—I'd find someone in there who was more interested in helping a stranger out than the policeman had been.

NEIDR

Snake.

No, really, not a wyrm or a serpent, but
a real, breathing, living snake.

A Tough People

I slipped back in through the door, remembering all the cop shows I'd seen that involved cameras recording people coming and going. I looked carefully around, but didn't see any. Granted, it was just as likely that I'd end up staring right at a camera and not recognize it here in the city. Still, looking up at the ceiling and the molding around it, I saw nothing but ceiling and molding—no wires, no bulky or round devices, and definitely no little red dots of light.

Fine. No cameras. At least, none that I could see. I realized there wasn't any particular reason to fear cameras, or to be happy for their absence. It just made me feel less—watched.

I climbed the first set of stairs up to a landing. Two doors branched off it, one to either side. I stopped and listened at each, craning as hard as I could, but didn't hear a sound.

Up the next set of stairs was another landing, this one returning to what I assumed was the front of the building. It, like the landing just below, held two doors, and each of them was as silent as the two below had been.

The door labeling threw me. On the bottom floor it was an A and a funky B, the latter almost lower case but with a bar across the top. Okay, fine, I got that. Next, though, came a regular B and a weird partial C, missing the bottom bar across. I climbed to the next floor and found a D and an E, which was good, but the D was shaped funky, sort of square-ish with legs. It seemed like somebody had taken a sort of graffiti-esque liberty with the letters. I listened at both doors, hoping to hear somebody inside moving around, but still there was nothing.

The next floor stumped me on its labeling: another E and an X, only the X had a vertical line through it. I wondered what the apartment manager could have been thinking. These apartments, though, were also silent, at least by their doors.

It started looking deliberate to have such weird symbols, as a 3 and a backward N greeted me at the next floor. I forgot all about it, though, as I got a real rush of adrenalin when I listened at the door with a 3 on it and heard voices. Lots of voices, in fact. It sounded like there was a girl party going on.

I knocked. What the heck, right? I figured they'd either let me in or they wouldn't, and it had to be much easier facing down a girl party than the crowd outside.

They let me in. It took a while, but they did. The conversation seemed to die down just a little after I knocked, and I could hear somebody's footsteps coming up to the door. A shadow passed behind the view hole, and then I could hear four different locks being thrown back. Finally the door opened, and I found myself face to face with a New York City girl.

I'm not sure what it was that said "New York City" girl about her so loudly. She was dressed about the same as I was, in pants and a tunic. She was wearing shoes, and I was wearing just sandals, and I could tell in her eyes that she'd noticed that fact even if I hadn't seen her looking down. But she was—hard, if that makes sense. Hard in stance, hard in facial expression, hard in how she held the door—just, hard.

Granted, I was used to elf society, where she would've thrown open her door, even distrusting magic-using princesses as they did, and invited me gleefully in for food and for talk.

She didn't.

Instead, she stood there, blocking the door, sizing me up. Her eyes flickered up and down my body, leaving me weirdly violated. They darkened, narrowing slightly, signaling disapproval. I'd been weighed and measured and found wanting. There were tough guys, and there were tough gals, and I was neither of those, her glare said. What business had I knocking on her door?

Still, she let me in. The other girls told her to. Then they started chattering, and even though my chest got dreadfully hot as a result, I was glad that Draignerthol could handle the translations. It was rapid-fire, and directed at me, and I barely kept up with it.

"Where you from?" the most common question asked, and I decided that was the easiest and safest one to try to answer.

"Up," I said, Draignerthol helping me say it in their staccato, guttural language. I pointed up, feeling a little silly. "Apartment above."

"Apartment *phlegm*," one of them prompted, and I nodded. Yeah, sure, what the heck, right? I guess every alphabet, especially New York's, needs a letter that sounds like phlegm. The elf language has one, as the team I'd watched competing in cylchoedd the other day proved. Only that was a gentle phlegm sound: *khe* mushed together with a little throat action tossed in. It shouldn't have surprised me at all, then, that the New York version of that was ten times as harsh, starting with a hard, quick *sh* sound and ending in a train wreck: *shchk* is pretty close if you growl a little and try to spit up at the same time you're saying it.

Honestly, it made me kinda scared just hearing it. But I couldn't show that; I had to be one of them. "Yes, Apartment *phlegm*," I said, and winced inside as they all gave each other these humorous, quizzical looks like I'd gotten it completely wrong.

"New resident from one of the farming districts," one offered, rescuing me. I nodded. "Well, come on in," she said, "we're just having our neighborhood morning chat, and we'll be glad to let you know all there is to know about the district."

I wasn't about to give up my newfound place, no matter how precarious it was, in the New York City society, and so I nodded, pretending to know what they meant by farming district, and followed them in. I heard the door shut decisively behind me, each of the handful of deadbolts re-engaged individually, forcefully. I started wondering why that was important.

One lock, I get. But four?

I spent the next hour or so listening in on the conversations of the seven other women gathered in the little apartment. I'd have been happy to participate, but nobody asked me my opinion, and at the same time, I really had no idea how. The topics were all beyond anything I'd ever known.

One, for example, had to do with size of breasts. Not that it was a glorious thing—oh, no, it couldn't be that simple. Instead, the conversation focused on one of the women getting a breast reduction. That threw me for a loop. The speaker was a normal-breasted woman now; she'd asked to be taken down to a normal cup size. I'd never heard of that before, so I listened closely to her logic. It turned out that breasts were heavy—a fact that I pretty well already knew—and got heavier the larger they became. There was a point, the woman said, where the weight of the breasts was a greater burden than any benefit having large breasts provided, and so she'd asked that they be taken down.

Her greatest pleasure, then, was her doctor's statement after the surgery that she had the most perfect C-cups he'd ever seen.

Meanwhile, a conversation behind me was focused on writing as a pastime; these folks liked to write. The conversation in front of me was about the school system, and it had to do with a teacher who—well, I kind of lost the details of what the teacher did to deserve their scorn while listening to commentary about breast size.

It was tough—no, it was pretty much impossible—to follow all three conversations at once even with Draignerthol translating. I tried for a while, and then just settled for listening in on the most interesting conversation going at the time. It turned out that the conversation that deserved the most interesting title was a rotating thing. For a while the exclamations about breasts entertained me, and then I lost contact with that conversation when the parent reached a particularly loud point in her ragging on the teacher they were discussing. I'd missed too much to know which school subject they were talking about, but whichever it was, this teacher apparently didn't know it. At least, she—or he, the translations from Draignerthol weren't making it perfectly clear—didn't know it well enough to be teaching it. Then, suddenly, my attention was drawn to the conversation behind me as the women in the kitchen argued about whether it was more important to finish writing a work quickly, or to take one's time in lovingly crafting each paragraph, where each chapter taking as much as a year, or maybe even two, to complete was a grand accomplishment.

I was just starting to get over being completely overwhelmed when all three conversations abruptly paused. It wasn't exactly simultaneous. Suddenly the breast-reduced woman looked over at me, smiled, and snatched up a plate of little sandwiches from the table, and then everybody else's mouths stopped moving as their eyes followed her to me.

"So, newcomer, you haven't told us your name," she said as she offered the tray's contents to me.

"Alyssa." I'd been going over that question already, and just decided to be honest. My name might or might not go with the sharpness of the language I found here, but it was just as likely that neither would any other name I could make up.

"Alyssa," she said, nodding. "I am Katrina. I'll let the rest of our little crew introduce themselves." They did, one at a time, rapid-fire, with just their names. No "hi sweetheart," no "welcome to our building," not even a "bless your heart."

"So where ya from?" Katrina asked once the name-rocket had gone full circle. It took the question a couple of seconds to register in the midst of the panic I felt over not catching any of their names in the hurry.

Finally Draignerthol told me what she'd asked. Where was I from? Right, well, I was from a place far, far away, having traveled through ley-powered teleportations to Kiirajanna, the world of elves and unicorns, and back to Earth to the middle of the largest, scariest city I could imagine.

They didn't want to hear that, nor did I want to tell them that. So I lied.

"Downtown," I said, hoping to just toss the subject aside with a generality and move on.

"Downtown? Really? You've come so far," Katrina said. I nodded, not sure how she knew that.

"What's it like, downtown?" a short brunette asked. She'd been one of the ones listening in on the breast reduction commentary.

"Well, you know, it's just normal," I made it up as fast as I could. Suddenly recalling the farming district comment earlier, I back-pedaled as much as I could. "Lots of people, for the farming district downtown. Got tired of working with my hands, though, so here I am in the big city. Are you a native here?"

"We're all natives here," Katrina explained. "Nothing near as exciting as downtown in the farming districts. Hey!" she said, suddenly brightening up. Her mouth gave me a huge, wide grin, though her eyes didn't reflect it. Strange people, these New Yorkers. "I have a great collection of art from downtown in the farming district, though. Would you like to see it?"

I couldn't turn down an invitation like that. Once, several years before, I'd turned down an elderly neighbor's offer to show me her thimble collection, because hey, who wants to see a thimble collection, right? But Momma did, or at least so she said, and after, she swore to beat me to within an inch of my life if I ever insulted somebody's hospitality like that again. I never did.

"Sure, I'd love to see it!" I lied. Some art is pretty, granted, but most of what I've seen that was called art was actually just abstract blobs and wavy lines intersecting other blobs, and I could never quite get why their blobs were any more artistic than anyone else's.

Besides, I had no idea how artistic these "downtown" folks were. I didn't know how much reaction I needed to show. Every little spidey-sense was tingling about how much danger I was stepping into, but....

But....

But you just don't insult somebody's hospitality.

She asked, and so I covered my eyes. It was so that I'd be surprised by the beauty of the art and the generous size of her collection, I was sure. I stepped forward through the door that I was led to and uncovered my eyes just as it shut behind me.

"Very funny!" I yelled and banged on the metal door. It didn't open; all I managed to do was hurt my hand. I banged a few more times and then gave it up. Downtown art, my butt. They'd just walked me out onto a narrow little balcony that doubled as a fire escape.

After several long minutes of beating my fist futilely against the cold metal of the door, I turned around to take in my predicament. It was still overcast and chilly, and though it had to be later on in the morning it didn't seem any lighter or warmer than my walk down the crowded street had been. Meanwhile I was perched five stories above the pavement of the alley below. The only other people I saw were a couple of bums slouched at the base of the row of buildings, one in each direction, and I couldn't imagine street bums being able to help me out much at the moment.

A few realizations smacked me in the head like blinding flashes of the obvious. First, I wasn't in New York City. I couldn't possibly be. Draignerthol worked, and it can't work on Earth because the magical energy isn't there. We'd already gone through that when the ley-line portal in the northlands teleported us to another spot in the same region. My brain just wasn't working at full capacity yet, unfortunately.

It also couldn't be New York City because I knew for a fact that they spoke English, not the weirdly harsh guttural tongue I'd already heard too much of, in the Big Apple. This I knew because of the trip Dad took the queen's kids and me on over the holiday. Granted, that was a harsh, clipped version of English, but it was recognizable, didn't require Draignerthol to interpret, and didn't contain nearly as much phlegm.

I had no idea where I was. It wasn't the elf language they were speaking, nor are there modern cities anywhere on Kiirajanna that I know of. So I wasn't on Earth, and I wasn't on any known point on Kiirajanna. Somehow, not knowing where I was got me even more anxious than when I'd thought I was on Earth.

Finally, I was about to freeze to death. I was really glad Dad had refused to let me go naked into the unknown, but the wind whipping through the alley way up above the street as it was drove every speck of warmth away from my body, straight through the thin garments I had on. I absolutely had to get down to the street, and sooner rather than later. Then, I wasn't certain what I would do, because I had no cash, nor did I know how cash worked in this realm. Buying a coat, or a sleeping bag, was completely out of the question.

I was pretty well screwed, to use the more vulgar but most appropriate term.

The cold metal ladder down to the ground was a little bent up and pretty rusty, but it looked like it would probably hold my weight. The other option was jumping, and that didn't seem very smart. Maybe, I figured, I could find a way to be a bum for six weeks. That, or try to camp out and sleep in the fetid water of the basement of the building I'd just been locked out of.

First things first, though. I reached out and took the frigid side bar of the ladder in my hand, swinging my feet in their flimsy sandals onto the even colder crossbars.

"This is gonna be great," I said to myself as I started climbing down.

PARC

A park.

Is it weird that the two languages use

basically the same word for it?

The Park

I almost managed to freeze my hands and feet completely off on the climb down. I was so cold, all I wanted was somewhere to sit and wrap myself up in a blanket, a cloak, even a large towel. I didn't dare stop, though, so as soon as my feet hit the ground I ran down to the end of the alley. I half-expected the bum I passed on the way to try to stop me and, I don't know, ask for money or wine or something, but instead he just stared at me as I ran past.

The street I emerged onto was the busy cross-way I'd walked across twice that morning. Luckily the traffic was mostly gone, the street nearly deserted. Apparently everybody from the morning rush had gotten to wherever they were going. Most everybody, anyway; there were still a couple of people walking, but they still ignored the heck out of me, bless their hearts.

Everybody ignored me, I should say, except for the snake charmer on the corner.

I think that the only thing that scares me more than big cities full of mean people is big, mean snakes.

Where there'd been a huge crowd that morning, everybody either waiting to cross the road or finishing crossing the road, there was now just a single guy and a large—a *very* large—snake. Very large, black, and undoubtedly more than venomous enough to kill me. The snake had to be venomous; what's the point of the charmer if it's not, right? Besides, no matter what else I've gotten myself into, one thing I can brag about is never getting close enough to a snake to ask it if it had enough venom kill me. Some people say they can tell based on the shape of the head or the size of the eyes or something, but to me all snakes are best just presumed bad that way.

In the movies, the snake is always contained in a pretty vase with just its head raised up and waving back and forth in front of the charmer, who in turn is always focused on the snake with all his energy. Which, I should add, is the only reason I ever suspect the charmer still possesses a lick of sanity. Plus, the charmer is always playing some kind of instrument like a recorder, creating spooky music like you'd expect to hear on Aladdin to convince Mister Snake that the best thing to do is rise and wiggle instead of strike and bite.

That's in the movies. It's not that way in Fake New York City, apparently. As I ran around the corner both the snake and its charmer stopped cold and turned, two sets of beady little eyes focusing directly on me. There wasn't even a basket or anything to contain His Hissyness, only a few yards of open concrete between it and my body, and I'd forgotten my snakeproof suit, too. The thin pieces of linen I'd put on suddenly felt even thinner.

The snake was huge, too, with coils about the size of a semi truck tire. The one full loop I could see was nearly two feet thick, vertically covering the distance between the ground and the charmer's knees. The rest of the snake twined around and on top of that, and the dinner-plate-sized head sat atop a tree trunk of a neck and met the charmer's at eye level.

Worse, there wasn't any sort of instrument.

I turned around immediately and jogged the other way. Unfortunately, it didn't take long to get close enough to the next street corner that I could see another semi truck tire of a snake with its human pet.

About then I figured that it was turning into one really bad morning.

I decided that I didn't care whether they allowed jaywalking or not, so I crossed the street in the middle of the block. Nobody seemed to notice, and at least that was good news. After I crossed I doubled back, heading toward Lexington once again. I don't know why; I just figured that was the road to be on. Besides, I needed to venture out in a way where I'd know how to get back to my basement.

The charmer at the corner stopped humming his little tune as I jogged up to the intersection again. This time I was on the opposite side of the road, though, so I sped up and was able to safely round the corner without being hassled.

Both charmer's and snake's eyes followed me once again, and I heard a long, low hiss from the snake. I turned and kept walking, forcing myself to keep my eyes directly to the front and not glance around to see how close the fangs were to taking me. Luckily, though, after a few steps the hiss faded and the imaginary fangs receded, and I was just cold and alone once again.

The cop wasn't there any more. I wasn't sure if that was a good thing or a bad one. I have to believe that he might have actually helped me out if he hadn't had so many other people around to watch. I mean, he was a cop, right? I don't know for certain, but I sure didn't see anybody else who looked like they might even try to be helpful. It was just a long, open sidewalk, a person or two striding along purposefully every couple dozen feet or so, and rows of what looked like more apartment buildings on the sides.

Oh, and a weed machine on the side of the street a little ways down. Now that was a shock.

It was the nicest, most well-kept appliance on the street, a big green shiny vending machine with a huge marijuana leaf painted on the side. As I walked, I watched a guy step up to it, drop a coin in the slot, and retrieve a green baggie from the chute on the bottom.

Boy, Fake New York City was one very different place from Mississippi.

I kept going. Every so often a spindly little tree grew through grates in the sidewalk, a city's way of apologizing to the forest that should be growing there. I passed a lot of businesses, mostly food places with their names written in the same strange squiggles and scrawls I'd seen in the apartment building. I found that if I pushed just a little energy, just the right way, into Draignerthol, the dragon pendant translated the name for me. When I tried it I came away with familiar-sounding names: Popeye's and Subway. But the businesses didn't look at all like Popeye's or Subway. What should be a sandwich shop, for instance, staffed by smiling and friendly sandwich artists, looked a lot like a sushi bar instead. At least the establishment with the word taco on its sign actually sold tacos, if the picture on the window were to be believed. It was all confusing. I kept walking, though; the last thing I wanted to do was attract the attention of the snake charmers or the cops or anybody else in power, at least before I figured out what was going on.

Meanwhile, the snake charmers seemed to be on every other corner. I couldn't figure out what they were doing there; I didn't see anybody walking up and watching a show or giving them money. No wonder, they all seemed hostile. The first couple I passed hissed, their heads tracking me as I walked by. By pointedly ignoring later sets, though, I managed to get them to ignore me, too.

Before long the left-most lane of the one-way Lexington Avenue became left turn only, and then it narrowed down to two lanes. I still hadn't seen any cars on the road, so I wondered what the lanes were for. On our trip to Real New York City I'd been amazed by the sea of yellow taxis, but there weren't any of those in this version.

The trees sticking up through grates on the sidewalk became bigger, both in height and in girth. They were still as leafless as the smaller ones had been, but then again, it was the middle of winter.

Up ahead I saw more trees, and that welcome view enticed me to pick up my pace even more. I ignored another snake charmer and his hissy semi truck tire, and once again I was rewarded by their lack of attention. The road narrowed even more, the new left-most lane turning off to the left as its predecessor had. It was all I could do to keep walking rather than breaking out into a sprint. The city was nearly at an end, it appeared. I said a prayer to anyone listening that the strange, rude city would end there.

One block more and the only remaining lane required a right turn, and then Lexington Avenue ceased to exist.

It wasn't the end of the city, it turned out. Disappointed as I was, though, I was glad to run into a park—an honest-to-goodness park with actual, living, planted trees. I hadn't realized how much my experiences with the forests and the elves had tied me to green things, but my heart soared as I forced myself to slow down and walk normally across the last few yards that separated me from the oasis.

Six-foot wrought iron gates stood open on the walkway that would have been Lexington Avenue if it had continued. I should say hung open, really; a hinge had long ago rusted apart and the gate, its black paint flaking off, leaned against its post at the top with its bottom tip wedged on the ground. The rest of what I could see from the entrance looked just as poorly cared for. Light plastic bags, the same type that the marijuana vending machine had spit out, littered the base of several trees, while the mostly-dead grass that should have lined the edges of the walkways grew in cracks within them instead. The stones of the path, the blocks of the wall, and everything else looked dingy and dirty, a combination of light brown moss, long-dead ivy, and multiple layers of dirt and grime.

I wondered who, if anyone, used the park. The bums had seemed perfectly comfortable in their alley. It looked like nobody was in the park at the time, which made it a promising location to house a six-week hideaway.

Five weeks, and five and one-half days, I reminded myself.

The plants in the park were just as much wintered-down as the trees on the street were, all their leaves withered and most of them gone. I saw green farther in, though, and so I walked along the wide path to get to the low evergreen hedges toward the middle.

In the center of the park was a round landscaped circle, and in the middle of that was a statue of a guy. He stood with his back to the entrance I'd used, and so I walked around, curious to find out who he was. I found a nameplate on the base of the statue, but it was blank.

I looked closer, but didn't see anything at all. No scratches, no worn lines, nothing. It wasn't that the nameplate was just old and faded. It was literally blank, and by all appearances it had always been blank.

The nameless statue guy looked down at me apologetically. The urge to speak up, to ask him who he was struck hard, but I held it in; even with nobody else around, I was nervous about doing anything that might mark me as crazy. Not that where I was didn't look crazy enough—a large park in the middle of an even larger modern, ish, city, where marijuana was sold from vending machines and people walked sternly everywhere. Meanwhile, here was a large bronze statue guy dressed in a weird-looking toga-like thing, weight entirely on his left leg, casting a serious expression downward like he was about to launch into a Shakespearean monologue.

I laughed at the absurdity. I couldn't help it, and I probably shouldn't have risked it, but I was glad I'd done it. I felt much better, thanks to a little bit of diaphragm action.

Looking around I saw that I'd entered along the shorter axis, north-south if I was reading the hazy sun's glimmer right. The rectangular park was about twice as long in the other direction, with an oval path along the longer axis.

I explored my way around the first half of the oval and then stopped at the far point of the second one. It was surrounded by scraggly evergreens and a thick cover of bare branches, leaving me feeling as safe as I'd been since my arrival. I plopped myself down on a bench to think.

I was obviously supposed to think that I was in New York City, for some reason. That's what it had to be, unless N.Y.P.D. meant something else. I was pretty sure I had the P.D. part pegged, and so that left N.Y., and I could only think of one city that started with those letters, and besides, this place was every bit as busy, as rude, and as huge as I'd seen of New York City on my one brief trip.

I couldn't be in New York City, though. For one thing, the residents of The Real New York City spoke English, last I'd heard. The people here didn't, not even close. The signs weren't in English, either. The restaurants seemed to be named after American restaurants, but they weren't the same. The only word that had been correct on the signs, if Draignerthol's interpretation were to be believed, was the Mexican one, which I supposed would have been funny in itself if the whole situation weren't so weird.

Also, last I'd heard, there weren't any snake charmers in New York City. Granted, I'd never studied the tourist attractions there, but the only thing I'd seen or heard on TV was about the food, or the lights of Times Square, or the Empire State Building, or that new Freedom Tower. I'd never, ever, seen or heard anybody talking about the snake charmers of New York City.

Topping it off, there were the pot vending machines. I mean, look, I don't care what anybody else does in the privacy of their own home—at least, not as long as they're not abusing somebody else—but near as I could remember, marijuana had only recently become legal, and that only in a few places. I was pretty certain that my memory was correct that those places didn't include New York, and they sure didn't include vending machines stocked with it.

I thought briefly of Amsterdam, where I'd heard they had a free drug thing going on. The city couldn't be Amsterdam, though. I don't think they speak English there, for one thing, but whether they do or they don't, surely their street signs don't have names like Lexington. That was a United States place from the Revolution, if I remembered correctly.

I thought about all the people I'd seen, the cop and the women in the apartment and all the folks on the street. All of them had a tall, angular appearance about them. They were more like me and my father than like Momma. Elves, then, they had to be. But Real New York City wasn't populated by elves. That castle in Wales I had lived my first few years in was, to be sure, but not Real New York City. So where did the elves here in Fake New York City come from?

I shivered and found myself wishing for the warmth of Draignerthol, and the little dragon pendant responded by heating up the little spot on my chest where it rested. Soon the air around me warmed up, too, and I was really happy when my teeth stopped chattering.

That was the kicker, I realized. This place had magic. Draignerthol was nothing more than a pretty silver dragon-shaped pendant with blue crystal eyes on Earth. That was why the powerful elf relic had ended up there in the first place. If I were on Earth at all, then, in Mississippi or in Real New York City or anywhere else, Draignerthol could not possibly have helped me out the way it had.

Kiirajanna, the realm of magic, was the only answer that made sense. I had to be there, with my fellow elves, instead of on Earth. Granted, I had no idea where there could be, as the priests had taught me nothing about any city anywhere on the planet. Elves didn't like cities at all, period.

Obviously, though, here they were, and in a very large number, living together in a huge, dirty city, and all of that somewhere on the same planet as Cysegredig, my father's glorious castle.

It briefly occurred to me to wonder if Sternyface even knew about this place.

The priests had taught me about the continent, about the vast lands and homes of the clans of the north, the south, the east, and the west. It was the largest continent on the planet, they'd said. They hadn't taught me about the other land masses, though, and they'd made it seem like they didn't because there weren't any to teach about. But the presence of the dark-skinned elves, and their stories about coming from another continent entirely, had messed that story up already.

So far I'd figured out that Dad and the priests knew about the dark-skinned elves. I had to assume that they knew at least a little of their lore, so maybe they knew about this place. Or, then again, maybe not.

Maybe their lack of lessons was because they didn't actually know anything to teach.

Maybe I was the first elf from the continent to find this place.

Maybe it was my destiny to bring these elves together with my own subjects.

Maybe all the prophecies about the disaster I'd bring upon the customs and the way of life of the elves meant I'd move these elves out of the city and back to the more comfortable, natural way of life. I could personally welcome them all as they joined their brothers and sisters in the forests. I imagined myself establishing crazy bonding parties and a sort of missionary effort to weave the cultures together. I could even find a way to incorporate the dark-skinned elves into the fold to create a single people, a single elf culture. There wouldn't be any marijuana vending machines, of course, but I wasn't about to start a drug war as the dragon queen. Nope, my policy would be that whatever happened in the comfort of your home, stayed in the comfort of your home.

My grand musings in which I was already installed as dragon queen were brought up short. "What are you doing on my bench?" a girl's voice growled from behind. She stepped out in front of me, hands on her hips and a glare on her face.

I gasped when she came into view.

It was Sephaline.

Druzhtane

"Get off my bench," Seph growled. Only, it couldn't be Seph; for one thing, my cousin had talked about her plan to return and then stay happily lounging inside the warm, dry castle through the remainder of the day after I walked through the stones to start my hunhymgais, and for another, the person in front of me dressed and smelled like a bum.

"*Get off my bench,*" the not-Sephaline growled, advancing toward me.

I smiled and held my hands up in the old gesture of submission. "Okay, okay," I said, not rising yet. "But first, tell me, please, how I can get a bench of my own to sit on."

"Like this," the girl said with a leer. Faster than I would have thought possible, she whipped a small-bladed knife out of her belt and put its point right underneath my nose. I looked down, crossing my eyes to see exactly where the tip of the knife was, and I didn't like what I saw. I was only about a quarter of an inch away from losing at least part of what I always figured was my face's best feature.

"Get off my bench," she repeated, her voice bouncy and sassy this time.

I nodded. When she put it that way, after all, I was happy to comply.

She sat down, folded her arms, and smugly said, "That's how you get a bench of your own."

"Oh. But I don't have a knife," I said. "Nor do I have the money to buy one."

She snorted. "You can't *buy* knives, stupid. Not here in the kingdom, anyway. Weapons are strictly forbidden. Where are you from, that you're so stupid?"

I bristled, but there was no point getting into an argument with the only person who'd actually talked to me so far. Besides, she had a knife, and I didn't, which makes for a much greater tactical advantage in person than it seems to in the action movies. I settled quickly on telling the truth. I'd tried lying once already, after all, and it had just gotten me a cold climb down a frozen metal ladder.

"Mississippi."

She shook her head. "Never heard of it. Must be a really stupid place."

I shook my head in return. "No, not stupid at all. Some of the greatest writers of all time have come from there."

"Writers? What good are they?"

"Mind if I sit here?" I gestured toward a dirty, but bare, spot on the concrete beside the bench, choosing to ignore her latest dig. I told myself that an even response was just the adult thing to do, that her having a weapon had nothing to do with it.

I lie to myself sometimes, I realized, and made a mental note to examine that later when I wasn't cold, nearly naked, hungry, and at the mercy of a strange girl with a knife.

"Suit yourself," she said with an almost-pleasant shrug. "Just not on my bench."

I didn't see a lot of difference between the hard wooden bench and the hard concrete platform, so I pushed Draignerthol's energy out to warm up the concrete and then sat down. When I looked at the girl, her eyes were wide and her dagger was pointed my direction again.

"Wh—what did you just do? You're a g-man, ain't ya?"

"I'm not a man at all. And no, I don't work for the government," I said, amused at the ancient term she'd used.

"Nobody but g-men use magic like that," she objected. My eyebrows shot up involuntarily. So magic did exist and was acknowledged by the people here, even if it was forbidden by the elves where I'd just come from—wherever that happened to be in relation to where I was at the moment.

I shrugged. "I use magic, but only for good. And I'm not a g-man."

"They teach you how in that Missikippi place?"

"Mississippi," I corrected, nearly laughing in spite of the dagger. It was funny, and a little calming, how this Sephaline look-alike mispronounced the name of the state the same way the real Sephaline had.

"Missiwhatevah." She started cleaning out under her fingernails, trying to make a point of ignoring me. I wasn't giving up the only conversation I'd been able to get going, though.

"What's your name?"

"What's it to ya?"

"I'm just trying to talk to you."

"Well, cut it out. It's stupid."

"You keep using that word. I do not think it means what you think it means."

"What's that?"

"Oh, nothing," I said. "It's a line from an old, funny movie I used to love. Look, you look an awful lot like an old friend of mine—a cousin, actually—named Sephaline. That's not your name, too, is it?"

"Of course not. What kind of stupid name is Sephaline?"

"I don't know; I didn't make it up. My name is Alyssa."

"Good for you."

"What's the big deal with your name? Do you think I'm going to use it to take over your mind or something?"

"Can you *do* that?" She actually looked frightened.

"No. Of course not. My powers are pretty much limited to warming up the concrete I'm sitting on, or the bench you're sitting on. I'll be happy to do that again if you'll just tell me what your name is."

"You still haven't let on what you want to know my name for," she said, glaring suspiciously at me.

"It's how I talk to people. I like to know, and to use, their names, is all. It's how we learned to communicate in Mississippi."

"Well, it's stupid."

"So is refusing to tell me your name," I said, tired of the failure I'd had in the attempts to be nice.

"Druzhtane."

"There. Was it that hard to tell me that?"

"No. Just stupid."

I sighed; she was hung up on that word.

"So what is this place I've come to, Druzhtane?"

"The kingdom, stupid."

"The kingdom of what?" I started to wonder if I was going to have to draw everything out of her, one or two words at a time plus the word stupid.

"New York."

"New York?" I was shocked! It really was named after the city. Why would elves bring part of Earth to Kiirajanna, though? And even weirder: why such a modern, congested part?

One of the better parts of the tour Dad had arranged for us in the Big Apple laid out the history of the bridges and trade. It was surprising to me how relatively recently the megalopolis of Manhattan had been a farming community, and then a trading community, and only a century or so ago becoming a major hub of commerce. The elves had been in the current epoch when the new world was founded by Europeans, and so I was curious how a modern city had been copied back to Kiirajanna.

"Yes, New York. Got any other stupid questions?"

"Where's Old York?" I didn't even know the answer to that back on Earth, but I was curious what she would say.

"Oh. Ha, ha. Showed me. Obviously you have plenty of stupid questions. Did your mother have any kids with a brain?"

"Is it even possible for you to talk to somebody without insulting them, Druzhtane?"

"Probably not," she said. "You could always stop trying to talk to me, and then I'd probably insult you a whole lot less, stupid."

"I could," I said. I wasn't going to, though. She would've cut me already if that were her plan, and otherwise her choices included either talking to me or leaving. "So you don't know where Old York is, I take it?"

"No. I don't. What difference does it make?"

"Not much, other than to see if you were really smart enough to be calling me stupid."

"I got a knife, and you don't, and so who's the stupid one? Stupid."

"We're both out here in the cold, deserted park. You do have a knife, and I do not. Only, I can warm your seat, and you can't warm mine even with the little flake you call a knife. Am I interpreting our situation right?"

"You keep talking about warming my seat. Seems like you promised to do it if I told you my name, which I did. You haven't warmed my bench yet, though, so you're a liar, too, in addition to being stupid."

I grinned; she was starting to come around. The magic flowed at my bidding, coming gently through Draignerthol to warm the bench.

"Okay, okay, that's enough," she said, squirming. Obviously I'd gone a little too far.

"Sorry. Let me know when it cools back down and I'll warm it up a little again, this time without frying your bottom. Deal?"

"Fine, deal. You still can't have it."

"I didn't say I wanted it. Does that bench over there belong to anybody?" I pointed to the twin of the bench she was on, just across the way.

"I don't know." She shrugged, her tone matching the expression on her face. Both said the question was irrelevant.

"So how did you get to being a loyal resident of the park here?" I asked. I didn't want to point out to my new friend, more or less, that she was, by all appearances, and smells too, simply a bum. A bum with a knife, granted, but a bum nevertheless.

"You sure you're not a g-man?" she asked, her eyes shifting nervously around.

"Quite sure. I only got here today."

"That explains your stupid outfit, then."

I sighed over the return to stupid. She was right on that one, anyway. "You're right, it was a silly choice of clothes."

"At least you had a choice of clothes."

"Right. I did have a choice. I take it you didn't? Why are you out here instead of somewhere—up there—" I gestured generally upward, into the great skyscraper jungle that loomed all around us, and continued, "using the marvelous intelligence that you have?"

"You're making fun of me now." She glared, and her knuckles tightened about the hilt of the knife.

"No, I'm being serious. You're obviously a smart girl, and you're pretty tough and resourceful, too. Why are you living on a bench in a park?"

"You don't have *zhopi* in Mississippi, do you?"

Zhopi. Draignerthol's translator had a hard time with that one. It meant bum, but there was a subtly noble ring to it. It basically labeled bumhood as a profession, when you called yourself a zhopi. Like being an accountant, or a lawyer, only—dirtier. And, if Druzhtane were evidence, smellier.

"Nope. No zhopi in Mississippi."

"Why the hell did you come to this stinking hellhole, then?"

I shrugged, and then answered honestly. "I don't know. It just sort of happened, and I found myself here. So how do you become a zhopi?"

She laughed. Apparently what I said had been one of the funniest things she'd heard in a long time, because she laughed long and hard. Finally she wound down, wiping the tears from her face. "You want to know how to become a zhopi, my stupid little princess from Mississippi? You don't. Zhopi takes you. I had a normal life, in a normal home, uptown, and then one day they came for me. I'd been selected for public service, right? Only, I didn't want public service, so I ran out the back and down the fire escape. I was lucky; I knew the alleys well, so they didn't catch me. And then, I was zhopi: outcast, not a member of the world, not a citizen of the kingdom, just—just zhopi."

The pain in her voice was sharp. She'd sliced through her original brusqueness and laid out an entire heart full of hurt. Then, just as quickly, she shut it closed again. I looked over to see her glaring back at me as though I were the one who'd forced being zhopi on her.

"I—I'm sorry, Druzhtane. Wow. That's—wow. How come you didn't want to go into public service?"

"You *are* new here, aren't you?" Scorn dripped from the word new.

"I am. We didn't have public service in Mississippi." That was a lie, sort of. We had public service, but I was willing to bet it was nothing like whatever had driven Druzhtane out of society.

"Stupid *and* lucky, then," she spat.

"If you must. But what is public service? I really am curious."

"Well, now, I don't know, do I? I didn't go. People go into public service and disappear. They don't come back." The last was said in a voice that was tiny, conspiratorial.

Oh. Well. I had a hard time keeping the chortle in over that little nugget. I managed it, but only by imagining Charlton Heston's super-serious expression as he whispered, "Soylent Green is people," in that old movie Momma had made me watch. But—really, though? People disappear for public service and don't come back? That was far-fetched for anywhere, and especially so for the beautiful world I'd come to know as Kiirajanna.

"I see you do not believe me," Druzhtane accused, her face drawn down in the exact same expression Sephaline used when I'd accidentally insulted her once. Or, maybe twice. Or a few times, but who's counting?

"No, no," I said, schooling my face to be completely neutral. "I do. I do believe you. It's just that—does anybody know where the people disappear to?"

"If we did, would we say disappear? What a stupid question."

"It was, yes. I'm just trying to wrap my mind around it, since we don't have public service in—um, in Mississippi. How many people have you known to disappear?"

"Several." She crossed her arms defiantly, holding the still-open knife carefully away from the other bicep.

So, several. Not a specific number, but several. Of course.

My stomach growled, pointing out that it was well after noon, and I hadn't had anything to eat since breakfast. Now I was really regretting turning down the sandwiches on the tray. "I don't suppose zhopi have anywhere to eat lunch, do they?" I asked, attempting but failing to add a light-hearted lift to my voice.

She snorted. "No, princess. Another stupid question, but by now I am getting used to them."

"You keep calling me princess. Why do you do that?" I asked, wondering if I had somehow been recognized. There wasn't any way these elves in Fake New York City would know about me and the whole dragon queen thing, was there?

"You keep acting like a princess. Why do you do that?" she retorted, and then added, "Stupid."

"So where do you eat?"

"Wherever I can find. Look, there's a soup kitchen that's run by a zhopi named Gleb just a little ways from here. Sometimes he's got food for a fellow zhopi, and sometimes not. We don't dare go out to it during the day, but I'll take you there tonight, after dark. Okay? Just don't say or do anything stupid while you're there."

"Got it. Don't say or do anything stupid. So what do we do till dark?"

"We?" she glared harder.

"You. What do you usually do during the daytime?"

"Whatever the hell I want, stupid. You don't get this whole zhopi lifestyle, do you?" She glared again, but I noticed it was lacking the shielded distrust from before. I guessed I'd broken through.

"Hey, I'm new here, remember? What is there to do till dark?"

"All sorts of things. Just don't get caught loafing around by the *chelovekzmee*. Reason I hang out in here is because they never come in to the park."

"Okay, so what's a chelovekzmee?" Draignerthol had given me its equivalent to a great big clueless shrug.

"No, stupid. It's a *chelovekzmeya*. That's one pair. More of them are a chelovekzmee."

"I see. What language do you speak here, anyway?"

She looked at me incredulously. "The same one you're speaking, stupid."

"No, I mean, what's it called?" I tried to recover.

She shrugged. "New York, I suppose. It's just the language we speak. What language do you speak in Mississippi—Mississippi?"

She had a point, strange as it was. I nodded, unwilling to go into how it was English but we weren't in England. "Yeah, I suppose you could call it that. But I really need to know what these chelovekzmee are in order to avoid them."

"They're hard to avoid during the day, but as long as you look like you have somewhere to go they won't bother you. At nightfall they slither back inside—too cold for their cold-bloodedness, I guess. If you've walked the street any distance at all you've seen them already."

"The snake charmers?" I guessed on an impulse. They were the part of my Fake New York City experience that still didn't make any sense at all.

"Charmers?" she asked, her eyebrows shooting up. "No, I wouldn't call them that. The man isn't charming the snake. The snake is the one in charge of the pair. The guy is just there to use the radio if needed, to call for backup or pickup. Snakes don't have any fingers, you see," she demonstrated the last by holding her hands up and wiggling hers at me.

"I do see," I said. This Fake New York City place got stranger by the minute. "So once they find and pick up a vagabond, where do they take him?"

Druzhtane shrugged. "Public service, I guess. Who knows? Why do you care, stupid?"

"Curious," I said.

"Well, don't be. Curiosity killed the mouse, right?"

"Cat," I corrected.

"Cats always kill mice. We were talking about curiosity, stupid."

"Oh, right." I let it go. I wasn't planning on being in this version of New York for any more than the required six weeks, so there wasn't any point trying to figure out their idioms.

Druzhtane reached over to the side of her bench and picked up the long, thick stick I saw there earlier. As I watched, she twirled it around in her hand several times, then flipped it over, and then twirled it around once again looking from the other end. She flipped it over once again, twirled a couple of times, and then suddenly and decisively went at it with her little knife.

I sat and watched her whittle for a while. It was impressive; the little girl really knew how to carve. With every wood flake that flew away, the chunk of wood became more of an intricate piece of art.

As impressive as the carving was, though, it couldn't hold my attention for too long. I started looking around. I was okay for the time being, wrapped in a little blanket of warm air as I was, but Druzhtane had brought up the cold of nighttime already, and its rapid approach scared me a little. I wondered if Draignerthol could help fashion a cloak—but out of what? I started looking around, and soon I found a fairly large oval-shaped fallen leaf, and then another just about the same size, and then several more. I started collecting them.

Before long I had enough of them to lay them out and completely cover the ground in about a six foot square. I stepped back and imagined laying the shape over my shoulders, and in my mind's eye I saw that I had the shape wrong. I shuffled the leaves around till I had more of a half oval, its much longer side straight to go over my shoulders and the other part rounded so that it would reach nearly to the ground all around me when draped.

"Here goes," I muttered to myself as I channeled energy into Draignerthol. I felt the heat wash over the leaves, binding them all together while adding a little moisture to soften them. I let the magic go and carefully picked up one corner—success! The next leaf, and the next one after that, were all attached to each other.

"I wouldn't do that too much if I were you, stupid," Druzhtane's voice came from the bench. I looked over; the girl was still furiously shaving at her wooden art piece. Without lifting her head, she continued, "They come after people who use magic, is what I hear. Anybody but a g-man uses magic, you disappear in the night."

"Who's they?"

"How the hell should I know? I don't use magic."

"I bet you could."

She stiffened a little at that. "I'd stab you for saying that if my knife wasn't so busy, stupid."

I sighed and looked back at the cloak I'd made. It was true; the ability to sense magic generally meant that you could also use it. At least, that was my conclusion. The priests and priestesses wouldn't even hear talk of magic without washing mouths out to rid them of the evil word. On the other hand, people figured out they were rangers early on by their ability to sense the "earth energy" around them, which I was pretty certain was the exact same thing as magic. Seph could sense magic from an early age, and she had grown into a pretty powerful ranger. Druzhtane could sense magic pretty well, so I was willing to bet she could use it, too.

Still, I couldn't see any point upsetting the girl with the knife. Literally, no point.

Proudly, I slipped my new cloak up and over my shoulders, letting it hang down. The smell of mildew was strong, but the warmth was nice, and I figured the aroma would go away eventually. I held the ends out and twirled around once, and then twice.

And then the cloak fell apart.

I sighed as I watched the leaves flutter all around, each falling back to the ground at its own pace. The magic I'd used as a glue had been strong, but apparently not quite strong enough.

"Nice try," Druzhtane said, still not looking up from her whittling.

"Thank you." I sat down and wondered where I could get a real cloak from.

"You can get a real cloak from the trash cans, stupid," she said, still not looking up.

"How did you do that?"

"Do what?"

"Read my mind like that?"

She shook her head, looking up at me for the first time since she'd started carving, her face a mask of confusion. "Read your mind? Ha, I can't do that. Ha, ha. It was pretty obvious, though, that you want a cloak. Right?"

"Right," I said, feeling a little silly.

"Stupid."

"Thanks."

"Mm hmm. Now shut up so's I can finish this."

I sat, then, and watched the leaves that had just been part of my magnificent cloak flutter around the park path, each transported a few inches at a time by gentle gusts of cold winter wind. While I watched, I wondered who it was that hunted magic users down, and where they took the magic users once they caught them. Then I wondered if that part were even true; it sounded like such a fairy tale kind of thing.

Then it occurred to me to be grossed out by what she'd said about where to get a real cloak from. The trash cans? Who does that? I shivered as the image of me diving head-first into an icky, smelly dumpster crossed my mind.

Just then Druzhtane said, "Ha!" and held up the project she'd just carved.

I took it from her, holding it carefully. It was quite good. She'd managed the old trick of carving something inside something else, and had done it much faster than I'd ever thought it could be done.

It was good, but it was disturbing. I've seen little balls inside of tubes, and roses inside of globes, but this—this wasn't so nice.

Druzhtane had carved a pretty fair representation of me, stuck inside a closed cage.

"Thank you," was all I could think of to say.

"Don't mention it, stupid."

"What's going on?" I asked, alarmed at the sudden increase in noise level I heard. I looked around and, through the trees and bushes, saw the same sort of mob of people marching in both directions along the roads that I'd seen that morning.

The question earned me another snort from Druzhtane. "Don't people have jobs in Mississippi?"

"Sure, they do. What does that have to do with thousands of people going this way and that on the street?"

"How do people get to their jobs in Mississippi? Does everybody teleport?"

"No, they drive. Most of them, anyway. Some ride the bus, I guess."

"They drive? Drive what?"

"They drive a...." Try as I might, I couldn't figure out an easy way to describe a vehicle. I didn't know if she'd ever even seen a horse, much less a carriage. "In Mississippi they have these things called vehicles, and everybody has one. It's large, about this big, and has four wheels—round things, that roll the vehicle along."

"Magic."

"Yeah, sure. You can call it that."

"So everyone gets their own vehicle? Just for one person's transportation? That's terribly inefficient."

"They're a lot more spread out in Mississippi," I tried to help her understand.

"Spread out? What do you mean by that?"

"Well, on a block about that size," I pointed to the block across the street just as an example, "you might only have six or eight families living. Not hundreds."

"You must have a lot of vacant buildings."

"Not really. They're just not as big."

"Not as big? You live in small buildings and you drive yourself to work? That is stupid."

I shrugged. "That is Mississippi."

"Mississippi is stupid."

I took a breath to defend my home state's honor, and then realized that nobody back home in Mississippi would even know, much less care, what an elf in Fake New York City thought of their intelligence. Instead, I just shrugged and said, "It is our way."

She met my comment with a cynical harrumph.

"So why aren't we hiding? Won't somebody look in and see us and wonder what we're doing here?"

"No. For one thing, the officials don't let anyone slow down enough to look side to side. For another, nobody ever comes in here except for us zhopi."

"Nobody? But it's so big, so well constructed. Why was it made in the first place? Surely not just for zhopi."

"How should I know?"

"I thought, as smart as you are, you might know some of the history of the place."

"Well, I don't. I can't know everything now, can I, stupid?"

"Guess not," I said, losing interest in the topic as I watched the crowds in the street thin in the dim twilight. Night fell quickly in between the skyscrapers.

"Now I'm hungry," was all she said as she jumped off of the bench and bounced away into the newly-dark streets of Fake New York City, leaving me to follow as quickly as I could.

The Soup Kitchen

"Wait," Druzhtane said, stopping me as we neared the gate and holding me back from exiting the park. "You look too clean. We have to dirty you up."

Dirty me up she did, ratting my hair out with her fingers and then spreading dirt vigorously on my face and clothes. I shook it out as much as possible, but the grime that remained was fairly well ground in.

"How do I look?"

"Terrible, but that's what you want. You still smell too good, but we'll have to go with it. Gleb is a careful man, and he could easily lose his place, and possibly even his life, if anybody found out he was feeding us zhopi. You may have to convince him you're for real no matter how much dirt you wear in, but at least the smears make you look less like a princess."

"How many princesses have you ever seen wearing dirty shirt and trousers?"

"You mean actual princesses? I've never seen any at all. But if I did see one, and she was wearing dirty shirt and trousers, she'd look just like you, I bet."

One of these days, I figured that I'd have to tell her the truth about the princess thing. Not this day, though.

I followed her out of the park into the dimly-lit sidewalks. The streets had taken on a completely different atmosphere from what I'd stepped out into that morning. Not that anybody smiled, or said hi, or even looked our way—it was, after all, the city, and nothing at all like Mississippi. But I didn't see any more snakes, at least. Also, the hustle of the morning was missing. People walked slower, and as they did they looked side to side into the shops and restaurants that lined this part of the avenue.

I did, too. I hadn't eaten since very early that morning, and there was a steakhouse along the way that smelled divine. I stopped by the big plate window and looked in, wishing I had a portion of the tiniest speck of the crown's wealth on me. As I watched, a portly gentleman by the window sliced a thin strip from the inch-thick steak on his plate and popped the pink, juicy meat into his mouth. My stomach actually fluttered.

A hand yanked me from the window. "C'mon, stupid," Druzhtane's voice whispered savagely. "If you stop and loiter, they'll call the coppers, and you'll be hauled away for sure. You, and me both."

"Coppers?" I asked as I let her drag me down the sidewalk. I hadn't heard them called that except in the *really* old movies. She'd used a different word in her language, of course, but apparently all Draignerthol could come up with was coppers.

"What do you call the police in Mississippi, then?"

"Cops. Officers. Police. There are other, more derogatory, terms, but I never use them. I just haven't heard coppers used in a long time."

"Oh, well, that's the regular term here. Now, can you start walking on your own, stupid? We look suspicious, you hanging onto me like this."

"Sure," I said, and shook my arm out of her grasp. She'd been the one dragging me, so the suspicious look was pretty much her fault, but she was taking me to a place where we'd both get something to eat. I didn't feel like arguing with her over minor stuff with food on the line.

It was a long walk. We crossed probably twenty streets on Lexington. As hard as I tried to keep track, though, I lost count. I'd like to blame it on the hunger, but the simple fact is that it was all too new to me, so I kept getting distracted.

We turned right and went a few blocks that way, only the blocks going that direction were about twice as long as the ones we'd been walking.

"Aren't city blocks supposed to be square?" I asked Druzhtane.

"Why would they be square?"

"I—I don't know. I always just figured that—oh, never mind." I'd seen the same thing in Real New York City, and shouldn't have been surprised at the copy here, but it was still pretty weird.

"Stupid," I heard her say under her breath.

We turned up the darkest street yet. Scary-looking people lounged around everywhere, but that didn't seem to bother Druzhtane, who just kept walking right by. They all ignored her, too. Just her; I felt their eyes following me down the block as we strode past. Before long I started to wonder if Druzhtane's princess jabs had any merit.

Suddenly Druzhtane opened and ducked through a small black metal door. I followed her in and up a dimly-lit metal stairway, the walls of which had graffiti layered on top of other graffiti. As we neared the top I could smell food, and that made my stomach twist around itself even though it wasn't anywhere near as sinfully succulent as the aroma that had emanated from the steakhouse.

Druzhtane stepped right past the burly guard at the door, but he moved quickly so that I couldn't follow. I started to squeak in surprise to get her attention, but luckily I didn't have to do much. She stopped, turned halfway around, glared, and stated, "She's with me."

He glared over crossed muscular arms for one, then two, and then a third heartbeat. Finally he shrugged and moved out of the way.

I tried to ignore the odor as we walked across the unevenly carpeted floor. I could still smell the food, and that hit my ravenous senses hard, but now that we were in what served as a precarious dining room I could also smell the sweat and caked-on-clothes aromatic of my fellow diners as well as a sordid helping of musty and moldy carpet. If I hadn't felt like my belly button was about to touch my spine I would have turned right around and left, but by the time I was fully into the room, the setup at the far side drew me like a tractor beam.

I accidentally bumped into a table on my way across, and the guy sitting at it actually growled at me, glaring up while he moved both arms to protect the meager piles of whatever he was eating from the cafeteria-like tray in front of him. He had the look of a starving hound protecting a bowl of kibbles.

"Sorry," I mumbled as we moved on down the room. It was a long, narrow strip; where we'd entered seemed about a third of the way back. The whole thing was only about twenty or twenty-five feet wide, at most, but it was probably seventy or eighty feet long, and the little square tables were crammed into this tiny space as tightly as they could be.

At the far end stood a man behind a serving bar. As we wound our way through the tables the picture resolved itself, and I cringed. It was a school lunchroom scene gone horribly wrong, with the glass separating the food from the diners greased over with smudges and drips. The food was set out in large unlabeled metal trays, and to the left rose a stack of cafeteria platters that might have been clean, or might not have; I couldn't really tell in the dim light. The food I wasn't sure about; the tray that gave me the most confidence looked like it was probably mashed potatoes. The second sure looked like mac and cheese, and I pinned my hopes on that guess being correct. Some sort of tomato stuff that had large chunks of ground meat in it rounded out the trio. At the far end was a table with a little stack of plastic tumblers, a few empty pitchers, and a spigot for water. A few dirty bins bearing some basic silverware leaned against the wall next to the spigot.

"Please let that be beef," I prayed as softly as I could to whoever might be up there listening. I didn't want to think what other type of meat might be in the red sauce.

Despite what my eyes and nose were saying about the generally disgusting state of the kitchen, my stomach was commanding me forward. I was starving, and smelling the meat sauce made the empty spot inside seem bigger.

"Heya, Dru, welcome back to You Slice 'Em, We Dice 'Em Restaurant," the jovial man behind the food said. He wiped his hand across his sweaty brow, pushing strands of dark curly hair out of his eyes, and then wiped both bare hands on a grease-stained apron. Smiling, he picked up a tray and asked, "Who's your friend there?"

She stepped up to the center of the counter, and I moved to stand at her left. "Friend's a stretch," she said. "We met today in the park, and she said she's hungry. Alyssa, meet Gleb. Gleb, Alyssa. Now my part's done, how about some of that yummy stuff going on a tray for me, Gleb?"

"Absolutely, sweetheart" he said, his hands moving on their own to fill up a tray. His eyes didn't leave my face. "Where'd you say you're from, Alyssa?"

I'd learned enough to tell the truth unless it was an obviously bad thing to do. Druzhtane explained on the way here, as we were walking, that we were headed uptown for the food, and so I had asked her, innocently enough, where downtown was. It was, she'd explained with only a couple of stupids thrown in, where we'd spent the whole day.

That had explained the women's reaction when I'd said I had moved there from downtown.

"I'm from Mississippi," I said, grateful for Draignerthol's help in translating. "Just got here today. I've been...."

"Out!" exploded from Gleb's mouth. His eyes grew huge as he looked at my chest where the pendant was, and his eyebrows went nearly to the top of his head. "Both of you, out! How dare you bring one of her kind into this establishment, Dru? How *dare* you?"

"What? I don't..." I started to argue, but a strong hand clapped me on the shoulder and started hauling me back. At the same time, Druzhtane ducked a hurled spoonful of mashed potatoes and turned to flee, herself.

"Out! Out!" Gleb's voice shrieked in rage as we sprinted back through the tables. Well, Druzhtane was sprinting; I was being hauled by my clavicle. She got there just before the bouncer did, and she stepped out and onto the stairs just far enough to catch me as I was launched outward

Druzhtane stood there for several minutes giving the now-shut door a solid piece of her mind, sending gestures as well as a string of epithets that Draignerthol didn't stand a chance with. Finally she wound down, gave me a glare that could have killed me if such things were possible, and marched down the stairs like a princess, albeit a dirty, smelly one.

"What the hell was that about?" I asked as I followed her.

She was silent all the way down the stairs, out of the building, and down and around the block. Finally she stepped into another, narrower, alley, grabbed me by the fabric on my chest, and shoved me roughly against the wall. Her other hand formed a pointer that was jabbed repeatedly into my face, a fact that was actually welcome considering that I knew she had a knife in her pocket. It was a small knife, granted, but I doubted I'd get the most basic of medical care in a place where I couldn't even get a plate of disgusting food.

"You just cost me my entry to the only food kitchen in the city, do you realize that?" she said, her voice quiet, intense, and very angry. "I've been eating there for years, and you—you!—just got me thrown out. And that, after I spent the day helping you out. What the hell are you up to?"

She ranted for several more minutes, all under her breath, and much of it unintelligible. I let her go at it, since I figured any sort of comment from me was as likely to escalate her anger to using the knife as it was to defuse anything.

When she finally ran out of steam, I held both hands in the air. "Please, put me down?" She did, and I continued, "I'm sorry, Druzhtane. I'm really, really sorry. You know I had no intention of doing that, had no way of knowing it was going to happen, right? Please tell me you know that. I'm probably every bit as hungry as you are."

She snorted, and I continued, "You know, I don't even know why we got kicked out. Call me stupid if you want, but please explain that reaction Gleb had. I've never had anybody jump at me like that."

"Your pendant, princess," she said. "It flashes a little when it's working. I could see it, but it didn't matter much to me since I've seen worse without the g-men showing up. Gleb, though, could lose his entire operation if the g-men raided him, and when he saw your pendant flashing with magic I'm sure he immediately imagined them following it to converge on his place. You were a clear and present danger to his little diner, Alyssa."

"Oh. I wish somebody had said something. I could've taken it off."

"Yeah, but then you'd'a just sounded stupider."

"Stupider isn't—never mind," I said. In the middle of a crisis was no time to correct the knife girl's grammar, right? "You do realize that the fact that he could see my pendant flashing means he's a magic user, too, right? Just like it means the same about you?"

"Nobody said we could or couldn't use magic, princess. We just can't get caught using it. Ponimayete?"

I nodded. Draignerthol couldn't quite translate the last word, but it sounded the same as when Italians on TV ask if you "*cappeesh?*" And I did. Cappeesh, that is. I cappeeshed that the elves here were the exact opposite of their cousins on the opposite side of the world. To Dad, it was a matter of honor that he did whatever was the right thing to do, whether anyone else saw him or not. To these folks, whatever they did was fine as long as they didn't get caught.

Might as well change the subject back to the hunger at hand, though. "So, okay, you didn't starve when you first became a zho-pi, obviously. And I can tell from what you've said that you haven't been going to Gleb's kitchen for long. So how did you eat before that?"

"I don't have the energy tonight," she said, and her comment made me suspicious. "Oh, give it a rest, okay? Neither of us will starve before tomorrow night, so we'll rest tonight, and tomorrow I'll show you how to do just that, and closer to the park to boot. Now, how 'bout we get back there before somebody else decides my bench is a good place to rest."

It wasn't a question. I followed her at a rapid walk back to Lexington and then back toward downtown. I looked all around at the towering buildings and wondered why one area with huge skyscrapers would be called uptown and the other downtown, when they both looked the same. I asked, and Druzhtane just shrugged and said, "It's because uptown is upwards of downtown. North, you know."

That just confused me more. What did uptown have to do with north when you were surrounded as we were with concrete and steel and rudeness?

I followed her the rest of the way back to the park in silence, the empty hole in my stomach growing into a pit, and then a canyon. I hadn't ever gone truly hungry before; Momma wouldn't have allowed it under any circumstances. Tonight would, then, be a first in that way.

It was a heckuva way to start a hunhymgais.

SARFF

Serpent or wyrm. Not the same as neidr, or snake.

A Familiar Symbol

Druzhtane, despite her anger at me for getting her booted from the soup kitchen, was an absolute blessing to me that first night. When we finally got back to the park, I felt like the breath that was whipping in and out of my mouth was the only thing keeping the sweat droplets from freezing on the tip of my nose. For that matter, I could see my breath pretty clearly in the moonlight, and I was fairly certain that wasn't ever a good thing when sleeping outside was in store.

By that point I was terrified to use Draignerthol. I didn't even talk much for fear of drawing attention to the flashing blue light on my chest. There was no way I was going to risk costing Druzhtane her sleeping spot in addition to her dining room by channeling some heat in the darkness.

Luckily, my new friend took pity on my shivering bones. She hauled a backpack out from its hiding spot in the bushes and produced a fairly ragged blanket for her own bed on the park bench. She tossed an even more ragged long overcoat at me as I stood there freezing. "Here, stupid," she said. "Cover up a spot with leaves, lay down on the leaves, and cover yourself with the coat. It might not be the most comfortable sleep you've ever had in your fluffy bed in your palace, princess, but it'll keep you alive till morning."

"Wouldn't the ground be easier to sleep on without the leaves, with less rustling underneath me?"

"Yeah, it would, till you wake up in the morning dead, stupid. The ground is cold, and it'll pull all the heat out of your body overnight."

Oh. I hadn't done much camping before; even on the three-day ride through the woods to and from the library we'd slept in cabins and, later, on cots in the king's fancy tent. I'd never done anything that could be remotely called roughing it. To be honest, then, I was kind of stupid when it came to spending a winter night in a city park.

"I don't suppose we can start a campfire, can we?" I asked, and got the glare I expected would be coming.

"You want the coppers to haul you off tonight?"

"Nope, nope," I said. "I'll be just fine right here in this wonderful overcoat you've given me."

I wasn't, but that wasn't her fault. At first, I kept envisioning the huge black snakes I'd seen that day entering the park to find my body laying on the ground, a ready-made snack. By the time I got that thought banished, my temperature had regulated enough that I had become uncomfortably chilly. It didn't help that just as I was settling in, Druzhtane whispered a special warning. "Oh, and make sure you sleep with one eye open!"

"Yeah, thank you very much, bless your kind little heart," I would have whispered back if I'd had the energy.

I finally got wrapped in tightly enough to support the illusion that I was warm enough to sleep, but then my stomach knocked up against that illusion. It reminded me rather forcefully that it was still empty, and that I'd never asked it to rest for the evening without a filling first. I was sure that its unhappy rumbles were plenty loud enough to get us caught.

Regardless of the cold, and the hunger, and the fear, I still fell asleep sometime during the night. I know this because I came to all in a start, all by myself, an old ragged gray overcoat still wrapped tightly around me, an empty park bench nearby.

"Druzhtane?" I called out softly, unwilling to raise my voice too much. No answer. I poked the bush from which she'd pulled her hidden backpack the day before, and then carefully leaned closer and peered in between the branches to see nothing.

With a long, drawn-out sigh I sat down on Druzhtane's bench. At least, I hoped it was still Druzhtane's bench. It was weird how much I hoped that. She wasn't much of a friend, granted, but she was the only person nearby who even came close. Honestly, I couldn't blame her if she decided to up and walk away from me after I'd gotten her kicked out of the soup kitchen. I figured that this Gleb person might even allow her back in if she promised that she'd left me for dead somewhere.

I sat for quite some time, hoping to see her smiling face bobbing back down the park path toward me. I didn't. Eventually, though, my belly button rattling up against my backbone, I realized I had to do something. With the danger I posed she probably wasn't coming back, and I still needed to find something to eat to keep my hunhymgais from becoming a much shorter, deadlier experience than normal.

I circled the park slowly, hoping to find something that looked edible. Seph had made sure I knew a couple of dozen Kiirajannan plants I could eat, but none of them apparently grew in Fake New York City. There were plenty of trees, but they'd all lost any sign of leaves or nuts long before I arrived. The evergreen bushes didn't look appetizing at all. There weren't even any of the more common tiny broad-leaf psyllium, nor even dandelion. I reached the bench again and shook my head; these Fake New

York City elves had managed to plant an entire park in vegetation that was completely useless.

But—it wasn't entirely useless, I realized. Stepping over to one of the denuded trees, I put my hands on its rough bark and reached out for the same arboreal world I'd found before, and found....

Nothing. I found absolutely nothing. The tree wasn't even really there, inside. It was just a tall mass of wood, dead in all ways but the most basic biological sense. I even tried singing, softly, raising my little happy sing-song in pitch to pull out the most stubborn of creatures from wherever they might be hiding.

Nothing.

I gave up and circled the park again, looking at the ways out. There were only entrances, and the one opposite the one I'd come in through was still gated and securely locked with a padlock that had seen better days but still looked pretty solid. I still tested it with a tug, and it proved as solid as it looked. One way in and out, then—fine.

I crossed the park and stepped out of it onto the barren concrete sidewalk.

It was silent. Apparently I'd slept through the morning rush hour in spite of all the noise, and most likely, given the placement of the sun that was glimmering through the clouds, I'd missed whatever noon rush hour they had, too. I slunk across the deserted street and went off to the right, walking down the long block beside the park.

When I reached the end I almost turned away from the park, but at the last second I saw a snake charmer down the way, and so I crossed the street to avoid him on the other side. I'd noticed restaurant signs farther down the road, and so I turned down the alley to walk behind them. Who knew what they might put out in their afternoon trash, right? I'd never eaten out of the trash before, but the other option wasn't feeling too great.

I glanced in the trash cans as I went by—nothing. I mean, actually, literally, nothing. The cans were empty. Obviously they were emptied earlier in the day. That plan crushed, I wrapped the cloak Dru gave me more tightly around my shoulders and hurried down the alley to the next block.

I turned the corner, hoping to head away from the park to find somewhere with a welcoming trash can, and walked right into a cop.

"Excuse me, officer, I didn't see you," I said in my friendliest attempt with their rough-sounding language, hoping that Draig-nerthol would make it sound convincing. Convincing, and unimportant. Convincing, unimportant, and very, very uninteresting.

Uninteresting to the point of being invisible, in fact, or so I hoped.

It wasn't. He stared right at my face, his eyebrows pulled down in concentration. I couldn't think of any way the dirt would have done anything but multiplied in my sleep, and in my head I prayed that he dismissed me as just another dirty, bedraggled youth.

I started to walk past, but his hand grabbed my upper arm in a strong grip. His calculating gaze swept up and down my body a few times. It was creepy, how his expression morphed more and more into one of recognition.

Finally, he spoke. "Well, Princess, how good it is to meet you. We've been searching the city, quite literally high and low, looking for you."

I started to relax. The guy spoke the word princess as though it deserved a capital P, and so he obviously recognized me. Even here, across the world from the castle and the abbey as I was, it was good to be recognized. Besides, Dad didn't say I couldn't accept any help at all. He just told me I couldn't come home for six weeks.

The words of the cop melded with all my swelling relief as he said, "Come with me, Princess, and we'll get you washed up and fed a good meal. Look at you, wearing such a ragged coat out here in the cold. You'll be wearing the finest furs this evening, I say you will!"

Maybe my hunhymgais wasn't to be spent in cold, tired hunger, after all.

Maybe my challenge was to be a political one, something that would test my wit and my leadership ability rather than my stomach.

Maybe....

I quit my useless musing and relaxed enough to look up unguardedly at his chest. Then, I saw it. This cop was wearing the same N.Y.P.D. badge the other ones had, but just above it, centered, was a small silver dragon pin.

I'd seen that dragon pin before, back in the Library of Alecsanddrha. And then again, at the battle of Ganolog.

It was the insignia of the Cult of the Wyrm. The folks who'd tried to poison me, and then failing that, to kill me and my friends. And failing that, they'd tried to take over an entire elf clan.

Yeah, those guys.

The Bad Guys.

"No! I'm not going with you!" I said forcefully. Well, the words weren't all that forceful, but the magic I pulled up and out of Draignerthol was. The cop's body flew several dozen feet, smashing satisfactorily into the plate glass window of a cupcake shop and shattering it. I watched, horrified, as a few long, jagged slivers of glass fell from the top of the window frame down, down, down, eventually connecting with the cop's gut that lay open as his body draped across the bottom of the frame, his legs laying outside and his torso dangling into the shop. The glass shards plunged in, slicing through flesh and organ, cutting him nearly in two and ending his life as he screamed a high-pitched trill.

I covered my face to avoid looking at the man I'd just killed. It was sickening, for one thing, and I wasn't cut out to be a killer, for another. Suddenly my better sense won out, and I uncovered my eyes enough to look up the street. Sure enough, the semi truck tire a few blocks up had resolved itself into a single black snake that slithered my way.

I turned and ran.

Somehow I found myself back at the wrought iron fence that surrounded the park. Quickly I glanced around; I didn't see any snakes, or charmers, or coppers either, for that matter. I took off toward it at a sprint, hoping to vault the fence with Draigner-thol's help. As I drew close I pulled energy to me and then pressed air underneath my steps and rejoiced as my feet left the surface just as I'd hoped. With the fence just ahead, I gave the energy a final light pump.

I managed to catapult myself several dozen feet into the park, flying past Dru's bench and flapping to a stop on the path, just barely staying on my feet.

Laying down, I crawled back to the edge of the bushes. I could hear shouts all around outside the park, and from where I lay I could see both snakes and cops milling about the street, all searching for something.

I had no doubt; they were searching for me.

I lay there in complete silence for several hours, willing everybody to just leave and let me be.

Finally, they did. Once I'd counted to a thousand without hearing or seeing somebody in black outside the fence, I sat up for a better view.

"Wow, princess, you sure do know how to make headlines," a familiar voice said behind me.

Overjoyed, I spun around and jumped toward Dru, grasping at an opportunity to hug her. She had another idea, though, one that she made obvious by baring her knife blade as I came close.

"Get away from me," she said.

"Look, I just—"

"Yeah, I know. You just got me kicked out of the only food kitchen in the city, and now just nearly got my park invaded by the coppers for the first time in years. That would've just gotten me sent to public service. I know what you *just*."

"I'm sorry!"

"Your sorry won't do me a lot of good in the company of the g-men."

"Please. Forgive me. I honestly don't know my way around, don't know anything about how to keep from getting caught. Don't even know where my next meal will come from. Help me, please. I promise, I'll be gone soon enough. For now, though, I need you. Please?"

"Well...." She eyed me up and down in the pretense of weighing my words, but I could tell I'd hit her in her soft spot. After one more quiet "please?" from me, she relented. "Okay, but no more stupid tricks. You ask me before you do anything, okay?"

"Okay."

"You better. You really better. You won't like public service any more than I would."

I felt the hairs on the back of my neck stand up from the way she said public service. I could tell from her tone that she was truly frightened of it to the bottom of her heart. Which was probably every bit as frightened as I was of the Cult of the Wyrm, I realized, and then wondered what the connection between the two could be.

"Now, get down low before somebody sees you," Dru spat, moving over to sit on her bench. I followed, feeling completely lost.

"Who *are* you?" she asked, looking at me with another of those elf whole-face expressions, this one of scrunched-up curiosity.

"I—I really can't tell you," I said. I didn't know that for sure, but it felt like telling somebody about the hunhymgais would negate the experience.

"You're not really from this Missikippi place, are you?"

"It's Mississippi," I corrected, thinking fondly of Seph who constantly made the same mistake. "Yes, I am. Really, I am. I've come here to do something, though I have no idea what that something is, if you can believe that. But that's all I can tell you, honest, and mostly because there's just so much that I don't know, myself."

"Hmmph," she grunted. "You're still stupid. Completely stupid. Totally. But I guess you're zhopi now, anyway. Very few of us have escaped the clutch of the public service recruiters, even in the unconventional way you did it, and so welcome to an elite sisterhood, Princess Idontknowwhoyouare."

"Alyssa. Look, my name really is Alyssa. Nothing I've told you has been a lie," I said, and then quickly scanned back over my memories of what I'd told her to make sure my statement itself was truthful. I felt better when everything checked out as far as I could recall.

"Okay, fine, then. Princess Alyssa it is. Want some food, Your Royal Majesty?"

As much as I wanted to ask her to drop the embarrassing princess title, the last part caught my attention and held it tight.

"Food? Goodness, yes. You have food?" I couldn't help it; when she mentioned the word my stomach had decided to remind me that it was, in fact, completely empty, and had been so for far too many hours.

She grinned and held out a package wrapped in paper. I snatched it out of her hands, more eager than I'd wanted to appear. For all I knew she was messing with me, and it was a messing with that I probably deserved after getting her kicked out of Gleb's place. Carefully, I pulled the edges of wrapping paper away and was rewarded with the sight of the first loaf of bread I'd seen in a couple of days.

Letting the paper fall, I turned the round loaf over and over, looking at it. I couldn't believe I was holding a fresh loaf of bread. My mouth started watering.

Druzhtane darted around me and caught the paper I'd dropped.

"You gotta keep the paper to wrap the next food in," she scolded as she returned to her bench. "Walking through the city carrying food out in the open is a quick way to get yourself taken in by the coppers. And please, Princess Alyssa, do go ahead and dig in. I have my own loaf." She demonstrated the fact by unwrapping the twin to the bread I held in my hands, pulling off a hunk, and popping it into her mouth. I quickly followed suit and was rewarded with the flavor of an aromatic, if somewhat stale, French roll.

"Good, innit?" Dru said around her own mouthful of bread.

"Mm hmm." I agreed.

"Bakery down the road throws away the old stuff early in the afternoon. I think the owner likes me; he always seems to have a loaf or two for me to pilfer. Sometimes I even get a meat pie or a ham croissant."

"Mmm" was all I could really say around the huge bite of bread I was chewing. But it was enough.

Benefits of Working

You could say that the next several days passed by uneventfully, if by uneventfully you mean sitting, confined, in a half-block deserted park in the middle of a strange city with a strange zhopi going out every midday to get us some discarded food to eat. After I told her about the ordeal with the cop wearing a Cult pin, minus the recognition part, Druzhtane had explained a little of how it worked from her perspective.

"That pin? Yeah, that's the insignia of the public service 're-cruiters.' It's a special group of the police department. They'll probably give up the hunt for you eventually, though. At least, they'll give it up here locally after they decide that you've moved on to a different area of the city."

"How long will that take?"

She shrugged. "Six weeks. Maybe eight."

"Oh. Great."

"Why? You got somewhere to be?"

"Can't tell you that, remember? But hey," I said, struck by inspiration, "if in, say, six or eight weeks or so, I were to leave— go back to my own place, where there are trees and forests and plenty of fresh food, and not anywhere near as many people, and none of those snakes or cops—"

"Missikippi?" she interrupted.

"Yeah, Mississippi," I lied, sort of. "If I were able to take you back there, would you want to go with me?"

"There's no city?"

I shook my head.

"No crowds?"

I shook my head again.

"Just trees and grass and dirt in an endless park like this?"

I nodded.

"So what's the point?"

"Well, it's…." I gathered my breath to tell her all about the joy I'd always found walking through parks, and was now learning to love in the well-kept woods of Kiirajanna that surrounded the most incredible castle in the realm, and then realized it would be like speaking another language to somebody who'd spent her whole life in a city. "It's, um, calm."

"Boring, in other words."

"Yeah, it probably would be to you."

Once Dru came back with a little plastic pouch in addition to the cheese and bread she claimed to have "found." I had stopped asking her where she was finding the food, mostly because she usually refused to answer, and when she did it just grossed me out. The gist, though, was that it was incredible how much food the restaurants in the area threw out because it got old before it got eaten. Plus, over the years she'd gotten in with a few of the workers, some better than others, and they would save her the choicest pieces instead of throwing them away.

The trash was feeding us pretty well, as long as I didn't stop to think how she acquired it.

"What's in the pouch?" I asked as we launched into our food.

"*Anasha*," she said, opening the little pouch and pulling its contents, two cigarettes, out. She smelled one and smiled a very contented smile, and then she waved it under my nose too.

"Pot."

"Pot?" Dru screwed up her face in a disgusted expression. No wonder; Draignerthol's effort at translating my English term was "sweat."

"That's what we call it in Mississippi. Pot, weed, Mary Jane, all words for the drug."

"You call it Mary Jane?"

"Yeah. Well, I don't, but some do. Don't ask; I don't know why. Did you get that from the great big green vending machines I've seen on the streets?" I remembered seeing a guy walk up to the machine and drop in a token, retrieving as a reward a little pouch just like what Dru had.

"Uh huh. They're spread across the city, every other block. More highly guarded than the banks, they are."

"You've gotta be pretty special to get a token, then, probably?"

"If you don't work, yes. You don't have them in Missikippi?"

I ignored her mispronunciation. "Oh, heavens no. Our kids have to buy their weed in shady back alleys."

"That's kind of primitive, isn't it?"

"I—I—" It left me speechless. I've heard Mississippi called primitive for all sorts of reasons, especially since coming to Kiirajanna, but not for its lack of cannabis vending machines. Finally, I managed, "I guess I never thought about it that way. So how did you get a token?"

"I told you, some of the guys have taken a bit of a fancy to me. One in particular doesn't always use his allotment, and when I give him something more interesting than his wife, he'll slip me a token or two."

"You—sell—?" I started to ask, horrified at the morality of what I was hearing.

She shook her head adamantly. "I sell *nothing.* We trade favors—little ones—kisses and, you know—for each other every so often, but that *doesn't* make me a *blyadth*," she said, her tone rising. My own face colored. Draignerthol obediently translated the word she'd used, but the translation left me with something I'd never repeat.

"I'm so sorry, Druzhtane. I didn't mean to suggest that. I was just surprised."

"Good. Don't do it again."

"What did you mean by his allotment, though?"

"I meant exactly that. Every worker receives twelve tokens with his pay at the end of every other week. How many tokens do you receive in Missikippi?"

"You get pot as a benefit for working?" I couldn't believe my ears.

"No, I don't, stupid. Everybody who works does, though."

"I don't believe it."

"You calling me a liar?"

"No!" I said, waving my hands to placate her. "I'm just having a hard time believing that society would be okay with everybody receiving a daily allotment of marijuana."

"Not everybody," she said and sighed, exasperated. "Just everybody who works."

"Oh. Well, that's better."

"Is it?" she asked, looking confused.

"No, not really. I just really don't get it. Why would they make sure everybody has pot to smoke?"

"I don't know, princess. And there's a second verse. I don't care, okay? Now, do you want this other one, or would you rather sit there asking stupid questions?"

I shook my head. I'd never been into drugs before, not at all. Granted, my dad had introduced me to some hard-core drinking, and I'd made a bit of a lush out of myself a time or two, but that wasn't something I wanted to continue doing long-term. It just didn't do much besides making me hurt the next day. I didn't want to know what a steady diet of cannabis might do even if it were pure, and who knows what was in the vending machine stuff?

"Suit yourself," she said as she settled into her bench and lit one of the cigarettes with a match from the pouch. With a long sucking sound she inhaled the smoke deep into her lungs, and then she leaned her head back and exhaled luxuriously.

"Sure is good," she said, her voice taking on the dreamy quality that I've always heard in movies and assumed was fake. "You sure you don't want a hit?"

"I'm sure," I said, and I was telling the absolute truth. I watched her smoke the entire first cigarette, and then the next one, as the sun disappeared behind the buildings. Toward the end all I could see was the red tip on the burning end as it bobbed up to her mouth and back down.

I thought I felt a little bit of a contact high, laying there in the darkness. I confirmed it by looking up at the lights on the surrounding high rise buildings that now seemed to be coming toward me slowly, through tunnels.

"Mmm, feels so—" she said as the little red dot winked out. "Mmm. Only problem is that now I'm hungry. That will pass, though. I love the way the lights on the buildings around us twinkle in the crisp winter air, don't you? They look...." She prattled on for several hours on a steady stream of topics that meant absolutely nothing.

Eventually I was tired enough to tune her out and go to sleep.

The next day dawned clear and especially cold. I woke with the ratty overcoat wrapped tightly around my neck and my feet feeling like great big ice cubes. I managed to unravel the cloak from around me and got up silently, pacing back and forth to get some feeling in them. Meanwhile, Druzhtane snored away on her bench. It was amusing to watch, since she had always been up and alert before me.

Then again, I realized, today was Sadoorn. That's Saturday, in the elf language, though I don't know what they call it in Fake New York City. They do, however, follow the six day calendar of the elves. Not as closely as we did back at the castle; the hustle and bustle that was already going proved they didn't follow our prohibition against working on the one weekend day. In fact, as I'd seen the Sadoorn previously, a lot of businesses remained open all week long. Even the snakes and the cops worked all day.

The week prior, I'd left the park for a walk, assuming incorrectly that the rule about working on Saturday applied and included the coppers and the snakes. Dru had yelled at me for doing it, of course. I tried to explain what I was used to, "back in Mississippi," but she seemed convinced that I was doing everything I could to get both of us taken in for public service.

I wasn't, but I didn't risk it again.

Instead, I launched into a brisk walk around the long oval path in the park. My legs needed the warmth, and it felt good to stretch them out a little even on a short track.

I drew up short as I came around toward the front area where I could see the gate; a zhopi friend of Druzhtane's stood just outside, talking quietly with a couple of cops. I'd met him before; his name was—Hektor, I think. Dru brought him in to meet me one night a few days prior. She'd explained something about him hearing of my expulsion from Gleb's kitchen and wanting to see the girl who'd upset the mighty Gleb. He'd even traded some actual meat and potatoes that made a great meal for the two of us. It had been an unmemorable meeting, other than the aromas. The food smelled great, but Hektor didn't. It wasn't just body odor; his very being seemed oily and disgusting. When he smiled, what looked like oil dripped from his teeth. Luckily that night he'd gone away quickly enough, and he hadn't been back since.

Now, though, Mister Oily-teeth stood at the gate to the park and gestured grandly in, obviously letting the cops in on something very important.

I raced back to Dru's bench. "Dru! Dru!" I shook her as violently as possible. It only took one shake; she wasn't as befuddled as her snores made her out to be. I barely managed to leap away out of slashing range as she came to with her little knife in hand, eyes quickly focusing on me.

"What? The world better be ending, Alyssa. You just woke me up from the best food dream I've ever—"

"Shut up, Dru. Quick, we need to run. The cops are at the gate with Hektor, and they look very interested in exploring the park."

Dru shot to her feet, her blanket falling into a heap. Her eyes darted to both sides as she quickly got control of herself. "Follow me," she murmured and set off at a low sprint, her entire body held below the bush line, down the pathway toward the back of the central circle.

She reached the edge of the bushes and peered around. Her groan confirmed what I could already hear in the stomping of boots that direction. We looked back the way we'd come to see a squad of half a dozen cops and a snake already at the bench and moving our direction. From the rear of the park marched another half dozen cops and a snake. They'd come in fast, too; even if we'd had an open path to run, we barely had ten feet of clearance from both groups.

"I got this," I said bravely, reaching for the powers contained within Draignerthol. Without the dragon pendant I was just another girl from Mississippi, but with it in my hands I commanded the ancient powers of the elf sorcerers to do my bidding.

Right then, my bidding was to show these Cult folks a thing or two. I stepped out from behind the bushes and grabbed the wind, looking to blast the guys in front with enough force to knock them completely out of our way, clearing a path for us to escape.

I felt the power of the magic sing in my soul and flow through my hands, and as I shaped it, focused it, readied it, I exalted in the joy that accompanied it.

Suddenly it felt like a wet towel was thrown over me. The power, the singing, and the very wind itself went silent. I screamed in frustration as I felt my feet knocked out from under me. The coils of a huge black serpent wrapped themselves around my body.

I couldn't feel the powers any more, which actually terrified me more than being wrapped up by a snake.

I could only just barely breathe.

Two voices were cursing for all they were worth. One was in a language I couldn't understand, but I recognized the voice as Druzhtane's. The other carried the most magnificent string of elf curse words that has likely ever been put together, and that in a screaming, high-pitched, frantic voice that I recognized as my own.

Both of the voices were squeezed out at the same time, my own by the constriction of what felt like a noose around my neck. Another voice took their place, this one a dry man's voice, clipped and bereft of all feeling. He said something in the strangely harsh language that had seemed so familiar just minutes before, a phrase that contained the word Druzhtane, and then he smoothly switched to the elf tongue.

"Welcome, Alyssa, to the multiple indescribable and wonderful honors of public service. The Crown would like to thank you through me for your willingness to serve."

A Guest of the Crown

What happened next is still a mystery. I could feel and hear movement, and I got the sense that we traveled for quite a distance. I couldn't see anything; somehow the serpent managed to keep a tight grip around my body while shielding my vision while undulating itself across the city blocks. All I could hear was a muffled but constant wail in Dru's voice from somewhere off to the side. I kept reaching out toward the powers contained in Draignerthol, but to no avail. The pendant was still there, but it had gone cold against my chest, and the absence of magical power felt like a strange wet shroud laid over me.

At one point the coils overhead opened to the sky, and the elf command for "behold" was whispered—or shouted? I wasn't sure, disoriented as I was, but they ended up in my ear somehow. My view cleared, and I realized that I was staring straight up at what looked like the Empire State Building. The skyscraper loomed above, and on the two sides I could see were the famous and picturesque scalloped risers that led up to a magnificent central spire. It was beautiful. I had only been granted a brief moment to see it on the visit with Dad, so I would have really thought it was cool if the snake hadn't kept tensioning my wrists together and ruining the moment, bless its vile little heart.

For the first time since our capture, Dru's shrieks of terror died down. We stood there mutely, tightly bound, and looked upward toward the magnificence of the building.

Then the tour ended, apparently, as the coils covered my vision once again and the serpent moved. The thrum of the city streets died out, and then I felt the vertical jolt of an elevator.

We rode upward quite some time before I finally felt the elevator slow to a stop, and then the door opened into a very quiet area. It was just another short bit of serpentine travel, and then the coils fell away.

I blinked, trying to get my eyes used to the bright, artificial light. Other than a hulking shape to my front, I seemed to be the only person in the room.

As the spots in my vision died away, my brain had trouble processing what they left. I found myself looking into the face of a creature that I'd have said was only a myth not too long ago. At the library I'd learned that wyverns weren't as mythical as I'd thought, though, and at the same time, I'd also learned to fear their magic-based power. I'd hoped never to run into another one, and yet here it was, trunklike back legs holding it in a standing position with its long, scaly, green tail wrapped around them for support. Its wings were folded neatly behind, with leading edge claws visible above the thing's shoulders. The beast's armored neck stood horizontal, putting the snout on the same level as my head. Intelligent black eyes studied me from within its vertical eyelids.

The shock was too much. I started to scream, but got cut off after only a second or two as scaly hands grabbed me from behind and something sharp pierced the skin on my shoulder. A nice warm sensation traveled quickly from there all over, and—well, that's all I remember of that moment, period.

When I came to, I was lying on my back on the first soft spot I'd felt in a couple of weeks.

My head hurt. It was obviously still attached, which was an awfully nice thing to note, but it felt like it was only a matter of time before it exploded.

My fingers moved when I asked them to. Nice.

My toes could move, too. Double-nice.

I moved my arms and legs side to side a little. It didn't feel like I was tied down. *Very* nice.

Silver linings were piling right up on my side, apparently.

Finally I decided it was time to brave opening my eyes. I instantly regretted it—the light hurt! I opened them again and forced them to stay open for several seconds as the light dimmed to a regular inside kind of glow. It turned out that I was looking up at a boring cement ceiling with a round incandescent bulb hanging in the middle. My eyes followed it to its edges, where I saw that most of the walls were made of white cinder blocks. The edge closest to where my feet were, on the other hand, met up with a prison grate kind of thing.

I was a prisoner, then. Not nice. Not entirely unexpected, of course; this "public service" didn't sound like a picnic in the park, after all.

It took a bit of effort, but I managed to sit up. The stiffness made me wonder how long I'd been down for, but I put that aside as I worked the muscles to banish it. I looked around. The cell I found myself in actually held a fairly nice mattress on a metal bed frame, as well as a table and chair set right out of the '50s and even a real porcelain toilet.

It could've been worse, I guess.

It was all white. Except the bars, of course, which were black.

There was some food on the table. It wasn't much, just some sliced meat and cheese and a hunk of bread, but it was fresh, and it looked a whole lot tastier than the stuff Druzhtane had been feeding me.

Druzhtane! I suddenly remembered how we'd been taken. In a moment of near-panic, I called out for her.

"Shh!" my friend commanded from her own cell across the hall. Her hiss for silence was not quite in time, though, as down the hall and into my field of view thundered one of the lizards that I'd been hoping I'd only dreamed about. It was no dream, though; there really was a wyvern staring into my cell. The thing, bless its blackened heart, was actually glaring at me for making a noise. At least, I think it was glaring. Its little beady black eyes glared hard, unblinkingly, at me, and the little slots at the end of its pointed, well-armored nose opened and closed rhythmically as it breathed. Otherwise its face was all bone and scale and ugly, glaring meanness.

It walked on two legs, each one terminating in long black claws. The two arms it held up and out, away from its body, also terminated in long black claws, though, so I wasn't sure if they weren't just two more legs. Its red leathery wings started from just above the joints on the front appendages and were held folded back against its body.

It was Scary, with a capital S.

The one at the library had been scarier, granted. It hadn't been confined to a narrow hallway between jail cells, for one thing, and it also hadn't had a set of bars separating it from us. Seeing the snout so close, it occurred to me briefly that I hadn't ever asked Sephaline whether wyverns, being the smaller cousins of dragons, could breathe fire, but then again it probably didn't matter. If the wyvern were going to roast me and eat me, it would have done that instead of injecting me with the knockout drug and leaving me on a soft padded mattress to wake up.

That was nice, sort of. Nicer than being roasted, anyway.

The wyvern ended its glaring session with a *whuff* as it turned and strode back down the hallway. I couldn't see all the way to the end, but I imagined that there had to be some sort of guard desk down there.

The image of a wyvern seated officiously at a metal office desk was funny enough that I snerked a little.

Dru glared at me.

"What?" I whispered across the way. Druzhtane looked at me with confusion in her face; apparently she hadn't heard what I'd said.

"What?" I growled, and then we both hurried away from the grates as we heard furniture moving at the end of the hall.

Several moments later, after nothing had happened, I sneaked up closer to the grates. Druzhtane did, too, and she mouthed words to me that were completely unintelligible.

Once again I whispered the word "what?" and, not understanding why it wasn't working, tapped my chest to activate Draignerthol for some translation help.

Sudden panic gripped me utterly. My chest was bare, Draignerthol gone.

My face must have said more than my mouth ever could, because Dru stood across from me signaling. "Whoa, there. Quiet, there. Slow down, there," her gestures conveyed. I almost ignored them, but reason returned quickly enough and I didn't.

Draignerthol was, according to what I'd learned, the most powerful magical relic ever created. Of course it was a desirable item. It had been taken, was all, and probably by someone who didn't even know how to use it. I'd take it back. "Y'all want the Dragon Queen, y'all get the Dragon Queen," I silently promised the rest of the world.

It was my Momma's pendant they'd taken from me. You don't do that.

"Can you understand me?" I asked quietly, willing my voice to move in only one direction across the hall to Dru and not down it. With Draignerthol I might have managed it, but the evidence that I hadn't succeeded came from the irritated-sounding *whuff* from my newest, scaliest friend at the end of the hall. Druzhtane, meanwhile, just shrugged and shook her head, wearing the same bewildered expression.

Obviously, the answer was no.

I grabbed the bar and shook, hard, trying to figure out how solid a cell I was in. My hardest shake couldn't even make the bars rattle, not even a little bit. It did, however, earn me another *whuff* from the end of the hall as well as an exasperated shake of the head from Dru.

I shrugged my confusion over to my friend, who just shook her head with the same expression she'd been wearing and sat down, facing away from me in her cell.

Ah, well. Heck. There wasn't much I could think of doing that would be productive, so I sat down at the table and sampled the food. It was, I found, as good as it looked.

So there I was. I had four weeks to go on my little coming-of-age quest, and I'd managed to get both myself and my only friend captured. By wyverns, at that. Wyverns who fed me when they could easily eat me instead. Wyverns who fed me and kept me captive up in the Empire State Building in what looked like New York City but where everybody talked a harsh language and received a ration of marijuana and where magic worked, or at least it worked as long as those black snakes weren't around.

It was all pretty strange—downright crazy strange, in fact. I turned it over and over in my head trying to make some sense of it, and when that didn't work I did the only thing my still-mostly-sane mind could come up with.

I started laughing.

Soon the wyvern stood outside my cell again making more *whuff* sounds of irritation at me. That just gave me more to laugh about, though. I couldn't get out, but from the way he was holding himself it looked like he couldn't get in, either.

At least, I assumed it was a he; not that it mattered. I tried imagining the beast as a her, a massive armored Matron Mama Morton from that musical, and that made me laugh even harder.

Before long another wyvern showed up, vigorously shooing its huffing and puffing colleague away. The new Matron Mama stood and glared at me quietly till I finally forgot what I found so funny and let my laughter die down. Then it surprised the heck out of me by speaking, and by doing so in nearly flawless elvish: "Princess Alyssa, it is a delight to finally make your acquaintance, though I wish we could meet under less restrictive circumstances. Welcome to New York City. I am Zhluskuh, chief adjutant to His Royal Majesty, and it is my pleasure to welcome you here as a guest of the crown, albeit a guest housed in a protective cell."

"A guest of the crown?" I ridiculed, giving him the dismissive gesture I'd been taught in Cysegredig.

The wyvern didn't even seem to notice.

"Absolutely, Princess," he continued in his too-pleasant, too-cheerful voice. "Unfortunately, His Royal Majesty is not available to meet with you until tomorrow morning, but in the meantime, if there is anything you desire within this adjutant's ability to provide, please, you have merely to speak my name aloud."

"Oh. Well, Zhluskuh, how about freedom for my friend over there?"

The adjutant craned his head around to look at Druzhtane, who was still sitting with her back to the whole mess. He turned back to me and said, "A zhopi—your friend? Interesting." Most interesting was how he dragged the *nnn* sound out in his pronunciation. "However, the release of zhopi is not within my ability to provide, Princess. I am sorry."

"What's in store for her, then? Is she headed for public service, or something else?"

"'Public service,' yes," he said, letting the last s draw out like a snake's hiss. "That is, in fact, precisely what is in store for your zhopi friend."

"What's the nature of this public service, then?" I asked, my suspicion raised. I remembered her explaining that people who left for public service never came back. I'd imagined and hoped it was something like Peace Corps, but the change in the wyvern's tone dashed that idea out of my head.

"The nature? Of public service? Why, Princess, it is when these zhopi find themselves of true service to the empire, for many of them for the first time ever."

"Doing what?"

I was amazed that a wyvern's scaly face could actually wrap itself up into a leer, but at the same time, given the present topic, I was disgusted with it. If I'd had Draignerthol, I would have burned the expression right off his maw as he said, "That is not for me to say, Princess. Perhaps you should ask His Royal Highness, tomorrow. Now, if there is anything you desire within this adjutant's ability to provide, please, you have merely to speak my name aloud."

With that repetition still hanging in the air, the wyvern clumped off down the hall and out of my sight.

"Am I here for public service, Zhluskuh?" I called into the darkness.

"You are destined for a higher calling," the rumbling voice returned from the shadows.

"Zhluskuh, where's my pendant?" I probed.

"In a safe location, held for return to you once His Majesty decrees. Now, good night."

Alone again, I looked around, wishing I could tell what time it was. I couldn't; there were no portals at all to the outside world, and no clocks on any of the walls either. I could have asked Druzhtane if either one of us spoke the other's language, but even if we could she probably would have been as clueless as I. Finally, alone in a world where suddenly nobody but an officious wyvern understood any of the words I spoke, I laid down and tried to drift off to sleep, hoping that I might wake up out of a horrible dream into a world that was right.

HUNLLEF

A nightmare. Literally, "self-cry."

Appropriate, no?

His Royal Majesty

I woke up the next morning after a pretty horrible night. Granted, the mattress in my cell was first-rate and felt incredibly good after sleeping on leaves and cold ground for a couple of weeks—yay, me. But sleeping in a cell, even when the great big wyvern had referred to it as being a "guest," didn't feel very hospitable. Add to that the promise of meeting "His Royal Majesty," whoever that was, first thing in the morning, and I had a fairly sleepless night.

And then there was Druzhtane, whose tough exterior finally shattered. She sobbed loudly all night, and every ragged breath of that tugged at my soul. Obviously, her predicament was my fault; if I hadn't moved into her spot in the park they wouldn't have come looking for me there, and she would still be a happy little zhopi. Now she was set for public service, and the happy little mental image I'd had of public service folks picking up trash on the sides of the road wearing cheap plastic orange vests had dissolved away in Zhluskuh's sneer. That vision was now replaced by a dreadful fear for her safety, and I knew that she hadn't even

understood enough of the elf language to get that much for herself.

Knowing all that made each wracking, blubbery sob another
nail through my heart. Unfortunately there was nothing I could
do or say that would change her plight, or even soothe her terror
in a language that she would understand, so I just lay awake listening. I spent what had to have been several hours doing that
while examining the light fixture on the ceiling, uninteresting as
it was.

Finally the lights went off completely. It was a little shocking
to plummet into total darkness, and I got up to look around.
There weren't any lights on at all, in either direction, that I could
see even the faintest glimmer of.

Obviously they didn't feel the need to guard us all night.

"Druzhtane, I'm sorry," I said softly, hoping that at least the
tone of my voice would mean something to her. But she didn't respond.

Eventually, she cried herself to sleep and the cell block fell silent. I figured the insides of my eyelids were every bit as interesting as the walls and ceiling that I couldn't see anyway, and so I
let my eyes flutter closed.

"Princess," a commanding voice roused me from sleep. I jolted
up, my body springing out of bed nearly entirely on its own in response to the surprisingly deep, reverberating tone. I blinked the
grogginess away and slowly took in my surroundings. I was still
in the cell, unfortunately. The lights were on, so I had to assume
it was the next day. The adjutant who'd spoken to me last night
stood outside the bars again, peering at me down his long snout.

"What do you want?" I asked, letting my irritation free to
slash its way into my tone. I was, after all, the Crown Princess of
Kiirajanna, the future Dragon Queen, capital letters included,
and I was perfectly justified to be angry over waking up in a cell.

It earned me only a brief snort. "What I want is unimportant. The time for your audience with His Royal Majesty approaches rapidly, and it is my responsibility to ensure that you are prepared for it."

"Oh. Does that mean I get a shower?" I asked sarcastically.

"Once you have finished eating your breakfast, yes. His Royal Majesty has an exceptional sense of smell, and we should not risk offending it."

"Of course not. I'd hate to risk offending anything about His Royal Majesty," I said, seething. We can't risk offending His Royal Majesty's sense of smell, but we can offend the crown princess all night long, apparently.

The adjutant nodded, either not catching my sarcasm or choosing to ignore it.

I was very hungry, I realized, and so I stepped over to the table. On it, while I'd been asleep, they'd left a tray of sausage and bacon, a bit of scrambled eggs, a platter of golden brown hash browns, and a few slices of tomato. On the side was a bowl that looked an awful lot like grits. Off to the other side there was a stack of pancakes, with a small pitcher of syrup beside.

It was just like Momma would have made. That scared me. I turned back to the adjutant and asked, "So tell me, Zhlu, how it is that here in New York City you have grits."

"We intend to provide you with all the comforts of your home, primitive though they may be, Princess. It is our desire to make you as comfortable as possible."

"As comfortable as possible before you eat me? Is that it?" I joked, hoping to draw from the adjutant an objection to the idea of eating me.

He didn't object, though. That scared me more. I felt like a caged bluebird looking into a rattlesnake's eyes.

"The crown is not to be kept waiting, Princess," was all he said.

Fine. I tried it. It really was—well, real. Everything was perfectly done. The bacon was salty and crispy and just barely greasy. The pancakes were light and fluffy and I swear they were almost as good as Momma's. The adjutant even had salt, pepper, butter, and a little thing of hot sauce to spice up the grits.

Once I finished everything and pushed my plate away the cell door opened and the adjutant gestured for me to exit. I stood and walked out as regally as I could, doing my best to remind them with my movements that I was, in fact, a princess. I had to wonder, perversely, if I had bacon grease or grits on my face, since they'd provided neither a napkin nor a mirror. Since I was apparently being marched to a shower, though, it didn't really matter.

I glanced into Druzhtane's cell. She sat there, dark rings formed around her eyes, glaring at me from her own untouched breakfast plate that looked identical to mine.

Maybe she didn't like grits?

I didn't have much time to ponder that, as the showers not far down the hall, off to the side. I wasn't hoping for any privacy from the massive winged lizard, which was good because I didn't get any. There was a small alcove in which to strip my clothes away, and as I did so I looked back at the adjutant. Sure enough, he was watching my every move.

"Are you going to watch me shower?"

"Security, Princess. I am afraid that I must ensure you are safe and well when brought up to meet His Royal Majesty."

"I don't suppose I could get a female guard, could I?"

"Why would you assume that I am not female?"

The great big lizard with wings had a point. The ones I'd seen so far were naked—not that they needed clothes, or even were likely to be able to find clothes that fit and would be safe from shredding on the sharp scales, I supposed. But I hadn't seen anything related to any sort of gender-specific, well, parts. I hadn't really looked, of course, but there was nothing obvious about a wyvern's anatomy. Its voice was in the baritone range, but then again so was Aerona's.

I shrugged and finished peeling off the nasty clothes I'd worn for over two weeks. "Okay, so are you?"

"I am not an egg-layer. Why does it make a difference to you?"

"Don't your kind have any sort of concern for modesty?"

"How many of my kind have you seen wearing clothing, Princess?"

"I've seen two of your kind so far. Three, if it was somebody else who greeted me so pleasantly with a hypodermic needle from behind when I arrived, bless his or her genderless heart. That's kind of a small sample size, don't you think? Now, if you'd bring me along to a party, then I'd be able to answer that better. Your kind does have parties, do you not?"

"You deserve to be warned that if you prattle on meaninglessly like that to His Royal Majesty, he is very likely to just eat you to shut you up."

"Why wouldn't he just eat me anyway?"

"He has his reasons, and they are his to divulge. Now, please do not risk keeping him waiting."

"Right, that whole eating thing." But I did shut up. I stepped further into the alcove, still in sight of the adjutant, and let the water cascade down my body. It felt incredible. Back in the palace I'd been treated to baths whenever I'd wanted one, which had been fairly often. There's something ultimately relaxing about a bath. Still, a good shower, with the hot water beating down on your scalp and then running down your body, can't be beat either, especially when your body feels like it has accepted a layer of dirt as a new hide. I found a bar of soap—smooth, creamy, and perfumed—in a lip on the wall, and with its help was able to remove enough dirt and grime that, by the time I did a final rinse and turned the water off, I actually felt mostly clean again.

I took the towel from the hook on the wall. It wasn't luxurious, but it was dry, and it was a towel. Then I examined the new clothes that were folded on the bench under the hook where the towel had been—again, not luxurious, but serviceable and very similar to what I'd seen the other Fake New York City residents wearing. My own clothes were gone, and hopefully already on their way to a burn barrel.

The adjutant led the way out of the shower area and to the other end of the hall to a set of elevators. These were bigger than the ones I remembered on the trip to Real New York City, and I saw why when the adjutant stepped on and took up most of the space.

We went up. I don't know how far, but it was several long moments of up. There weren't any buttons or indicators to show where we were along the path, so I started wondering if we were ever going to stop.

Finally, we stopped.

In that moment, I wasn't sure whether to cheer for stopping or to cower in terror at whatever might be coming next.

The doors opened into a huge and mostly dark room. Sunlight filtered in from above lending some relief for the eyes, but at first I couldn't tell much about the floor level.

Zhluskuh's hand—paw—claws, whatever—hit my back with just a little more force than was really necessary, bless his heart, and I found myself staggering out into the room. The elevator door behind me closed before I could regain my balance, and when I turned around I saw that I was alone.

Well, not quite alone.

I could hear scraping sounds from deeper in the room. I shook off the terror that suddenly invaded my heart and mind and stepped forward, determined to prove that the Dragon Queen wasn't scared of anything, despite the fact that I was actually pretty dang terrified. At that moment I could literally feel the weight of Draignerthol absent from my chest, and I felt naked.

But I squared my shoulders and strode forward anyway.

As I pressed into the room, my eyes started adjusting to the strange lighting. I could see that the opposite end of the room was illuminated, dimly, by light from above, as were the two sides, and I realized that the shape of the illuminations outlined the huge arches in the dome of the Empire State Building that I'd been shown from below.

I also saw a lot of junk scattered around on the dark floor, most of it gathered together in large piles. Somebody needed to do a good cleaning of His Royal Majesty's chamber, I thought, and then my foot kicked something near the bottom of one of the piles. I reached down to pick it up.

It was a leg bone. From its size I was pretty certain it was a human leg bone.

I craned my head to the side, my eyes trying to penetrate the darkness to look into the pile of garbage better. Sure enough, as my eyes got used to the dim light and the outlines sharpened, I realized that the pile of garbage was actually bones—lots, and lots, of bones. All human bones, near as I could tell.

I wanted to scream, but somehow I knew that would be a very bad idea.

"Princess," a booming, lyrical, deeply resonant voice filled the chamber. "Or is it Dragon Queen I should be calling you? It is unbelievably good to make your acquaintance. I have been looking forward to this day for much, much longer than you have been alive, I must say."

The sound of scraping, of sharp edge against stone, drew nearer. Two reflective orbs flickered into existence a few feet above me, resolving into eyes and transfixing me in their gaze. They drew closer, their coal-black color enhancing the intensity of the intellect that shone from within.

They finally lowered to my level. Each eye was easily a foot in diameter. Between them dropped a scarlet-scaled hill that ended in a dark snout that I imagined could cover me in killing flames the moment it desired. To either side of the eyes stretched more armored plates. The monstrosity undulated in front of me, a wicked smile on its huge serpentine face, its sinuous scaled neck looming from the darkness beyond.

"Welcome to my home, Princess," the creature said, its hot smelly breath washing over me. Suddenly I felt a weirdly intensified, gripping need for dread, a vital hunger for terrified retreat backward. My mind came up with the image of me beating on the elevator doors, screaming for their safety, begging for anything and anyone to help me.

No, I decided. No, I wouldn't let it take me. I hadn't read nearly as much as I needed to about creatures like this, but I'd read enough to prepare for its fear spell. I knew what was in front of me, and far from fake, magically-induced terror, that knowledge of actual, present danger frightened me to no end. I'd faced down wyverns before—albeit with some help. But wyverns aside, some types of creatures were supposed to be dead. Gone. Forever. Some creatures were supposed to be nonexistent. They just flat weren't supposed to be around anymore, not in Kiirajanna, not in Fake New York City, not anywhere.

Supposed to be around or not, though, there wasn't any mistaking it. His Royal Majesty was, in fact, a dragon.

A Lesson or Two

"Princess? You seem to have lost your voice. Are you feeling well?" The dragon's deep, cool, lyrical voice seemed to be mocking me.

Indignation welled up in my heart, thawing my terror-filled veins. How dare he mock me? The little I knew of dragons told me they were huge, incredibly powerful not just physically but also in the arcane. Worse, they were obscenely evil creatures. This one, a mature red that could end my life in a mere moment in any of several different ways, truly had me at his mercy, disarmed as I was and surrounded by his wyvern minions. Yet he had the nerve to make fun of me. How dare he?

How dare he, I thought one last time as I felt my face flush. The fear dropped away.

"Look," I mustered the courage to sneer, and was proud of myself that I managed to put it out there without my voice breaking in the process, "I'm pretty sure I know what kind of creature you are. If you're going to eat me, then just go ahead and eat me."

The dragon snorted, searingly warm air flowing out of its nostrils and backing me a little more into the alcove. I started sweating.

"Princess.... My dear, sullen, little elf princess, if I wanted to eat you, then you can rest assured that I certainly would have by now. Unless, of course, I wanted to toy with you. That is, I admit, a minor foible of mine, this playing with my food before finally breaking it apart and slurping it down. I do so love it, you see, when my prey reaches the point in its terror when it begins perspiring heavily—oh, look!—much as you are now. I love the aroma and the flavor of fear, I guess you might say. Yes, that is it. The flavor of terror—all terror, but especially elf terror—is—divine."

An incredibly long tongue snaked out of the dragon's mouth, which was by that point only about seven or eight feet away. It slithered toward me slowly, a thick slab of red muscle from which large drops of dragon saliva dripped to the floor and left murky splatters. As repulsed as I was, I stood my ground, though, repeating *how dare he* in my mind.

It licked me. The tongue was hot and sticky-slimy. It felt like an electric blanket covered in petroleum jelly and turned up on high. I probably should not have been surprised at the heat radiated by the tongue of a fire-breathing monster, but I was, to the point that I jumped before I could stop myself.

The tongue followed, starting at the base of my neck and winding its way up the side of my face to finish by slurphing the beads of perspiration from my forehead. It was gross, and that plus the heat brought more beads of perspiration, which in turn brought more slurphing.

Finally the dragon's tongue slithered back into its wide maw, and the dragon somehow managed to crank its armored visage up into a smile.

"Mmm, yesssss," the dragon hissed. "Tasty, your fear is. Buuuuuut—" it drew the word out as it slowly shook its huge head back and forth, "as much as it disappoints my taste buds to say this, you can put your fear away, Princess. I have no desire to harm you. Trusssst me," it hissed again in response to my skeptical expression. "I have nothing—other than a quick meal, perhaps, tasty as that might be—to gain from eating you. I have much to gain from a mutual pact of understanding, however. That is my desire, Princess Alyssa. That is why you have been invited to be a guest of the Crown."

"A pact? As in a partnership?" I asked, still skeptical. Why would one of the most feared creatures in all of elf lore—probably in the entire universe—have anything to gain from a pact with me? What could I possibly bring to any bargaining table? It was huge, armored, strong enough to rip me into little pieces of princess meat, and glimmered in a blue haze of arcane energy, while I was small, only marginally competent with a bow and arrow, made entirely of the creature's favorite meat with no scales to protect it, and currently bereft of the one relic that had been on my side. Why I remained uneaten was still a mystery in spite of his high-sounding words.

"Yessss," it said, its head bobbing up and down by several feet in what would have been a humorous gesture if I'd been in the mood. "A partnersssship."

"I, um—okay," I stumbled, not sure where the conversation was going and even more unsure where I was hoping it would end up. Freedom? Not likely. But I was curious. "But if you were so interested in a partnership, why send your minions to attack and cage me and my friend? Why bring me up here to sit in your prison cell? Why not just use those massive wings to fly down to the park and offer up a partnersssship there?" I admit, I was poking the bear a little, but it was obvious that I wasn't likely to become dragon kibble yet.

The tongue snaked out at me again, catching a few more beads of perspiration off my forehead before I managed to slap it away.

"You can just stop that right now," I demanded with as much of a glare as I could manage while working hard to keep my voice even.

"Oh, fine. I shall forego the finer pleasure for the time being, in the name of our understanding-to-be. Yes, I am sorry for the abuse you received in our retrieval, Princess, but I try not to visit the ground level more than I absolutely have to. You see, the citizens of my great city are a little bit frightened of my majestic form."

"Yeah, ya think? Perhaps you don't know this, dragon, but your kind is awfully frightening in general."

The dragon's voice roared in laughter. "I do know this, Princess. Your reply reminds me, however, that I started the conversation on an all-too-confrontational basis. Allow me to start again as your gracious host by introducing myself. The name I most often hear, the one by which my followers refer to me, is His Royal Majesty, though that is certainly not a title that I might expect one of your exalted rank always use. Please, call me by my name, or at least the part of my name that is pronounceable using your fleshy mouth and teeth and tongue. I am Xlixi, king and ruler over all of this realm, and it is my pleasure to welcome Alyssa, Crown Princess and future Dragon Queen of Kiirajanna, to my home."

The formal introduction didn't do much to calm me down. Nor did the way Xlixi pronounced the name of my home realm, with a much stronger *k* than was necessary and a *jzsh* sound instead of the *j* I'd heard everyone else say.

"Thank you—I think, King Xlixi," I said, doing my best to wrap my mouth around his name. If that was the pronounceable part, I was scared to learn what the unpronounceable part might be. Still, it was probably best to compliment the beast. Dragons in the books and movies were always terribly vain, and this one seemed just as bad, so petting its image of self just might keep me alive longer. "This city you rule over is beautiful." And full of drug addicts, but I chose not to bring that up. "Where, if I may ask, is it located on Kiirajanna? It looks, and is named the same as, a major city in my former realm, but I know that it is not that city."

"Ahh, yesss!" the dragon hissed, sounding jubilant. "You have come to appreciate my masterwork, then?"

"Um, yes. Yes, definitely. Yes, I appreciate its magnificence a great deal. But, I am curious, Your—or His—Royal Majesty, King Xlixi, why did one with your amazing powers decide to replicate New York City on Kiirajanna?"

"You are not on Kiirajanna, Princess," the dragon told me smugly.

"Not on—" I said, shocked. I recovered quickly. "But not on Earth, either, right?"

"No, not on Earth."

"Because your kind cannot exist on Earth," I said, meaning it as more of a question than a statement, but I got it wrong.

I'd forgotten to play the ego game, and regretted it immediately as the dragon snorted, exhaling another hot, nasty breath my way. He said, "No, Princess. My kind do not *bother* existing where our magical powers are unavailable, and that useless little rock which you call Earth fails to provide that pleasure. Do not think it is because we *cannot*."

Something about the way Xlixi said it made me question his honesty. Not aloud, though—I still feared being eaten, at least a little, despite his assurances otherwise.

"So if I'm not on Earth, and not on Kiirajanna, where am I?"

"Pazhbojanna."

"Oh," I said, a little disappointed that his answer hadn't been more useful. "And where is that?"

"*When* is that, I believe you meant to ask, Princess."

"Oh, right." I hadn't, and he knew it, and I was pretty sure that he knew that I knew that he knew it, but I might as well play along with the big guy's ego game. "So, *when* is that?"

"You really do not know about the space-time continuum, do you, Princess?"

"No, I didn't read enough of Isaac Asimov's seminal work in school," I replied. It was a lie. I'd read lots of sci fi growing up, and Asimov is one of my favorite classical writers. It's called science fiction for a reason, though, and I halfway hoped Mister Big-and-Scaly would catch my sarcastic reference.

"Well, if you had kept up with your studies, little one," he said, obviously missing my point. I was a little disappointed, truth be told; it had been a nice, subtle one. "Then, Princess, you would know that each of the realms exists in its own space and time, and that the energy pathways are all that connect one to another."

"No TARDISes, hmm?" I asked, hoping he'd at least catch one reference.

"Do not toy with me, Princessss." I wasn't sure whether the hiss at the end meant that he'd caught it or not. "The ley-gates are, as you know, the only way to pass from one realm to another, and my brethren have ruled those pathways for eons. We created them, in fact."

That went directly against what I'd been taught in my elf training by the high priestess and her sisterhood. According to that lecture, the pathways were part of the natural forces, a naturally-occurring duct that the massive power of our assembled race had managed to close off at the end of the first, incredibly violent, epoch of Kiirajanna's history. Then, in their wisdom, they re-opened it as the third epoch began. Not much there lent itself to dragonkind ruling over the paths, but I didn't have much to gain by telling King Windbag that he was wrong, especially not when said wind would be hot enough to kill me.

"So, how many realms like this are there?"

"How should I know? Each of the other realms like this is cultivated by one of my race. I do not go on tours, and neither do they."

"Cultivated?"

"Well, yes, of course. Cultivated. That is the term in your language for the planting and reaping of food, yes?"

I thought about it for a bit. He'd used the infinitive form of the verb *tyfu*, which was indeed the elf word for planting and reaping of food, but that wasn't what surprised me. My objection was in his thinking of the realms as something to be *planted* and *reaped* in the first place. It was both a scary and a disgusting thought, but as scary and disgusting as it was, I was still curious about it.

"It is the correct term, yes. Your command of the elf language is perfect, King Xlixi. But why do you use that verb to describe your rule of the realms?"

"Well, a dragon needs to eat, Princess," he said, a pretense of bashfulness in his tone. The implication made me sick to my stomach.

"So you created this city—" I started, unsure how best to finish the thought. I figured it probably didn't matter much; the giant dragon-scale-clad ego in the room would finish it for me.

Xlixi finished it for me. "To raise food, yes, Princess. Pazhbojanna, in my own, ancient tongue, the true language, actually means breeding land. A breeding land, for elves. I came up with the name myself, as a matter of fact. Is it not fitting?"

As much as the admission chilled me, it was overridden by a sudden memory of the time I'd asked my father about the weirdness of the name of the realm of the elves—Kiirajanna. When I'd re-learned the elf tongue, it had struck me as very strange to be in a realm whose name, Kiirajanna, was entirely impossible to spell out in its own language; the elves had no k's, nor j's, nor double i's nor n's. His explanation that the name of the realm had come from an older, more fundamental language had reassured me then, but hearing Xlixi's exposition filled me with dread, bless his draconic little heart.

"It, um—it is. Fitting. Quite fitting. What, if I may ask, does Kiirajanna mean in your ancient tongue?"

His simple answer sent chills up my spine. "It means feasting land, Princess." The dragon managed a grin once again.

"You named it that?" I wasn't sure what I was going to do if he answered yes.

"Not I," the dragon said with a full, throaty chuckle. "Kiirajanna has been around for far longer than I have been. I believe my ancestor responsible for naming your world was the mighty and magnificent *Xchstlsrwstchrltzstlklkltrwntntntntntndrtklt*. What a fierce lord he was."

I couldn't have even come close to making the same clickity-clicks that came out of the beast's mouth. "You weren't kidding about dragon names being impossible to pronounce, were you?"

"Oh, no. My kind prides ourselves on the length and complexity of our names. In fact, we rename ourselves every few hundred years, adding letters to indicate how long we have survived in our harsh existences. Why, my eldest—"

I interrupted, too horrified to care about the lecture on dragon naming conventions. "So my world, the realm over which I will one day soon be ruler, was named by a dragon for the fact that he liked to feast there. On elves, I must presume."

The dragon nodded. I suppose it was easier for the beast than shrugging would have been, and it served the same purpose. "On elves, yes. Dragons dine on other creatures, too, of course: deer, cattle, griffins, and—"

"Wyvern?" I interjected. I was curious.

"No!" I could tell I'd hit a nerve; the beast's head sprang up several feet in shock. "Never wyvern! They are our younger, smaller cousins. I do, though, know of one dragon who managed to cage and raise a herd of unicorn specifically—"

"Unicorn? You eat unicorns?" My horror settled into the pit of my stomach.

"Do you *ever* let your fellow collocutor finish a sentence, Princess?"

"Well, yes, but not when he's talking about eating elves and unicorns, bless his heart." I risked a glare at His Royal Carnivore.

"And what do you eat, Princess? Twigs and leaves?"

"I eat meat, too, but not from my own kind, and never from unicorns! They're sacred!"

"To you, perhaps. They are a very tasty dinner, to me."

"Eww," I said, my whole body shuddering in revulsion.

"Oh, please. You can lay off the little girl routine, or else I may decide that you are not worth the title of princess. Your kind is annoying in this regard. You are often the top of the food chain as far as you are aware, and you have no issues with raising lesser beings for slaughter. Nor do you have a problem watching beasts lower than you on the same food chain devour beasts lower than they are for dinner. But as soon as you find out that you might actually make for a fine meal for another creature, you always melt down with indignation and revulsion."

I considered his words. He was right about my never having thought twice about eating pork or beef. Still....

"But the beasts I eat don't have consciousnesses, don't have souls," I objected.

"Pah!" he said in a half-laugh, half-snort that blasted me once again with hot air. "I could say the same of your kind, little one."

"No! No, you can't! How dare you suggest that civilizations responsible for libraries and space travel have no consciousnesses?"

"Space travel? You use the pathways my kind created to travel between the worlds. You build libraries, we build worlds. Your accomplishments are as much beneath my race's works as the slough of a pig is beneath your own. How dare you even try to equate elves to dragons?"

I considered his words. While we had, in fact, landed humans on other places in space, which was something, I was certain His Royal Dismissiveness would find a way to claim credit for the accomplishment for his own species. No matter what I said, that path of the conversation wasn't going to end well, so I decided to switch it up. "So you created this world?"

"I did." If the dragon was shocked by the abrupt change of direction it didn't show it.

"Why did you emulate New York City, then?"

"The city you call New York serves as an excellent model for growth of live—shall I say, humans—to a high density of population."

"But I thought you didn't *choose* to visit Earth."

"Do not test me, Princess. I do not so choose, but pictures and stories abound. My servants go in my stead and return with wonderful tales of high-rise efficiency. I have but replicated that efficiency here in my own poor little experiment in food cultivation."

"That's disgusting, you know."

"I would expect you to think so."

"So, these servants you mention. Are you talking about the Cult of the Wyrm?" I remembered the little dragon pins worn by the cult members back on Kiirajanna, and the same pins here in this replica of New York City.

"The Cult of the Wyrm, you call them. What a humorous title. Yes, I am referring to those fools."

"They're the same fools who tried to poison and kill me at the Library of Alecsanddrha."

"I know. The bumbling idiots were supposed to have brought you here to meet me when you visited the library, but they failed. Miserably. And when they failed, they resorted to primitive approaches involving poison and arrows. And then there was the absolutely deplorable attack in Ganolog. Princess, what you went through was never my intent."

"Your intent? So you've had this all planned out from the beginning?"

"Of course."

"I have a hard time seeing you taking a planning role in the prophecies."

"The prophecies were my creation, Princess."

I had a very hard time believing that, having read most of the prophecies myself. For one thing, there were obscure passages that could easily be interpreted as me gaining rulership over the dragons. His Royal Arrogance would not have written that in, I was pretty certain. Plus there was the timing thing; the prophecies were written back in the First Epoch, thousands of years ago, while His Royal Windbag didn't seem like he could be that old. Old, yes, but he'd chosen a pretty modern city to build, so it just didn't seem possible.

But I decided to leave that be. "So what, then, are the snakes?"

"The snakes—oh, the serpents? Ah, my serpents. Yes, yes, my serpents. Yes, they are quite a special treat for magic users, are they not?"

"You have a strange definition for treat, but yes, they are quite special. Where did you find them, or did you just create them?"

"You give me too much credit, Princess. One of my ancestors bred them initially. All I have done is keep the line going. They do make excellent keepers of the peace, do they not?"

"I suppose so. Look," I said, getting tired of the conversation with Mister Hot-and-Smelly, "what do I need to do to ensure the safety of my friend?" Druzhtane may have been raised in a city where elves were basically cattle for the lord dragon, but that didn't mean I had to sit back and watch her be eaten.

"The young elf you were brought in with?"

"Yes, that one."

"Fascinating. You are worried that I might eat her."

I stepped back involuntarily. That was exactly what I'd just been thinking, complete with a nasty visual image. Could the dragon read my mind? It wasn't something I'd read they could do, but then again, the power to create fear implied other mental abilities as well. That gave me a whole new level of concern.

"Yeah, that's pretty high on my list of worries right now."

"Do not worry about that, dear Princess. Your friend is safe." I tried hiding my relieved sigh, but then he continued, "For the time being. She is too skinny. Nothing but sinew and bone and skin."

Shocked, I thought about Druzhtane—and he was right. She was very, very skinny. Body by Poverty, I would have to say. Then I thought of the rest of the people I'd met, including the group of women in the apartment I'd visited my first day. None were what I'd consider fat, but none were that skinny either. They were all pleasantly plump.

"You fatten the elves up, don't you?" I asked, and then thought of the marijuana dispensing machines. It clicked into place. "You keep them drugged, using a drug known to inflict a certain amount of hunger pains, the same way the chicken breeders on Earth stuff chickens full of food, don't you?"

"Princess, Princess, Princess...." The huge tongue flicked out toward me again but I batted it away, an interplay that brought a grin to the beast's lips. "You know, I would hate to have you thinking badly of me—oh, wait. No, no, I must amend that sentiment. I do not really care what you think of me. Yes, I do manage my city in a manner which will provide me the best possible food source. Because yes, I admit, your elf friends represent my tastiest and, currently, most easily obtainable source of sustenance."

He allowed that to sink in for several long moments of silence. Finally I broke that, asking soberly, "And so what do you want of me, considering that I am but the lowly future queen of your food source?"

The eyes the size of dinner plates stared at me like a cobra's eyes might stare at a rodent. "You are the future Dragon Queen, Princess. There is nothing *lowly* about that. What I want *of* you is nothing more, and nothing less, than your destiny. I want you to rule your people in Kiirajanna in direct subordination to my own rule. I want you to strongly and peacefully usher me in to my rightful role as overlord of all of Kiirajanna and its inhabitants."

I froze. What the dragon was suggesting was for me to subjugate my father's people, an entire realm of free elves, to a life as his personal cattle herd.

"You don't want to rule the elves of Kiirajanna; you want to feast on them," I said, horrified.

"You would be surprised, Princess, how little feasting I would need to do with two whole realms to choose from."

"That doesn't make much sense. You'll still need to eat the same either way. With two realms, you just divide your— snacking—between Dru's people and mine."

His silent grin sickened me.

"Why do you need me, though? As powerful as I've heard dragons are, surely you could just swing right on over and start dining. Or am I missing something?"

"I could, indeed, Princess, just swing right on over and start dining, but as you know, your people are proud. Foolishly so. There would be—resistance. Strife. Your people would fight me, and many would die. Under your orders, it would be a much more peaceful transition."

"You've said that word twice now. A dragon, interested in peace? You really don't care about that, do you? You just want to keep the number of salad bar stations maximized."

"Well, if you wish to phrase it in that manner, I shall allow it."

"And so, to prevent a war, you expect me to waltz in and say, 'okay, my loyal subjects, from now on this little dragony-pooh over there is going to be around, flying and swooping overhead. Don't fear, and don't feel the need to fight. I expect you to let him eat you if and when he wants'?"

"Bah. What would be the difference between that and the way rulers in your lands send their subjects off to war to die for a strip of land somewhere? At least this way, they contribute to the great circle of life, so to speak."

"I don't have a good answer for that right now, but I'll come up with one."

"Ah, I am sure that you will, Princess. And in the meantime, I do grow hungry, and so you should probably be seen back down to your room now."

The door opened behind me and the two wyvern arms, claws extended, snapped around my shoulders and yanked me into the elevator before I had a chance to reply. We rumbled in silence back down to my cell.

Confinement

Dru gasped and looked at me like I was a ghost when Big-'n-Ugly brought me back to my little cell. Not knowing how to tell her anything in the harsh language of Pazhbojanna about what I'd just been through, I settled for a wistful smile and a wave. She waved back, and ever so slowly she started to return the smile. That widened my own smile; apparently she'd been worried about my safety, though probably in part due to what it meant in terms of her own.

A hot pot of soup was on the table in my cell, a loaf of soft, squishy bread beside it. Smelling it made me realize how hungry I was—had I been in the dragon's chamber that long?—but it also brought with it flashbacks to the poisoning in the library. When the librarians had tried to poison me with their soup I'd been protected by Draignerthol's power, but here I didn't enjoy the same shield. As I thought it over, though, I couldn't come up with any reason the dragon or his wyverns would try to poison me. After all, if Xlixi wanted to harm me, he could have easily just feasted and called it a day.

But no, I was probably too skinny for him, too. All skin and sinew, as he'd said. I looked back across to Dru's cell to see her sopping up her own bowl of the same stew I had with another loaf of the fresh bread.

Maybe he was trying to fatten us both up?

I thought briefly about ways to warn Druzhtane not to eat so much, but there just wasn't any way to get that message across in pantomime that wouldn't be insulting. Heck, most ways I could think of to speak it would've been just as insulting.

I gave in and ate it. It tasted even better than the meat and cheese had the night before. It was hot, for one thing. It had been weeks since I'd had hot food, and beef stew was one of my favorites.

I drew up short at that thought. I hoped it was beef. The other alternative was—I just didn't want to think about the dragon's version of cattle. But no, he said he preferred to eat elf, and I doubted that His Arrogant Puffiness would share his favorite meal with me no matter how much he might enjoy my horror at learning I'd been tricked into cannibalism.

Not having anything else to do once the bowl was empty, I laid down on my bed. It was good to be warm, out of the elements. It was good, too, for my stomach to be full of warm, tasty food. It was good to have a nice, soft bed to relax on.

Yes, I was in a completely different space-time than I was supposed to be in, and I was imprisoned in a mock-up of the Empire State Building under the watchful glare of a creature that, till today, had been the scariest type of creature I'd ever seen, and now ranked only the second scariest type. Momma's pendant, my own source of power, had been taken away. Meanwhile, I was imprisoned as the "guest" of an actual dragon, and his desired "partnership" involved me giving him permission to eat my own people.

All things considered, though, it could've been worse. I tried to get myself to believe that, anyway. The dragon could've been more interested in me as a tasty morsel of humanity than as the future queen. I was, at least, still alive and kicking. Not kicking very hard at the moment, but as I lay there pondering, I convinced myself that I'd find a way to kick when it mattered most.

As I lay there I also wondered if, and how, Xlixi had made it so I traveled here rather than a hunhymgais spot on Kiirajanna. He'd bragged about his kind creating and controlling the ley-gates, after all. Maybe the jerking around sensation I'd felt was his exercise of that control? Maybe that was how he populated his breeding experiment here, by redirecting travelers and capturing them? I decided to ask him, even though I already knew that the odds of him telling me the truth were low.

Once I got home—if I got home—I'd also have to ask Dad, or Sternyface, or maybe both, how often elves disappeared on their dream quests and were never heard from again. The elves would probably take it as a risk of the rite of passage, but what if it were caused by draconic interference?

A light scrape surprised me alert. I sat up and looked out just in time to see a wyvern's tail moving down the hall toward the guard desk at the end. I had to shake my head—had I gone to sleep? For how long?

Then I noticed what had caused the sound. On the floor just inside the cell bars was a leather-bound book, apparently left as a gift.

A gift? From whom? More important: why?

I walked over and picked it up. It was a large book, nearly a foot and a half tall and a foot wide, and over an inch thick. The impressive leather cover was unmarked.

It covered nearly all of the table once I moved the bowl out of the way. Carefully—who knew what kind of a trap the dragon might try to set?—I opened it.

Near as I could tell, it was in ancient elvish. The words were familiar, but the script was straighter, more rigid than the books I'd read. The title page read "The Mabinogion." It sounded a little familiar, actually, though I couldn't place it.

I started reading. It was interesting, but immediately I ran into some differences between the language it was written in and elvish. It wasn't hard to puzzle out, but the conjugation was a little different, as was the lenition, or transition of hard consonants into softer ones. I had to be reading Welsh, I realized—some old form of the Welsh language, too, that didn't use the standard Latin alphabet. The stories seemed ancient. I read it, though, in spite of the difficulty. Heck, it was all that I had available to do, and besides, it was an interesting set of stories.

They brought supper sometime later, and I finally saw how they had managed to do it without waking me before. One smaller wyvern—I guessed smaller meant younger with wyverns, but that was just a guess—padded along with an elf on a leash, and the wyvern opened the door while the elf slipped in to each room to deliver food. It was another large bowl of aromatic soup, in this case, with another forearm-sized loaf of fresh bread.

They obviously weren't trying to starve me. And if the dragon could be believed—a big if, but worth considering—they weren't trying to fatten me up, either.

I looked up when the girl came in and smiled. She returned a quick half-smile that contained more fear than anything else, and then she set the tray on the table and darted back out like a deer sensing a hunter's sight.

My smile followed her out but then shifted to sadness. I couldn't help but wonder how long the poor girl had before she was considered "ripe" to the dragon. A shudder of revulsion passed through me; I couldn't imagine eating a thinking, feeling being at all, much less in the livestock-y way that Xlixi was raising elves like cattle.

Druzhtane and I ignored each other for most of the day. It hurt me a little bit to do so, but there just wasn't any way for us to communicate. She'd stopped crying, but that just left plenty of room for stone-cold silence.

Once, by accident, our eyes met. It was right after the little serving girl on the leash darted out of my room. Dru was served just before me, so she was already seated at her table sipping on the warm soup. She glanced over as the girl darted out, and the head motion from across the way caught my attention.

I smiled.

Dru smiled back.

I shrugged my most sincere "well, this is about the best we could expect" expression.

She nodded.

The next morning was a repeat of the previous one. The adjutant came and got me, rushed me through a shower so that my body aroma, which I thought had been gotten rid of the last shower, wouldn't offend His Royal Windbag. Then we rode the wyvern-sized elevator to the top of the building for another audience with the dragon.

"Ah, Princess, how good of you to join me again. Have you considered my offer further?" he asked as soon as the door slid shut behind me.

"I'm not sure you can reasonably call 'if you let me only kill and eat a few of your people, I won't kill more' much of an *offer*, Xlixi."

"I am royalty, the same as you, Princess. If I can give a lesser being such as you the privilege of an honorific, I would expect you to render the same respect to me."

I didn't dare tell him how much it sounded to me like he was whining. My father, I was certain, would have just continued the conversation without demanding specific words. Heck, I'd seen him do it. But, fine....

"Your Majesty, King Xlixi, I am certain one of your immensely powerful intellect could see the difficulty I would have in considering your offer to murder and eat my people with any degree of felicity."

There, I finally used that spelling word in a sentence, the absurd thought struck. With it came the image of Ms. Norbury, our senior English teacher, clapping in the ridiculous way she always did when one of us used a word correctly. I wondered whether, were she present, she'd be more inclined to think "wonderful, Alyssa finally used felicity in a sentence" or "holy jumpin' Jehosaphat, Alyssa's talking to a dragon." Probably the former, as much as she was into her subject. But all that's beside the point.

"Don't patronize me, Princess," the dragon's roar brought me out of the thought. I suppose I *had* been doing that, after all. I was going to have to put my sarcasm tongue back in my back pocket for the time being, at least for as long as I had to be in audience with a being that could eat me whole in one bite.

I nodded and chose my words more carefully. "I apologize for the slight, King Xlixi. My imprisonment rubs my patience a bit raw, but I will diligently attempt to speak more suitably."

"Oh, my dear Princess, you are not imprisoned! You are my guest. Did you enjoy the reading material I had delivered to you yesterday?"

I shrugged. "Belle got a whole library," I said, kind of hoping I would get to explain that movie reference, but he ignored it so I went on. "I have enjoyed reading it, but I am curious as to why you selected that work."

"It is the story of dragons battling on Earth. I thought you might enjoy the history of my race as it pertains to the realm of your birth."

"Oh." I did remember reading that, but it had seemed like a sideline to the story being told. "There wasn't a lot of information about either the red or the white dragon in that story, though. Do you know their names?" Granted, I didn't really care about their names, but I wanted to keep him talking about the story. Somehow, I figured, it had something important to do with the reason I was in his not-prison behind bars.

"Of course I know their names! Regrettably, however, the names of those two dragons are impossible for a fleshy one such as yourself to pronounce."

Of course they were. I didn't push it, though; I'd already irritated him enough. "Well, it is good to read the tale, regardless. Those with whom I grew up considered that story to be a fable, and I always considered that silly." I hoped was no way he could have known that I'd completely made that up. "I have enjoyed reading the true account of it. Do you have any other works that give further account of your race's history, King Xlixi?"

"Of course I do, Princess. It is my hope, though, that you are not my visitor for long enough to read them."

"I see. And, so, for you to release me from your—your hospitality, I presume you require me to agree to let you enter Kiirajanna in the future?"

"Enter it, as its rightful and true king. Yes. And I require you to swear it. More specifically, you must swear upon your future crown that when the times comes for me to join your world to this one under my own overlordship, you will not merely allow it, but will publicly welcome that occurrence with open arms."

"Wow. That's a lot of swearing to take in."

"If it is too much to be sworn today, then our discussion is over, Princess." Immediately, the door behind me opened and I felt claws reaching for me. I made a mental note that either the dragon could communicate telepathically with its adjutant, or the wyvern made a habit of listening at doors.

"Wait!" I gasped, coming up with a desperate plan and going with it.

"You wish to make the oath?"

"I—I might, but I have had a hard time concentrating since I arrived, Your Majesty. Everything I had with me of importance has been returned, all except for a little bauble that is precious to me. It was—it was my mother's, you see, and her mother's before that, and it is how I keep myself grounded and focused while I face the world without her comforting presence. Might I ask that the pendant be returned to me so that I might more clearly make such a significant decision? It is just a small bauble, except to me."

I'd been hoping he would bring it up so that I wouldn't seem too needy. I really did feel naked without the power of Draignerthol on my chest, and I was hoping to be able to talk to Druzhtane again at some point. But if the dragon sensed I needed it for anything significant, I was pretty certain it would become a bargaining chip. I wanted to keep Momma's gift off the negotiating table, tilted as that table was toward His Royal Halitosis.

"Ah, Princess, yes," the dragon's head levered up and down like a seesaw. "You must be referring to the powerful relic known as Draignerthol." Well, heck—there went the bargaining chip. "I was wondering when you might bring up that ancient talisman of arcane power. You are aware that you were prophesied to be the one to return the pendant to Kiirajanna, are you not, Princess?"

"I am aware, Your Highness, of a lot of prophecies regarding me. So many, in fact, that I have a difficult time keeping them all straight," I replied, still careful to avoid showing too much of my hand.

"Well, congratulations. You have indeed returned Draignerthol to Kiirajanna. Excellent work, Princess. Now, I think, it is time for the wondrous relic of an age gone by to spend some time on Pazhbojanna. Do you not agree that would be a good thing?"

"It already has spent some time here, Your Highness. I believe it is time for me to return it to its original home."

He laughed a deep, evil, throaty chuckle. "In due time, Princess, you may. Say, once your oath to me has been duly executed, and I am ready to return you to your land?"

I just glared at him. I knew it was the wrong thing to do, but I couldn't think of much else. Everything I thought of to say at that moment was likely to get me eaten.

"Take her," Xlixi told his adjutant, and that quickly I was whisked back onto the elevator and the doors swooshed shut.

CARCHAR

A prison.

Or, to a tree, a city.

Settling In

Xlixi sent me a message later on that morning.

After settling down at my table to read more of The Mabinogion, I heard another light scrape and looked up. This time the wyvern pushed not one, but three books under my door. I realized as I ambled over to see what they were that His Royal Windbagness was telling me that he was in it for the long haul.

It sent me another message, too, though—one that was subtle and probably unintended. What I heard loud and clear from the gesture was that, for some strange reason I couldn't see, he needed me. For all of his talk of his own power and going in with or without my approval, he was anteing up strongly for my cooperation. I'd have to figure that part out.

I'd have to get out of the cell first, though.

I looked at the new books. One I already had, just—not with me. It was the book of prophecy that I'd taken out of the Library of Alecsanddrha as it had burned down, only this one was bound differently and scribed by a different hand.

I shot a silent breath of thankfulness upward. Multiple copies *did* exist! The revelation brought a strong sense of relief, not so much because I now owned two copies of the same prophecy, but because it meant that many of the other works that I hadn't been able to save were probably also duplicated elsewhere. The guilt that had perched on my shoulder like a damning raven eased up just a little. Yes, I'd burned a library, but maybe, just maybe, that fire hadn't in turn caused the loss of countless volumes of priceless information.

Maybe.

Worth hoping for, right?

The other two were written histories, one of the realm of Kiirajanna that reached back into the first epoch, and the other a tale of the Cult of the Wyrm. Obviously he was trying to show me some level of goodwill in providing me the sordid details of his allies back home. That still seemed strange considering the fact that I was a prisoner in his tower, one who could easily be disposed of in a single gulp.

I flipped briefly through the history of Kiirajanna, marveling at what a treasure the work was. Elf history was divided into four epochs, according to the history teachers Sternyface had assigned. The first epoch, one spanning many thousands of years, was one in which magical creatures—dragons, included—had roamed the land, and the elves had used magic with abandon to bend both the world and each other to their ways. It had gotten so badly out of hand that eventually huge scars from magical catastrophes scored the land. Meanwhile the elves were bringing the more primitive, non-magic-wielding humans over to be their ground troops. Finally a courageous group of elves got tired of the desolation and bloodshed and ended it forever, or so they thought, brokering a peace treaty and then cutting Kiirajanna off from the only other realm they'd known about at the time.

Thus began the golden epoch, the time most elves regard as the best of their history. After the concerted effort to cut themselves off from Earth, they'd settled down to a fairly comfortable and peaceful lifestyle. Magic was around and still well-regarded, but the strong rulers of that epoch placed strong penalties on the offensive use of spells, and in doing so avoided strife and warfare, at least for the most part.

That could only last so long, of course. As peaceful times generally do, I suppose, that epoch ended with the outbreak of a powerful, world-wide war, one that ignited old hostilities and created new ones. Once again, war wracked the realm for centuries, tearing both the people and the land physically into pieces. Finally a treaty was negotiated that not only ended the war but also forbade the practice of magic, and thus was the fourth epoch launched.

It was the fourth epoch that I found myself in. Some said that I was prophesied to bring an end to that epoch in my role as the Dragon Queen. I knew I would cause some turmoil, but I wasn't sure about the epoch-ending thing. I hadn't found anything mentioning epochs in the actual prophecy, though to be fair I hadn't made it completely through the whole thing yet. All the interpretive stuff I'd relied on at the library had burned with the building. At least, that was what I'd thought. I was pretty certain most of the historical knowledge of the realm had burned at the same time.

In the book I'd just been given, though, the little-documented first epoch and the almost entirely undocumented third epoch were each described in pretty stark, sometimes gory detail. If I'd been in a better situation I would've cheered out loud for the gift.

The other book, the one on the history of the Cult of the Wyrm, was a lot more disturbing. Some of it I already knew, like the efforts of both the staff of the Library of Alecsanddrha and the traitors in the northlands to disrupt the prophecy. But it also told of agents—more than one!—who had infiltrated the inner circle of the royals. It didn't give any identifying information, unfortunately, but it rapidly became clear that I had to be careful who I trusted in the castle once I returned.

If I returned, a little voice inside my head tried to say, but I shoved that back with all the mental force I could.

I took to reading as my sole activity. It wasn't that hard. I'd always daydreamed of being able to do nothing but sit around and read all day. If I tried and concentrated, I could actually forget about the cells and the bars and the hungry dragon upstairs, and in so doing actually enjoy the peace, quiet, and solitude of my little white room and the books it now contained.

I didn't hear much else from Dru. Since she didn't have anything to read, she started an exercise regimen. I'd listen every morning and every evening to her huffing and puffing as she did pushups and situps and jumped in place.

The interrogations by Xlixi continued as well. Every morning I'd be roused after breakfast, taken for a shower that, as far as I could tell, Dru hadn't had the opportunity for yet, and then taken up to see His Royal Hot-air-ness. Each time I'd be asked if I were ready yet to make my oath and walk free, and each time I replied that I wasn't yet. I was careful never to say no outright. I was pretty certain if I did he'd just decide that keeping me around wasn't worth the effort.

The third day was the worst. I'd asked a couple of times about the nature of the elves' public service, and both times I'd gotten a simple response of a chortle and a gleam in his eye. The third visit, after we went past the standard preliminaries of "have you decided" and "no, not yet," he asked if I was sure that I wanted to know the truth about the elves' public service.

"Yes," I said firmly, probably overplaying it. I wasn't all that sure, really.

The dragon silently looked off into the distance, and suddenly, after a few long moments of quiet, the elevator door opened behind me. Before I could turn around, an elf boy in his early teens was shoved past me.

"Ah, my public servant for today," Xlixi growled. The young elf regained his balance and faced the dragon, and then he went completely rigid. I saw the light blue magical aura connect the dragon and the boy, and I sensed the same terror that Xlixi had foisted on my consciousness at our first meeting, and then I noticed that the elf boy was fully ensnared in the arcane thrall. Xlixi's huge eyeball glanced my way, and I could tell in that brief look that he knew that I knew it. It was obvious that the dragon's deep, evil-sounding chortle was at my expense, not the boy's.

"This is the nature of public service, Princess. *You* may not be entirely susceptible to my powers, but rank and file among your kind are. Scratch your head, son."

The elf boy scratched his head. I stepped forward so that I could look at his face and blanched from the stark terror radiating from it.

"What a mighty dragon you are, scaring a little boy like this," I observed, the statement earning me another deep, evil-sounding chortle.

"You have yet to see my true might, Princess." The red tongue snaked out and caressed the boy's neck and face, lapping up the huge volume of sweat that was cascading down the poor kid's front. "His terror is delicious."

"You're going to eat him, aren't you?"

"Oh, of course. After all, I must consume calories in order for my basic body functions to continue. Surely you can understand that, can you not? He has been fed very well, on some of the finest elf dinners that can be created in this city. He has been kept comfortable, warm, and dry, and for the past week he has received massages and showers, and even anointing of oil. I am told that makes elves feel special, honored, and I have had him honored above all. Today he will take his place as the source of my own continuation of life."

"Look, mighty King Xlixi, what can I do to save him?" I wasn't ready to swear an oath of fealty yet, but I couldn't watch the poor kid die, much less be eaten by a dragon.

"Save him? You wish to save him? From what?"

"From death," I answered quickly. Too quickly, I guess. It earned me a loud bark of laughter from the dragon.

"Dear, dear confused little elf Princess, do you not know that everyone dies? Everyone except me, I should say, though eventually, once I have lived a few thousand years, I may choose to finish my life as well. But all of you lesser creatures are born, you live, and you die, all of those milestones occurring within a few mere decades of each other, and so death is the one constant in your lives. You cannot cheat death, so why do you even try?"

"He's so young." I shrugged, wondering if I might make more of an impact if I assumed the dragon's cold demeanor.

"Of course he is. The young of your species are far more tender than the old. Why would I make him live several more years when the end result will be the same for him but less satisfactory for me?"

"But—"

"But there is a time to grow, and there is a time to harvest what has been grown. That is the way of the world. It is the way your food manufacturers on Earth treat their crops and livestock as well, yes? Why must you be so sentimental? Oh, I must confess, Princess, I am deeply disappointed. I thought that one known to prophecy as the Dragon Queen would be sterner of countenance than this simpering little girl I see before me. Perhaps what this is telling me is that I should eat you now, along with your public service friend there, and look for someone else to install in your place?"

"No. No, I am the Dragon Queen," I said, resigned to the fact that there wasn't going to be anything I could do for the poor kid to my side. "At least give him a fair, sporting chance?"

"A sporting chance...." The dragon's voice rasped over the words, tasting them as they went. "Princess, I would *love* to endure your explanation as to what you mean by a sporting chance."

"Oh, mighty King Xlixi, I do not seek to have you endure anything long or drawn-out. I simply mean a chance, however slight, that he might alter his own fate."

"And not be eaten? How silly an idea. Are you suggesting that I might allow my dinner to go uneaten, thus making myself hungry, or are you suggesting that this elf that stands rooted in fear might find it within his power to escape me?"

I tried more, stronger, diplomacy. It had, after all, bought at least a little time for the kid. "Oh, mighty King Xlixi, I do believe that you can certainly be magnanimous in sparing the life of one little elf, and yet I would not suggest that you cause yourself to go without needed sustenance. Nor do I hold any hope that this young lad might escape your clutches. I merely suggest, as is our tradition as elves, that you give your prey the opportunity to run, to hide, perhaps to make the game a little more difficult." It was the best I could do for the kid, and though I was being honest when I said I didn't give him strong odds in any case, I hoped the dragon might give him at least the chance to run. That way if he died, as he most probably would, at least he would die attempting to defend himself from a dragon rather than shivering in terror and, sadly, in a pool of his own urine.

"Hmm," the dragon gave a show of considering my suggestion. "Okay, Princess, if such a display would please you, then I shall grant it as the magnanimous and mighty king that I am. Boy, you may run now. You *should* run."

Suddenly the boy's body jerked as he came back into his own senses. Terrified, he glanced at me. I shrugged and pointed to the far corner behind us, hoping he could get to the back of one of those and somehow lose the dragon's pursuit.

He took off at a sprint.

"How long does this sporting chance last, Princess?" the dragon asked as we both watched the poor kid run.

I sighed. "As long as you believe is sporting, I guess."

I was resigned to the kid's fate. I wasn't prepared for what happened next, though. I sensed a ripple and saw a blue flash of power as the dragon's arcane energy suffused the room. With a speed that should have been impossible, the dragon's head whipped around and toward the runner. The kid had even less of a chance than I'd feared. I watched the dragon's teeth grab his torso and then, in the simple continuation of the earlier move, fling it back my direction. The poor kid's body ricocheted off the wall and ended up in a heap right where he'd started, legs bent at insane angles, eyes entreating me to somehow find a way out.

The dragon hummed with pleasure as its great head rotated slowly back around. It reared as a great snake might, and then struck, ending the boy's life as it removed the head and shoulders from the remainder of his body. Bones crunched in the dragon's mouth as the beast chewed, huge eyes watching me for my reaction.

I refused, angry and disgusted as I was, to even reach up and wipe the blood spatters off of my arm.

The dragon reached out with its tongue and lifted the rest of the corpse to its open maw, chewing with relish so that I could see the bones and flesh ground into paste. He swallowed, and then said, "Ah, yes, Princess. I must commend and thank you. This sporting chance tastes quite delicious. I shall use it with more public servants from here on out. And now, for today, you are dismissed."

The great elevator door behind me slid open and I was yanked into the car once again.

I didn't let myself sob my revulsion out till I was safely back in my room.

The next day, I spotted Draignerthol. I just barely kept myself from falling to my knees in relief when the blue glimmer caught my eye. I'd been worried that the dragon had Momma's pendant up in his horde of treasure. Granted, I hadn't seen a horde of treasure up on his floor, only piles in the darkness, but it was a huge room and I hadn't seen but the closest bit of it   I figured he had to have one somewhere, though, since all the books about dragons described a horde of treasure.

But either Xlixi didn't have a horde, or he chose not to keep Draignerthol in it. As I walked back down the hall in front of my little prison-cell-away-from-home, I saw that the wyvern guard who normally sat at the desk was gone, and behind where he normally sat, right there on the wall, hung a little silver dragon-shaped pendant with bright shiny eyes that glowed deeply with magical power. It beckoned me, the promise of the power that was hanging just right over there. I could feel it. Draignerthol's call, hereditary or otherwise, coursed through my veins. I wanted it.

But I wasn't ready to make a move yet.

So I took the disappointing right turn into my cell and smiled at the adjutant while he shoved the cell door closed. That was when I discovered something—apparently the cell doors were treated the same way the snakes were, which made them impervious to magic. Now that I knew Draignerthol was right over there, I felt its presence and its magic right up to the moment when the door closed, and then the sensation went out like a light bulb.

Maybe it wasn't that the snakes carried anti-magic powers as part of their makeup. Maybe, instead, it was something the dragon could do, a spell to be cast.

I added that to my list of stuff to find out.

I didn't have to wait long. The next morning, as Xlixi started to ask me whether I'd yet decided to swear the oath, to support his opening the dragon cafe of Kiirajanna, "Elves Served Your Way," I interrupted him.

"Something has been bothering me, Your Royal Highness, and this might impact my beautiful world of Kiirajanna and thus my decision. As I am certain you know, we do not have any snakes on my world." When he nodded, I cataloged that as another important data point—apparently he was pretending to know more than he did. I hadn't actually seen a snake, but that night in the woods I'd sensed one, and besides, you don't get a "Swadda of the Serpent Veils" if there are no serpents. "So, Your Highness, are you planning to bring those big black snakes with you to Kiirajanna? And when you do, will they still serve as the magic blockers that they are now?"

Again I got to hear the dragon's deep, throaty chuckle. "Do you believe that I should, Princess?"

"I assume you'll want to stifle the use of magic among your subjects there just as you do here."

"Oh, my future subjects on Kiirajanna have already pretty well stifled magic. That is what my Cult leadership tells me you have discovered, in quite a difficult manner, yes? You are prophesied to unstifle it, as a matter of fact, but clearly you have done little toward that end other than a few simple jumping tricks."

"Why do you say that, Your Royal Highness?"

"Majesty, not Highness. I say that because the spell of magic repulsion is an old and quite basic one. If you'd come here knowing it already, you would have recognized the danger my serpents posed to your abilities, and you would also have known the counter to it. Odds are that some in your priesthood will recognize it, though, so of course I will be much more subtle when I enter Kiirajanna. So no, to answer your question directly. I will not be bringing the serpents there with me when I consolidate my power on both worlds. Does that make you feel better about your own realm? I do hope to please you, as I am certain that you know. A partnership is, after all, a two-way street. And speaking of two-way streets, now that I have answered your question, it is time for you to answer mine. Will you give your oath to welcome me, and my status as overlord, among your people?"

I gave the same answer, and predictably got the same response as a wyvern yanked me backward and an elevator door slammed shut in my face. But I'd learned something key. I just didn't know how to use it yet.

Something else brightened my step as I was herded back to my cell. As I turned the corner and the guard desk came into view, I saw that the spot where Draignerthol hung was blocked from my sight as usual by a very large wyvern. Knowing it was there, though, I could actually sense its presence.

Maybe, I wondered, the magic I'd always credited Draignerthol with might actually be possible for me alone, without the pendant? Elf wizards, particularly the dark-skinned ones, had clearly worked magic on their own. Their spells weren't anything nearly as powerful as what I had been capable of, either at the library or in Ganolog. But that gave me hope, regardless. Maybe, just possibly, I had it in me to launch a spell without the relic's assistance.

I promised myself that I'd find out.

ONNEN

Ash tree.

It is pronounced as though there were only two single n's, but the double-n is a good measure of the ash tree's self-importance.

An Unlikely Ally

One evening the next week, I gained an unexpected ally. I didn't mean to, trust me. It was an accident—a happy, unfortunate, strange, terrifying accident.

I was sitting in my cell reading, minding my own business, when they decided to serve supper once again. It was the same bowl of soup and loaf of bread that I'd become used to, but it was served by a different pair. Not the elf—the elf was always someone different, and I had started assuming they just picked someone at random from the pool of "public service" elves. But it was a different wyvern this time, too.

Must have been a different "feed the princess" shift, I figured.

I looked up when the cell door opened. In walked a timid little boy who couldn't be much past puberty. He wore the typical leash, and he kept his eyes downcast as he served me my bowl of soup and then left.

I watched him go, sad to see a young cherub so downtrodden, and then I looked over at the wyvern. Our eyes made contact. I saw the dark black orbs partly hidden by the vertical lids contract ever so slightly.

And then—well, then it happened. Whoosh!

Sephaline, a ranger who'd bonded with her familiar on her own vision quest, had told me a couple of times about how the bonding felt. It was a whoosh, she said, a sudden exchange of energy that left you dazed and confused and more than a little blurry-eyed. All of a sudden the ranger went from looking out of her own eyes to looking both directions, experiencing the sight of her new familiar while also experiencing the sight provided by that same creature, out of eyes that happened at that moment to be looking back at you. That was the most confusing feeling of the whole process, she'd told me. The other senses worked that way, too. Seph told me that wolverines like Booboo had a particularly keen sense of smell. That, she'd said, was the hardest thing to get used to over time, the smelling of everything around her, herself included, and that ratcheted up dozens of times more intensely than she'd been able to smell before.

I looked into the wyvern's eyes, and suddenly I saw myself looking back. The boy scampering out into the hallway suddenly became nothing more than a minor distraction in the confusing double-vision of the moment. I was...lost. And so, apparently, was she.

The wyvern was a she.

I'd be willing to bet, based on my first moments of experiencing my new bond, that wyverns' senses, smell included, are way more acute than even a wolverine's. Suddenly, completely, I could smell things. I could smell the sheets, which had been laundered with a soap laced with something acrid. That laundry had happened fairly long ago, so it smelled more like musty me than like laundry soap. I could smell the decaying paint. I could smell the steel of the bars. I could smell myself, and that wasn't a good thing. I mean, it wasn't a bad thing—I didn't really stink, no matter what snide comments the adjutant made. But suddenly I could smell myself far more sharply than ever before. The reason I stood out among the other occupants of the cell block was that I'd showered once again that morning. The adjutant kept telling me that His Royal Highness didn't want to be offended by the aroma of a nasty unclean elf that he wasn't going to go to the trouble of eating, and now, as I vividly experienced the flowery aroma the soap had left on my skin and compared it to Druzhtane's sweat, I understood the difference. It hit me right square in the nose.

The other elves—now, they were a little ripe. More than a little, to be perfectly honest. From behind the wyvern wafted a particularly stinky elf smell that I knew to be Druzhtane. I had never smelled her quite the same way I could now, of course, but it was unmistakable. Down the hall in the empty cells, I could tell there had been other elves just from the sweaty, gross aromas still wafting from the blankets and mattresses.

It was intensely weird. I felt like a bloodhound.

There was something else, too. In the fringes of my vision, I could actually see magic.

I'd sort of seen magic before, granted. Every time it had happened around me, or I saw where it had been done, or I tossed the energy around myself, I'd sensed it as a blue aura.. But that was for active, actual magic. Now I could see latent energy. The bars of the cell glowed, for example, and I was sure that if I asked the wyvern—my new familiar, apparently—to look directly at them—

She looked directly at them. She—she knew what I was thinking through the bond. Amazed as I was by the richness of the connection, I still noted what I needed to about the bars. I saw the spell that had been worked on them. Better, I saw the cracks, the small imperfections, in the energy. The spell weaving had relaxed over the years, I realized. Given my new ability to view magic specifically through the wyvern's eyes, I was pretty sure I could shatter the weaving, given the time.

And yes, she was a her. I'd been guessing, not knowing how to tell the gender of a wyrm, but through the suddenly-opened door of mutual sensitivity I could easily make out her gender, her essential femininity. That, and her confusion. She was more bewildered than I was, and that was saying something. I saw, racing through the wyvern's mind, the mental imagery of the stories she'd heard. I saw her fears. Bonding to an elf was the subject of speculation, of younglings' tales, one she hadn't really believed possible up to this moment, and bonding to a prisoner, if it could happen at all, was *not* supposed to happen, not ever.

She was–she was terrified. Completely, abjectly terrified.

I have to admit, I was, too. I had no idea what had just happened, how it had happened, or what to do about it.

After a while, the young elf boy ended our mutual moment of shock. He didn't do much, just looked up in surprise at the wyvern who held his leash but wasn't moving on as normal. The wyvern, sensing the kid's motion, broke eye contact with me and glared at the kid. She was angry at the insolence inherent in his eye contact. I could tell. She wanted to smack the kid hard enough to bounce it off the wall. At the same time, Kluzhka sensed my own horror at the thought of hitting such a young boy who was only wanting to get on with his work. She recoiled inwardly, never having thought about the elves as anything more than subjected, lesser creatures. We were basically food, to her.

And now, here she was, bonded to food.

And–I knew her name, I realized: Kluzhka. It was a pretty name. I remembered that Seph and the old ranger Owain had both told me that a familiar was the one who chose the name, not the ranger. I'd giggled at that; after all, how can a simple beast like a wolverine or a cardinal have enough coherent thought to know its own name? As I understood pets–and I'd never really had one, but I thought I knew enough about it—they only came to know their name after some training by their humans. They had it trained into them, in other words. They didn't come to you knowing their name like a familiar did.

Like Kluzhka did.

Kluzhka wasn't a pet. As her thoughts clouded over and started taking on a red tinge, I realized that I could tell through our bond that my thinking about her in parallel with birds and beasts was vitally insulting to her. She glared at me, and through her mind's eye I saw her taking out her anger on me, ripping me apart, and immediately after that vision I had the strangest wave of remorse wash over and through the bond that now held tight between us.

She wanted to want to kill me, but she couldn't.

Ha!

Mumbling in the strange, harsh, guttural, draconic language that I hadn't realized wyverns could speak, Kluzhka slammed the door shut and shoved the boy on down the hall, moving toward the elevator that would take them back down to the group pen that the boy had been chosen out of, and that would successfully end her shift. With a grumpy expression on her face—*now how did I know that?* I wondered—she glared over her shoulder and shuffled toward her lair.

She was looking forward to solitude to consider what had just happened, just as I was. First, though, came the task of eating supper—for both of us. For me, the soup seemed to be the same variety they'd served every other time. It consisted of meat that I still really, truly hoped was beef, mixed with some vegetables in a thick, rich broth. Now, though, it smelled different. I figured out after a little bit of sniffing around it that the difference was Kluzhka's nose, which had picked up the scent of the soup from where she'd been at the door. She could tell exactly how much pepper there was in the soup thanks to her superior nostrils, which was nice, but the whole mess seemed disgusting to her. Something about her reaction to the disgusting slop smell convinced me that she would never, ever, eat soup, and that reaction nauseated me in turn.

Suddenly I wasn't hungry. And that was a good thing, I realized, as I started getting whiffs and vague views of what Kluzhka was being served. I blanched; in front of the wyvern was either the long, muscular, raw leg of some sort of fair-skinned beast, or....

Or I didn't want to think about it. No, I thought as I clamped my mind's eyes shut–I really, truly, completely, wholeheartedly didn't want to think about it.

The thought that she might be eating part of an elf made my stomach do somersaults while it tried to climb up through my throat. I was glad I hadn't eaten my soup at that point, because I was pretty sure whatever bites I'd taken would have come right back up.

The interesting thing was how she reacted. The first sensation she broadcast was of defiant hunger; I guess she'd been looking forward to her hunk of flesh for as long as I'd been looking forward to my bowl of soup. Somehow, though, my horror got to her, and she paused. The pause surprised me, since I hadn't realized how deeply we could influence each other. It was real, though, because the more I thought about how disgusting the raw meat was, the stronger the sense of revulsion I felt through the strange bond that passed between us.

Through Kluzhka's eyes I saw the hunk of meat raised from the food bowl, then dropped back down, then raised again, then dropped back down, and then raised again and held for a few moments. Finally she tensed her muscles in frustration and then tossed the meat away in disgust.

I got the feeling that she'd never been unable to dive straight into a meal before. At the same time, I remembered that I'd never been flat out denied, either, until I'd come to the strange and twisted version of Fake New York City. I didn't want her to suffer, I came to understand. Still, a little bit of hunger seemed pretty fair in comparison to eating raw elf.

Kluzhka settled down into her little nest, grumpily glaring at the wyverns, her clutch-mates, who were hungrily taking advantage of the portion of food she'd tossed across the room. With a wyvern-sized sigh, she laid her armored head next to her wing, closed her eyes so I couldn't see anything else, and throttled both her thoughts and her breathing.

The gesture clued me in that it was obviously time for me to get some sleep, too.

CAETH

Bonded in the way rangers and their

familiars are.

Literally, "strict." Go figure.

A Sleepless Night

Who are you?

You can speak?

Of course I can speak. Did you think me an animal?

Of course not!

Yes, yes, you did. I could see it in your thoughts.

How can you see my thoughts?

How should I know? It is this strange spell you cast upon us.

I didn't cast anything.

Then what is this sorcery that allows elf and drakonikya to see into each others' heads?

I—I'm not sure.

You know of it, though. I see that in your thoughts.

How can you see my thoughts?

Do you always repeat yourself like that, elf?

Not always. But it is an effective technique when a question is going unanswered.

If you continue asking unanswerable questions, you will continue having your questions go unanswered.

Fair enough. I just find it weird that you can see into my thoughts, but I can't see into yours.

Oh. Well, now, you did not ask me that question, Princess.

Please don't start calling me that.

Princess? But I have been led to understand that that is your title, elf.

Yes, it's my title, as I've been told over, and over, and over again, and for all sorts of reasons. But since you seem to have taken up residence in my mind, I'll just ask you to cut it out.

'Cut it out'? An interesting idiom.

It means—

I am already aware of what it means.

Oh, right. That mind reading stuff you do, again.

I do not do 'mind reading stuff.' There are those in this city who do, however, and His Royal Majesty is one of those, and so it would behoove us both for you to figure out how to end this spell, or at least to shield your thoughts, before tomorrow morning.

I just saw—

...the consequences of His Royal Majesty finding out about this bond that has inexplicably formed between us. Exactly. I opened up my own thoughts to you to let that out, hopefully giving you an example of how your mind looks to me without any sort of shuttering effort on your part.

Would he really kill you like that? Just—rip you into pieces?

Oh, no, probably not like that. Ripping me to pieces would be much too nice, too simple, for an expression of the Lord's displeasure. No, it would be much, much more violent. I don't believe I can bring myself to imagine the violence, in fact. Regardless, hopefully the scene I showed you illustrates the importance of keeping your mind blank while you are speaking with him.

That's all there is to it? Just keep my mind blank?

For the most part, yes. Just fill your eyes with, and then let your mind see, an image of a blank wall. You do have a few of those in your cell, yes? Oh, that's good. Just—do not focus as closely on the grout between the blocks. You need to present a blank mind, not a cinder block wall pattern. Ah, better. Now remember that vision, and think on it while you speak with the king.

He wouldn't eat you, would he?

No, of course not. Well, probably not. To my knowledge, he does not have a history of eating drakoniki.

Oh. And your kind, that I call wyvern, are what you call drakoniki, I saw through the mental image that you passed.

Oh, good. Even a stupid elf can be taught.

Hmmph. Thanks.

You are most welcome.

I didn't actually mean to express appreciation.

I know. I am not stupid like an elf. I am curious, though, about the emotion I felt passing through with your question. You would be sad to see me eaten by the king?

Well, yes. Of course.

Why? Not long ago I sensed your horror over my contemplation of the enjoyment of my dinner. You and I are not friends, elf, nor are our races allies.

Don't you feel an emotional connection?

I wish that I could say I do not, but I do. It is—strange.

Yeah, well, welcome to the club. It's part of the bond, I think.

What is this bond you are referring to?

The ranger's bond. I don't know a lot about it, but what I've read tells me it always happens first during hunhymgais, which is—

I have seen in your mind what it is. Go on.

Oh, right. Let's try this the easier way, then. This image I'm sending you is my cousin, Ranger Sephaline, with her familiar Booboo. This one is the great Ranger Owain with his familiar— um, I forget the bird's name.

Very interesting. So—so if your images are true, then I must be one of these rangers?

Well, no. I am. The elf is the ranger, and the beast is—

You think me a beast? You already said you do not.

Well, you're—kind of beast-like. I had never even heard one of the drakoniki talk, in fact, before today.

Of course you hadn't. Why should my kind deign to speak with yours? Elves are, after all, but one miniscule step above cattle.

Thanks.

You're welcome.

I was being sarcastic.

I know.

Well, aren't you just the mouse that got to keep the cheese?

…. Okay, you stumped me on that one.

I know.

Listen, elf princess, this has been a charming talk, but now we must find a way to break this spell.

Why?

WHY? Are you daft?

You just said I was but one small step above a cow.

And now you intend to bumptiously try to prove me right?

No, now I intend to get you to explain why you believe this spell, if you must call it that, should be broken.

Oh. Silly me, to have thought the answer to that should be obvious to even the most logic-impaired of food-beasts.

Maybe if you stop insulting me and return instead to having an actual conversation, your logic might shine through.

I'm not sure I know how to explain the matter to you in a manner that you will not find insulting, elf.

Try me.

Okay. Fine. You are an elf. An elf princess, for all of whatever exalted goodness that means among your kind, but to me, an elf. I am a drakonikya, descendant of a long line of elf-hunters, one very small evolutionary step down from the drakoni themselves, who make up, as I am sure goes without saying, the mightiest race that has ever existed. I should be hunting you, not swapping tales with you through a strange telepathic bond all evening. It goes very much against the natural order of things, for one issue: I am the hunter, and you are the prey. For the second issue, as I've already told you, the king will take a very dim view of the procedure and will likely kill us both. For the third, I feel myself actually succumbing to the spell and feeling—emotion—for you, and that is entirely against everything for which I have ever stood. You must tell me how to end this, and immediately.

You feel emotion for me?

Ah. And now it is time for you to attempt to make me regret admitting to that, is it not?

Not in the way you think. I'm surprised that one who thinks so highly of herself would admit to it, yes, but that's not why I asked. Lookit, Kluzhka, as little as a year ago I thought your kind were nothing more than myth and legend. A few months ago I learned otherwise in an encounter with a—with one of your kind. You're not legend. You're lizards—great big flying lizards, and now that I've come to know you, I know you're great big flying lizards who can think and feel. You're powerful, granted, but I've seen one of you bested by elves working together. You're not a weak race, by any means, and yes I should label you race instead of species in recognition of your status as sentient beings, but you're not all-powerful either. Now, I'm pretty sure I couldn't beat you in a physical battle, and I don't know if I could best you magically, but the individual contests don't matter. Your race has no business looking down on mine as anything inferior. You got that, Kluzhka?

I am not certain I agree with your premise, having lived my entire life so far looking down upon your type as both a good source of protein and an excellent source of sport. I do appreciate your spunk, Princess, and be glad for that admission. However, I am still more than a little hung up on what will happen when the king learns of our connection.

He can't learn of it.

He's a drakon. He will.

No, he will not.

You have no idea what a drakon is capable of, elf.

I have read of them—

Read? You have read of them? What exactly do your little fantasies say of the mighty drakoni? That they fly around and spit out fire?

Well, yes, that and—

That, and they are grand masters of the arcane arts. King Xlixi has been reading your thoughts, and manipulating your emotions accordingly, since you arrived. His very gaze can cast fear into your heart such that you merely stand and tremble as his jaws end your life. And he has seen many centuries, and possibly even several eons—over which time he has undoubtedly honed his killing prowess.

You've met him?

No! Of course I have never met the king. For me to do so would mean either a very unlikely promotion of several ranks at a single bound, or else death. Why do you ask?

It's just that—if you haven't met the king, how do you know his powers?

His powers are well known—

Well known? You haven't seen them yourself? And you ragged on me for having just read of them?

I suppose that you might have a point.

Oh, I might have a point. Wyverns.

Elves.

Look, Kluzhka, I admit that I have no idea, really, what we're up against, bless its thrice-damned heart. I admit also that I am scared out of my ever-lovin' mind. All I know is—all I know is—I know—look. Kluzhka, you and I have only been bonded for a matter of hours, yet it seems as though we are old friends. I know this isn't logical. I know it's dangerous, and to both of us. I also know that I have no idea how to break it, or even if breaking a ranger bond is possible. So as logical as it sounds to break the bond and go back to being wyvern and elf at war with one another, I honestly don't know whether it's any use to even look for that. You can't just ask your friends because they'd kill you, and even if I could get to the elf priests to ask, their response wouldn't be much friendlier. Might as well, instead, find a way to be compatibly joined.

....

....

Your logic—makes sense.

Hey, lookie! The mere elf managed to make sense to Her Mighty Lizardness. So that's good. Now can we get back to what's important?

**sigh* And what, if I dare ask, is it that you deem important?*

I'd say that getting to know one another is important. I'm assuming, granted, that the state of being bonded is permanent, but at this point we have no evidence that my assumption is invalid.

Correct.

So—so getting to know one another is important, right?

....

....

....

RIGHT?

....

....

Oh, fine.

So who are you?

I am Kluzhka.

And?

And what?

And—I don't know. Your favorite color? Your parents? Your brother and sister? Your dreams? Your aspirations? Your first boyfriend?

You ask a lot of silly questions.

What would you ask that is less silly?

How about—let's see. Do you know what actually hunting for your food is like?

You called my questions silly?

That was not a silly question.

Was, too. My cousin taught me a lot about fending for myself—including hunting—while I was getting ready for this trip. Little did she know I was gonna end up in a white cell being served stew by terrified elf servants, right?

Your cousin, the ranger? The one bonded to the wolverine—it is that word, a familiar? Yes? Good. You seem to care for her a great deal.

I do care for her a great deal.

She is a cunning hunter?

She's competent, I guess.

Competent is good. She is the one who held off the drakoniki with the wind storm?

How did you know that? I haven't told you that whole story.

You were broadcasting again, envisioning that encounter while telling me of her. Those sorts of things are easy to see through someone's thoughts.

What's that like? Can you envision your parents while you tell me of them?

No.

No?

No.

Well, why not?

Because I do not know what you are asking about. The concept of parents is—foreign to my kind.

Wait! Wait! Was that a mental image of a hatchery you just sent?

Indeed.

So that's—oh—you're—you don't—

Correct. I know as little about which drakonikya laid the egg that became me, and which male fertilized it, as you do about finishing sentences.

Hey! Well, I guess that's fair. So what was it like growing up in a hatchery?

There was not much to it, elf.

You don't have any mental images of soaring among the clouds the first time, of hunting in the woods?

It was not allowed.

Going outside wasn't allowed?

That is what I said, yes.

Surely you've been out of the tower since—no, I guess not, from the images you're sending. See? I'm getting better.

I am thrilled beyond description.

Sarcasm, again?

You seem to enjoy it, Princess.

I guess. So why haven't you been out of this tower?

Complex, actually. The tower is just the tallest part, His Majesty's roost. But my kind are housed in several adjacent buildings, all interconnected through a tunnel system. As for the rest, no, I have not been out there. It is not allowed. Only the king and a few of his closest advisors enter and leave, and that only under cover of darkness.

But—why?

The king does not wish for his cattle to be frightened, it would seem.

So the elves never see their king?

I do not believe so. The only elves who ever meet him are those selected for that level of public service.

And public service means getting fattened up to be the king's food, right?

The king's food, or ours. We in the king's retainer must eat, also.

Oh, right—what I saw earlier was you about to chow down on a piece of elf, wasn't it?

Yes, and I am still quite hungry. What do you expect me to eat?

I don't know; I was thinking maybe a tasty cow, or a pig? Ever had a perfectly grilled flank steak?

Those are for the drakoniki who are sent out from the tower. They say they are not as tasty as—

I do not want to know.

Right. So, as useless as this questioning is, I have nothing better to do so I will turn it around to you. What was your hatchery like?

A lot different from yours. I spent a lot of time out in the woods growing up, and since I came to Kiirajanna I've been out there even more.

I see two very different kinds of forests in your thoughts. Why are they so different?

Well, one is the southern forest on Earth, and the other is the elf-tended forest on Kiirajanna. The first is wild and free, with a solid dose of kudzu to make it look even more unkempt than it would be otherwise. The second set of images are from the woods where the elves literally tell the trees to grow in straight lines.

They're both—beautiful.

Thank you. I doubt you could ever visit the southern forests, since magical creatures like you apparently can't go to Earth. But the other forests are my home now, and once I get out of here we'll make sure you see them.

Once you—um, elf, I must tell you that you are not going to—

Get out of here? Yes. Yes, I am. I will find a way. And when I do, I'm taking you with me.

Strong words, but foolish, especially in the last.. I cannot leave.

Why not?

For one thing, you have shown me your people's reaction to the last wyvern they met. Would I not receive a similar reception?

Probably, at first, but you do know who I am, right?

I do! You are an elf princess. A surprisingly smart one for such a stupid race, though I admit that is not saying much.

Yeah, thanks. But no, I am more than that. I am Alyssa, the future Dragon Queen of Kiirajanna.

Oh. I see. What is a dragon queen, exactly?

The queen of the elves to whom the dragon prophecy refers.

Oh. And that queen is you?

Yes.

How do you know for certain?

I am the one born with the dragon birthmark.

Well, that is pretty telling, I would say.

More sarcasm?

Of course. I am so proud of you for recognizing it.

The insults really aren't helping. But no, your own king recognized me, which is why he's been talking to me every morning about swearing an oath of fealty to him.

Why haven't you done that yet, then?

Because he'll eat my people if I do.

He will eat your people whether you do or you do not.

Probably. But if him eating my people is such a given, why does he seem to need my approval?

That—is a good question, elf. Another one. I am surprised, and quite proud of you.

I'm going to start ignoring your insults.

I was hoping that you would. But back to the topic—you say that King Xlixi knows of the prophecy, and it stands to reason that that is why he is so intent on seeking your oath. So what does this prophecy say about your future?

That I am going to burn the library down.

Why would you burn a library down? Oh…. I see in your mind that it has already happened.

It's—it was—a long story.

Of course it is. And so you are called—or are to be called, if I understand it correctly—the dragon queen because you burned a library down, like a dragon might?

No, that's not why.

Then why?

I don't know. I haven't gotten that far into the prophecy.

I—I see. So, if I understand correctly, you do not entirely know who you are, and yet you asked me if I know who you were, and when I answered your question, you corrected me with a title you do not yet understand, and yet through all this you expect me to believe that there is something in the title that would protect me if I were to return to Kiirajanna.

Yeah, I guess. Now that you put it that way it sounds a little silly, but that's pretty much it.

Your Highness will understand, I hope, why I remain skeptical.

Your—or is it My?—Highness's father is also the current elf king.

I see. So your father has but to order his royal subjects to be comfortable in my presence, and they will be so?

No, that's not how it works.

I see.

You keep saying that, when I'm not sure you see at all.

Well, I do see something, but I am not certain that what I see is what you wish me to see.

Do you see this?

The image you are sending to me? Yes, I see what you believe my soaring above a beautifully forested landscape might look like. Neither of us has ever actually been witness to that vista, though, so I understand the hesitancy in some parts of the image. I admit to the yearning in my soul that your image creates, but I am still stuck on your inability to explain why your people will allow me, one of your most fearsome foes, to exercise such freedom.

You'll be the Crown Princess's, and soon the Queen's, familiar. That will be enough, among my highly-ordered elves.

I—see, if I can use that word properly—doubt in your mind even as you attempt to convince me. And we still have not settled the familiar part, actually. A familiar is a beast. I am not beast. I believe that you would be my familiar.

Yes, well, I'm not a beast, either.

Okay, so if we take the argument at face value and ignore, for the time being, the obvious inferiority of your species, then we can agree that neither of us is a beast, so it seems as though the title of familiar should fall upon the lesser being.

Okay, that's fine.

So I shall be the first drakonikya with an elf queen as a familiar.

No!

Why not?

An elf can't be a familiar.

Well, by the same logic, or unfortunate lack thereof, neither can a drakonikya.

Look, I didn't realize till tonight that you wyverns could even talk.

Your ignorance of my race's abilities serves little to prove your point and much more to prove mine, elf.

Okay, so can we just be bonded, as equals?

Equals? In what universe? I am stronger than you, faster than you, and smarter than you. How can we be equals at all?

Smarter? Bless your heart.

Why does the mental image I receive when you project those words have nothing to do with the words themselves?

No reason. But look, I'm going to be the elf queen, while you're just one of the wyverns in the employ of the king.

You refer to luck of birth. Your father was a king, while whoever inseminated my egg was not. I can still eat you in just a few bites.

Look, I'm getting tired, and I need to be at least a little bit rested to face Xlixi in the morning. Also, we're obviously going to have plenty of time to debate this in the future. Can we table the who is superior to whom discussion for later?

We can. It is probably best that we do so, in fact. Tomorrow, please be very careful to shield your thoughts regarding the bond and me, but do not shield them completely. If you suddenly show yourself capable of actually shielding something, the king will become suspicious and probe farther. Trust me, the king is adept at probing minds. Do you understand the balance of which I speak?

Yeah, I do. Makes sense. I'll get through the conversation with him, and then tomorrow evening you and I can continue our discussion. This has been cool, by the way.

Cool. Yes. If I am correct in reading the meaning of the term you used, this has been cool to me, also. I never thought I might consider an elf interesting, much less a friend. Thank you.

No. Thank you.

He Built This City

As I clomped with Zhluskuh onto the elevator, and then let him shove me into the dragon's lair, I couldn't help feeling like my feet weighed a few hundred pounds each. I was terrified for this next meeting, worried that I'd fail Kluzhka, that Xlixi would be able to sense that something was different about me.

"Something is different about you, little one," the dragon's voice rumbled even before the massive armored head snaked around the support column. "Your thoughts are more guarded from me than before. Tell me, what has happened overnight?"

Because I'd feared this moment, I'd prepared for it. That meant coming up with a plausible lie, unfortunately, and lying wasn't my strong suit. Still, I gave it my best. "Last night I remembered my training in the mental disciplines, oh mighty dragon king. I am pleased to say that, though your magnificence had me off balance when I arrived, I am returning to my normal, disciplined, self."

I'd figured that playing to the dragon's natural arrogance might have the best chance of working, and I waited anxiously to see whether I was right.

Xlixi seemed suspicious for a breath, and then for two, but finally he nodded and sighed. "Yes, yes, I am glad to hear of your abilities in the mental discipline of blocking. That said, I would prefer to be able to monitor your concerns and worries, Princess. At least, I should add, until you have sworn your fealty to me. It is for your own protection, you see."

"For my own protection, mighty Xlixi? I don't understand."

I did understand, sort of. While he'd been talking, I also felt his hypnotic magic trying to take over my mind, addle my senses. The dragon wanted to control me, a realization that left me pondering the difficult choice of whether or not to pretend like he was succeeding. On one hand, he might relax and tell me what he really needed me for if I pretended. On the other, he might decide I was weak and just start probing, and I doubted that I could fend off a direct mental attack from His Royal Ego. So instead I rolled along and played dumb, hoping for a clue.

"Oh, it is simply that I would not want untoward thoughts to bother you in your contemplation of the orderly and pleasant reign that a future involving my overlordship will present."

"Of course, Your Majesty. I contemplate that often, already, and I feel closer than ever to a decision to proceed. As for the monitoring of my concerns and worries, of course an exalted being should already know that you can do so if you need, and at any time. You have but to ask. Or, should you choose, I am certain that you, a great and wise dragon, are powerful enough in the arcane to break through my primitive mental disciplines even without my permission."

"You are correct in your assertion, Princess, that I could easily break through your primitive mind's barriers to view your thoughts, but that is an imposition I am loathe to impress upon you," he said, his tone sounding uppity.

"You would rather I leave my guard down so that you can impose yourself upon my thoughts without the effort of breaking through, then, Your Majesty?"

"I should probably eat you for the impudence of asking that question, but I shall not, as I do still intend to see the Dragon Queen elevated to a position from which she can welcome the Dragon King into my rightful place. Thus, since I am not disposed to eat you, at least not at the current moment, I will just reply with a negative. I would rather you not leave your guard down, in other words, because the challenge of breaking through it, undetected even, is stimulating to me."

"I see," I said. "I stand, as always, at Your Majesty's pleasure."

"Do not presume to make such challenges to my authority a frequent matter, however."

"I will most certainly not," I agreed, feeling like I'd won a battle but not really sure what the prize was. "Your Majesty," I added, a little bit too late for proper courtesy.

"Hmm." His deep-throated rumble shook the floor, and I once again felt him imposing his will upon me. Certain I'd pushed him as far as I dared, I went down on both knees and put my forehead to the floor.

"Please forgive my insolence, oh mighty king!" I called out. Yes, it was corny, but I figured it would work.

It did. The mental pressure eased.

"So, Princess, are you ready to swear the oath I seek?"

I was ready for that one, too. If I could keep him talking about his wondrous creation, we'd skirt the whole topic again.

"Oh, Your Majesty, please tell me once again how huge this incredible city that you have built is."

"I believe, in the units they use on Earth, it is twenty-two square miles, the same size as the area they call Manhattan."

"You created an island that large?"

"I saw no need to create an island. A large wall circumscribing it seemed enough to restrict the outward flow of people. The interesting thing, though, Princess, is that in hindsight I can see the wall was unnecessary. The people are comfortable here, and do not wish to leave. Here they are born, and here they thrive. It is a good life for them. While it lasts, of course, but no one was meant to live forever. It will be the same for those on Kiirajanna."

I ignored the obvious baiting. "But why New York City? Surely you could have created just about any structure."

"Ah, you see, that is indeed a key monument to my wisdom. In my youth I studied how those who had come before me had hunted for food. They had even enjoyed it, flying about and searching for suitable little elves to feast upon. The terror, the battle—the joy of the circle of life. And yet there was risk. My kind is powerful, but as I am sure you are aware, little elf, we are not omnipotent. Some of my kind would sustain injury, and on the limited occasions when the elves would band together in their huge hordes, sometimes my kind would even lose the battle. That is why my egg was spirited away to this realm, in fact; they rose up and actually caught many of my kind unaware. While that certainly shall never happen again, it caused me to reconsider the method we used to obtain our food. I experimented for a while with different ways to draw elves to me, but that seemed to only bring the strong, sinewy ones. I tried establishing villages and caves of various configurations, to varying levels of success, but then I sent agents to Earth, primitive though it may be, to learn how they raise animals to support that society's large carnivorous appetite. Their methods were simple, obvious, if you will. Simply bring the animals in the herd closer together, to live in smaller pens, but the key is that you must make them feel happy, satisfied."

"And a city was the obvious answer."

"Correct, little one."

"Why New York City, then? Why not Tokyo, or London?"

"I chose New York City because of what I was hearing of it. For one thing it ranked very well in terms of population density; the residents of the New York City on Earth, I realized, must truly enjoy living in tiny little livestock pens. Plus, and equally important, my agents spoke of a vibrant multi-cultural feel, one where anyone could be happy. And since the happiness of my subjects is paramount to me, as I am certain you will soon see in your own realm of Kiirajanna, that was the design I chose."

"Must be hard to create a multi-cultural feel, though, when you only have one culture."

"You have only seen the very tip of it, Princess. I shall have an agent give you the full tour, once I have your oath. With an occasional twist of the ley line transporters I was able to pull youth from all the clans on Kiirajanna, and there were also many rural communities already on this world to pull from."

"So you set them all down in a mostly empty city, gave them plenty of food and marijuana, and now they're all happy little cattle."

"Yesss," his self-satisfied rumble ended in a hiss. "I shall arrange for you to enjoy a tour of the marijuana growing facility, also. I am particularly proud of my horticultural efforts. Those elves are the happiest of my little flock."

"I bet."

"I will have your oath now."

"I—I'm not ready to give it, Your Royal Majesty. Just another day or two of thinking on it? We both want to wait till I'm truly ready to give of myself, don't we?" It was another corny line, but it had worked several times already.

"I am sure that you enjoy this grand game, but I tire of it, Princess. You have until tomorrow to either become my vassal or my lunch."

Once again I felt the air pressure change behind me as the elevator door swooshed open, the adjutant's hands roughly grasped my shoulders, and I got yanked backward and out of His Royal Puffball's presence.

Lunch that day was a surprise. Instead of the hunks of sausage, cheese, and bread I'd gotten used to, the little servant elf brought an actual steak, cooked nice and medium-well with a baked potato and salad in the other compartments of the serving tray.

"This is cow, isn't it?" I asked suspiciously as the elf slipped out. The poor kid jumped at my words and fled, but he probably didn't understand the question. His wyvern handler glared at me for opening my mouth, but it didn't give me the satisfaction of an answer either. A moment later I asked Dru the same question, knowing that she wouldn't understand but burdened with a gnawing curiosity anyway. She looked over and shrugged from her own steak supper, but the gleam in her eye and the way she dove right in made me feel a little safer.

I tasted it. It was good. It could've used more pepper, I think, but beef steaks used to be the ultimate of treats in our house growing up. I kept hoping it was beef as I took bite after savory bite.

I wanted to assume that I'd know elf if I tasted it. Of course I'd know elf, right? But the slab of meat on my plate definitely tasted like beef.

If the dragon was playing a fast one on me, I didn't see what he might stand to gain. He and his wyverns loved the taste of elf; according to Kluzhka, it was far superior to beef. I got the sense from her that they fed me soup made from prime cuts of beef in the same way that some people buy the best pet food for their little pets. Granted, the example didn't work all the way through; I couldn't imagine a cat or a dog feeling the same revulsion to a good steak fit for human consumption that I felt toward the thought of eating my own species. Plus, cows are herbivores, so they wouldn't consider a steak a treat in any event.

I finally gave up the mental game and forced the wicked specters out of my head. What I didn't know about the meat's source wouldn't hurt me, after all, while starvation would definitely do some damage. I wolfed it down.

Soon after, I heard from Kluzhka. *If you give us away, little elf princess, I swear that I will eat you myself.*

Hi! Great to hear from you, my friend! Yes, my day is going wonderfully! I hope your day is going well, too!

Just—shut up.

I could already hear the scraping. Within moments Kluzhka came into view, followed by the adjutant. He let himself into my cell and bowed slightly.

"Good afternoon, Princess. I trust you found your lunch enjoyable?"

"I did," I said simply. If it was a trick, I wanted him to have to bring it up. To my relief, he just nodded.

"His Royal Majesty has requested that you be given a tour of our horticultural facilities here. He said you were particularly interested in the herb that we grow. This is Kluzhka, who unfortunately does not speak your language, but she is a manager of that facility, and she has proudly offered to sacrifice her time off this afternoon to show you around the greenhouse. No, believe me, Princess, it is her pleasure to do so, and it is my pleasure to insist," he said as I started to object. "Perhaps you would enjoy a pouch of the herb, yourself?" The adjutant held out one of the baggies I'd seen come out of the street vending machine. I had absolutely no desire to partake of the drug, but I remembered how Dru had cherished the bag she'd gotten.

I nodded and took the packet from him, laying it on the table. "Later, thank you. Right now I look forward very much to this tour."

The two wyvern spoke in a strange series of audible clicks and hisses, and then the adjutant turned back to me. "Kluzhka will guide you from here. Remember that she does not speak your language, but she reminds me that two of our kind will likely scare the workers too much for their productivity, while she and you together will probably have the opposite effect. She is wise. She is also under orders not to kill you should you try anything untoward, but the orders say nothing about whether or not she may inflict pain. I would advise you to stay within whatever lines she directs you to."

The adjutant huffed and shuffled back down the hall.

What a jerk, filtered through the mental connection Kluzhka and I now shared. I grinned at the mutual statement as I silently tossed the baggie across to Dru, who I knew would enjoy it much more than I would. She caught it deftly and actually shot me back a smile in return.

He seems nice enough.

So why were you imagining me hurting you in all sorts of horrible ways while he was talking in that strange language you use?

He put the images there when he warned me that you were under orders to cause me pain if I get out of line.

Oh. Well, that's true. Don't get out of line, as I would hate to see what this "bond" would do for transporting pain between us. Let's get moving, though, before someone suspects something. And please do try to guard both your mind and your facial expressions. It's quite easy just looking at you to tell that you're involved in a conversation.

Lead on. I followed the thought with a hand gesture. Kluzhka nodded and stomped down the hall.

A Tour

What powers the elevators? I asked as the car hurtled downward. I hadn't been on a lot of elevators in my life; most of the buildings in my home town only had a single story, and the ones that weren't, like the high school, had stairs that I'd been expected to use. The elevators I'd ridden, though, had all felt mechanical, with a jerk at the start or stop and sometimes even while it was in motion. I hadn't felt anything but a completely smooth ride here, though.

She confirmed my suspicion. *Why, magic, of course.*

And yet the snakes can ride on them without harm, apparently.

Why would they not?

They're anti-magic. Aren't they?

No, not at all. They just have magic disrupting spells cast on them.

Oh, right. The king had explained that when I'd arrived, I recalled a little too late. The stress got to me, I guess.

Can you cast magic, Kluzhka?

All of my kind can. Though—"cast" is not entirely appropriate, as we are magic, and when we use the energy, it is just that—using magic rather than casting it. Now, remember to walk right next to me and to school your expression, she chided me as the car slowed smoothly to a stop and the door opened.

I failed the moment I stepped out of the elevator. Schooling my expression went right out the window as I turned and gaped in every direction, and because my head was swinging like a tent flap in a tornado, my feet stopped and anchored themselves in one spot.

Kluzhka proved her strength by yanking me through the air by the hem of my shirt. My suddenly-chastened feet had to paddle back and forth quickly to stay under me. The wyvern just huffed and held on to me as she marched deliberately down the walk-way.

I said to stay with me, not stand and gawk like a newborn.

I couldn't help it. This place is amazing. It looks like the sub-way tunnels I rode in once back home, only there's nobody else down here.

There are plenty of others down here. My kind use these tun-nels as our main transit. We're just lucky that we have not run in-to anyone yet, and so no one else has seen the idiotic expression on that face of yours, Princess.

Do trains ever run down those tracks?

What tracks? Oh, there aren't any tracks down there, she said, reading my meaning by looking at what my mind was seeing. I glanced over to where, in Real New York City, tracks would run to guide the subway trains along through the tunnels, but she was correct. The floor at the bottom was bare.

Is that what your kind use those inset paths for? She was good at reading the images from my mind.

I nodded, and then glanced into the path again. Then I thought back to the statue in the park with nothing on the name plate. It seemed as though Xlixi had carefully used the images his agents had sent to build the structures, but didn't have any real understanding of what the things in or on the structures were for.

In here, she said, pulling me into another elevator. The doors closed and we went upward. When it stopped, we exited and I gasped again.

You really are very easy to impress, Princess.

But this is huge! I argued. To me, it was. We had stepped out of the elevator onto a landing that was about eight feet wide. It was made of something like plexiglass, which gave me a weird vertigo when I looked downward at my feet. It appeared to go all the way around the growing area, which was easily as large as five or six of my high school's gymnasiums put side by side. Above, a clear, arched roof let sunlight directly in. Below was a horticulture operation grander than any I've ever seen.

How many plants do you manage here?

There are sixty thousand holes, though not all are currently occupied. Some are awaiting new seedlings, while others are under maintenance. She had a hard time conveying a large number like sixty thousand; neither of us had ever thought about how to express a number in the thousands through mental imagery when the Arabic numerals both humans and elves used were foreign to her. She ended up showing me six marks, and then a ten-by-ten square that increased ten-fold in one direction and then increased ten-fold again in the other direction.

Xlixi had found a way to use hydroponics to his advantage. Every four feet or so a rack of pipes ran five high, the bottom a little above floor level and the top nearly even with our walkway, eighteen or twenty feet above the floor. A single small pipe carried water from the ceiling down to each set of racks. Holes for the plants ran about a foot apart, and the water trickled by each one till it reached the opposite end, where it cascaded down and returned along the next lower rail, back and forth across the huge greenhouse till it reached the end of the fifth rail, at which point it just dripped into a drain in the floor.

This is enough for the whole city? That was impressive to consider.

Of course not. This is but one of our operations. There are dozens. You elves consume a vast quantity.

You wyverns don't partake? I asked, the query answered with a derisive snort.

We started walking since standing there together silently would have looked too weird. The elves working the floor glanced up at us as the massive shadow Kluzhka cast through the transparent walkway passed by them. Many did a double-take when they saw me with their supervisor, but nobody seemed willing to stare too long. Instead, each just took us in silently and went right back to work. There must have been a hundred of them scurrying about, some on the floor and others on ladders.

What are they all doing?

Different things. It takes a lot of effort to efficiently manage growing operations on this scale.

Well, duh. That girl down there, the one in the brown shirt. She's just walking down the row. What's she doing?

Asking to be eaten by a hungry supervisor.

You wouldn't.

Well, yes, I would, but I was joking about her. She's checking the new plants on the bottom rung. See how she just stopped and plucked something? We plant a few seeds per pod, and usually the seedlings are selected early on. Sometimes the selectors miss one, or a seedling waits a while to sprout, so her job is to cull the pods a final time.

Why don't you just let both plants grow?

We get less out of two plants in one pod than we do out of one, believe it or not. We let the strongest stay, and we remove its competition.

You make it sound so—brutal.

Life is brutal, Princess.

What do you do with the seedlings you cull?

There's not usually a large volume of those, but all of our waste, including clippings and cullings, is dried and chopped to make animal food.

Ah. And what do you use for plant food for these? I let the question slip out before examining it to see whether I really wanted to know the answer. I didn't, but by the time I realized that it was out there anyway.

Oh, that! You know how sausage is made, Princess?

No, I never really thought about it.

It's all the parts of the elves' food-beasts that aren't good enough for steak, ground up with other ingredients and fed to the elves for breakfast and lunch.

Oh. That's appetizing. I let sarcasm flood my mental tone.

They seem to like it. But we don't make sausage out of elves. Those parts get used to feed my plants.

Revulsion gripped me, and I let my face blanch. Kluzhka huffed a few times in her weird way of laughing.

It's not nice to mess with me like that, I accused.

I never claimed to be nice. Not to anybody, and much less to my familiar.

Uh huh. So you're still saying that I'm the familiar, eh?

Still not admitting that I am the superior one? After seeing this marvel? I can hunt, and I can supervise large-scale growing operations. What can you do?

I can put this discussion off for some other time, is what I can do. We don't need this competition. We need to figure out how to get out of this.

There is no way to get out of this.

I can't accept that, Kluzhka.

I am not certain reality cares what you can and cannot accept, Princess. You could always stay here. Come work for me; I'd treat you well. You know, most of your fellow elves fight to get assigned to work here.

They do? Why, the fringe benefits? Is your profit sharing plan that awesome? Or is it so that they can scurry around and check for seedlings to cull?

No, none of that silliness. It is my workers who get extra shares.

Oh. I hadn't thought of extra pot as a side benefit.

It's not obvious. I think it's one of my best ideas. You'd like that, no?

No.

Why not?

I don't do drugs.

She snorted.

All elves do drugs. This drug that my team grows, at least. There's no harm to you, and I hear that it can make you feel much better after a long day at work.

No.

But—

No.

Suit yourself.

You're not doing them any favors. You're just numbing them before the slaughter.

Circle of life, Princess. Circle of life.

While I'd been paying attention to the banter, she'd led me three-quarters of the way around the growing area and then off down the side hall. It wasn't really interesting, just a conveyor belt that moved buckets full of green stuff to another room. We walked around this one too, Kluzhka offering a running commentary on how they carefully dried the harvest and packaged it all by hand. It was about as boring a job as I'd ever heard of.

You know there's no way we can break this bond, I said as we stepped into the elevator to take us back up to the floor on which I was being "housed" as a "guest" of the Crown.

No, Princess, I do not know that, at least not with the thoroughness with which my kind likes to know things. Unfortunately I am coming to suspect that your assertion may be accurate, but to state that I know it is a falsehood.

Fair enough. You know there's no way Xlixi will let me leave without giving him an oath that he knows I'll never break.

Same answer, Princess.

You know I'm never going to give him that oath.

That one, I'll agree to knowing. You are, after all, the most stubborn pack animal I've ever seen.

You know what that means.

Kluzhka demonstrated that a wyvern could sigh.

Yes, Princess, I am fairly certain that I do know.

MEITHRINFA

A nursery of little baby plants.

Heaven, in other words.

A Break for It

The next night, I was ready.

Truth be told, I was ready for a lot. I was ready to get back home to a nice orderly land where powerful magical creatures didn't threaten to eat me every day.. I was ready to sleep once again in my father's wing of the royal palace under Aerona's careful watch. I was ready to bring both Druzhtane and Kluzhka back with me into my own world. I was ready to deny Xlixi the oath he so desperately sought.

Most importantly, I was ready and itching to warn my people of the dragon's plan. The elves needed to know of the danger ahead. They needed to drop their silly concerns about me or the dark-skinned ones working magic and realize that they had to take up their most ancient of weapons, in order to beat their most ancient of foes.

According to Xlixi, Kiirajanna had served as the feasting field for the ancient dragons. I would die before I'd see my world, my new home, turned into that once again.

Kluzhka had told me how the hunting went. Every week, once per week, Xlixi, bored of the ease of feasting on elves who were brought to him, left the tower at night to soar over and hunt the surrounding areas. He was happy enough with wildlife, but he really wanted elves—elves who were in shape, who could run and hide and dart about and, when cornered, could scream. Several settlements surrounded the city, settlements that for the most part contained zhopi who'd escaped the "island," and they were the prey that Xlixi desired.

While he was gone, the tower was always on highest alert, since none of the wyverns wanted to be the one in charge of the tower when something happened. When he returned, though, the wyverns stood down, and Xlixi, in turn, slept off the food that was in his belly.

After he returned, then, was the time we decided we would make our break for it.

Luckily for me, it meant I'd gotten a reprieve from the usual ultimatum, as His Majesty wished to avoid the unpleasantness of eating his little elf princess on such an auspicious hunting day. "The king asked me to tell you to have a good day. He said, 'Sleep well. I will most likely kill you in the morning,'" the adjutant said.

"Some day I will be the dread pirate," I replied, putting attitude into my voice. It earned me a confused look.

Tomorrow morning it is.

Yes, Princess. Tomorrow you will be free, given a little good fortune.

As will you.

I—doubt that. But we shall see.

I'd gotten her to agree to go with me to Kiirajanna, but she—and I, also, I hated to admit—feared she would be no better in my homeland than I was in hers. Not much better, anyway, though she gave me the point that my king wasn't an ancient, terrifying magical beast who loved feasting on her kind.

The only thing I wasn't certain about was the six-week hunhymgais timer. I'd spent two weeks in the park with Dru, and I thought I'd been in the dragon's tower for four weeks, but I hadn't been counting since I'd had more important things to worry about. I couldn't imagine it would matter that much, really.

Surely Dad wouldn't say, "Nice to see you, my daughter, but you're early. You should have stayed to be eaten instead of coming back to warn us about the dragon." The other elves, maybe, bless their dark little hearts, but the King of Kiirajanna, never.

We prepared carefully. She got herself the night off, whatever that meant for her growing operation. What it meant for us, though, was that she would be free to wander the prisoner hallways in the early morning hours after the master returned.

Meanwhile, I'd been practicing my spell weaving without the benefit of a magical pendant. It wasn't easy, but it was possible— I went into the efforts knowing that it had to be, since the elves who made Draignerthol did so through tremendous application of magical power all while not actually using the pendant they were crafting. I realized that Draignerthol's help was like those tongs people use to lift ice blocks; by hand, it was both slippery and cumbersome to wield the flows. It was weird, relying only on my own spell power, and I couldn't get much oomph behind it, but at the same time it was exhilarating to touch, feel, and manipulate the energies myself without going through the pendant. I had to sit way back against the wall thanks to the anti-magic spell on the bars of the cell, but I managed.

As the lights went off in the cell block I tested myself by reaching into what I'd seen of the chinks in the spell and tapping gently. The spell held, but only barely. I grinned, and I waited.

The signal finally came from Kluzhka: mighty King Xlixi returned to the tower to sleep away his now-full belly. As she transmitted the message, I thought I heard his screech approaching from off in the distance. It was a truly terrifying sound that I doubted I'd ever be able to forget.

I smiled as I carefully wrapped my new books up in a sheet and tucked them under my shirt. Soon, we knew, the wyvern at the end of the hallway would waddle sleepily away from his desk for a break, and then we'd be ready to roll.

Several long minutes passed. Kluzhka sent me a panicked vision of the wyvern at the guard desk not leaving.

I started to panic, too, but settled down almost instantly. I'd had enough, and I didn't really care. One way or another, I was getting out of that tower.

I sent Kluzhka the image of us moving forward, and I felt her coming up to the floor in response. In one swipe of magical power I reached out and grabbed the spell that had been clumsily laid upon the bars. I pressed the chink full of my own energy, twisting and pulling, and as Kluzhka rounded the corner I could see, through her eyes as well as my own, the magical energies cast on the cell door shatter and fall away.

Suddenly I felt—full, is the best description. Full of power and strength and might. Powers which I'd only sensed through Draignerthol roared directly through me. In a couple of long strides I found myself standing in the hallway, shoulder to shoulder with my new familiar, facing down a befuddled wyvern guard.

I knew I had to keep him from calling reinforcements. In breaking the anti-magic spell I'd seen how it was cast, and so I replicated it in a bubble around the guard, wrapping that in turn in a sound-proof bubble of stagnant air. It was surprisingly easy, and I started congratulating myself.

Kluzhka urgently thrust her will into my little mental celebration and sent me an image of klaxons going off and wyverns racing to intercept us.

Right.

There would be plenty of time to congratulate myself once we were back on Kiirajanna. Now, it was time to *move.*

As much as I reveled in the vitality of my newfound personal connection to the power of magic, I really needed Draignerthol's boost. Besides, that was Momma's pendant they'd taken from me. I reached out with a slippery, rebellious finger of energy to pull the pendant toward me, and I nearly cheered out loud as it sailed obediently right past the wyvern's shoulder and into my out-stretched hand.

I slipped the dragon pendant's chain over my head.

Suddenly everything was louder, stronger. Sharper. Over the course of the month or so that I'd been without it, I'd forgotten the feeling of Draignerthol gently amplifying my senses. At the same time I'd slowly become accustomed to the sensations of having a magic-wielding wyvern familiar. I found myself reeling, then, from the dual wave of Draignerthol's enhancement adding to Kluzhka's keen senses.

We didn't have time for that, though. I left Kluzhka to watch the wyvern at the guard desk, and I turned to Druzhtane's cell. Within moments I had the magic block crushed, and then it only took a second to figure out and break the physical lock on the door. Her cell sprang open.

"What—what are you doing?" she asked, caught up in her early morning sleepiness.

"Rescuing you," I said. "Now, get out here and help us out."

She did. Sort of, anyway. Kluzhka didn't have to work the wyvern at the desk very hard; he'd seen me basking in the relic's radiance and was more interested in retreating than anything else. Druzhtane, meanwhile, stepped out of her cell and followed me the twenty feet or so down the hallway to where my rearing familiar was frightening off the competition.

"Now what?" Dru asked. Rejoicing in the ability to under-stand her once again, I said, "Follow me." I ran over and jumped on Kluzhka's back. Dru, to my relief, did the same. Kluzhka opened her wings with a snap and launched us toward the only windows on the floor. It was exhilarating, at first. The only problem was, those windows were closed.

Acting on instinct, I pushed a blue-tinged amorphous mass out in front of us and then flung it at the barrier. Sure enough, the closed windows opened right up in a flurry of glass shards. We flew rapidly through the crystalline fog and entered the early morning, still-dark, air above Fake New York City. It was exhilarating. One moment we shot through the hole in the oppressive wall that had been my prison for so long, and the next we were hurtling through the chill night air. I felt Dru's arms tense around me as the cold hit her, and I reached out to wrap us in warmth.

Only then did I look down at the ground. I had already figured, from the feeling in the pit of my stomach, that the pavement was hurtling toward us at, literally, break-neck speed, and my eyes confirmed it.

Kluzhka's thoughts, mostly her glee, infiltrated my consciousness, and I realized that she wasn't just dropping like a rock for the tactical advantage that being able to duck around buildings presented. She was actually enjoying it. It terrified me, this falling like flour sacks into the darkness with a city beneath us, and that terror, in turn, added to Kluzhka's enjoyment of the moment. Some day I'd have to lecture her on that, I knew, but it would wait till after we were safely back on Kiirajanna.

If we made it safely back to Kiirajanna, anyway. We'd made it out of the tower, but that was the easy part.

Within moments we came down even to the tops of the neighboring buildings. The wyvern's broad, bat-like wings popped outward with a *snap*! Suddenly my stomach was the only thing that still hurtled toward the ground, through from Dru's loud *whoomph* I was pretty sure hers was busy performing the same stunt. With a powerful surge, Kluzhka pressed her wings backward, propelling us forward at an unbelievable speed through the still night air and, happily, level to the ground.

I transmitted a mental image of the location of the ley-gate to Kluzhka. She banked, wind whistling over her wings and past my head, around the high rise and down toward the street I had indicated. I hoped, desperately, that it was the right one. I couldn't read the street signs at all, and most of the buildings looked exactly alike.

Behind and above, I heard a dragon's shrill, powerful shriek of rage cut through the night air. My life blood froze at the sound, and I felt despair for the first time. I only had the vaguest of ideas where and how far we had to go, and I couldn't sense the gates at all, and we were flying pretty much blind through a city that neither Kluzhka nor I had ever flown over before.

I held on tighter, willing Kluzhka to fly even faster. The city was completely dark, which was the opposite of what I'd seen in Real New York City, but the part of my brain that wasn't running on terrified understood that now. It made perfect sense, but the unfortunate fact was that the pervasive darkness played heavily against us. The city looked so different from above, entirely uniform. Every street looked the same, every doorway similar. I started to wonder what we would do if we weren't able to find the right apartment building. We hadn't made a Plan B, and that was starting to scare me more than ever.

Guiding a flying wyvern, on the other hand, seemed pretty easy. It was just like riding a horse, believe it or not, only falling off was a whole lot scarier to consider. Plus, the surges that I'd felt as my horse galloped were amplified greatly as the wyvern's huge wings beat. It was truly an incredible sensation, one that I desperately hoped to live long enough to feel again.

We looped around the neighborhood I thought contained the building with the ley-gate in it as the dragon screamed again. I looked for the magic mark I'd left on the door when I walked out the first time, but I didn't see it.

I wanted to panic. The escape wasn't going at all like I'd imagined it.

The park! I suddenly realized that I knew exactly where the building was in relation to the park Dru and I had lived in. I transmitted the image of the park, and felt the wyvern acknowledge it. It was difficult; the wyverns were never let out of the tower, after all, so she'd never seen the city, especially not from the vantage of a couple of dozen feet above ground whipping along through the air. She could, however, see the park nearby, and so she angled her body toward that treed strip of land.

I heard Dru's sigh from behind me as we flew over the rectangle of empty trees of her former home, spun around, and headed back north. I wondered the same thing she was obviously thinking: were we going to make it in time?

A third scream erupted from the tower, this one louder, angrier. I risked a glance up and saw, for a moment, the moon's radiance blocked out by a huge wing.

Xlixi, full belly or no, had taken flight to come after us.

There! I saw the door, just up ahead. Somebody had closed it in the weeks I'd been imprisoned up in the tower, of course, but the tiny magic sigil I'd thought to leave on it was still present and burning a welcome to my eyes. I angled Kluzhka toward the little diamond, sending her a picture of it that I knew would jive with her draconic mage-sight.

I risked another glance up and sensed, more than saw, a dark shape gliding down from the top of the Empire State Building. It angled directly toward us.

There was no time to be fancy, then. We set down directly in front of the door, Dru jumping off at the same moment I did. There being no point for subtlety any longer, I gathered up as much magical force as I could and blasted the door open.

"C'mon, Druzhtane!" I called as I darted inside.

I heard the reply clearly. "Nyet," Dru said, and I didn't need Draignerthol to tell me what she meant. The tone of her voice froze me in my tracks.

I spun to look; Druzhtane was already backing away into the darkness, eyes wide, legs clearly tensing to run. She waved her hands at me in a shooing motion.

"Come with me! Be safe!" I called.

She shook her head. "Safe," she pronounced meaningfully, jabbing her thumb back into the dark heart of the city. That was the last I saw of my savior and friend as she darted off into the pitch blackness of the very early morning.

I called after her, once, pitifully, though I knew it was useless. I wanted to cry, but I didn't have time for that. I spun around and led the way down the stairs.

Kluzhka and I both cringed back from the murky water that I'd forgotten flooded the basement. Fear pressed us on, though. We splashed through it, and as my staff came into view I breathed a sigh of relief. My main fear had been that the carved control rod I'd brought from Kiirajanna would be missing. I reached for it, and then realized with horror that the wyvern wouldn't fit into the alcove that contained the ley-gate.

Very close by, from just outside, trumpeted a dragon's battle cry. Fire bathed the stairwell, rolling down the dingy metal stairs and setting the sewage water at the bottom to boiling. At the same time, I heard clomping footsteps on the pavement above and knew the police, and likely the snakes with them, were right on our trail. I was pretty sure that with my new discovery I could handle a snake or two, and Kluzhka was big enough to fight off the men, but I really didn't want to test any of that, to risk going back to captivity inside the tower.

At the same time, I feared that Kluzhka wasn't ready to come to Kiirajanna. She would be feared—reviled, in fact—as an evil creature. Her kind had been banished before, and the sighting of one of her kin months before at the library had caused enough of an uproar that I knew her arrival would make headlines.

You don't have to go, you know, I sent. It pained me to say that, the idea that we might be separated across time and space despite our newfound bond. That was a horribly empty feeling.

In response, she sent me a panicked set of images, most of which involving a dragon ripping a wyvern's body apart. She was right; whatever she faced on Kiirajanna, it was easy as a summer walk at the lake compared to staying here after helping me escape. I looked frantically at the small alcove, and then back at her girth. She—she shrugged, a gesture I hadn't imagined a scaled wyvern could make.

Make sure you are touching me when you activate your staff, she sent, surprising me even though it shouldn't have.

Right. She was a magical creature. She could very likely teach me how to do several new tricks.

Another draconic scream, this one even closer, pierced the night. It was accompanied by the sound of boots on the metal stairs, and that spurred me to action. We were completely out of time. I reached back with my right hand and touched her snout, and with my left hand I pushed the staff into the gate.

I'd never been so relieved to feel a discomfort as great as the lurch to my midsection that told me I was going home.

Return

Transport through the ley-gates was normally unsettling, and downright weird the previous time, but this time it rocked me backward, and as the air exploded bright blue and then slowly returned to black around me, I stumbled backward. Luckily I was leaning, straight-armed, against something behind, and the firm base it provided kept me from toppling over onto my butt.

Teleport done, I listened—silence. It was the silence of Kiira-janna, I hoped. Slowly, cautiously, I peered around and rejoiced as in the light of the moon I saw stately, uniform trees, well-regulated grass, and the circularly-planted stones surrounding the now-dormant gate—the tell-tale signs of Kiirajanna, indeed.

I was home.

I heard, and at the same time felt, a warm, moist snort from above and behind. I glanced back—oh, right. A wyvern. Kluzhka stood right behind me, blinking in surprise at the sudden change of scenery. As she focused, my own vision split into two sets of eyes and then slowly refocused into my own view.

A slight motion drew my eyes outward to where the wyvern held her right foreleg up in the air, well away like Momma held bugs she was removing from the house. Looking at what the wyvern found so distasteful, I realized how close we'd come to not escaping at all. In her claws Kluzhka held the severed head of a huge black serpent, the tongue still flickering in and out of its now-lifeless mouth. It was gross. It was awesome, though, as a still-quivering symbol—a trophy, even—of what we'd been through. I sensed a grin on her face that I couldn't completely see in the dim light.

I guess that was closer than I realized.

Yes, Princess. The serpents are fast, but they're no match for my kind. Still, his presence would have made the trip more difficult if I had allowed him to live. She flicked the serpent's head off into the darkness.

We should probably head— I started, but then I heard the unmistakable sound—unmistakable to an elf, anyway; I doubted that the untrained Mississippi girl I'd come to Kiirajanna as would've heard anything—of a runner coming our way. Several runners, actually. I'd been hoping against hope to hear that reaction, honestly. A little part of me feared that nobody would be waiting for my return. Somebody was, though. Dad, I was pretty much counting on, and I figured Seph, as well, but I have to admit that I was also hoping to see a certain dark-haired cylchoedd-playing prince rushing to the stones to greet my return.

I wasn't disappointed at all. Out of the woods bounded the dark-haired Prince Charming, followed closely by my father and then by my cousin, her loyal familiar Booboo right at her heels. Not far behind, surprisingly, ran a pair of ancient elves, High Priestess Naissa and Exalted Master Ranger Owain.

My happiness turned to confusion and shock immediately, though, as everybody stopped at the edge of the clearing and snarled. Keion pulled and knocked an arrow, as did my cousin. Dad, meanwhile, jumped protectively in front of Naissa and

Owain and brandished the dagger he always carried hidden in his belt.

That wasn't the reaction I was expecting.

It was me! I was back. What were they so afraid of?

I felt Kluzhka's panic as she perceived several immediate threats to her—and, not knowing any better, to my own—safety, and it clicked into place. The elves were terrified of the wyvern, just as she'd said they would be, and they were fighting back. Meanwhile, she was confused at the combination of the danger with the relief and joy she got through her link with me.

"*Stop!*" I yelled.

They didn't, of course. At least, not immediately. I can't say that I blame them. The entirety of elven historical lore describes wyverns as fearsome creatures, monsters that were nearly as terrifying as their cousins, the dragons. To have one just pop right in, this close to the castle, and right behind their beloved crown princess must have been a few levels beyond unnerving.

We had a standoff. I let it go, thinking that everybody would eventually figure it out.

I was wrong. Keion released his arrow first, Sephaline sending hers just behind. At the same time Booboo displayed the acceleration and flat-out speed that wolverines are famous for, making a beeline toward Kluzhka's knees. Behind, the wyvern braced for the arrows' impact, shifting her stance just slightly so that the points of the projectiles would ricochet off of her hardened scales while putting her body into a position to charge the one she saw as the most dangerous of our foes. That just happened to be Prince Charming.

I wasn't having any of it, though.

I yanked the energy through Draignerthol, thumbing back through my memories to the shield spell I'd read in the books Xlixi had provided. It turned out to be pretty simple to erect the constructs after I'd seen them explicitly spelled out, and the adrenalin of my own stress coupled with the anxious feelings from Kluzhka made darned sure I wasn't lacking any will. Instantly a bright blue bubble popped up between me and the elves. Arrows clattered against it and fell to the floor, which caused both archers to relax their pulls on the second arrows they'd nocked, confused expressions springing to their faces.

I felt bad for Booboo. The wolverine had great acceleration and sprint capabilities, but it was apparently paying such close attention to the wyvern's knees that it didn't see either the blue bubble or the arrows. With a *whoof* Booboo crashed into my spell and collapsed, going down hard enough for Seph to gasp aloud. Then, luckily for both me and my cousin, and, I suppose, for the wolverine itself, her familiar rose back up on all four legs, shook off the collision, and changed its tactic from an energetic charge to a frightening high-pitched growl.

"*Stop!*" I yelled once again.

Luckily, everybody did stop the second time. Both bow wielders lowered their weapons, and my father stood up, quitting his defensive stance. Apparently Seph's new attitude affected Booboo's too, as the attack beast's neck hair settled and it trotted back to her side. That was good. It was better when I sensed Kluzhka stand down also; the attack posture fixing to spring at Keion relaxing into a more benignly protective attitude behind and above me.

That was very good. I didn't have any idea what I would have done if I'd had to fight everybody present to keep them all from fighting.

"Alyssa, that's..." my father said, his voice trailing off. His lips kept moving, but it was obvious he wasn't going to be able to finish the sentence anytime soon, so I finished it for him.

"A wyvern. Yes, Dad, Your Majesty, I know. Her name is Kluzhka, and I brought her back through the portal with me. On purpose, even."

"Kluzhka? That's—how do you know a wyvern's name?" he asked, an incredulous look on his face. "I didn't even know the blasted beasts *had* names."

Kluzhka, who was listening in on the conversation through our link, hissed at being called a beast. I sent her a quieting bump and replied, "We're bonded, Dad."

"*Bonded?*" he cried. I wasn't sure if his cry was of anguish or disbelief, but either way it was forceful. And loud. Loudly forceful.

"You can't..." the king, the high priestess, the prince, and my cousin the ranger all started saying at the same time. They stopped, and after sharing meaningful glances with each other, the group decided to let Dad complete the sentence for them.

"You can't join with a wyvern in a ranger bond, Alyssa."

"Why not?"

I tried not to be too challenging. He was my father, after all, but the simple fact was that I had already done what he was telling me I couldn't do. It was the first time I'd ever heard him speak informally, though, so I could tell that his rudder was way off kilter.

"Well, I—it—not—a wyv—" he stumbled, obviously unsure of his words. As he kept going, though, his tone and wording regained its regal formality. "It's—well, look, Alyssa, it is a sentient being, from everything that we have been taught. A sentient, *evil* being. Our kind have fought—um, that creature's kind—for millennia. Now, to go and join, in a sacred ranger's bond, one of our kind to one of their kind—well, that is—it is impossible. Inconceivable."

I grinned in spite of myself. My father was completely beside himself, to the point where a normal person would have been rendered speechless. In all my daydreams, my memories, and my recent interactions, it was pretty much impossible to imagine him ever being like this. Here I'd just gone and done it.

Seph, meanwhile, had moved closer by several cautious steps. Her eyes transfixed Kluzhka's in a weird ranger stare, and her head tilted sideways in contemplation. My own eyes saw Seph's intensity in her expression, while my link to Kluzhka gave me the wyvern's side of the connection. I could feel the mutual respect that radiated between the two of them. Owain did the same, though he didn't tilt his head as dramatically.

"Apparently, uncle, she *can* join a wyvern in a ranger bond," Seph corrected my father. I nearly gasped out loud; it was the first time I'd heard her refer to my father as anything other than Your Majesty. I was proud of the newer, more confident version of my cousin. My father, meanwhile, took her comment in stride, nodding thoughtfully.

Owain nodded slowly, the ancient ranger lord's wrinkled face openly displaying a degree of awe I wouldn't have expected from anyone in the realm. "Ranger Sephaline speaks the truth, Your Majesty. Unheard of as it is for a ranger to bond another sentient being, your daughter—a ranger now, it seems—appears to have done exactly that, and to none less than a *wyvern*."

High Priestess Naissa cleared her throat. "I mean no disrespect for your profession, Owain, but she is quite a bit more than a ranger. She is the crown princess, after all, and the future Dragon Queen. Plus, she has not built a reputation for worrying over the appropriateness of her decisions, has she? Is it altogether surprising, then, that she returns to us bonded with a wyvern?"

I looked around, seeing through both my own eyes and those of Kluzhka. The expressions of fear and loathing I'd seen earlier had changed, morphed into admiration and wonder. Even Booboo stopped growling and joined Seph in an attitude of respect.

I dropped my shield spell and shrugged. "It's not like I chose this," I stated flatly. Nobody responded to my attempt at modesty; they seemed too busy, instead, trying to take in my new familiar.

Meanwhile, the waves of joy I received from Kluzhka were a little surprising.

Yay! Kluzhka, I'm just as happy as you are for the acceptance and love you're receiving from my friends.

Acceptance and love? The two bow wielders have not even put away their arrows yet. Your kind has a strange way of showing acceptance and love, I would say.

Well, at least you're happy that they're going to welcome you into the realm.

Who said I was happy over that?

You are, aren't you?

I'm glad I won't have to fight off five elves and that little toothy beast while trying to keep you alive, Princess. Not to mention that the two spellcasters are old and sinewy—not tasty at all.

Well. At least you care about my welfare.

I would be terribly sad to lose my familiar.

I sighed in dismay, but inside I was happy. Not only weren't we going to die, but in a small strategic victory I noticed that she correctly identified the high priestess as a spellcaster. I'd known that I'd eventually have to win Naissa over to my argument that the healing gifts of the priesthood were as magical as any of my own casting efforts, but I'd pretty well lost hope of any chance of doing that. The recognition by the wyvern, a strongly magical being, rekindled that hope.

My father cleared his throat loudly, and then said, "Well, Alyssa—crown princess, future Dragon Queen—that was an impressive shield you erected. An impressive *magical* shield." I remembered that my father hadn't actually witnessed my spellcasting abilities first-hand. "Consider the power of Draignerthol rightfully acknowledged, my daughter, but that was a serious and complex spell you cast, if my senses and the high priestess's gasps are to be believed."

Sternyface nodded. "It seems as though you had an opportunity while on your quest to study the long-forbidden arts."

I shrugged. "The dragon lent me part of his library while I considered his offer. I didn't return them," I admitted, pulling the sheet-wrapped bundle from my shirt and unwrapping it so all could see.

Expressions of joy turned to confusion, and then to disbelief, and ended up in panic and horror. At the mention of the word dragon, all five smiles were doused in cold fear. Round, joy-filled eyes narrowed and darkened. Cheeks collapsed in on themselves. Teeth vanished, other than the slightest wedge of a grimace, with an unvoiced growl on five pairs of lips.

All five took to glaring at me.

"Why are you glaring at me like that? I'm—I'm not the dragon," I reminded them with a shudder.

"Alyssa, there are no dragons," my father said, his voice dark and dangerous. "You will hopefully not mention that part of your visions again. It is too painful a portion of our past. A portion that is done and over now. As—well, as you should know."

The high priestess shot my dad what she must've thought was a hidden, hurt look, but I caught it.

"I do know that dragons are a painful part of Kiirajanna's past, Dad," I said. "The high priestess and her followers have taught me a great deal of the histories of our realm. But what I learned on this trip was no vision. I was caught and imprisoned on another realm, one that is beyond our ability to see, by an evil and quite powerful, and completely real and alive, dragon. I barely escaped, and that only with the assistance of both Draignerthol and Kluzhka. I return with dire news, but I also know that our people have succeeded in defeating dragons before, and I have no fear that we will do so, again."

"It seems you have much strange, foreboding news Princess," Owain piped up from the side. I was glad the old ranger held onto enough of his senses to intervene; both Dad and Sternyface looked like they wanted to explode. "Perhaps we should retire to a more private, more comfortable area to discuss it?"

Everybody seemed to nod at once, and all but Dad turned toward the castle and started walking. I moved forward to catch up, but Dad motioned me to slow down.

"Alyssa," he said, his voice quiet and almost halting. "I—um—I know that the bond between elf and familiar is strong, but...." He left the last part unspoken as he looked meaningfully back toward Kluzhka's hulking form.

I saw what he was hinting at. I nodded and turned toward the wyvern, trying to express in mental images what the elf king was suggesting. It turned out that my fear that she would be hurt over not being welcomed into the castle was unfounded, though.

I am quite hungry, Princess, and I doubt that your little fruits and nuts would settle my stomach's desires.

Well, I don't want you to feel—oh, that was just disgusting. I tried to get my stomach to settle itself after the mental image of her talons rending a fat buck, moist flesh hanging from her jaws.

Circle of life, Princess. Circle of life. Besides, it's dark, which makes it prime hunting time for me. Trust me, I shall enjoy this greatly. And if you need, I can return to your side almost instantly. No harm can come to my familiar.

Thanks. Just no elf eating, okay? But you still seem a little bothered.

I am. It is nothing to worry over now, though.

What is it, Kluzhka?

Nothing to worry over.

Kluzhka!

Fine. It is just that our escape was—

Miraculous.

Too miraculous.

Not too miraculous. I am a powerful mage, and you are a magnificent flier.

You know that dragons are powerful mages and magnificent fliers, yes?

Of course I do.

Did you also know that dragons can teleport?

No. That might have been nice to know before we planned to fly out of there.

My kind can too. We couldn't, because you were not certain where you were going. But Xlixi should have been able to follow us much faster.

Oh. You're right.

I am?

Yes. This is terrifying, but nothing to gain by worrying over it now. But we do need to discuss it later.

You actually are a little bit smart, Princess.

Go feast. Maybe dulling your hunger pains will do the same to your tongue.

Ha! Enjoy your little elf meeting.

Turning, the massive smart-aleck lizard lifted off and sailed toward the hills in the distance. I could feel her—I could actually see her, in my mind's eye, come to think of it—looking forward to chomping on some fresh animal flesh.

Silently wishing her safe hunting, I turned back to my father, who'd watched the silent interchange closely. "Lead on, Your Majesty," I said with a smile.

Breakfast and New Beginnings

We did a fast march back to the castle, during which I couldn't help swinging my head side to side to marvel at the beauty of the elf-tended forest once again. I hadn't realized how much I would miss the orderly vegetation during my quest, and it was such a shockingly different environment from the cramped civilization of Fake New York City that I rapidly fell back in love with my home realm.

The first thing I wanted to do upon entering the castle, after visiting Little Treebeard, was pay a visit to the huge brass tub in the bathing chamber that sat across from my room. The dragon's shower was clean enough, but I still couldn't get the sensation of the adjutant's watchful eyes out of my head. I longed for the feeling of warm water pressing in around my entire body, of soap bubbles covering the surface and obscuring me, my being, and my very soul from the rest of the world.

It would just have to wait, though, as my father made clear. I'd shared enough of my experiences on Pazhbojanna, including what I'd learned from the dragon, with my father on the walk that he propelled us all directly into the royal throne room and shut the door solidly behind us. The queen was already there, though it was still in that weird hour between late at night and early in the morning. Lady Meredydd, the queen's Lady of the Bedchamber and an indispensable source of knowledge to me so far, stood behind Her Majesty and refused to make eye contact. An elf produced chairs and folding tables from somewhere while I wasn't looking, and the entire group of us sat in a weird circle— King and Queen on thrones of gold, grizzled old Ranger Owain and High Priestess Naissa on some of the nicer chairs, Prince of the Realm Keion, who looked quite sure of his qualifications to be present, right next to my cousin who looked the exact opposite of Prince Charming, and, finally, me.

I sat down last after genuflecting with both my hands and my upper body to the queen, earning a sly sideways nod from Lady Meredydd. The queen gracefully nodded her acceptance. The congregation remained silent as more butlers appeared with food from the kitchen: fruits, ham, bacon, and eggs, all served individually on platters set onto the folding trays, one for each of us.

The servants, their jobs done, melted out, and within a few moments the seven of us ate in silence. Even Lady Meredydd was absent, though I had a hard time believing she wasn't listening in from somewhere.

"Alyssa," the queen spoke, her voice making a tinkly sort of chiming sound in my head, "you have—such a beautiful name, my girl. Alyssa. Have I ever told you that? It rolls itself right off of the speaker's tongue in the most delightful way. Alyssa," she said a final time, letting each syllable linger. Then she continued, her voice still kind and light, "So, Alyssa, your father tells me that your quest was a bit more enlightening than any of us would have suspected it might be. Would it be too forward of me to ask you to tell us the story?"

Wow, I thought to myself. The queen of the elves was using formal structures of respect in addressing me. I wouldn't, couldn't, presume to be her equal—not yet, anyway, and probably not for a very long while to come—but I'd come a long way from my coronation, when she'd addressed me as a child.

Then again, I *had* just faced down a dragon.

But how, I wondered, had my father managed to tell her anything? We'd walked into the palace in silence, and I had been in their company the entire time. He hadn't said a word to her.

Somehow Dad read my mind, or at least the expression on my face. "Crown Princess Alyssa," he said formally, "you should be aware that the king and queen share a certain sort of mental bond associated with the office. It is not unlike, in nature at least, that of you and your, ah, *familiar*, but it is less attuned to senses than what I have heard of the ranger bond, while being better suited for carrying conversations. Trust me, it improves the governing process substantially."

"Thank you. I did not know that, Your Majesty the High King of the Elves of Kiirajanna. The knowledge you have chosen to impart upon me will serve me well in the future," I replied in a similar tone. It dawned on me that that bond must've been how Dad had managed to still rule the kingdom while he was away on Earth, cavorting with Momma. When he'd explained it away as "messaging" before, I hadn't thought to ask if he meant telepathic. I wondered briefly what the mechanism was, and how it didn't qualify as magic to them, but I put that out of my mind quickly. It wasn't useful. Later, maybe, it might be, but for now there wasn't anything to be gained.

I looked around at the faces of the assembled group. My dad and the queen were concerned far more than the tone of their voices let on, and it showed in the wrinkles in their faces where wrinkles shouldn't be yet. The two more ancient elves were also listening intently; I'd say they also looked very concerned, but their faces already featured entire networks of wrinkles even on good days. My cousin and the prince, meanwhile, just looked a little bit out of place. Seph's eyes kept darting nervously to the door that now served as the barrier between the ruling folks and the rest of the population of Kiirajanna.

I wondered how the elves of the realm would take the news, especially given their desire to see me exiled not all that long ago.

A gentle clearing of his throat told me that Dad was still waiting on something. Oh, right—the story for the queen. I thought about it for a few more seconds—where to start? Would she react better to, "Well, you see, I went, and I saw, but I didn't buy any t-shirts, and then I met this dragon," or to a long, full, detailed account?

I settled on something between the two. "So," I started after taking a deep breath, "The ley-gate didn't teleport to where I was expecting it to. I know, it was silly to build expectations before starting, but all I've ever known is Earth, and for the past few turns of the moon, Kiirajanna. I ended up, though, in a third place, a different realm entirely."

I could tell my story had already hit a nerve when the queen shot a sharp look across to Sternyface, who just shrugged and looked even more pensive. "We have long suspected, Your Majesty," she started, "but—"

The queen cut her off with a sharp gesture for compliance, made a little more gentle by the smile that followed. "I was seeking confirmation rather than accusation, Naissa. Now, Alyssa, forgive my interruption and continue."

"Yes, ma'am. It didn't seem like a third realm at first. Instead, I thought I had been brought back to Earth, in a massive city called New York." Both the king and the queen's eyebrows shot up over that, and I remembered that she had grown up on Earth, herself, and so she had probably visited the city. Meanwhile, I knew he had, because I'd been with him.

I described the gateway location first, telling them about the deserted basement room and the fetid water it contained. I got several crinkled noses in response to that bit. Then I briefly told them about the cop, and about the group of women, and then about the walk that followed. Both Dad and the queen gasped when I mentioned the park.

"In the real New York City, it is a private park, where only those who live nearby and are wealthy enough to purchase them have keys. I do not recall the name, but it is reportedly a beautiful span of landscaped trees, shrubs, and flowers," Dad said, and his comment was answered by a nod from the queen with a quiet, "It is, indeed."

"You have been inside?" he asked her.

She nodded again, her eyes staring wistfully off into the farthest corner of the throne room. "I have. On one of our trips to the Big Apple, we were given a tour of Gramercy Park by some merchant friends of my grandfather's. It is an incredibly beautiful park, but it is always held closed and locked against public use. You say you were able to just run in, Alyssa?"

"Yes, Your Majesty. The park is not at all like what you're describing. The wrought iron gates are not only unlocked; they dangle off of their hinges and drip rust flakes onto the path. It's a deserted area, and it's where I met Druzhtane."

At their prompting, I told them about the young elf, my only friend in a strange new world. Seph looked uncomfortable when I said that the two were spitting images of each other, but Naissa took her turn to butt in and explain that duplicates should be considered pretty normal on separate worlds, and that it also wasn't surprising that we had run into each other given how close I and my cousin were on Kiirajanna, and she concluded that it was also likely a good thing she'd chosen to remain behind, as there was no telling what might happen if the duplicates met each other.

I told them about the food kitchen, and how we were thrown out. Keion and Dad both clenched their fists in anger at that part.

Then I told them how Dru managed to find us food—he little fa-vors, which earned a naughty grin from the men and a very dis-approving look from the queen, who I guessed had never been hungry in her life. Then I remembered her brief tale of her own hunhymgais, and that led me to wonder whether she would feel differently if she'd been in our shoes.

I told them about Dru's first bag of pot, and then about the tour of the marijuana growing operation. Dad and Sternyface seemed impressed at the population control method, while I could tell that the queen felt uncomfortable and a little scandalized—not at the tale, but at the other two's reaction to it. She got over it quickly and slammed her regal face back down, but I had been able to see the concern for just a moment.

I told them about our capture, and about the snakes and the Cult members. I described the horror I'd felt in waking up in a cell with Draignerthol missing from my neck. I told them about meeting the dragon the first time. I described his offer to me, and then I told them about how I'd spent nearly a month telling the dragon that I didn't want the term Dragon Queen to mean the same thing he wanted it to mean.

In careful and thorough detail I described the sacrifice of the young boy to make Xlixi's point to me. I didn't leave anything out, not the hot, fetid breath, nor the dragon's silky, menacing voice, nor the boy's abject terror. I described the mix of the complex aromas of urine and blood as the kid died, ripped neatly in two—the acrid tang and the unmistakable stench of ammonia—and felt a bit cruel for my own enjoyment of the queen's discomfort as she blanched and pressed her breakfast plate away. It wasn't my in-tent to make anybody sick, but I had to make sure that the image of the dragon as an epically evil creature stuck.

I told them about our escape, too. I tried not to make it into bragging about how I could competently do magic even without Draignerthol, but I think that came out a little. It was, I reasoned, part of why I was back in Kiirajanna, alive, and more important, it was a large part of who I was and who I was to become. There wasn't anybody in the room, after all, who didn't already know I could competently do magic, and it didn't seem that big a stretch to me that I was capable of doing so now even without the fabled relic. I was rewarded by almost no reaction; everybody took the "I reached out with my power and called Draignerthol to me" bit without protest.

That led me to the moment I found myself facing off against the majority of the ruling caste of Kiirajanna, and so I ended the story there.

"A good telling of your grand adventure, Alyssa," the queen said, and then silence filled the room like a shower's mist on a humid day. Everybody had been anxious to interrupt me—everybody but Keion and Seph, that is, and they both looked like they wanted to just disappear—while I was telling the story, but now that I was done everybody seemed to just want to sit and think.

And sit, and think, I thought as the silence extended. We were all done with the contents of our breakfast trays, so even the sounds of biting and chewing were absent.

"So what are we going to do about it?" I asked when I could no longer sit and watch them sitting and thinking.

"About what, my dear?" the queen asked.

About what? Did you miss the part about the dragon wanting to eat you and all of yours, lady? I wanted to scream, incredulous. Instead, I schooled my voice and said, "About the imminent invasion by the dragon, Your Majesty. It seems we should be doing something to prevent that."

She shrugged and said, "Alyssa, if what the dragon told you about the ley-gates is correct, and I have no reason to believe otherwise, I do not believe we can do anything to prevent the dragon lord from traveling across them and entering our realm. Do you know something that would suggest otherwise?"

She had a point. "No, Your Majesty. I misspoke. I feel that we should be doing something to prevent, or at least lessen, the slaughter that will happen when he does travel to Kiirajanna."

"Such as?" my father interjected. *Thank you, Dad*, I did my best to project to him. By switching the conversation to between us he was allowing me to drop the formality a bit and just speak my mind.

"I don't know. Such as marshaling the troops, sharpening the bayonets, crafting more arrows. Something."

The comment earned me a snicker from Keion. When I leveled a glare at him, he shrugged and said, "Crown Princess, you should leave the preparations for fighting to the fighting men of the realm to worry about."

"While my son makes a valid point about your inexperience in preparing troops for battle," the queen interjected with storm clouds on her face, "I am certain he is only phrasing his comment sloppily and not intending to suggest that a queen, or even the crown princess, is unable to or unsuitable for leading troops into battle. We have all read enough of our race's history to recall the grand battles against mighty foes that were led by Queen Rhiannon, for example."

Dad jumped in. "Indeed, an elf queen should be just as knowledgeable in battle as an elf king. We shall have to add that to the list of training that lies ahead for you, Alyssa. Not that you have not already been through some significant battles, but you do still have more to learn. As for this specific situation, though, I am aware that you were being facetious when you said to sharpen bayonets. Rest assured that we maintain a suitable stockpile of already-sharpened arrows and javelins. In regard to marshaling the troops—that actually is a problem, my daughter, and for more than one reason. The dispersal of our troops under regular circumstances—those in the north, under Padrig, are in the north, while those—well, those others may not be ours to command in any event. But let us not dwell on that for the moment. The simple fact is that the dispersal of our forces may not be a negative thing, for when the dragon lord decides to visit us as you say he will, it is unclear where he will make his entrance. We have many ley-gates spread through the land. Also, as we are all fully aware, the Cult of the Wyrm exists and is likely passing him information as we speak. They would of a certainty notice any large gathering of armed forces, and so while the dragon would know where we are, we would have no idea of his whereabouts. So, you see, keeping our forces distributed across the land is undoubtedly the best approach."

I nodded; I did see. Then I decided to address the elephant in the room.

And no, there wasn't actually an elephant in the room.

"What about magic?" I asked.

"It is forbidden," Sternyface intoned immediately after I finished asking the question, like one of those automatic response systems on the phone.

"Not for the dragon."

"The dragon will fight according to his moral compass, and we shall fight according to ours. We have defeated dragons before, and we will do so again," the queen pronounced, the expression on her face suggesting that the topic of conversation was over.

It wasn't, though. This wasn't an issue I was willing to concede on—the future of my race depended on it, after all.

"In the histories I've read, Your Majesty, the fight against the dragon has always been led by sorcerors and enchantresses. I've never read of a dragon being defeated by—no offense, Dad—bows and arrows and javelins." His sideways grin told me no offense had been taken—at least, not by him. I wondered if now would be a good time to bring up the dark-skinned elves I'd met.

The queen sniffed. "We shall find a way, then, that is not written in the historic journals."

I shook my head; there just wasn't any way that I could see to win the battle without magic. "Your Majesty, with all due respect, I have met this dragon. This dragon is huge, and extremely powerful. He doesn't cast magic; he is magic. You're—we're—going to have to fight fire with—"

"No," the queen stopped me with both her sharp word and an even sharper gesture of dismissal. After a few moments of dank silence stretched across the room, her face softened and she said, "Alyssa, dear girl, trust me that I heard what you said about the dragon's capabilities the first time. We should now adjourn and consider the alternatives as we understand them. Meredydd, signal the servants to remove our trays and prepare the room for court."

"Yes, ma'am," the lady said, materializing from behind the curtains and sailing out of the room. Meanwhile the queen disappeared behind another curtain. I'd followed my father similarly, through the one that led to the king's private chamber, a few times for some good heart-to-heart father-daughter talks. But that sure wasn't going to happen today, I figured.

I left. Important priorities called to me, and none of them were in the throne room.

After a Respite

I sighed. I couldn't help it, really. I'd remained submerged in the waters contained in the deep copper tub for as long as they stayed warm and soothing, but finally I had to either accept that they were cooling down to room temperature—a chilly thing, at best—or limber up my magic and use it to warm them back up. Because I still didn't feel all that comfortable using magic so close to the monarchs and the high priestess, I chose the first option.

I didn't really want to go back in my room yet. I'd stopped by on my way to the bath, meaning to send L.T. a quick smile and a song, but that little elm tree was insufferable. Where before it expressed the fact that it missed me by tremendous, noisy slapping of branches, this time I got little angry twitches and snicks. And each time I tried to excuse myself to take the bath, the tree erupted into an angry whirling dervish that reminded me of the tree near Hogwart's. I tried calming it down, I really did, but L.T. was having none of my song as it let me know just exactly how horribly scared and alone it had been. Finally, I gave up; I left it to whirl its branches in anger and walked out, shutting the door solidly behind, leaving Aerona smirking at the whole cattywhom-pas scene.

Now, though, the bath water was doing nothing for me. Rising from its tepid depth, I accepted the waiting servant's offered towel. It was soft, luxuriously so, and a great deal more than the towels I'd used in captivity. I sighed again. It was good to be back. It was good to be completely clean, finally. It was good to be able to speak and have people understand my language.

It was good to be the crown princess, I thought with a flip of my hair into a second towel.

Growing up distinctly middle-class, I never could have imagined that I'd say that last phrase. But I'd done a lot of thought in the dragon's cell, and I'd done even more thought while submerged in the sensationally hot water of the bath that had been prepared for me. I'd been through a lot, journeying to the library, reading what I could, and casting my first spell to save us all. Then there'd been running through mud, battling a horde of barbarians in the frigid north. And then, captivity that quite nearly broke my spirit. And the future? It didn't look to get much easier, what with a dragon preparing to invade my home realm. Years and years of war, of stress, of death, was all probably written directly into my destiny, and so, for the first time since I'd arrived at the castle, I allowed myself to really sink in and enjoy the bath as something that I deserved.

It was over. That was okay; I could always take another bath later. And, frankly, another after that one, if I were that kind of a person. But that was the kind of thing I imagined the queen's daughters doing. I had friends who wanted to see me, to talk to me, after my long absence, and I wanted to spend time with them as well.

I dressed as quickly as I could and headed down to the main dining hall, where I was sure Seph would be waiting.

She was. So was Booboo, who let me know with a low but unmistakable growl how displeased he was that I was joining them at the table.

Seph swatted at the wolverine. "Booboo!" she loosed her own sort of growl.

"It's okay, Seph. I probably still smell like wyvern to him." I meant it as kind of a joke, one that Seph humored with a single chortle, but we both quickly realized that it wasn't really a joke at all.

"Actually, you smell like the princess's bath water," she said, and I was pretty sure that that description was meant as a bad thing. My cousin did, after all, prefer to spend nights on the trail. She continued, "But, speaking of that, how is your familiar doing?"

I liked Seph a lot. Not only was she my cousin, and she'd been a really great companion on the journey to the library, but she was also—and most importantly—the only elf I'd run into who didn't called me princess.

"As well as can be imagined, I suppose. I'm fairly new to the whole familiar thing," I said, honestly. I'd been horrified when, while I'd been eating breakfast that morning, I received mental imagery of Kluzhka finding, hunting, and ripping a deer into bite-sized pieces. Wyvern bite sized, that is, which is a pretty big bite. The wyvern was both incredibly strong and fast, as I could tell by seeing her pounce through her own eyes, and I was awfully glad that Seph managed to beat the wyvern we'd faced with the strong wind currents she'd kicked up through—

Through magic. She hated the term, just like everybody else did, and we all knew it. But it was magic. There was no arguing with that fact now.

"You've watched her feed, haven't you?" Seph asked, correctly gauging my expression. I nodded. She said, "It shocked me, too, the first time I saw Booboo eat. The savagery of the animal kingdom can be overwhelming to a new—a new, um, bonded person. Oh, don't look at me that way. You're a princess, not a ranger."

She had a point, and I nodded to it. The ranger lifestyle, traveling around with none but a familiar for company for months or years at a time, was one that despite my country upbringing didn't suit me in the slightest. Not, I added to myself, that I was necessarily all that perfectly suited to the princess lifestyle, but darn, that bath had been nice. Sometimes having servants was nice. Sometimes even knowing that the watchful gaze of Aerona rested over me protectively was nice, strange though it felt.

I hadn't told her about the other bit, my strange experience of pushing my awareness through the trees and through the earth and, in doing so, sensing all around me. I sucked in a breath to do so.

"So, Sephaline—"

"So! Princess," Keion said, striding up and then plopping himself down at our table. I looked at him, amused and curious. For once I could see right through the bravado into the maelstrom of emotions he was trying to hide. Some of those emotions, visible in his troubled eyes, were still rooted in a series of kisses he and I had shared. He'd been worried about me, I could tell. When he'd come running in the woods early that morning to see a fearsome—he thought—wyvern behind me, his eyes had lit up with a crazy fire and he'd beaten everyone else, including the ranger, to loosing the first shot in my defense.

And now that I was back, and safe, and by all rights an adult now who actually outranked him, I could tell that the cocky prince wasn't certain how he wanted to react.

Well, neither was I.

"Hello, Prince," I greeted him with my jauntiest smile.

The lines around his eyes tightened in confusion. He'd apparently expected something else instead allowed himself to go speechless. I waited for him to regain control and continue, or at least explain, but he never did.

"So what have you been up to for the last six weeks?" I asked, clearing him of the need to find something to say.

He shrugged. "Oh, this and that. Archery, you know, and cylchoedd."

"Oh, right," I said. I'd gone six whole weeks without hearing about his sporting position. "How are the Bs doing?"

"Winning. As usual. We've won the last three cups."

"Of course you have."

"Sarcasm, Alyssa?" he asked.

I shook my head. "No. Heck, no. I don't know enough about the sport to be sarcastic. Are the cups annual things?"

"They are. My mother told us about your World Cup competitions every year in a sport called football back on Earth. I believe it's much the same."

"Oh. I thought it was called the Super Bowl, but whatever. I've never been all that big of a sports fan, honestly. So your team has been the best for three years, then?"

"We have."

I wasn't sure how the conversation could possibly get much more broken.

"So how are you going to keep a wyvern familiar safe?" he asked, proving that yes, it could get more broken.

"Oh, I suppose I'll just wrap her in bubble wrap and duct tape and tell her not to cross the street without looking both directions first."

"Now that was sarcasm."

"Ya think?"

"Sometimes you're insufferable, Alyssa."

"I've had good teachers," I said, tossing a sweet grin his way.

"Uh huh. Speaking of, when was the last time you practiced your archery, Princess?"

"Several weeks. They wouldn't let me have a bow and arrow in—" I started, and then stopped as I realized that several elves were paying attention to us. "On my quest," I finished, not willing to mention the dragon or any of the other scary details in front of others just yet. That had actually been a private request from both the king and the queen, each of whom had sent messengers to interrupt my bath with it. *The common people have enough to worry about already while we determine how best to meet the threat,* both messengers had said.

"I will be out there tomorrow morning. You—I would—I hope to see you join me then," the prince said, stumbling over his words. I had to work to hide my smirk.

"I will join you," I promised, and got angry at myself as I felt my own pulse quickening. He was awfully good looking, though.

"I will join you," Seph mimicked with a leer after he'd left. "You two are—" she let it hang, but the silence said enough as she eyed the group who'd congregated to watch us. "Well, you are."

I sighed. "I know."

"Can we go for a walk?"

I leaped up, happy for a chance to be away from the other ears. Booboo joined, and the three of us strode along easily toward the south, our rapid pace keeping us warm despite the chill in the air. Silence was our companion for several long minutes until we came to the ley-gate I'd passed through some hours before.

Seph shook her head and started casting magic.

No, not magic. Ranger energy.

Whatever. It was blue, and I could see how she worked the flows. I was pretty sure I could work the same spell whether you called it magic or not.

As she gathered her own energies and then put them to work, I saw the tracks of our encounter, including the huge, three-toed, claw marks that Kluzhka had left behind, slowly evaporate from the landscape. Soon she was done, and the turf surrounding the stones was left completely clean of evidence.

"Nice job," I said.

"Was that sarcasm, Alyssa?" she asked, mimicking the prince's comment earlier with a wide grin.

"Yes. Yes, it was."

"Sometimes you are," and she paused to let out a long, playfully exasperated sigh, "insufferable."

"Yeah. Yes, I am. And Cousin, other times, I'm scared." And I was scared. Not so much for my familiar; Kluzhka had already transmitted images to me that showed a vast unpopulated range of foothills, fairly close by, where she could live and hunt at will. The idea clearly thrilled her, as she'd only ever known the inside of a tower as home.

She'd do fine. I was scared for my fellow elves. I'd seen, firsthand, the power of a dragon, and even if the queen was right and elves could prevail over it using primitive weapons, many would die when the evil one chose to invade.

"I know," my cousin said, meeting my eyes with her own solid, confident gaze. I knew she understood what I was talking about. "But you have me and the prince, and Booboo too, by your side, and many others also. We'll make it through, Alyssa."

"You sure?" I really needed the reassurance, I guess.

"Yeah. I am. Let's get back before we freeze, though."

Together, two cousins on a single purpose, we walked back to the castle. Having her, and her familiar, and my own wyvern, by my side for whatever might come did make a tremendous difference. With that, I was ready for whatever the future held.

OLEUNI

Light, which is breakfast to a tree.

Magic Apologetics

The day finally arrived, no matter how much I willed it to stay away. Word had gone out quickly that I'd returned, successfully, from hunhymgais, and my adversaries to the east, west, and south had been just as quick to call a council to declare me unfit for the crown. The travel for them wasn't a huge deal, since they hadn't bothered going very far in the six weeks I'd been away. It was more of a planned inconvenience for us, really, since they demanded the council to be held outside the castle complex.

Neutral ground, they had said.

They picked a grand clearing to the south and west of the castle. It was reachable in less than an hour via the magically-powered horseless carriages, but instead of that we all decided to march on horseback so that Dad and the rest of the ruling triumvirate could show up with a column of black-armored King's Men behind them. It wasn't that Dad wanted a fight, but he wanted to show that he was ready for one if the others did.

A little way out from the meeting point, I called for a halt. Dad, surprised, led his men to obey.

"Second thoughts, Alyssa?" Seph asked quietly. I could see concern in her face as she pondered everything that might or might not be in our immediate future.

"No. Not really. But—look, I need to get something off my chest. Dad, Your Majesty Queen Taliath, High Priestess Naissa, Keion, Seph, Ranger Owain, could I please get you all to step away with me for a minute?"

Everyone looked surprised at that. Aerona looked the question at me, but when I didn't answer she took it upon herself to follow, also, as I tromped down a path to the side just far enough to be out of view of the armsmen.

"Look, I'm not sure there's any point in me facing this, if—"

I held up my hands to quiet the general chorus of disagreement that sprang up immediately. Once it died back down, I continued. "As I was about to say, I'm not sure there's any point in me facing these other rulers down when my own family, my own supporters, still look at me sideways over the possibility that I might cast a spell. I mean, if *you* can't support me, why should I expect them to?"

"Alyssa, we support you, all of us do. We just wish you'd listen to reason and stop working magic," the high priestess said.

"No! I—I'm sorry for how vehemently that came out. But no, it's not going to work that way. I can work magic, and as you've pointed out yourself, there are battles to be faced in the future if there is any truth to the prophecy whatsoever. And you know I believe it, and I know you do, too. And there's no way I'll let friends and family go down without using every tool in my arsenal to help us win."

"Alyssa," my father said, "no matter what the result of such a battle would or might be, using magic in spite of centuries of tradition will lose our side the war."

"But—"

"We support you," the queen said, her beautiful voice ringing through the chill air. "But we cannot support your use of magic any more than they can."

I gritted my teeth in frustration. "Ranger Owain, would you give up your ability to reach out to the trees or to speak with your familiar?"

"No, of course not. Why would you ask such a question?"

"Because it's the same thing."

"No, dear, it is not," the high priestess began in her too-condescending tone. I reacted more to the tone than to the words.

"Yes! Yes, it is. Seph, step forward." My cousin complied with the command, her puzzled expression deepening. "See that seedling at your feet? Make it grow by an inch."

Seph shrugged, bent down and touched the seedling, and pushed her ranger powers into it. Obediently, the tiny plant grew an inch taller.

I didn't bother bending down as I pushed my own magic into a nearly-identical seedling to the side. It grew an inch taller, and I turned a satisfied expression to the onlookers.

"See? No, you don't," I added quickly to forestall any arguments. "Dad, your dagger, please."

I took the king's nervously-proffered dagger and, before my pain centers could rebel, used it to open a slice across my palm. Holding the wince at bay—the dagger's slash hurt!—I challenged, "High Priestess, surely you can heal this."

"Yes, of course I can. But why should I, since you inflicted it upon yourself so willingly?"

"Just heal it. Please. Humor me. And watch closely."

Sternyface looked over at my father, and when he nodded she complied. Her expression made it clear how much she disdained having to heal a self-inflicted wound, but in spite of that she pushed blue-tinted magic into the wound, causing the flesh to knit itself together.

"Thank you," I said, stepping back, and then held my hand out for all to see. They gasped as I slashed it once again, blood spraying out from the twice-opened skin. With what had to be a feral grin, I pushed my own healing energy into the flesh, healing it exactly as the high priestess had.

"See?" I challenged, holding my hand up, palm outward in defiance. "It is the same. You heal with healing energy, I heal with magic. Tell me, Seph, that you did not see the same blue tint surrounding both exercises."

"I did," she said quietly, apparently scared of invoking the high priestess's wrath. It was an unfounded fear; the high priestess was too busy glowering at me.

They were stopped, but not completely won over yet, so I decided to try something that I had no idea would work. It was a long shot, I knew, but I managed to convince myself that if, by some miracle, it worked, it would hopefully clinch the deal. I dug deep into Draignerthol as I pushed out my magical senses, seeking certain creatures I knew would be close.

Suddenly both Seph and Owain gasped. Seph, eyes wide, accused, "You—you spoke to Booboo!" Owain remained silent, but I could tell he was just as tense, and over the same bit of taboo that had gotten Seph's hackles raised.

It was, after all, rude to reach out to attempt a takeover of a ranger's familiar. That much was known, though whether a takeover was even possible was more conjecture than anything else. Still, it had never to anyone's knowledge been attempted due to the rudeness associated with the action.

I wasn't worried. I had no desire to take over either Booboo or the master ranger's little dove, and I trusted both rangers to understand that. Still, I hoped that they would see that for a nonpractitioner to be able to even touch a familiar's train of thought required ranger power—magic—and thanks to my pendant, I had that in spades.

It almost worked, but then Seph's eyes narrowed. "Alyssa, we have already determined that you are qualified to be a ranger. Why you would attempt this is beyond me, but the ability to speak to my familiar does not make that ability magic."

I sighed, sensing defeat. "I know. I know. I have a ranger's powers, which you just saw me use. I have a healer's powers, which you also just saw me use. I am also, apparently, a cursed magician. That you are willing to believe those three exist separately rather than the obvious conclusion that they are all the same—it saddens me, but...."

After several long moments looking up into the trees, I lowered my gaze, passed it solemnly around the circle, and quietly said, "I guess I am done. Let's get this over with, so that I can be banished for once and for all and go back home to Momma. At least she believes in me."

"No," the high priestess stated. Arms crossed and eyes narrowed, she didn't look like she was ready to say the words that came out of her mouth anyway. "Alyssa. Crown Princess Alyssa, I should say, you ask a great deal of us. We are your supporters, no matter what. We—and I am fairly certain that I speak for all standing here—will fight to prevent any sort of exile, and not for your benefit either. You are the Dragon Queen of prophecy, of that there is no question. Your leadership is necessary, painful though it may be, to guide us through the coming storms. We have accepted that, and to a certain extent, I believe that we are all resigned to our fates, whatever that might mean in the near future. But now—now you ask us to ignore centuries of teachings, centuries of beliefs, built up in our heads and our hearts and accept that the cursed magic is the same as the wonderful skills we use every day."

"I do, because it is. It is the exact same! The actions, the blue tinges around the flowing energy—surely you've seen it yourselves! You have to see the blue energy if you can use it, right?

Ranger energy, healing energy, magical energy, it is all the same blue energy. I *know* that you have seen that yourselves."

"That—may be," she acquiesced with a narrow nod. "I must confess that I am leaning toward believing you, myself, after your displays just now. But you are asking us to abandon years—decades—centuries of tradition."

"Yes. Yes, I am. You know what? I have to. The prophecy you keep throwing in my face said so. But you know what else? You have done the same, to me. I have, for years, believed that unicorns couldn't really exist, and yet Dad showed me one. The creature let me pet it, even. Unicorns *do* exist. I know you know it, and you're probably as surprised that I doubted it as I am that you doubt my points. And then there's wyverns, too. And now, even, I have seen an actual dragon, with my own eyes, and I've heard it with my own ears. I've felt its hot, fetid breath with my face. I've seen it eat an elf, joyfully and greedily. Weeks ago you would have told me that dragons do not exist, and by all that's right I would've agreed with you, and yet you all believe me now. Why is it so hard to also believe me about the nature of magic?"

"Our culture, Alyssa," Keion said, and then he moved into the center of the tiny ring to stand beside me, raising my healed hand into the air. "I—I am just a warrior," he announced to the rest of the party. "I cannot heal, nor can I grow plants. I cannot even see this blue tinge that many of you keep speaking of. But I saw gashes in her hand closed up the same way by healing and by magic, and even if the power came from two different sources, her hand is nevertheless healed in both cases, regardless. Meanwhile, I have seen the good that the crown princess has done using her magic. I, myself, stand here today only because she saved my life, and more than once. Whatever you think of her abilities, I shall stand by her side and with her, now and in the future."

My eyes misted over at the sudden show of support. Dad stepped across to take my other hand. "As do I. In spite of the magic. No—no. I correct myself. I stand by my daughter's side because of the magic."

"And because she is your daughter," Sternyface observed, her expression matching her tone in dryness.

Dad nodded once as Seph and Master Owain moved over to stand behind me, each with a hand on one of my shoulders.

"I think it would be dishonest to hide that we rangers have always thought our powers were special, while being dangerously close to the powers of sorcerers," the ancient master said. "In the absence of any other explanation, I have to agree with the crown princess."

The queen stepped forward and hugged me, leaving Sternyface standing by herself.

"I hope you all realize that this is blasphemy at the basest meaning for the term. It will very likely mean my replacement as high priestess." She glowered now at everybody, including Dad.

"They will never find anyone who is a match for your abilities, Naissa," Dad argued. "Can you at least agree that what she has said might have some truth to it?"

"No, I—sorry, Cadfael, but your daughter is actually correct in every way. As difficult as it is to utter these words, I and many of those who serve under me have known that the boundaries between our arts and magic are tenuous at best, and primarily exist only to scare people away from working the forbidden side of nature's gifts." She sighed, and then turned toward the road where the King's Men still waited.

"Now that all of that is said and done, can we get back on the road and see an end to this episode?" she asked over her shoulder, and when we all started following, she moved to lead the way.

BRWYDR

Battle.

Or conflict.

Pretty much the same thing

to the elves.

Epilogue

Crown Princess Alyssa, the central figure and focus of the turmoil that swirled about her, stood rooted, a pillar of self-doubt and uncertainty set in the middle of a storm of chaos. On every side hundreds of elves shouted and tempers flared. Only a centuries-old tradition of peace kept blades in their scabbards, and that, clearly, was only temporary.

"You said you would banish the demon child!" Swadda of the Serpent Veils screamed, her shrill voice piercing her many layers of fabric and the distance between them while her hand made the most obscene gesture known toward the crown princess. Several of the elves gathered around her shouted agreement. Meanwhile, the several hundred elves who stood ready to defend her cheered.

Alyssa's father stood calmly beside her, the glow of his eyes the only betrayal of the temperature of the fire that raged within the king of the elves. "No," he growled, the power behind his voice quieting the crowd somewhat, if only briefly. "We agreed to table the discussion until after she completed her coming of age ritual. Now, in light of the news—"

"A dragon? You expect us to believe that story?" Hefin called out with a chuckle. The elves from the east, a thick, burly bunch, threw up hearty chortles behind their leader. "It is ridiculous at best."

"Convenient, is what it is," Swadda inserted, her voice sly. "What a magnificent way you have found to scare us into submission, make us follow along blindly thanks to this dreamed-up threat to our safety. We're so terrified now that we can't think for ourselves. Aren't we?"

"I'm not!" Hefin cried.

"None of us are," the nearly-naked Glynis called. "You're not, are you, Padrig?"

The newly-arrived bennaeth of the northern clans held up his hands in protest. Grigor, advisor to the mighty bennaeth and, secretly, uncle of the king, shook his head in open dismay. Padrig said, "Come, now. Honestly, I have not even had an opportunity to speak with the girl yet. Give me time—"

"Bah!" Hefin bellowed. "We have given the king, his whelp, and his sycophant from the north too much time as it is!" A loud cheer rose from the honor guards from east, west, and south. We will have a decision this day!"

The elf king assumed his most charismatic smile and stepped forward, hands up in a calming sign. "You—we—shall have a decision, and on this day. Please, though, let us retire to the comfort of the throne room to calmly discuss the matter—"

"No!" Swadda's voice sliced through the king's like a sword through a pillow. "We pulled you out to this neutral ground for a reason, Cadfael. We will tolerate delay no longer. What will it be, mighty king, your daughter or your crown?"

"You would have us destroy centuries of peaceful tradition just for fear of violating another tradition?" the high priestess asked. She stepped forward to stand united beside the king, the queen joining to her other side, the three members of the royal triumvirate forming a shield in front of Crown Princess Alyssa, who watched silently from behind.

The subject of the raging argument stood like a statue in the middle, seemingly distracted. Her lips fluttered as though speaking to herself.

"It is already broken, as it is, a result of your bringing the witch into the castle. Now, we must ask you to step down and allow wiser leaders take charge," Hefin said.

The leader of the east stepped forward and pulled his sword six inches from its sheath with a sneer. The king's eyes widened at the obvious martial challenge. Face frozen in shock, he shook his head, hands lowering toward his own weapons. "You—you would...."

Suddenly Alyssa's voice sliced into the swirling rage of emotions, silencing all. "No!" the crown princess cried, peering off into the distance with unseeing eyes and punctuating each word of her statement.

"I. Am. Not. *Your*. Familiar!"

CYTGORD

Harmony. Agreement.

Pretty much the opposite of what exists

in Kiirajanna at the time of this story.

A Note from Little Treebeard

Hi, y'all!

I got that right, I hope? I think that's how Alyssa does it.

I sure do appreciate everybody reading these stories. You get to hear about *me*!

I wanted to sneak a little blurb in here at the end to let you know that I am as disappointed as you probably are in how little I and my brethren were featured in this story. I mean, sure, this part of Alyssa's journey had to be told, but....

But.

This is not a story about trees. In fact, it's a story about the very anti-forest, the monstrosity you call *city*. And worse, I didn't get to go with her.

In the name of balance, then, I snuck in while Alyssa wasn't watching and changed the little word-lessons at the beginning of some of the chapters. She wanted them to be about dragons and magic, but you'll get plenty of that in the *next* book, I promise. For *this* book, I made them about trees!

I hope you enjoyed!

About the Author

Dean by day and writer by night, Stephen H. King grew up being asked whether he was "that Stephen King." "Not the author," he'd say until his writing addiction took hold and made that into a lie. Now he writes and reads and blogs as The Other Stephen King--you know, the one who writes fantasy and science fiction. When he's not writing, he enjoys thinking about writing while going on hikes or long road trips. When he's not thinking about writing, it's usually because he's fishing.

Find other Stephen H. King works at:
http://TheOtherStephenKing.com

Read his ongoing thoughts about writing, authorpreneurship, and other key parts of life at his blog:
http://TheOtherStephenKingOnWriting.blogspot.com

9 780999 893555 3